DOWN
IN
CUBA

Also by Vincent Meis

Eddie's Desert Rose

Tio Jorge

DOWN IN CUBA

VINCENT MEIS

Printed in The United States of America

Fallen
Bros

www.fallenbros.com

FIRST EDITION
Fallen Bros. Publishing
6010 Pacific Coast Highway #9
Redondo Beach, CA 90277
ISBN-13: 978-0615812205
ISBN-10: 0615812201

FOR
MY SIBS

ACKNOWLEDGEMENTS

My thanks go out to the people of Cuba for sharing their stories with me as well as their joyous spirit and frankness while I was doing my research for the novel. There will be some who will say I was too hard on Cuba, and others not hard enough. This was in no way, shape or form, intended to be a political novel.

The members of the Guywriters prose writing group were of great help, offering solid advice and suggestions when I workshopped many of these chapters with them.

Donna Hanelin shared her wisdom on an early draft and has always been a source of support. Richard Hack has again provided excellent proofreading and editing.

Bill Meis has shared his writing expertise as well his steadfast encouragement since the beginnings of this novel. My other siblings, Michael Meis, Mary Hardcastle, Monica Wellman, and Marcia Meis have all given their support in different ways. Of course, none of this would have been possible without the love of reading and writing that our parents, William A. Meis and Virginia C. Meis, instilled in us.

Yo visitaré anhelante
Los rincones donde a solas
Estuvimos yo y mi amante
Retozando con las olas.

I will visit longingly
All the places where unseen
My lover and I have been
Playing with waves by the sea.
                    -José Martí
                    Versos sencillos

1

I had fled the country and sworn I'd never go back. Yet three years later, I was on Havana's seaside walk, the Malecón, where the island had first captured me in its delicate but inescapable web. On one side of me was a low wall holding back the choppy sea, and on the other a multi-laned drive where old cars, kept together by will and ingenuity rather than genuine spare parts, bumped over potholes with a thump and a rattle. On the bike path, clunky Chinese two-wheelers pedaled by with a regular click. I knew all these sights and sounds. I knew the way the sun shone down like a heat lamp too close to my head and the way the sluggish air painted a salty solution of Cuba on my skin. And I knew the feeling of the city trying to take over my brain, pushing it into the lane of memories probably better left untraveled. It was a combination of things that sapped my strength. But a lot had happened in those three years. I was different and, I believed, stronger.

Down the way a chorus of young voices shouted, "*Vamos!*" I looked up to see a pack of unruly boys on the move with wet, threadbare T-shirts plastered to their frail bodies. They weaved around groups of listless walkers and headed directly toward me, a wild intent in their black eyes. I stopped short and braced myself for impact, wondering why they intended to knock me down as if I were a bowling pin. Just as they were upon me, the group split into two wings, flanking me on both sides so close I felt a spray from their soaked clothes. Their sneakers squished as they passed.

I whirled around to watch as they raced for the next spot where waves crashed over the seawall. The older boys stopped and held out their arms as if receiving a shower of baptismal water. The smaller ones, some clad only in dripping briefs, scrambled up on the wall and danced a little jig. Then one of them again shouted, "*Vamos!*" and the wave-chasers took off like a flock of birds, landing at a spot a few yards down the wall.

I laughed off my moment of alarm. I still wore my American big city defenses, no good in Cuba. Here, what appear to be situations of potential danger often turn out to be nothing. It's what sneaks up on you that you have to watch out for. I continued walking with my head up and listened to the low, secret voices of lovers as they sat embraced on the drier parts of the wall, the shouts and laughter of children at play. And I caught out of the corner of my eye the exaggerated gestures of teenagers in the tireless ritual of flirting. From a distance the heavy sea breeze carried the faint chords of a guitar mixed with muffled singing from a group of young people on the wall. They were in shadow as the sun ducked behind a bank of rapidly forming clouds.

A drop of sweat rolled over my cheek and hung on my jaw. I needed to get back to the air conditioning of my hotel. I picked up my pace and promptly stubbed my toe on a rock. Under my feet were chunks of the seawall that had been knocked to the pavement by the force of the waves. The Malecón was crumbling, and the splotchy facades along the waterfront served as an eerie backdrop. The whole city, it seemed, was bent on returning to rubble and dust. It was an ancient theater in ruins, a stage where comedies and tragedies were still played out year after year. I thought of my own drama of love, hope, and betrayal that had begun and ended on these very stones. But again I was convinced of my toughness, the older and wiser me, happily attached and enjoying a modicum of success back home in Los Angeles with my book, *José Martí: Apostle of the Everyman*.

In the distance I saw a little girl walking between two men, holding both of their hands. They lifted her up, and she swung between them.

Then each time her feet touched the pavement, she begged for more. Up again she went. Their happiness, even at a distance, was infectious, and I found myself fantasizing something similar in my future.

Their game brought them close to the wall just as a large wave pounded the rocks and splashed over in front of them, making the men instinctively huddle around the child. She screamed with joy and the men laughed, one of them with hunched shoulders, a momentary stagger in his step, and bended knees as if his whole body were collapsing under the amusement. It was Leo. I recognized the gesture, the precise way his shoulders curved up and forward, his head down, his free hand cupped to his stomach, holding something in. His laughter was painted on my memory like an indelible mark. The sound of it wrapped around me and made running away impossible. Cuba, part-temptress and part-prankster, was working its dark magic again.

They were now just a few yards in front of me, and I stared at the child with her long dark hair in pigtails. She was wearing the pink Gap Kids overalls I had sent her on her last birthday. I had received no thank you, no response.

Leo looked up and saw me. His sweet laughter faded, and his face turned dark. "Martin," he said with a mixture of disbelief, and what I guessed were painful memories for him, too. His black eyes danced a rumba under arched eyebrows.

I approached with palms turned up, as if running into him were a marvel beyond comprehension, and with an openness to what the universe would put in my hands. "Leo, what are you doing here? I—"

"Anabela, *dale un beso a tu tío* Martin," he said. He released her hand, and the other man did, too. I went down on my haunches and wrapped my arm around her. She moved into my embrace and pecked me on the cheek. Her skin was creamy smooth, and she smelled freshly scrubbed.

"*Hola,* Anabela. You don't know me, do you?"

She reached up, touched the small gold hoop in my ear, and frowned. "No," she answered in a coy, small voice.

"I met you when you were just a baby."

"She knows you," said Leo. "From pictures."

I looked up into his eyes and held on to the girl to steady myself.

"You showed her pictures?"

"She loves looking at our old photos."

Anabela tapped my shoulder with a pudgy finger and announced with glee, "*Tío* Martin." Then she rotated her body to point at Leo. "*Papi.*"

"*Sí, mi amor,*" said Leo.

He then turned toward the other man, who had been standing at a distance, and said, "Oh, I'm sorry. Alfredo, this is Martin. Martin, Alfredo. "

With tightness in my gut, I rose up to shake Alfredo's hand, detecting a South American accent in his "*Mucho gusto.*" He had a weak handshake and was much older than Leo, average-looking, balding and slightly overweight. In beige slacks and a blue button-down shirt, he looked too formal for the Malecón. I disliked him instantly.

"Alfredo, why don't you and Anabela walk on ahead," Leo said. "I'll catch up."

"Where did you meet *him*?" I muttered when Alfredo and Anabela were out of earshot.

Leo smiled, enjoying my uneasiness. "Don't worry. He's not with me. He's Sulyn's husband. She and I haven't been together for a couple of years now. Sulyn met Alfredo about a year ago and moved to Argentina. They're just back for a visit."

"Anabela lives there with them?"

"Yeah," he said with downcast eyes. "I'm waiting for my visa. I'll go in a few months. Alfredo is getting me a work permit."

"You look good," I said.

"You weren't going to call me?"

"I didn't know how. Three years is a long time. I… did you get the book?"

"Yeah," he said in the same bored, unreadable way that used to drive me crazy.

"So?"

"It was nice, the dedication and all. That's funny, my name in a book. Sometimes I take it out and read that page over and over, wondering why you never came back." His voice was losing its hardness, faltering the tiniest bit.

"How's your mom?"

"We're leaving for Holguín tonight. Why don't you come with us? She would love to see you."

"I can't. I'm just here for a few days, a Martí conference. I'm presenting the book."

"And you weren't going to call me," he said again, shaking his head. Our eyes locked, held for a minute. His were the first to let go and fell to examine his shoes. "My mom said it's my fault."

"No fault."

He nodded.

"Do you have time for a beer?" I said.

"We're supposed to meet Sulyn. We're already late."

"Anabela is so… beautiful. She looks just like you."

"Thanks." He lifted his chin, and our eyes met again.

"When you get to Argentina, let me know where you are. I want to keep in touch."

"I should go." He put out his hand, but I pulled him to me. I put my arms around him and held him tight to let him know it wasn't a lack of love that took me away. He was tense and it began to feel awkward, but I held on. Then, for a brief moment, his body relaxed and the years melted away.

He pulled back, and as he turned to go, gave me a neat little wave before he ran to catch up to the retreating silhouettes of his daughter and Alfredo.

I found a dry place on the low wall and settled myself onto the sun-warmed concrete. The water splashed against the rocks just on the other side, and I gazed up at the Hotel Nacional on the hill, realizing that I was sitting in our old spot, the place where I met him some five years before. Without warning, a big wave came up and slapped me on the back, the spray falling all around me like a fountain. I coughed and jumped back down to the sidewalk, drenched to the bone. Like a dog I shook myself off and trotted toward my hotel.

2

Five Years Earlier

The Russian-made YAK-42 plowed at 400 miles per hour through wisps of clouds in an inky, moonless sky and dipped toward Havana. It wasn't fast enough for me in a rush to make up for lost time. One day I was a youth hunched over a guitar in a crowded college dorm room, belting out "Guantanamera," full of wide-eyed notions of peace and rebellion. The next day I woke up in an empty house on a cool, damp Southern California morning, slouching toward middle age with the heavy boot of failure pressing down on my chest. I was unable to summon up a single reason to get out of bed. Then the phone rang, and the dean told me that my sabbatical had been approved.

Now, three months later, my head vibrated against the double-paned Plexiglas, and I had a jitter in my leg that wouldn't quit. The plane shuddered, and my heartbeat ratcheted up a notch as the twinkling lights of the city came into view. The other passengers, too, were restless, craning their necks to look out the windows, their bodies tugging against the seatbelts. We were a planeload of refugees, anxious for our deliverance, ready for a new life or to recapture an old one. Everybody on the flight seemed to have a purpose, and I had mine.

"I'm going home. I'm going home," a woman across the aisle blurted out in a voice that sounded as if she were drowning. Earlier in the trip

I had seen her laughing, throwing back her head of straw-colored hair, so solidly coiffed that it looked like a helmet.

From behind me I heard Mexican Spanish in the tentative accent of the Yucatán say, "That girl, Dorita, better be there at the airport."

"And her friend, too," said his companion. They laughed, but their laughter had a shallow ring to it, and I pictured their round, brooding Mayan faces going silent while they contemplated the love of their sweet Cuban girls.

The woman next to me shook her head of thick hair—proudly let go to gray—in disapproval. From the first moment I saw her I had a feeling she was American by the way she was dressed. In sharp contrast to the Cuban women on the flight who had donned their best designer knock-offs, she wore loose-fitting natural fiber clothing: linen drawstring pants, a cotton flowery peasant shirt and braided leather sandals.

Her pale eyes were sporadically focused through frameless glasses on a page in Carlos Fuentes' *Christopher Unborn*. I felt her glancing at my twitching knees and my constant shifting in the seat, but I avoided conversation with her. She was frighteningly similar in appearance to my wife.

And then she broke the silence in a grating voice that could not be ignored. "Is this your first trip to Cuba?"

"Yes. And you?"

"Me?" she said with a laugh that was part cough. "I've lived here for twenty years. I'm a journalist and have just come back from a U.S. speaking tour. Somebody has to counter all the propaganda put out by the news media about Cuba." She was solid in her attitude, but her chilly manner made me doubt she won a lot of converts. "You're traveling alone?"

God, so American. She jumped from cold and detached to a question that was too meddling.

"Yes. I left my wife at home." A nervous grin took over my face. People frequently misinterpreted it as guilt, and I watched in mild panic as her expression turned to disgust.

"Not another one," she mumbled, turning back to her book.

"What?"

She ignored me, her eyes stuck on the page.

"Excuse me. What did you mean?"

She slammed her book shut and twisted her body to confront me. "You think I don't know the score? Look around. Most of the men on this plane are married, but how many are traveling with their wives? You should all be ashamed, treating Cuba like it's a big brothel just because people are desperate to feed their families."

I sat up straight. "I'm not here for that!" I gave a backward nod to the two men behind us. "I'm on sabbatical and I'm carrying donations of medicine. You thought I...?"

"You're a teacher?" she said. Her cheeks flushed. "Oh, dear!"

And then I was offended that she backed off so easily. As if teachers were so prim they didn't cheat on their spouses.

"Latin American Studies. I wrote my dissertation on Martí. I'm here to soak up real Martíism."

"I'm truly sorry. You must think I'm awfully rude. It's just that there is so much of that going on."

"Martíism?"

The corners of her mouth turned up in a half-smile. "You know what I mean." She relaxed her frame and hugged the book to her chest, still turned in my direction. "I think it's wonderful you're interested in Martí."

"This is a scouting trip, research. I plan to come back for a longer time to write a book."

"About Martí?"

"There's so little written about him in English. I want to bring him to the English-speaking world the way he brought English literature to the Spanish-speaking world."

"In Cuba all school children can recite Martí from a very young age. She began to recite, and then launched into a discourse that I only half-heard.

My own journey to Martí had begun twenty-five years earlier in a dorm room with Che Guevara posters plastered on the walls and the smell of dirty laundry coming from the corner. We would pass around the guitar, and I would launch into my most practiced song. "*Yo soy un hombre sincero, de donde crece la palma.*"

One day a friend thrust a small book in my hand. "If you are going to sing that song, you should at least know where the words come from." He caught me off-guard.

The book was José Martí's *Versos Sencillos,* Simple Verses, and on its pages I came across the lyrics to "Guantanamera," quite stunning on the page even without the melody. I couldn't put it down. With each year my Spanish got better, and I went deeper into the garden of his images, where under each leaf lay a new emotion, all of them bound by roots to his homeland. And year after year I dreamed of visiting a place that could inspire such undying love, a love Martí laid down his life for on the battlefield. I carried it with me still, the book.

And after so many years with the images of Cuba swimming around in my head, I was on the eve of discovering Martí's land, sitting next to a woman who looked like my wife, telling her about my book project. After she finished her Martí speech, she asked questions about my research: Where had I heard about him? What where my favorite poems? She listened to my answers just like my wife would, fascinated, so different from the usual reaction I got when I told people about my work. She gave me a renewed hope that there might be people interested in a man who had been dead for over a hundred years.

The jolt of the tires hitting the tarmac set the passengers to clapping, first a few tentatively, then more joined in. My neighbor handed me a card.

"Sorry, I never introduced myself. I'm Laurie Bronstein. That's my phone here in Cuba. I have some friends who are professors at the university and they might be able to help you with your research."

"Very kind of you. I'm Martin. Martin Vandenberg."

The plane taxied past a new terminal, a modern structure of glass and steel looking like something that might take flight itself, and instead headed for a large prefab warehouse that appeared as if it had just been dumped down at the end of a runway.

We descended the well-worn metal steps of the rolling staircase bathed in the sweet fragrance of the tropics, and stepped into a sea of uniformed officials with a new smell of diesel invading our nostrils. Led as if to an execution with blaring lights in our faces and armed guards at our sides, we reached the terminal doors.

Once inside we were treated to salsa music, at full volume, coming out of five TV monitors, one for each line leading to the immigration booths. They showed a welcome video with Tropicana showgirls dancing across the screen, forcing wide smiles and garbed in multicolored outfits sporting sequins and feathers.

The immigration officer stared me down through bulletproof glass an inch thick. She was a young, attractive woman with dark shoulder-length hair and a drab olive uniform designed to let me know that pandering to tourists was a bitter pill for true revolutionaries like her. Her questions were terse and her manner gruff. She looked at my passport photo, and then centered on me. She again stared at my passport, then up at me, repeating this action several times. I wondered if there was something wrong. She looked down at my hands gripping the ledge under her window and narrowed her eyes.

"Name?" she barked and my heart skipped a beat.

"Mar...uh..Martin...Vandenberg."

"Date of birth?"

"July 26, 1953." My voice got its strength back.

The edges of her mouth began to soften as if my words were a soothing tonic. It was impossible for a Cuban not to react to the date, the exact day Fidel Castro and his band of rebels launched an attack on the Moncada army barracks in Santiago de Cuba, the beginning of an uprising against the U.S.-backed Batista regime.

"Your birthday is big holiday in Cuba," she said in careful English. "You will celebrate it here?"

"I plan to." It was less than two weeks away, and I was eager to spend my birthday away, away from everything.

She stamped my tourist card, tucked it into my passport, and returned it to me. "Enjoy your stay." She buzzed the outer door open, let out a sigh, and looked toward the next passenger.

"*Gracias*," I said. Her response was to raise her hand almost imperceptibly off the counter and let it fall back down.

After gathering my bags, I approached customs with a pounding heart. One of my bags was full of recycled drugs—medicine that could no longer be used by the patient it was prescribed for, but still within the expiration date. My neighbor in Los Angeles, Tomás, had asked me to deliver the medicine to a doctor in Cuba, his way of circumventing the U.S. embargo against the island. I agreed to take the drugs and Tomás arranged for me to stay with one of his friends, Gerard, who helped with the recycling project. Tomás insisted that I wasn't doing anything against the law. Yet I approached the tough-looking customs officials still wondering if it was technically legal to transfer prescription drugs from one country to another. I began to sweat as if I were a real drug-runner.

The agent stared at my bags, but then caught sight of the traveler behind me, who had a great deal of luggage. He waved me by, and I hurried out the terminal doors.

When I gave the taxi driver Gerard's address, he grunted and started the meter. So far I hadn't exactly felt welcome in Cuba.

"Do people not like Americans here?" I asked.

"You American?"

"Yeah."

"We love Americans. It's just that we don't think much of the government. Anyway, people here wouldn't recognize you as an American right away. Just a tourist."

"People don't like tourists much?"

"Are you kidding? We love tourists. How would I feed my family if it weren't for tourists?" He snickered and pulled out a pack of Marlboros. "Do you mind?" he said, holding up the pack for me to see.

"Go ahead."

The Avenida Rancho Boyeros was tedious like most thoroughfares passing through the outskirts of a major city: boxy warehouses with corrugated metal roofs and whitewashed factory walls. In most countries the walls are covered with advertising and graffiti. Here, there were faded revolutionary slogans like *"Viva la Revolución."* The billboards, too, were plastered with similar phrases: *"Socialismo o Muerte," "Con Fidel Siempre."*

As we came to a more residential area, I leaned out the window and gazed at the people as they walked, stood, or bicycled along the side of the dimly lit road. They were casual, many of the men without shirts and the women in shorts and tank tops, comfortably dressed against the heat that radiated from the dust and gravel around them. Their bodies were thin, shapely, none of them overweight, with rich skin tones from white to chocolate brown. They moved sensually, proudly, almost seeming to float along, not with great speed, but forward. Others stood in large groups at bus stops, leaning on each other or perched like large birds on the crumbling cement blocks that once supported a bench. I was anxious to jump out of the taxi and walk among them, know them. The lyrics from "Guantanamera," the words of Martí, came to me again. "*Con los pobres de la tierra, quiero yo mi suerte echar.* With the poor of the earth, I cast my lot."

Once out of the drab outskirts, the taxi approached the lush, wide-open streets of Vedado, the unofficial heart of modern-day Havana. We rolled along under a canopy of leafy old trees that added a hush to the already quiet boulevards. The air was still and hot, and the moist essence of the city dampened my California skin, still dry from the hot Santa Ana winds blowing on the day I left Los Angeles.

On the Avenida de los Presidentes, I peered out the window at what seemed an exact replica in real life of a photo I had seen in a National Geographic spread about Cuba—a single bike transporting three people. A shirtless young man was precariously balanced with a foot on either side of the back wheel center bolt, while a young girl sat sideways on the crossbar and a slight man in his forties pedaled the bike. They were so close I could have extended my arm and touched them. I *wanted* to touch them, touch Cuba. I smiled at the girl, but she stared blankly into my taxi, uninterested, distant, remote. The traffic light changed, and the older man put all his might into the pedals while my taxi sped effortlessly past them down the almost empty streets.

We pulled up in front of a high-rise that looked as though it hadn't been touched since the fifties, each year falling into greater disrepair. Paint was peeling from the walls and a few of the windows were boarded up. I nodded to a shabbily clad man, who was leaning back precariously on a rusty chair by the door, and entered the lobby under a fluorescent lamp that was tacked up on the dingy wall. Most of the ceiling panels were missing, and several of the marble tiles along the lower wall were gone, revealing splotches of petrified glue.

"Does that elevator work?" I asked the man.

"Sure does. Well… most of the time."

"I'm looking for Gerard Monfils."

"Tenth floor."

Gerard was a French-Canadian from Montreal whom I had met through Tomás not long before he left Los Angeles to live in Cuba. I remembered him saying one night, "The left in the U.S. is dead." I wanted to argue with him, but I knew I couldn't. Like many others, my radicalism of the seventies had settled into the complacency of the nineties.

Tomás gave me a rundown of what to expect at Gerard's posh—by Cuban standards—three-bedroom apartment. There were often a lot of people in his house due to his open-door policy to both foreign and Cuban visitors. It had gotten him in trouble with the local CDR, the Committee for the Defense of the Revolution, who kept a watchful eye on the neighborhood, making sure that everyone was adhering to the principles of socialism. I wondered if the man at the door was keeping track of who was coming and going.

Tomás also warned me to watch my valuables as things had gone missing in the apartment. Still he felt it would be a good place to start, and he assured me that Gerard was a great host. I could stay there a few days until I found a place of my own. "You must not stay in a hotel," he said. "Hotels don't offer you the Cuban experience, and there is no point in going there if you don't have that." I wasn't quite sure what he meant by the Cuban experience, but I trusted his advice.

The elevator door creaked open.

3

I have a fear of elevators, and the one in Gerard's building proved a formidable test of my will. If it hadn't been ten flights with heavy bags, I would have walked. The car wobbled as I set my bags down on the worn linoleum. There was no button marked ten, only a black, broken-off stub where the ten should be. I pushed it, and the door banged closed, sending the car upward with a jerk. To distract myself from horrific visions of falling elevators, I read the messages and names scrawled across the walls in black marker or etched into the layers of old paint. The single bare bulb flickered, cut out for a few seconds, and then came back to life. Squeaks and thumps and scrapes announced the passing of each floor.

By the time the elevator rattled to a halt on the tenth floor, I was gasping for breath. I quickly pushed my bags out into a claustrophobic landing by the door to 10A. On the largest of the bags, I sat down to rest my shaky legs for a moment.

After a series of knocks, the door opened. A short, muscular, dark-skinned young man in gym shorts gave me a blank look and said, "*Sí?*"

"*Soy Martin, amigo de Gerard,*" I explained.

"*Soy Giovani,*" he said in a subtle mocking of my Spanish. He waved me into the living room without bothering to help me with my two large bags and backpack. I stumbled into the dark room, the only light coming from a small television. I could make out three other people crowded around the screen, and before retaking his seat, Giovani made a quick introduction.

"This is my sister, Yanela; her daughter, Odet; and Osmani, a friend who is visiting from Camaguey." I shook each of their moist, limp hands while they looked around me at the TV.

"*Voy a matar ese pinche cabrón,*" shouted a nasty-looking guy on the screen. "I'm going to kill that fucking asshole."

I moved out of their way and ended up next to a large potted fern that tickled my neck with its fronds. "Gerard is expecting me, right?"

After a brief delay so that the mean character on the TV could finish his next line, Giovani said, "Yeah, but he had to go out of town."

"Out of town?"

"Family emergency."

"When will he be back?"

"Don't know."

This was not the warm and friendly Cuba I had read about. So far I had gotten hostile looks from officials, cool receptions and weak handshakes.

"*Siéntese,*" said Osmani. "Sit down."

I looked around, but there was no place to sit.

"Maybe I should go to a hotel."

Osmani jumped up. "Gerard wants you to stay here. You are to sleep in his room." He grabbed one of my bags. "This way. You're probably tired, right?"

I followed him into the large bedroom just off the living room. He went to the bathroom linen closet to take out some clean sheets.

He removed the old sheets from the bed and began to spread out the new ones. I went on the other side to help him, though it felt awkward to be sharing a domestic chore with someone I had only just met. We fluffed the sheets up in the air and as they settled, I caught him smiling at me. I bent down to tuck in my side. After we finished with the bed, he got me a towel and laid it gently on top of the crisp, clean sheets. I dropped down on the bed, and he sat next to me, very close, our legs almost touching. He asked me about my trip, and I gave him a long, meaningless description of the delays and extended layovers at the airports. With a sudden upswing of his arm, he gestured toward the bathroom and with a glint in his eye said, "It's so hot. Do you want to take a shower?"

I stood up at the abruptness of his question, the unexpected inflection of it, which sounded like an invitation. Tomás had told me jokingly to be careful with some of the guys who hung around Gerard's apartment, but Osmani hardly seemed like someone I might have problems with. He was short, with undernourished arms and legs, and pasty skin. Wisps of his long hair were stuck to his forehead as if he had a fever. His ears were elfin, framing a kind though homely face. He looked very young.

"The shower's a good idea. Thanks." I picked up the towel off the bed, walked into the bathroom, and closed the door.

I took off all my clothes, but as I pulled back the curtain I realized that this was unlike any shower I had seen before. The showerhead was larger than normal and had two wires running from it, taped to the spigot, and connected to a switch on the wall. It looked hazardous. But with the way Osmani looked at me, I was reluctant to ask him for instructions. I could figure this out. There were three settings on the head: *fría, tibia* and *caliente.* It was set to *tibia,* so I left it there. I turned on the water and it came out cold. Eyeing the switch suspiciously, I flipped it and the lights dimmed for a second. After another thirty seconds the water got lukewarm, but there was almost no pressure. I put myself under the tepid dribble and began searching for soap. I found only a sliver.

Used to a hot shower no matter what the outside temperature, I reached up to change the setting to *caliente.* As soon as I touched it, a pulse of electricity shot through my body.

"Shit!" I screamed.

Osmani popped his head in. "Are you okay?"

I peeked out from around the curtain. "Yeah, I guess."

"You can't touch anything metal when you are under the water."

"Now you tell me," I mumbled.

"And I forgot. Don't use too much water. All we have until they turn on the pumps tomorrow is in the tank just over your head."

I hurried to finish my shower with the image of a cascade of water crashing through the flimsy ceiling above me.

I threw on some shorts and went out to the living room where they were still mesmerized by the screen. Osmani made room for me on the sofa, wedged between Yanela and Osmani with his arm stretched behind me touching my shoulder. Odet was sprawled across Giovani and Yanela with her head half in my lap. The closeness of so many bodies, the humidity and the heat weighed on me, so accustomed to space and the cool evenings of California. But I didn't want to seem like an uptight American, so I sat and chewed on my travel-dried lips.

As soon as the movie ended, I stood, announced that I was going to bed, and escaped into my room. A strong sea breeze rattled the glass-louvered windows and sent the wall hangings dancing in the moonlight. Despite my fatigue, I stared at the phantom shadows of the blowing fabric above me. I felt alone, awkward, drifting out at sea with no anchor. Outside the window laughing, shouting, and whistling rose up from a crowd of teenagers outside a nightclub ten stories below, as clear as if it were next door. I got up to investigate. One youth shouted to another, "*No me toques, maricón.* Don't touch me, faggot." The harsh words were amplified in the dense air. I backed away from the window and fell back on the bed.

The sun streamed in through the uncovered windows, burning a swath of light across one side of the bed, and I moved my body out of its path. It continued to creep toward me and made sleep impossible. In the bathroom I splashed water on my face and let the excess cascade down over my chest and back. In the mottled mirror I caught a glimpse of my haggard face. I looked like I hadn't slept in days. All my emotions seemed reflected in my skin—the anxiety of being in unfamiliar surroundings, my uncertainty about the Martí project, my confusion about the state of my life.

I had nurtured great hopes for this trip, my antidote to the mundane life I led back in Los Angeles, where I bumbled about the empty rooms of our home in a tattered robe and worn slippers. Lizzie was away a great deal, taking care of her parents in Santa Barbara. Her father had Alzheimer's and her mother was too frail to handle him. My daughter, Jenny, the light that kept my life on track through the years, had graduated from college and was headed for a summer internship in a law firm to carve out her own life without me looking over her shoulder.

Now my dream of being in Cuba was real, and my savior was the book I planned to write. In my most buoyant moments, I imagined it the consummate work on Martí in English. Yet when I sat in front of my blank computer screen, a paralysis took over my brain, making me despair that my project was doomed from the start. I wanted to excite the English-speaking world about a man who died over a hundred years ago, a man who wrote poems about bees and bluebirds and honeysuckle rose and then rode into the thick of battle untrained and probably knowing that he would be killed. He was passionate about life and ideals. He became the voice for the downtrodden, the standard-bearer for the exploited. In everything Martí was a romantic, from the simplest act of turning over a leaf in the garden to his insistence on fighting in a battle against the oppressors. Life at the end of the twentieth century seemed comparatively flat, full of cynicism and instant gratification. Even if I was successful in diving into the sea of this man's life and capturing the pearl of his existence, who would be interested in reading about his sort of passion?

I ran my hand through my blond, thinning hair and looked into my blue eyes. What made him do it, jump on a white horse and ride into the thick of the battle against the heavily armed, well-trained Spanish troops? The rebel generals had ordered him to stay in camp, knowing that if they were able to throw off the yoke of Spanish rule, Martí would be the one to lead the new nation. A single bullet struck his frail body and knocked him from his horse to the ground.

I had done nothing with my life remotely so grand as Martí. He was physically slight of frame and had suffered most of his life from an injury that occurred as a teenager, when he was imprisoned and forced to do hard labor for his ideals. My body was still strong as I pressed on to my late forties, already older than Martí when he gave his life for something he believed in. What would I give my life for?

I resolved to start my day by visiting the giant statue of Martí in the Plaza de la Revolución and the museum devoted to him next to it. Inspiration was what I needed.

I shuffled in my flip-flops and gym shorts into the living room. Odet, who had been playing on the floor, jumped up and ran away. I walked past Osmani sleeping sprawled out on the couch with his mouth hanging open and his brown hair tousled. He looked even more like a child than the night before. I stepped out onto the terrace and took in the sweeping view of Havana's skyline. Only a few high rises built during the fifties and sixties interrupted the view to the sea. The wind, tasting slightly salty, whisked the heat rising off my skin. At this hour the city seemed innocent and sleepy. Patches of green were scattered between the wide avenues, and I traced Línea Street down to the end where it met the blue-gray water.

In the kitchen Yanela was washing dishes with Odet squeezed in between her mother and the sink. As I walked in she announced, "*Hay café,*" without turning around. "*Pero no hay pan.*"

The coffee sounded good, but I needed my morning bread. "*Dónde puedo comprar pan?*" I asked Yanela.

"*Pan cubano o pan extranjero?*"

"*Pan cubano.*" I had no idea they made special bread for foreigners. I wanted to eat what Cubans ate.

From the Cuban bakery down the street, I brought home the *panecitos,* small squares of bread that looked like dinner rolls, made from unbleached flour. I had them with *café con leche.* By the time I finished breakfast, I had abandoned the idea of going to the Martí statue. I hid in the apartment from the heat, which dragged the midday hours slowly toward afternoon. I would venture out when the sun went down.

An hour into a sweaty afternoon dream that had me drooling into the pillow, Yanela called me to the phone. I stumbled out and picked up the receiver, and with bleary eyes noticed that the outer layer of enamel was almost completely worn off. It looked unsanitary, and I held the mouthpiece at a distance from my lips.

"Hello."

"This is Luka."

"Who?"

"Luka. I'm supposed to pick up the medicine."

"Oh, yes. Of course."

"I'm here in Vedado. Can I come over now?"

In a few minutes, a young man was at the door. He looked like he had walked out of an Italian fashion magazine, and I stared at him for a moment.

"I'm Luka," he said.

"Please come in."

He stopped in the middle of the room. The sunlight streaming in from the balcony played a light show in the ringlets of his shiny black hair. His eyes were the color of dark chocolate, and his skin gave off a warm brown glow.

"Hope I'm not disturbing you," he said in rapid-fire Cuban.

"I'm a little groggy from the trip. I had fallen asleep when you called."

He smiled, wide lips, white teeth, an open smile. "Your Spanish is good. Where did you learn it?"

"I used to spend a lot of summers in Mexico. Come out on the balcony. There's a little breeze."

We walked to the edge and looked out over the city.

"How do you know Tomás?" I asked.

"I met him when he brought medicine before. And you?"

"He's my neighbor...our neighbor."

A gust of sea breeze came up and rustled his loose-fitting white shirt. I looked down at his brown hand close to mine on the railing.

"I would offer you something to drink, but I don't know what's here."

"I know a place nearby where we could get a beer if you want."

La Fuente was an open-air restaurant just a few blocks from the apartment, the cool garden a welcome relief from the sauna of the street. Trees and towering plants leaned over and cast their shade on the tables that were gathered around a small pond with large multi-colored goldfish. At one end of the pond, spouts sent arcs of water down on the surface, creating a steady, soothing music.

We sat down with our beers and he told me about his work with the HIV community in Cuba. He said it was quite small compared to other countries in the Caribbean. The government did its best to provide free medicine to the patients, but the HIV combination therapy was very expensive. "Because of the U.S. embargo, we can't buy meds from you guys, our logical trading partner, so we have to get them from other countries. It increases the cost even more," he explained.

"It's insane. Forty years of bad policy. The only thing the embargo seems to achieve is to keep Castro in power."

Luka looked over his shoulder and lowered his voice. "I don't agree with everything the government does, but it *is* trying to take care of people with the disease—well, all diseases for that matter. And of course, healthcare is free."

"In the States I read something about people with the HIV virus being forced to live in camps."

His eyes again darted to the neighboring tables. "They aren't camps and people aren't forced…at least not anymore. When the first cases were discovered, the sanatoriums were mandatory. I lived at a sanatorium for years and it was very comfortable."

"Oh," I said and looked down at the table.

"Did I shock you? I thought Tomás probably told you. Anyway, I'm fine thanks to you guys sending me the meds."

"At least I get to meet someone who will benefit from my smuggling operation," I said with a smile.

"Tomás told me you are married."

"I have a daughter who just graduated from college."

"You don't look that old."

"My wife got pregnant when we were *very* young," I joked.

"You came here alone?" He took a sip of his beer and a line of foam sat on top of his grin.

"I'm taking a break…from everything."

"Cuba can be good for that." He licked off the foam and grinned again. "Sometimes I wish I could take a break from everything."

After the second beer my head started falling forward, and my eyelids became unbearably heavy.

"You'd better go back and take a nap," he said, and laughed.

"You've been so kind to put up with me. I feel like an idiot."

"Here's my number." He handed me a small scrap of paper. "Give me a call before you go back. I want to send a letter to Tomás."

"Maybe we can have another beer sometime when I'm more with it."

"I'd like that."

4

After a nap I went back to La Fuente for a dinner of pork, salad, a mix of rice and beans called *congri*, and fried green plantains called *tostones*. I thought about the conversation I had with Luka earlier, about how casually he revealed his infection with the virus. Bringing medicine to Cuba had started out as a favor for a friend, but after meeting Luka, it felt more like a mission. I promised myself to find a way to keep him supplied with medication.

With a full belly and fortified conscience, I headed up Calle F, looking for the main thoroughfare of Vedado, Calle 23. The streets were dimly lit by tarnished old streetlamps, and branches of ancient oak trees hovered in the air above me, adding mystery to the dense air. Shadowy figures were nearly upon me before I could see them or realize where they had come from. They went on. A bicycle clicked by, and then the big circular headlights of a 1955 DeSoto rounded the corner. The car shifted into third and crawled up the block. I gazed into the brightly lit windows of the elegant but tired old homes, and for the first time since I arrived, felt the enchantment of the city. Even the gigantic cockroaches darting across my path didn't break the spell.

Walking past stately mansions with their rich details—large-columned porches, stained-glass windows and marble staircases—I began to understand why the upper class, mostly white Cubans who fled to Miami, were still so incensed. The people that left these homes after the revolution expected to be back in them within a matter of months; forty years later they were still waiting.

And then, a punctuation mark to my thoughts, everything went black. Almost immediately from the window of one of the houses came the lament, "*O por dios!*" From another window I heard, "*Gracias, Fidel,*" in a weary, sarcastic voice. It was quickly followed by a harsh, "*Cállate.* Shut up." Tomas had warned me about the *apagones,* or blackouts, quite common since the fall of the Soviet bloc, when Cuba lost its source of cheap oil.

Within minutes candlelight began to appear in some of the windows, and in others a flashlight beam could be seen jerking around the room. Old women came out on their porches and balconies in threadbare housedresses, and I heard one ask in a tired voice how long the blackout would last. An argument ensued about who was to blame, and the voices jumped from weariness to indignation, the sound getting louder and louder until someone admonished them.

I reached a wide avenue, and in the passing headlights I read the street sign: Calle 23. A few blocks away an illuminated, multi-storied hotel stood triumphantly against the blackness, the words "Habana Libre" in big blue letters illuminated at the top. Major hotels, it seemed, had their own source of energy. I was drawn to it as if to a lighthouse beacon, a refuge where I might pass the blackout.

The entrance was above street level, and as I went up the steps I got a strong sense of leaving pedestrian Havana. The transformation was complete when I stepped through the doors from the dark into the light, from heat into coolness, from dingy into polished, and from the peso world into the dollar one. All appeared normal with the reception area full of activity as guests, some in their finery and others in vacation wear, glided back and forth to the elevators while still others sat in intimate conversation in small groups around the vast lobby.

I settled into one of the few unoccupied plush lobby chairs. Next to me a bald German with a beer gut and glacier-blue eyes was speaking halting Spanish to the delight of a much younger *mulata.* She sidled up to him on the sofa, and giggled her way into his arms. Across from them a young mother was keeping one eye on the German-*mulata* couple and the other on her two small children, who tussled on the floor. I caught the Canadian accent as she tried to reel in her children with strain in her voice. Her husband blocked out everything behind a deep-sea fishing brochure. Around me was the new Cuba, the Cuba of tourism. I was on an island within an island.

A large group that had been sitting in the Polynesian-motif lobby bar began moving en masse toward the exit. A tour bus was parked across the street and beyond that a building now had lights. The blackout was over.

Back at Gerard's I stood in front of the elevator and listened to a cacophony of sound as it made its way down. Was I going to get on the shaky contraption right after a blackout? Then I heard steps coming my way through the garage. It was Osmani. As my elevator fear was somewhat lessened when not alone, his company was welcome. But his downcast eyes and blasé greeting told me that he was in a foul mood.

"What's wrong?" I asked when we stepped into the dim elevator light.

"I went to this going-away party in Havana Vieja for a student group from Chicago. A girl I met on the street invited me, but when I got there she ignored me. It's always the same with foreigners. They treat us badly. They take advantage of us and leave us with nothing. I don't mean you and Gerard."

"What were you expecting? She just invited you to the party, right? Or was there something else?"

"I spent all my money on a taxi to go to that stupid party and then nothing. There was a Mexican boy there who liked me, but he said he couldn't even afford to buy me a beer because he spent all his money. What a waste of time! I've got better things to do."

I wondered what those better things were. He spent most of the day on the sofa in front of the TV, and I had heard Giovani call him a lazy bum. I was curious about his casual flirting with both sexes.

"Are you bisexual?" I asked, though the question caused my face to redden.

"I'm married," he said in a rising voice. "I have a baby back in Camaguey."

"Okay," I said, noting that he hadn't answered the question.

The elevator arrived at the tenth floor, and as soon as we were inside the apartment, he said, "I've got an idea. Why don't we go for a walk? You can buy me a beer."

"I'm tired." I edged toward the bedroom.

"Come on, man. You're in Cuba. You can sleep at home. We'll just go out for an hour."

He did have a point. I hadn't waited half my life to go to Cuba so that I could crawl in bed before the clock struck midnight. It wouldn't hurt to go out for one beer. Giovani must have heard us talking because he came into the living room and glared. Osmani explained that we were going out, and Giovani curled his lip in disapproval before turning around and stomping back into his room.

"What was that all about?" I asked when we were back in the elevator.

"Nothing. He thinks he's the master of the house when Gerard's not here and he's into everybody's business. Just ignore him. Gerard told me to be nice to you."

We walked to the end of Línea, bought beers at the Cupet gas station, and then walked across to the Malecón, the seemingly endless seaside promenade that skirted the curved figure of the city. A delicious, cooling breeze hit my face as I gazed at lovers walking hand-in-hand and small groups talking, laughing, smoking, and passing around bottles of rum.

Up ahead along the seawall a large crowd had gathered across the street from a fountain the size of a small swimming pool. Osmani quickened his step and dragged me along until we were at the edge of the gathering.

"What is it?" I asked. "A party?"

"Sort of a street party."

"Is it a holiday or something?"

"Every night is a holiday here. It's where everyone hangs out."

Two ladies of the night in skimpy shorts and tall boots walked toward us. One had long blonde hair that hung like a waterfall and the other a short, jet-black bob. "*Nena, no hay nadie aquí más puta que tú*. Nobody is more of a whore here than you," I heard the blonde say in a high-pitched taunt. They were almost in front of me, and the dark-haired one caught my eye. I tried to look away, but she had me locked in. It was not until she was standing right in front of me that I realized they were two men. Still, I was powerless to avert my eyes.

"*Hola, joven*," he said to me in a sultry voice. "*Dáme un beso.*" His face was so close that I could see the makeup that covered a shaved chin. The thought of kissing him sent a shiver up and down my spine.

I took a step back, shook my head, and croaked, "No."

"See you make-a him 'fraid, *puta*," said the blonde in English.

I hurried to catch up with Osmani.

"Go wit' you *pinguero*," said the rebuffed one.

When Osmani stopped laughing, I asked him what a *pinguero* was.

He looked at me as if I were a child. "You know, it's a guy that sells his *pinga*."

"His what?"

This time he groaned. "*Por dios*, man. This thing." He grabbed between his legs.

I looked at his crotch and then quickly away.

"Some of the guys here are prostitutes," Osmani explained in the monotonous voice of a guide. "And some are just *jineteros*. The *jineteros* are like hustlers. They could be selling themselves or anything that might separate a foreigner from his money. They would be just as happy overcharging for a bottle of street rum or cigars, though there is more money in sex."

I looked around and felt that everyone was staring at me as though I was a mark. A young boy sitting over on the wall put a hand between his legs and stared at me vacantly. I turned my head away.

The sexual vibration of bawdy laughter and voices in a battle of decibels drew us to the center of the crowd of young men, women, and a few foreigners. Part of me wanted to flee, and part of me was transfixed, immobile. I spotted a few of the older foreign men, leaning toward younger men, ready to fall, with anticipation buoying their drooping faces.

A youth in a NY baseball cap, a sleeveless T-shirt, and tight jeans stopped in front of me, pointed to his wrist and said, "*La hora?*" He looked like one of my students.

"12:15," I answered abruptly and we walked on.

"You don't like him?" Osmani asked.

"Osmani, what is this all about? I don't know what Gerard told you, but—"

"It's cool."

"No, it's not *cool!*" I pictured Laurie, the woman on the plane, and wondered what she would think if she drove by and saw me. How could I explain this to her? I couldn't explain it to myself.

Osmani looked at me like I was a sad case. "So you want to go home?" he said with hurt in his voice.

"I'm tired."

For a moment he wrinkled his face, and then went back to the pitying look. "All right. Let's go."

About halfway back through the crowd, he stopped again and said, "Wait a minute." He left me in the middle of the sidewalk and approached a thin young man sitting on the wall. Then he called me over and introduced me. I didn't catch the man's name, but he held my hand just a moment too long with an inquisitive look on his handsome face. His features were somber with full lips, the lower one hanging down slightly and looking a little puffy. Dark eyes peered out from barely open lids, like the slit eyes of a cat adapted for night hunting. At the same time he didn't seem like the others, obviously on the make. More of a friendly drunk. I was the first to look away, and then, when my eyes came back to him, they rested on the lion's head tattooed on his right bicep.

"You like my tattoo?" His voice grabbed me and made me want to talk to him.

"Is it a friendly lion?"

"Sure. Like a little pussycat. I have several more. Look at this one."

He was wearing a red Nike T-shirt with the sleeves cut off. The one on his other arm was a long fire-breathing dragon crawling up to perch on his bicep.

"Does it...uh...hurt?"

"Not now." He laughed.

"I mean when you get it."

"It doesn't hurt much on the arms. Some of the ones in other places hurt a lot more." He winked, and for a moment I thought he was going to show me the other places.

His friends edged closer, waiting to be introduced. Osmani indicated that he wanted to talk to his friend in private, and they walked just far enough away to be out of earshot. The other friends came still closer and offered me a swig of rum mixed with lemon soda in a small plastic cup. It was three parts rum to one part soda, and I winced at my first taste of the biting street rum. They laughed and offered to put in more soda.

"That's okay," I said. Out of the corner of my eye I watched Osmani and his handsome friend moving their hands and positioning themselves like boxers, speaking forcefully. I wasn't sure if it was an argument or just the way Cubans talked to each other. I *was* sure I didn't want to be in the middle of a confrontation. I started to move in the direction of the apartment. But Osmani and his friend finished their conversation and blocked my path. The tattooed guy brushed past me, swiping his hand gently across my back as he retook his place on the wall. His unexpected touch sent a shock up my spine. I stepped back and Osmani took my arm, turning toward me, so that the others wouldn't hear. "He's very nice, huh? You like him?"

"Were you guys talking about me?"

"No, man. We had to clear up some old shit. I think he likes you, though."

"Look, Osmani, I need to go home."

He clucked at my answer. "He's a good guy. He won't ask you for money like the others here."

I looked at him with outrage. "Money? Are you serious?"

"Okay, but we can't be rude. They invited us to drink a little with them."

We turned back toward the group and Osmani's friend held out the plastic cup in my direction. With a half smile he tilted his head in the form of a question. I walked over and took the cup. "What did you say your name was?"

"Leonardo. Just call me Leo. And yours?"

"Martin." I pronounced it "Mar-TEEN" like in Spanish, so that I wouldn't have to repeat it several times.

He stuck out his hand and we shook again. "We already did this," I said, looking down at our joined hands, his a creamy brown and mine a rosy white.

"Yeah, but a person worth meeting once is worth meeting twice."

I produced a shallow laugh, the nerves around my mouth twitching. "What makes you think I'm worth meeting?"

"Because you're from somewhere else. Because you can tell me about the world out there." He swept his arm toward the dark sea behind him.

One of Leo's friends, Ricardo, butted in and asked, "Where is your boyfriend?" Osmani had drifted away.

"He's not my boyfriend."

"You don't have a Cuban boyfriend?"

"Not Cuban, not any kind."

"Where are you staying?" Ricardo continued.

Leonardo saw that I was annoyed with the questions. "*Ricardo, déjale en paz.* Let him be."

I gave him a smile of thanks and took the cup again. Already feeling the rum, I leaned back against the wall. Leo patted the seat next to him and I hoisted myself up on to the cement still warm from the sun of day.

In passing the cup back and forth, he let his hand fall on my leg. It felt heavy and the heat of it seeped through my jeans like a hot iron. My thigh twitched and he took it away.

"Sorry," he said.

"It's just…"

"Just what?"

"Nothing. I arrived last night, my first trip to Cuba. It's all…different." He passed me the cup and I drank some more. It didn't taste strong now, just soothing.

"Let me see your hand." He took my right hand and joined the palm of his left with it. "Look, they're the same size."

I started to say, "So what?" but I remained quiet. Terrified quiet.

"You have nice hands," he said, now holding mine between his.

"I'm a teacher," I said as if that explained it. I took my hand back.

"See, when I first saw you, I knew you were a person who could teach me something. I would like to be in your class. Sit in the first row." He sent out flashes of light with his eyes and his smile was contagious.

"You don't even know what I teach. I might teach something like nuclear physics."

"I doubt it. You look too nice for that. I'd say something to do with languages or history."

"Osmani told you, right?"

"I just knew." He casually let his hand fall again on my leg, but this time on top of my hand. His fingers slipped perfectly into the grooves. It felt good, normal, until I thought about what I was doing. I pulled away.

"What's wrong?"

"Nothing." I tried to sound casual, and then he enveloped his arm around my shoulders, pulling me toward him so that my head was touching his. I could feel his hair, gelled into a spiky do, stiff against the side of my head.

"Don't worry. It's okay." His voice was like a foghorn, full of bass and vibrato. I tried to laugh off my predicament and imagined this was a game that no one took seriously. All I had to do was get up, walk back to the apartment, and escape into a dreamless sleep. It was so simple. I grabbed the cup, took a big swallow to fortify myself, and handed it back to Leonardo. I stood up ready to leave.

"What are you thinking?" he asked.

"Nothing. And you? No, let me guess. You're thinking about your wife and kids back home."

"*Coño!*" he said, his voice shooting up toward the sky. In a short time I had come to know his range from gravelly low to squeaky high when he got excited. His eyes pierced the film through which I viewed the world. I was hypnotized by the movement of the crowd around me, the rum, and Leonardo's penetrating stare. I leaned back against the wall, and he had his arm around my shoulders again. I closed my eyes, listening to the sound of voices, the faint lapping of the sea behind the wall, but louder than all of it was his whisper in my ear: "*Tranquilo.*"

Osmani reappeared and winked at Leo. "What are we going to do?" he said.

"I gotta go to bed soon," I said and stood up straight.

"Alone?" Osmani asked.

I looked at Leo. "Maybe we can do something tomorrow. Have lunch?"

"Have lunch?" He shrugged, and in a cool shift of gears said, "I think I'm busy."

"What are you going to do now, Leo?" asked Osmani.

"It's too late to go back to where I'm staying. Just stay here. I have no place to go." Leo's voice was neatly shaded with disappointment.

"See," Osmani said to me, "he doesn't have a place to crash. He can at least come back to the apartment, sleep on the couch or something."

"I don't know. It's not my apartment," I said. I thought of Gerard's drill sergeant roommate, who wouldn't be happy if we dragged somebody home. "It's not a good idea."

Osmani took charge and had us all on our feet, heading toward the apartment. I threw up my arms, but protested no further. We walked in silence under a nearly full moon, Leo walking very close to me, our hands sometimes bumping.

At the apartment door Osmani fumbled with the keys. He tried one after another until they slipped from his hands to the floor. Leo, who had had more to drink than any of us, picked them up, examined the lock, fished out a key, slid it in, and opened the door within seconds.

5

In my wet clothes I sat in the Habana Libre lobby bar, sipping a glass of Havana Club Añejo Reserva with the air conditioning blasting down on me. A pair of shivers rattled my icy back. For three years I had imagined what it would be like to see Leo again, but I never came close to predicting the gut-wrenching pain, the pure misery of looking into the eyes of a lost love.

In those grim days following the break with Leo and the hopeful but still shaky change in my relationship with Lizzie, David came into my life and lifted me up from my despair. He was good for me, and I would be the worst kind of fool if I jeopardized my relationship with someone who gave his blessing to this trip, knowing the story of my time in Cuba. Though ten years younger than me, he was more mature, more solid, a person to grow old with.

I downed the rest of the rum and went up to my room. With my eyes on the phone I peeled off the damp clothes, put on a hotel robe, and picked up the receiver.

"David, it's me."

"Well, this is a surprise. I thought you said it was too expensive to call."

"It is, but I wanted to hear your voice."

"Are you okay?"

"Fine. Have you thought any more about adoption?"

"Is that what you called about?"

"I just wondered."

"You sound strange."

"A bit lonely, I guess."

"It's only been two days."

"Two days and a lifetime."

"Martin, you're being weird. What's going on?"

"It's probably the heat. You can't imagine how hot it is here."

"I had dinner with Jenny and Jack last night. She's showing, Grandpa."

"You are cruel. Maybe adoption isn't such a good idea."

"Would you stop already with the adoption? We'll talk about it when you get back. You *are* coming back, aren't you?"

"Very funny."

"I miss you."

"Miss you, too."

As soon as I got off the phone with David, I called Cubana Airlines and booked a flight to Holguín.

When Madelin showed up at Los Amigos Restaurant, I didn't recognize her. It had been three years, and her signature wild blonde curls had been transformed to shoulder-length brown waves. Her style of dress was also more discreet—a beige pantsuit with a string of pearls at her neck.

"A new look for a new life," she explained after a double-cheeked European kiss. "Rafael has asked me to marry him, and we're going to Spain."

"That's great, what you always wanted. Will you be near your brother?"

"It's a dream come true, marrying Rafa and being close to my brother in Barcelona. And what about you? Did you get everything sorted out with your wife?"

"We separated…amicably. I have a partner now, David."

"Tell me about him."

"He's a grade-school teacher, patient, very nice-looking. He grew up in California, Mexican-American. My Spanish is better than his."

She gave me a funny look and poked at the salad with her fork. "You don't sound very…excited."

"He's a great guy. He really is. It's just that…"

"You can't forget Leo, right? Are you sure you just came to Cuba for the conference?"

"I would have been fine. I would have gotten through this all right if I hadn't run the hell right into him on the Malecón."

"You ran into him?"

"I was walking along nearly delirious with the heat, minding my own business, and almost at the exact spot where I met him, I looked up and there he was, walking with his daughter and another man. I freaked."

In a moment her eyes were moist, absorbed in my dilemma. "Another man?" She sniffed and scrunched up her beautiful nose.

"He's an Argentinean who's married to his ex-wife, Sulyn. They live in Argentina now with Anabela. That's the saddest part. Leo doesn't even have his daughter with him, his one true love."

"Another Cuban family torn apart," she said with disgust.

"But Leo is waiting for his visa so he can leave. The Argentinean is arranging it, which I think is rather magnanimous."

"What was it like seeing him again?"

"Devastating. I felt like I always did in his presence, weak and overwhelmed. But I did a good job of hiding it. We only talked for a few minutes and then they had to go."

"And the baby? What is she like?"

"She's a little girl now, almost four years old. She's adorable. She looks so much like him it's scary."

The main dish arrived, and we both took a deep breath and exhaled at the same time, then laughed at our need to let the air out of the past.

"What about your other friends here in Havana? Have you seen them?" she asked.

"Gerard finally left Cuba. He's in Venezuela doing translation for the government. I don't know about Luka. I've called his house a bunch of times, but no one answers."

She put down her fork and raised her hand to her mouth still partially full of food. She swallowed hard. "You don't know?"

I stared at her a long time over the edge of my wine glass, her large brown eyes now swimming with tears. A choking sound escaped from my throat. "When?" I managed.

"About a year ago. I ran into Monica on the street and she told me."

"It's my fault," I groaned. "My fault."

"I'm sure it's not."

"I stopped sending medicine. I tried to make sure Tomás's people were getting it to him, but I didn't follow up. I had just met David, and Cuba couldn't be part of my life anymore if we were to make a go of it."

"I don't think the medicine had anything to do with it. Monica said he got pneumonia."

My mind drifted back to the first time we met, when Luka burst into Gerard's apartment like a shining star, full of life and an ear-to-ear smile. We stood side by side on the balcony, and his hand so close to mine on the rail opened a tiny door.

We finished the bottle of wine, but little of the food. On the corner I put Madelin in a taxi and promised to visit her in Spain. I didn't tell her that I made a reservation to go to Holguín. I hardly believed it myself. After my book presentation the following afternoon, I would head to the airport.

6

July 2001

There was a single lamp in the corner of the living room casting a soft amber light as Leo and I stood awkwardly in the no-man's-land between the door and the sofa. Osmani had disappeared, and Leo was bent forward with his hands in his pockets, waiting for me to say something. After a tense few moments, he asked for the bathroom. I took him through the bedroom and turned on the bathroom light. I stepped back into the room and sat on the side of the bed, letting my head fall back onto the mattress. He didn't close the door and I was shocked how loud the stream hitting the toilet water sounded. Then there was pressure on the bed and I opened my eyes. He was sitting on the bed at a respectable distance with his hands between his legs. I ran my eyes over the curve of his back, his bones showing through his T-shirt, the back of his head with its thick black hair.

"Where should I sleep?" he said, looking at the double bed and surveying the room. I lifted myself up and noticed that the door to the living room was closed. I had a moment of paranoia that he could rob me, beat me up.

"Did you close the door?" I asked.

"I think it was Osmani. We could sleep toe to head."

"Do what?"

"You know. You have your head at that end and I have my head down there."

"Then I get to smell your feet. Great."

"They don't smell *too* bad," he laughed.

"Just get in bed normal. I'm going to the bathroom."

I spent a long time in the bathroom with the door closed, sitting on the seat cover of the toilet, waiting for him to fall asleep. I knew I wouldn't be able to sleep even though I was drunk and wanted nothing more than to pass out. At home I slept by myself and was used to getting up and going to bed when I wanted, taking over the whole bed if I wanted, farting if I felt like it.

When I emerged from the bathroom, the bedside lamp was on, the red shade giving a rosy glow to the white sheet covering his body. I looked down at the pile of clothes on the floor—shoes, socks, T-shirt, jeans…and underwear, nondescript gray bikini briefs. I stared at them in panic, and then looked again at the shape of his body; he was on his side facing the far wall. With a feather touch I lifted the sheet and got a brief glimpse of his hairy buttocks before I stretched myself out along the very edge of the mattress, reached up and turned off the light. There was no noise from the bar down on the street, and no air passed through the room. I was hot in my tank top and boxers, afraid to breathe for fear of waking him. A small clock ticked. Why couldn't I hear his breathing? There was a rustle of mattress material, movement, skin sliding on sheets, my held breath, the darkness, the heat, my body damp with sweat, the touch, muscles tensing up, arms wrapping around, a body pressed up against my back, my fists clenched. It was one smooth motion, like a mother scooping a child into her arms. But I was not a child and I felt trapped, trapped in tenderness.

"Relax," he whispered. "Sometimes you just have to let what is going to happen happen."

"No," I whispered back. He must have felt my heart thumping. He must have known that I didn't want to be wrapped up like a package.

"Yes," blew into my ear and through my body. He licked my earlobe. I tried to move out of his grasp, but he held me tight. He was much stronger than I had imagined. He pulled me closer to him.

"Let me go," I said through my teeth and tried to free myself from his arms. He had one hand under my shirt and was rubbing my chest.

"Tell me you don't want this and I'll stop."

"I don't want this."

"Say it to my face. Look at me and say it to my face."

I turned my face to him and said, "I don't want this."

In the pale light from outside I could see his smile begin to fade, but there was still a certainty in his eyes that I was lying. "All right. Have it your way." He separated himself from me and stretched out on his side of the bed, facing the wall. Instead of relief, I felt loss. I stared at the shadows on the ceiling as the abandonment drained the life out of me. Every cell in my brain was telling me I did the right thing while every fiber of my body was aching to be held. My heart was pounding hard against my ribcage, a wild animal trying to escape.

"Leo?"

"What?" he answered in an uninterested voice.

"Can we talk about this?"

"Talk? There's nothing to talk about."

I moved over closer to him and put a hand on his shoulder. He shook it off, but then sighed. He turned his face to mine and kissed me before I could object. Our lips parted and I touched the stubble on his face. He touched mine. He smiled. I frowned. He started to kiss me again, but I turned my head to the side.

He put a hand on the back of my head and nestled it into the crook of his neck. "*Tranquilo,* baby. It's okay." Rather than calm me, his voice was pure oxygen and I was riding new sensations, plunging down white-water rapids. Then he lifted my undershirt over my head and pulled my shorts down. When they were down to my knees he pushed them to my ankles with his foot. I did nothing, could do nothing, to stop him.

Our bodies were entangled so that I wasn't sure whose hands, arms, legs, cocks were whose, so much skin on skin, so many points of contact and each one firing. The ride was going too fast, and he sped it forward by going down to my nipples with his tongue, licking them, flicking them. I didn't realize I was moaning until he told me, "Shh. You'll wake everybody."

My world was burning and on the screen of my tightly shut eyes the flames lapped at the bridges to the past. My head was spinning. My hand was burrowed into his thick black hair. I held on, not knowing how far I was willing to go, but on the edge of a great fall. And then his head went still on my chest. I opened my eyes and heard the breathing of slumber. "No," I said. "It can't be."

"Huh?" he mumbled without regaining consciousness.

I awoke in a new world, lying on my side with Leo spooning me from behind, his arm across my chest. I gazed at a grayish smudge on the closet door, the faded Indian bedspread draped over the chair by the bed, the crooked shade of the bedside lamp. I pondered in disbelief what had happened and took a deep breath. He gave me a squeeze, touched the back of my neck with his lips, and then was gone again. In the sobering dawn my heart was still pounding like I had been running in a dream, pursued by shadowy elements that wanted to do me harm. But what harm had Leo done to me? He held me sweetly like I hadn't been held for a long time, his breath a feather tickling the back of my neck.

I wiggled out of his dead-weight arms and got up to pee. When I came back, I fell into the bedside stuffed chair and watched him sleep. He had turned on his side facing away from me, and in the mirror that ran the length of the bed along the far wall I could see his fluttering eyelids and parted lips, the lips I kissed a few hours before. I stared at them, finding it difficult to believe it happened. In the diffused light of breaking day, I saw a long scar on the side of his neck. There was another peeking out above the sheet on his upper back, and I was certain the lion of his tattoo winked at me.

As if in response to my hard stare, Leo stirred and his eyes creaked open. He saw me looking at him in the mirror and rolled over. "What are you doing?"

"Just watching you sleep."

"Come here." I stayed put. With his head he pointed to the space next to him. His smile was almost a sneer.

I shook my head.

"Come on. I won't hurt you. Just want to hold you."

"Just hold." I rolled onto the bed beside him and he put his arms around me, kissing me on the top of my head. "*Tonto*," he whispered. As soon as I was in his arms again I felt like I had taken a drug, fireworks snapping and popping on the surface of my skin up and down my body. He dozed off, but I felt like I was at the circus, bombarded by unaccustomed sights and raw smells. I was five years old and I couldn't sit still.

"You're not going to let me sleep?" he groaned.

"All right, you sleep and I'll take a shower." I started to get up, stopped, sat on the side of the bed with a hard-on. "God, this is not right," I mumbled

After a cool shower I pulled back the curtain and saw him standing over the toilet, shaking off the last drops. He grabbed the towel off the rack and brought it to me as I stood dripping, my arms hanging heavily at my sides.

"Come on, get out."

I stepped onto the small faded carpet and he started to dab me with the towel. I got a good look at his scars, but I tried not to stare. He had a six-inch-long one that began at his sternum and traveled down to the center of his navel. I could clearly see the hatch pattern of where they had sewn him up. There was another two-inch one on his upper chest, a similar one on his arm that had healed in an irregular pattern, and the clean five-inch slice on the side of his neck that I had seen before. When he finished drying me off and went to hang up the towel, I discovered six more gashes on his back.

As the light streamed in the bathroom window on the wounds of his otherwise beautiful body, I was rocked by a mix of repulsion and empathy, wanting to shy away, to not imagine the pain that was once there. At the same time I had an equally compelling impulse to touch them, like an unconscious primitive attraction to someone who had survived an attack by a ferocious beast. He was someone to latch onto in the wild jungle of this world, someone who carried himself with the self-assurance of having looked death in the eye, unafraid to confront what life might put in his path.

As he stepped past me on his way to the shower he gave me a quick kiss on the lips and the normalcy of his action astounded me. His breath was sour, tobacco-laced, his hair tousled. All his imperfections—and mine—were in full view, and yet he was striking in the way he moved, a natural man at ease with himself. I lingered outside the shower curtain, listening to the water patter down on his skin.

With my towel wrapped around me I went back to the bedroom and stretched out on the crumpled sheets. I was sober and yet I was getting a merry-go-round effect, the spinning in my mind of things that didn't make sense. My gut was twisted in a knot. I didn't have much time to be in my misery for even with my eyes closed I saw his nakedness enter the room, his dampness come toward me, and then he was straddling me. "Wake up, sleepyhead."

He leaned down to press his lips to mine, and then quickly withdrew a few inches. I opened my eyes to the sight of his head at an angle, questioning. Like a spider getting ready to devour his trapped prey, he leaned down, down, down until his face blurred and our lips met. The kiss melted away all the thousands of reasons that we should not be together. Minutes went by and egos were suspended. There was no difference in age, in culture, in language, in body types, in economic levels, in education. There was no intrusion like sexual orientation. There was no *me*. But then I remembered I had to breathe, and when I gasped for air, the little bits of my surroundings began to fall back into place. He had shifted his legs so that his weight was full upon me and parts of my body were feeling pain. Again I smelled his breath.

My mouth was pressed against the scar on the side of his neck and he scrunched his shoulder to his cheek, and started to giggle. "You're tickling me."

"Oh, sorry."

"It makes me weak," he said as if I were seducing *him*. Then he took my hand and put it between his legs.

Once when I was in high school, I slept over at Ronny Blake's house and we got drunk on his father's whiskey. He said if I jacked him off he would do me after. It seemed fair enough. It was just a thin pole and in the dark it didn't seem to have any connection to a body. I stroked it. And then there was warm liquid shooting over my leg. He passed out and left me betrayed. We never talked about it or did it again. I started working on Leo, but I couldn't forget that this one *was* attached to a body, a person.

"He's a little shy," Leo said. "He might need more than that." He pointed with his head down there and raised his eyebrows slightly. I froze.

"What? You don't do that?" he asked.

"No. I mean, I don't know."

"You don't know?"

"I am being born again. Gimme a break."

"Turn around."

"No way."

"I won't stick it in. I promise."

"Only the tip, right?" I said sarcastically.

"What?"

"Never mind."

In the end we rubbed up against each other, our bodies moving in sync until we both came. I rolled over on my back and stared at the ceiling, floating on the essence of soap from our showers, now mixed with sweat and the musty smells of sex.

"That wasn't very satisfying," he said. "It's not really sex if you don't...you know."

My body tensed up, and I felt a surprising chill in the warm room. I was caught between a fear that he would flee in disappointment and a resounding wish that he would. It was so quiet I could hear the traffic and people talking down on the street. I ventured a look at his face and noticed his eyes were closed. And then from his lips, "Are you okay?"

"I don't know."

"You're full of I-don't-knows today. What was that you said about being born?"

"Nothing."

"All right, I'm going to take a shower. Maybe you'll know something when I get back."

I took my turn in the shower and when I came back to the bed he was stretched out facedown, his elbows propping himself up over a book he had picked up from the headboard bookshelf, a children's book in Spanish called *El Cuento de Ferdinando* by Munro Leaf. I lay down beside him, and he pushed the book over so that I could see it. On the inside cover was a large poster on a wall of a Spanish town that said, "*El Toro Ferroz: Ferdinando*. The Ferocious Bull."

"Why don't you read it to me?" he said.

"You want to make fun of my pronunciation?"

"No, I want to hear you read."

"*Todos los otros toritos con quienes él vivía corrían y brincaban y se daban topetadas, pero Ferdinando no. Le gustaba sentarse en simple quietud y oler las flores. Tenía un lugar favorito afuera en la pradera debajo de un alcornoque.*" Leo helped me with the pronunciation of "*alcornoque.*" It was a story about a little bull that didn't like to run and jump and play rough like the other bulls, but preferred to sit under his favorite tree and smell the flowers. One day a group of men came to look for the liveliest, most ferocious bull to fight in the bullring. As they examined the bulls, a bee stung Ferdinando and made him go wild, so they chose him to fight in the ring.

I continued reading. "*Cuando llegó al centro de la arena y vio las flores que las hermosas damas tenían en el cabello, todo lo que hizo fue sentarse en quietud y olerlas.*" When he got to the bullring where he was expected to fight, he saw the flowers in the hair of the pretty women and all he wanted to do was to sit down quietly and smell them. In the end he got to go back home and lived quietly ever after.

"*Que mariconcito!*" Leo said in a joking way. "What a little gay boy!"

"You didn't like it?" I wanted to defend Ferdinando.

"I *did* like it. He was a little gay, but really smart. After some bad luck, he came out all right in the end." We went back and looked at all the pictures, making comments about the different expressions on

Ferdinando's face, and had a good laugh at every one. Holding the book, we were connected, and he took it a step further by draping one leg over the top of mine, dragging our legs closer together. I was baffled by his ease that allowed him to wrap me in his private world, though I still looked at myself with outside eyes, rattled by self-conscious shaky emotions that flowed over me like the tide, dragging me in and pulling me out.

It was the time of day that the heat was most brutal, but the *paladar*, a family-run restaurant of a few tables and chairs set up in the living room of an old home on Línea, was like a deep freeze. Leo and Osmani, unused to air conditioning, sat on their hands and shivered. Then Leo removed one hand to lift up his shirt and show how his unusually flat stomach had gotten even flatter. He and Osmani compared notes on the last time they had had a decent meal.

When the pasta dishes came they attacked the food and washed it down with gulps of beer. I stared down at my pasta alfredo. It looked like a heap of cardboard strips covered with paste. On the other side of the table Leo put his fork down, took a sip of beer, and reached for a cigarette. The he burst into laughter at something Osmani said but I didn't catch. I remembered when Lizzie and I used to go out to eat after we first met, and how she would smoke as soon as she finished her meal. She loved to drink beer and would often break into raucous laughter. It embarrassed me and I resented that she could be so free, a leftist who knew how to have fun.

Under the table Leo put his hand on my vibrating leg and forced it to stop.

"Martin, where are you? Come on, eat. The wind is going to blow you away." He made me laugh because that's what they used to tell me when I was a skinny child.

"I don't think there's any chance of that now," I said, looking down at my stomach.

"Anyway, I wouldn't let it," Leo said. He held my knee and batted his long eyelashes.

At Gerard's building we stood in the lobby waiting for the elevator. Leo and Osmani patted their full stomachs and faked moans of complete satisfaction, and though I felt lost, I was strangely content. Leo stood so close to me I sensed the warmth of his skin. The elevator door opened and several people came out, including Giovani, who glared at us and then went off in a huff without a greeting. Inside the elevator I looked at Osmani and shook my head.

"Don't worry," he said. "When Gerard gets back I'm going to tell him everything. You don't know how mean he has been to me."

Out on the terrace we sat around the glass-topped metal table, which reflected the blue sky above us. Leo and Osmani resumed their conversation about life in the provinces, how hard it was and how there were no jobs. Though Havana presented more opportunities, they agreed that the city had other problems. The people were different, unfriendly; everybody was out to get you, not like the people back home who were always there to give you a helping hand.

"What about it, Leo?" said Osmani. "Do you prefer to live here or back in Holguín?"

"No doubt about it. Holguín. As soon as I can, I'm going back. I haven't seen my mom in a few months and she misses me a lot. She's alone." He pulled a small snapshot out of his wallet and showed it to us. She was a pretty, dark-haired woman with a youthful smile.

"How old is she?" Osmani asked.

"She's forty-two, no, forty-three."

"She looks much younger," I said. He took the photo and lovingly put it back in his wallet. We hadn't discussed age, though I imagined him to be in his mid-twenties.

"She depends on me a lot. My father left—she kicked him out—shortly after I was born. He drank too much and she got sick of it."

"Do you still see your father?" I asked.

"Oh, yeah. Everything's cool now. He comes over to the house with his new wife and my half-brothers."

"You're lucky to at least have half-brothers," commented Osmani. "I have a sister, but she left a long time ago with my mom to the States. I don't have anybody."

Leo glanced at his watch. "I have to go back home."

"To Holguín?" I said with a squeaky concern in my voice.

"No, man, to my place here," he said laughing. "What are you doing tonight?"

We agreed to meet at 10 p.m. at the apartment, and he gave me his phone number, "In case you change your mind," he said. Down on the street we shook hands and I took out my wallet to give him five dollars. "For transportation," I said uneasily. He hadn't asked me for anything as Osmani promised. He looked at the bill blankly and muttered something about helping the woman in his house. I assumed that he was staying in a woman's house and that he had to contribute for food and household expenses. I knew so little about his life or what he was doing in Havana.

I came back from a walk in the afternoon and spied Osmani sitting on the street outside of Gerard's building with another young man whom he introduced as his brother, Jorge.

"What are you doing down here in the heat?"

"Just talking."

"Wouldn't it be more comfortable upstairs? God, I'm dying."

Osmani and Jorge gave each other a cautious look and then Osmani blurted out, "There was some money missing from Gerard's apartment, and he thought Jorge took it."

"It wasn't me," Jorge whined.

"Anyway, he's banned from the apartment."

"Martin, can you buy me a beer?" asked Jorge in a syrupy voice.

"No, not now."

But I did sit and talk with them. They wanted to know where I lived, what my house was like, what kind of car I had, how much my watch cost, what I paid for various things. I was planning my escape when I noticed a man crossing the street wearing a tight black T-shirt, and red-and-white-striped jeans. As he got closer I recognized Luka, and was pleased, though confused, to see him again so soon. He came over and we shook hands.

"I was visiting a friend nearby, so I thought I would stop and see how you're getting along."

"Let's go get a beer," I said. Jorge gave me a nasty look.

We went back to La Fuente and ordered a couple of Bucaneros. The last two years had been tough for him, he told me. He met a Spaniard who was going to help him leave the country. They did all the paperwork and he had his visa, but two weeks before he was supposed to leave, Luka came down with a rare virus that left him unable to walk for almost six months. He looked fully recovered, but I could see in his eyes how hard it was to be so close to leaving and instead have to spend months in terrible pain, getting around in a wheelchair.

"There will be other chances," Luka said with false confidence. "What are you doing tonight?"

"Me? Uh…I sort of have plans."

"Did you find a girlfriend already?"

I stared at him, shaken by his question. "No, nothing like that."

"Oh, that's right. You're married." He was looking at me with that same devilish grin that he had the day before.

"I am. Married. But I got drunk last night and…"

"Don't tell me you did something with one of those guys I saw you talking to?"

"No, but I did go with Osmani to the Malecón. Let me ask you, do all those guys just go there for money?"

"Not all of them. I go there. Lots of my friends go there. Did you meet someone?"

"Osmani introduced me to a friend of his."

"What did you do? Bring him home?"

"Not like that. I mean, he didn't have a place to stay and we were drunk. He offered to sleep toe to head…"

"The same old story," he said and shook his head in disbelief.

"Nothing happened." I lied, disturbed by the look on his face.

"Then why are you seeing him again?"

"He's nice. He invited me to have a beer with his friends."

"Better be careful. You don't know what you're getting into." His tone had changed and he sounded angry with me, or at least disappointed. When we parted he was cold, distant, not the carefree young man that I had met the day before.

   I only had an hour to shower and get ready before Leo was supposed to arrive. From my room I heard Osmani and Giovani arguing in the back bedroom, muffled voices rising, interrupting, rapid-firing Spanish that eluded me. A few minutes later Giovani came in my room with a determined look on his face and a puffed-up chest. "Gerard doesn't want *jineteros* in this house, and I saw you bring that guy up in the elevator. We've had too many problems."

   His use of the word I only learned the night before left a cold stone in the pit of my stomach. "Do you know Leo?" I threw back at him.

   "No."

   "Then how do you know—?"

   "I don't have to know him. I am Cuban. I know. Please don't invite him to this house again." He turned and walked out, my protest still stuck in my throat. I was furious he had been so rude while at the same time I wondered what he knew, what he saw. Was I missing something? Was Leo out to fleece me? *Jinetero* sounded harsh, even felt harsh inside your mouth when you said it. As much as I wanted to throw his remark aside, Giovani had taken me off my cloud and made me look at myself in the mirror; I hated him for it. Everything spun around in my head and the only thing that was certain was that I had to intercept Leo before he came up in the elevator and caused an awkward scene. Then I had to figure out what to say, how to tell him I couldn't go out with him. Of course he would see right through me. He was good at that. He would grab me, hold me, beg me to be with him again. I laughed at my own insane fantasy. He probably needed some money. All that act about missing his mother. I would buy him a bus ticket to Holguín, give him some money and then say goodbye. I didn't need distractions. I had work to do.

   I sat on the same low wall by the building driveway where I had sat earlier with Osmani and his brother. Cars stopped and people got out, but none of them turned out to be Leo. In the distance I spotted a young guy walking toward the building, yet as he got closer I realized it wasn't him. I tried to remember exactly what he looked like, but I had lost some of the details.

In the fresh air I began to see things differently. My new approach was to be cool. Why couldn't we be friends, and maybe sex? I couldn't believe I was even thinking about that, though I had hardly thought about anything else all day. In the echo chamber of my brain, over and over I kept hearing the sound, the one that started as a low, crude moan and ended up a muffled shout when I made him come.

Several times I stood up to go back upstairs, and then sat down again. He was forty-five minutes late and a new anxiety set in—he wasn't coming. All this raking myself over the coals had been for nothing.

Osmani came around the corner. "Where's Leo?"

"You tell me."

"Why don't you call him?"

"It's late. If he had wanted to come, he would have. Anyway, I don't need this."

Out of the shadows appeared Jorge. He was the devil materializing out of nowhere to tap you on the shoulder and whisper some smarmy bargain in your ear, which, if you agree to it, would solve your problem. Maybe he would offer up Leo if I agreed to sell him my soul.

"*Hola, compadres,*" he said.

"Leo didn't show up," said Osmani.

"Too bad, but you've got us." He sniggered.

Osmani gave me an embarrassed grin. "Why don't we go to the Malecón? He's probably there."

The three of us headed for the Malecón and I walked hesitantly, pushing each step forward and holding back with the same force. Jorge was drunk and started in on me immediately. Though he told me he was nineteen, he looked about twelve, which made all the pick-up lines coming out of his mouth seem ludicrous. "What do I have to do to be your boyfriend? I can give you a great massage."

I ignored him. He was like a pesky fly that I wanted to swat away. Osmani was more like a little puppy dog that followed along in hopes that one day you would notice him and scoop him up. Walking between them and a head taller than both, I imagined what I must look like to others. Again I pictured Laurie happening along and catching me with two boys less than half my age.

Leo wasn't on the Malecón though we ran into his two friends, Ricardo and Humberto, from the night before. They were sober and not very friendly. "Where's Leo?" Osmani asked. "He had a date with Martin and he didn't show up."

"It wasn't really a *date*," I said.

"I talked to him earlier," said Ricardo. "He's not going out. Hey, Martin, can you buy us a bottle?" I gave them a few dollars and said I was going home.

"I'll go with you," said Jorge.

"No, you won't. I know the way back." At least I thought I did.

7

The one thing I knew was that I had to get this trip back on track, get back to my mission. "Idle hands do the devil's work," my grandmother always used to say. Martí awaited me. I had abandoned him, not done a single bit of research, not written a single note, not even gone to see the grand statue in Plaza de la Revolución. On my second night in Havana I had gotten drunk and lost my head. Why did this happen here, now? I had had opportunities before, young men and women coming into my office and looking at me in a way that could open a door to something beyond a discussion about the Mexican Revolution. I had caught dreamy-eyed stares in my lectures, but getting involved with a student would not only have been inappropriate, it just didn't interest me. The change I needed in my life was to write this book and get it published.

I needed to escape from Gerard's apartment as if it were cursed, and I turned to Osmani for help. He acted offended that I wanted to leave, and only reluctantly wrote down the address of someone he knew who rented rooms. The house turned out to be full of offbeat characters and wasn't clean. I turned it down.

In front of Gerard's apartment, there was a stout woman with cropped hair walking a miniature poodle on a short leash. She had stopped to let the dog do its business right in the middle of the side-walk. She looked me in the eye. "Are you the one searching for an apartment?"

I looked at her suspiciously. "How did you know?"

"That young man told me. I have an apartment with independent entrance right here in a secure building. Do you want to see it?" She pointed toward a boxy three-story 1950s building right next to Gerard's.

"How much?"

She didn't answer, only waved for me to follow her.

The dog hadn't quite finished dumping, but she yanked the leash and led the way.

The apartment had the basics: air conditioning, hot water, telephone, TV, and a separate living room. In the main room there was a refrigerator, counter, and sink, but nothing to cook on. When I told her I wanted to cook, Rosa offered to get a hot plate and promised to bring it by no later than the following day. We shook hands on our agreement.

I stood on the cracked, baking asphalt in the middle of the Plaza de la Revolución and looked up at the monstrous white marble statue of Martí—in life a diminutive man, in death a giant. He stared down at me, and I felt small, confused, insignificant. I weaved my way across the street through heavy traffic and moved toward him, around the massive white pedestal, his stern eyes following me, sizing me up, as if knowing how I had spent my time in Havana. I escaped through the glass double doors into the cool of the five-point tower that rose up behind him. In the marble lobby, I apprehensively bought a ticket to ride the elevator up to the highest lookout point in the city. Several tourists were waiting to go up, and I forced myself to believe that at the Martí monument they would have to keep the elevator in top working order. I was sweating profusely by the time we reached the top.

The sun beat mercilessly through the observation windows while vultures circled around the top of the tower, their wings gliding within inches of the thick Plexiglas windows. I was dizzy, and with the heat, close to passing out as I gazed down on the vast square and the official buildings that surrounded it, and then out to the patchwork of green interwoven with drab-colored structures. Out there somewhere was Leo. What was he doing? I pictured his slightly drawn face and how his head hung down when he had walked away the previous afternoon.

I heard voices speaking in French, coming from one of the other five points of the star, each one forming a small observation area. Then I heard a rough, gravelly voice that sounded like Leo, and I moved quickly through the other points of the tower until I found the one where they were gathered. I rushed in and stopped short. They turned to look at me. The voice I had heard was from a squat, hairy Cuban explaining the history of the monument while one of the French women translated.

"Sorry," I said and moved on.

I took the elevator down with two Japanese girls, who giggled at my fidgeting and flustered breathing. I stepped into the lobby and found Martí staring at me from a series of portraits in a gallery off to the right. Each of the artists had attempted to convey the power of the man, and all seemed to have failed. Still the eyes had their effect, and I fled the lobby as I had the statue. How could I write about this man? He was so great and I was nothing, less than nothing. I was squandering this opportunity of being in Cuba.

By the time I got back to the apartment, I had stopped beating myself up and resigned myself to being a lowly creature without scruples. I spread out the scrap of paper on the table with Leo's phone number written neatly across it at an angle. My heart was thumping an irregular beat. I punched the numbers slowly, precisely, forcing myself to be completely conscious of what I was doing. A woman answered and when I asked for him she said in an aggressive voice, "*De parte de quien*? Who's calling please?" I couldn't tell if she was a protective landlady, a nosey neighbor on a shared line, or a jealous wife.

He came on with his uneven voice and an unreadable attitude. I quickly felt like it was a mistake, but took a deep breath and dived in. "Are we going to, you know, see each other again?"

"Tonight." It was not a question.

"Where?"

"I'll meet you on the Malecón at 11 o'clock." Not the slightest hesitation in his answer.

"See you later then on the…uh… Malecón."

"What? No kiss for me?" he said.

I went blank at his question.

"That's okay. I'll get my kiss later."

An awkward laugh escaped my throat. It sounded so horrible I hung up.

It started to rain soon after I left the apartment, and by the time I got to the empty Malecón, it was pouring. I headed up the street known as La Rampa and tried to stay under trees and overhangs so as not to get drenched.

Outside a cafeteria on the corner of Calle O, I saw a large group, the crowd that would normally be on the Malecón. The rain had fallen off and as soon as I crossed the street I saw Ricardo and Humberto. They spotted me as well and motioned to Leo. He greeted me with a big smack of a handshake, acting cool, but with a beaming smile.

We went inside, a place was full of young Cubans milling around in tight, rain-spotted, shiny outfits, and several foreigners looking lost, their skin insipidly white in the bright lights. We got a bottle of rum and some cola, but Ricardo and Humberto were soon up greeting friends and sharing their drinks. They started flirting with a trendily dressed Spanish youth with blond streaks in his longish hair. The Spaniard's Cuban date sat brooding while they circled the table like sharks, eventually engaging him in conversation, inviting him to our table and introducing him to Leo and me.

We shook hands with the Spaniard, but then ignored them and talked about what we had done since we last saw each other. Before long his leg rubbed against mine, and his hand moved down to my knee. I put my hand on his and felt his calm energy pass through me. After we finished the bottle, Leo and I left, headed back to my place. Neither of us said where we were going, but his smile was wide and catlike when I reported I had rented my own apartment. On the street he turned and said, "Do you consider the five dollars you gave me the other day *ayuda*?" He said it without malice, but a punch in the stomach would have caused me less discomfort. We were stopped in the middle of the sidewalk and he looked at me with his lower lip jutted out like a challenge. I wanted to crawl away, and I let my eyes wander in search of an escape route.

"What? You want money for what we did? That's not…Osmani said…oh, shit. This is absurd! When I said the five dollars was for your transportation, I meant just that. I'm not stupid. I know people need help, but I thought we could talk about it if I saw you again. You didn't show up."

He took a step back. "*Tranquilo.* It's just that most guys like to help their friends because life is so difficult here. Anyway, we can still see each other until you leave."

"Who told you I wanted to hang around with you the whole time I'm here?"

He gave me a neat little smile and put his arm around me. "You called me, didn't you?"

In the dim light of the apartment I came out of the bathroom. Leo lifted up the sheet and I crawled in as if I were going into one of the living room tents my siblings and I used to make with sheets and blankets when we were kids. He wrapped me in a tight embrace and my sighs were audible as he hummed a tune we had heard in the bar earlier. The money discussion had been banished to a far corner, and though I was still petrified about the next step in this intimacy, I was confident that he would guide me through it. And then I felt his body settling, his arms relaxing, his mouth go slack.

"Leo?"

"Hm?" he mumbled.

"Nothing."

"*Mañana.*"

It was late morning and he held me. He wanted to sleep, but I was wide wake.

"Is there something that you want?" he grumbled.

I took his hand and moved it down so that he would be able to feel how hard I was, but his arm locked with his hand over my stomach. "No, I can't," he said.

"You can't what? You can't touch it?"

"No," he said as if it were the most logical thing in the world, as if he were expressing his preference for potatoes over carrots. The other night he had been a free spirit ready to kiss for hours and touch me all over, but to touch me there, the place that made me a man, was taboo. I was supposed to be the inhibited one, the neophyte dependent on him to show me the way. It had taken all my courage to make the bold move with his hand and now I was confused. I lay back and looked up at the ceiling while my erection faded.

"It doesn't mean I don't like you. It's just the way I am." He gazed down at me, trying to get into my eyes, but I looked past him. Then he bent down and started tonguing my nipples. He had already seen me go crazy over that. I tried to roll over, but he held me down and pinched my right nipple while he chewed on the left. I closed my eyes, but I had stopped resisting. We both had erections and his body was pressed on top of me.

"I want to give you something," he whispered. He was positioned now so that he was pushing it between my thighs.

I shook my head slowly from side to side. "No, I can't"

"I promise I'll be gentle."

"No."

He put his mouth against my ear and breathed with a desperate rhythm. Then desire caught us up in its wake and things became hazy. I opened my eyes and observed as if from a distance his casual motions— tearing open a foil packet with his teeth, spitting in his hand, kissing my knees and putting them on his shoulders, telling me to stroke myself. I closed my eyes in a futile attempt to block it out. He was probing, pushing. I pretended it wasn't happening, until a sharp pain made it undeniable. I tried to move back, force it out, but he kept on pushing and I thought I was going to die it hurt so much. Then he took my jaw in his hand and held my head steady, peered deep into my eyes, willed me to relax. I tried to obey, but the pain persisted, persisted as long as I fought it. And then I stopped fighting. Almost against my will, I came. He shouted and I shouted. He threw back his head, not looking at me anymore, but out there in some wild place.

We both began to laugh when we saw how far the bed had slid into the middle of the room and I wondered if Rosa had heard us. My head hung off the end of the mattress and he was again looking down on me, this time with dark satisfied eyes. I felt shame, but it was more manufactured than real, as if a beast that had been pursuing me for years had overtaken me, and it was less ferocious than I had imagined.

After we had showered and were sitting in the main room in our shorts, the door separating the two parts of what had once been one large apartment burst open, and Rosa advanced into the room with the hot plate tucked under her arm, pressed against her large breasts. "I told you I would bring you something to cook on," she said.

Everyone froze, and then she went over and put the contraption down on the counter. I introduced her to Leo, and if there was any surprise on her part, she didn't show it. She kissed him on the cheek, saying, "Come on, young man. I need your help to connect this thing. I don't see very well."

Leo easily transitioned to handyman, got under the counter, and connected the tube to the tank of gas. They began talking about Holguín like they were old friends and soon were laughing as they told me about a donkey that drank beer. Rosa explained that outside of Holguín at a hilltop hotel, a donkey sauntered up to the bar, and you could give it a drink of beer. Tourists love it.

"I hope Martin can come and visit me in Holguín," Leo said. It was the first I had heard of it and I didn't take the invitation seriously.

"Yes, you should go," said Rosa as she started rattling off the names of all the places to visit.

"That's all fine, but right now we need to get something to eat before this boy starves to death," I said, pointing to Leo.

"Yes, I imagine you *do* need some nourishment." She winked, and I rolled my eyes at Leo.

With the traditional lunch of fried meat, rice, and beans lodged like a brick deep in our stomachs, we walked along the Malecón at the steamiest part of day. We were on our way to the Melia Cohiba Hotel because I needed to break a 100-dollar bill, and a large hotel was one of the only places that would deal with it. Leo saw some phones on the street out front and said he wanted to call his mom. I gave him my phone card and headed for the smoked-glass doors of the modern glass and cement tower.

It was a five-star hotel run by the worldwide Spanish Melia hotel chain, but the woman, the only woman in the entire hotel who could change the bill, was out to lunch. European excellence meets Cuban laissez-faire. I had an espresso at the lobby bar and waited. From my perch on the bar stool, I looked out the floor-to-ceiling windows and watched Leo talking on the phone in the tiny glass-enclosed telephone kiosk, leaning over with his elbow on the ledge, a cigarette dangling from his other hand.

When I got the bill changed and came out of the hotel, Leo was sitting on the ground, leaning against the kiosk in the shade. He looked worried.

"What's the matter?"

"It's my mom. They found something on her breast and she has to go back to the doctor on Monday. I need to go home." He took the photo out of his wallet again and looked at it. "She's so young," he said.

"Don't worry. I'm sure she'll be all right. Most lumps like that don't mean anything."

"Why don't you go with me?"

"When?"

"Tomorrow."

"I can't. Maybe I could come next week."

"I'll look for a place for you to stay. At my mom's house there's no shower, just pour water over your head. And the bathroom, well, it's outside."

"Let me think about it."

He nodded. "What are you doing tonight?"

"I have two tickets for the ballet. I was going to ask Luka to go with me. Would you want to go?"

"I've never been to the Gran Teatro. Sure, let's go. What time does it start?"

"Eight o'clock."

"I'll go get my things for the Holguín trip and be back by six." He assumed he was going to spend the night. It was all casual, normal. But I was glad he was going back to his hometown. It would give me a chance to clear my head, figure out what was going on, and most importantly delve into my work.

Leo called to say he was having a problem and wouldn't be able to get back before 7:30.

"I guess we can't go to the ballet."

"We'll go. I promise I'll be back at 7:30. We'll get a taxi and be there by eight. Wait for me."

I believed he would try, but I already had a feeling for the way things worked in Cuba, and I doubted we would make it on time.

A couple of minutes before 7:30, he was at the door, and I hugged him. He winced. "Ouch," he said.

"What's the matter?"

"Nothing. It's just my arm."

Then I noticed that he was empty-handed. "Where are your things?"

"That woman I live with burned my backpack and tore up my clothes." He was nonchalant. Then he showed me places on his upper arm and shoulder where she bit and hit him. I could see the teeth marks and bruises. The nosey landlady theory was definitely out.

I cleared my throat. "Is she your girlfriend?"

"My wife, but we are not living together like a couple." He rubbed his two index fingers alongside each other and shook his head to make sure I got the point. "She is more like a friend now."

"Some friend!"

"When I said I was going to Holguín, she went crazy. Every time I go there, she thinks I'm not coming back. I had to call the neighbors to help me control her. That's why I am late." He dismissed the incident as though it was just one more in the constant daily struggle that was living in Cuba.

"You still want to go to the ballet?"

"Do you have a shirt I can wear?"

I gave him one of my dressy shirts, a light fabric in colors of tan and black, and it looked as if it were meant for him.

On the taxi ride I tried to imagine the woman biting and hitting him, and all that it said about his life. He was so easygoing, but seemed to provoke strong emotions in other people. I touched his leg. "Are you all right?"

"I'm happy. This time it's over."

The rhythms in Cuba were so unlike other places I had been. When you were trying to get served in a store or restaurant, things moved at a snail's pace. People sauntered along the crumbling sidewalks or sat back on beat-up chairs on porches with their eyes half-closed, mongrel dogs curled up in the shade too lazy to look for food, and tired old cars chugged along and belched out black smoke. Juxtaposed to the everyday movement of the country, you had the emotional life that moved at a frenetic speed. In a few days, Leo and I had reached a plateau of closeness that might take months back in the States; he had had a big fight with his wife and said their relationship was over; and his mother had called him home to a medical crisis. Out the window a *camello,* the pink camel-shaped extended buses pulled by a semi tractor, inched along with more than a hundred people jammed inside. You could get married and divorced in Cuba faster than you could get from one side of town to the other on a *camello.*

In the taxi our legs were nearly touching and my right hand was resting on the seat. He moved his leg over on top of it, wedging it between his ample thigh and the plastic upholstery. He continued looking forward, lost in his thoughts, but a slight smile cracked the edges of his mouth.

We pulled up in front of the elegant Gran Teatro de la Habana where a small crowd had gathered. Rising above us was the façade, all arches, columns and niches lifting our eyes up to the corner tower topped by a winged figure. It made me think of a wedding cake with all its curvilinear details promising hope for a fruitful life, a life that few Cubans had, though they *could* go to world-class ballet for about 30 cents. This was the home of the National Ballet of Cuba, and in the Sala Garcia Lorca we were going to see the Ballet Español de la Habana, a performance by eight recent graduates. I had gotten prime seats—fifth row center.

The first half of the performance offered selections from flamenco to a fusion of more traditional Spanish dance with modern steps, from pas de deux to the eight dancing together in the final number before the intermission. The second half was more remarkable with a dance interpretation of "La Casa de Bernarda Alba," a work by the theatre's namesake, Garcia Lorca. The costumes and set were minimal, but the brilliant lighting and passionate dancing brought to life the story of an Andalusian household in mourning. The total control that Bernarda wielded over her five daughters was a foreshadowing of the Franco regime that came into power shortly after the play was written and Garcia Lorca was assassinated by fascist forces.

I had a feeling this was all lost on Leo, but he did sit with his chin in the palm of his hand staring intently at the stage. Afterwards he said he liked it, though his stomach was doing its own little dance near the end, calling for food.

"Let's go eat. I told my friend Luka to meet us in front of the theatre."

Even though Luka had behaved weirdly when I told him I had met someone on the Malecón, I wanted him to meet Leo. Maybe he would tell me that I was out of my mind to get involved. Maybe being with them together would give me some perspective on what was happening, or listening to them talk might give me a sign I had missed before.

Luka was out front, and as we walked past the Capitolio and through the dark Parque de la Fraternidad, they took off in their Cuban *Oriente* Spanish. Before we got to the restaurant on Reina, they seemed to be friends.

We ordered beers and the only plate they were serving—fried

pork, congri, tostones, and salad. Leo was open about what happened earlier in the evening and Luka was fascinated by the story. He asked Leo how he had met his wife.

Leo had met Yudith waiting in line at Coppelia, a huge open-air ice cream parlor where everybody, rich and poor, could eat ice cream, that is, if you were willing to wait up to three hours in the lines that snaked out of the entrances and down the block. So there was plenty of time for Leo and Yudith to flirt. She had her own place and invited him home. After living with her a short time, he decided that the city had its advantages and he was through with country life. In telling the story, he said that he had actually been married four times, the first one being at the age of sixteen. Cubans used the word *casado*, married, very loosely, Luka explained to me. Yudith was the only one that Leo had been officially married to. In Cuba that simply meant filing some papers.

"What about men?" Luka asked.

Leo wasn't at all fazed by the question. "I had an Italian friend. I would see him when he was in town, every few months for a year or so. It was while I was living with Yudith and she knew about him. One time the three of us even went out to dinner together."

"What happened?"

"It was a disaster."

"No, I mean with the Italian," said Luka.

"I don't know. He just didn't call anymore. I have failed at all my relationships." He laughed self-consciously without sounding too upset about it.

"Are you going back to Yudith?" Luka asked.

"No way. She's crazy and she called me *maricón*." He said it like it was the worst possible insult. "Several times we broke up and I went back to Holguín, but she always came and got me. But not this time. It's over." He looked at me and winked.

We fell silent and they attacked their food. Leo looked up sheepishly from his plate and put his hand on my leg. "*Come, niño*. Eat, baby."

"Martin, are you going to Holguín?" asked Luka.

"Maybe next week."

"Why don't you come with him, Luka?" said Leo.

Luka looked at me. "What do you think?"

"Sure, why not? I mean if I go."

After dinner Luka convinced us to go to the Malecón with him. The large crowds of the previous nights had been scattered as there were three police cars lined up along the curb. Officers randomly asked people for their IDs and detained some for questioning. We walked along the seawall and witnessed a boy with a hangdog expression standing with two policemen. He gave one-word answers to their questions as he shuffled his right foot back and forth. His friends sat nearby and commented like spectators at a show. One young man in tight Capri pants and a lime-green gauzy shirt tied at the waist taunted the policemen in a high, drunken voice. They ignored him. Luka told me that all the regulars at the Malecón were sick of getting hassled by the police and some showed their contempt by mouthing off or taking their time to move on when the officers tried to clear the area. I thought back to the night when Tomás gave Lizzie and me a little lesson in gay history. He told us about the Stonewall riots in New York where it was the people most on the fringes, the drag queens and transvestites that had the courage to stand up to authority, starting the modern movement for gay rights.

The main group of the Malecón, the less bold, had moved away from the police, and we followed like sheep. I felt like we were abandoning the defiant ones, but I didn't want Leo to get in trouble.

At a safe distance, we sat on the wall and he had one arm thrown over my shoulder. I was still uncomfortable about public affection, but with another beer it faded. He would be gone the next day, I reminded myself, and I would have my life back. Luka wandered off to talk to some friends.

"That was funny what you said the other night about me thinking of my wife and kids back home," said Leo. "You didn't even know me and you said that."

"It was a joke. You don't have kids, do you?"

"No, but my mom is crazy to have grandchildren."

"You're going to have kids because your mom wants you to?"

"I like kids. Don't you like kids?"

"Sure. I have one. A daughter."

"You have a daughter?"

I wished I hadn't mentioned Jenny. Things were complicated enough. "She just graduated from college."

"So she's about my age," he said, goading me.

"No, she's much younger than you."

"I like younger girls."

I moved out from under his arm. "That's not funny."

He grabbed my arm and pulled me back. "I'm just kidding. Tell me what she's like."

"Some other time." I imagined her face, the way she looked at me when I did something that embarrassed her like the time I got in an accident that was clearly my fault when I was driving her and her boyfriend home from a dance. God, if she ever found out about this!

"I'm sorry. Don't get so upset."

"I should go home."

"Martin, come here." He took my hand and held it. "You are being silly. Come on. You can't go home without me. I have no place to stay."

"That again?"

"This time it's for sure. I want to hold you all night, not do any bad things. Just hold you."

"You think it's bad?"

"Oh, you like it?"

"I didn't say that."

I gave him a beach bag, some of my clothes, a toothbrush, and a package of trail mix for the trip. We went down to the street and I put him in a taxi to go to the bus station. From inside the car he shook my hand and looked out at me with his sad, half-closed eyes, at least I thought he was sad. He had a perpetual shadow under his eyes so that if he wasn't outright laughing, a brooding look took over his face. "Call me when you get there," I said.

He reached his hand out the window to touch my hand one more time, his lips curling into a half-smile as the taxi pulled away from the curb. I watched the car fade and felt a sense of losing something that I never had, like waking up from a sexy dream that you want to go back to, but can't.

8

Every day after Leo left, thunder cracked and the skies tormented us with nearly constant rain. But then we might have a break, the sun stepping out in all its shine, and I'd hurry out to the store through the steamy heat rising off the pavement. Rivulets of sweat ran down my arms and torso when I did nothing more strenuous than walk casually on the shady side of the street.

One afternoon it cleared up for several hours and I ventured out to the Martí Study Center on Calzada. I sat out in the shade of the small palm garden, reading one of the books I had purchased and taking copious notes. The day kept my mind occupied, but that night I became twisted in the sheet, sleepless with Leo on my mind.

Gerard called, saying that he was back in town after his sister's funeral, so I rushed over to see him, desperate for someone to talk to. He greeted me at the door with a drink in his hand. "Would you like one?" After he put ice in my glass he seemed to forget what he was doing and stared at a roach crawling up the wall.

I stood silent and watched, too.

He let out an agonizing sigh. "It has been the worst week in my life. It's not easy to lose a sister. We were very close."

"I'm sorry."

He had more gray in his full head of dark hair since I last saw him, and his high cheekbones and straight-backed posture clashed with the relaxed garb that he had adopted in Cuba: old shirts with sleeves cut off and baggy shorts. He poured some rum in my glass. "I want to apologize for what happened with your friend. What's his name?"

"Leo. It's no big deal." I didn't want to get into a discussion about him.

"Giovani was being overly protective because of a series of robberies that have taken place recently, some of them involving people whom I trusted completely."

"I guess people get desperate. By the way, I would appreciate it if you didn't say anything to Tomás about, I mean…"

"Don't worry," he said, giving me a hard stare. "I won't say a word." He suppressed a smile. "Do you want to talk about it?"

"There's nothing to talk about."

"All right," he said with an unbelieving blink. Odet's laughter rang out from the other room. She, Giovani, and Yanela were on the sofa playing cards. "I don't want any of your friends treated badly. I would like Leo to come over some time so I can meet him, and Giovani can get to know him better." Giovani heard his name and looked over at us.

"He went back to Holguín."

"You're not going to see him again?"

"Why should I? He's just a friend that I met through Osmani."

"It's okay. I don't mean to pry. Nobody's going to judge you here."

I was on my second drink and chugging it, clinking the ice around in the bottom of the glass. The three over on the couch broke into laughter as somebody slapped down a card. The TV was on and I heard the trumpet signaling the midday news. We sat down at the dining table and stared into our empty glasses.

"I'm in a bit of a jam," I blurted out. I immediately regretted saying it.

"Do you mean with Leo, or are you saying in your life in general?"

"This is all new to me, Gerard. I'm not sure what I'm feeling."

"I think you know what you're feeling, but it's too scary to comprehend. As you have seen, Cuba can be quite enchanting, can take you places you probably didn't expect."

"You hear people talk about, you know, being in a closet. What does that mean? I never felt like I was in a closet. Leo is an attractive guy. I was drunk. I swear to God, this is not going to change my life." I looked up at Gerard sitting with his chin resting on his entwined hands. He appeared amused.

"Don't look at me like that. You remind me of my mother," I said.

"I'm not your mother or your confessor. I'm just here to listen."

"We had a good time together. It doesn't have to be a life-changing event!"

"No one is saying you have to change anything."

"He invited me to Holguín."

"Are you going?"

"It's probably not a good idea." The doorbell rang and Gerard jumped up.

"Just watch yourself," he said on the way to the door. "I mean your heart as well as your wallet."

It was the start of a stream of visitors and the conversation was put on hold. It was just as well. I didn't like the way Gerard and Luka looked at me when I talked about Leo. I could hear them thinking, "You're one of us now." I was not. I was not like them.

After two rum drinks, it was hard to think of doing much but sliding into the afternoon haze that everyone else was in. The Sunday movie was in English with subtitles, the second Harry Potter movie, and I sat with Giovani, Yanela, and Odet, and stared dumbly at the screen. About halfway through the film, I forced myself to get up and go out on the terrace for some fresh air. It started to rain again. Within seconds great silvery sheets of water were pouring down from the sky in an *aguacero* like I had never seen before. The rain pounded the streets far below while cars inched through the rapidly-forming puddles. In minutes the puddles turned into flooded streets. I wondered if it was raining in Holguín and if he was out in it, if he was with a girlfriend and they were clinging to each other under an umbrella, happily dancing through the puddles like *Singing in the Rain*, with me a million miles away from his thoughts. Rainy Sundays and rum: a dangerous combination.

I sat back down and watched the rest of the movie. Four more people arrived, introduced as reporters from the BBC working on a documentary about green medicine in Cuba. I gathered that Gerard would be occupied for some time. The rain had dwindled to a light patter, and I got ready to leave. Osmani appeared from the back bedroom and said he would accompany me downstairs. In the elevator he told me in a dramatic voice that he was going back to Camaguey, back to the family that loved him, unlike the people here.

When we arrived at the lobby, the skies had opened up again, so we sat on a ledge to wait it out. "Those scars of Leo's?" I asked. "Was he in an accident?"

"Accident? No…" He paused, letting the anticipation build up. "Let me tell you the story. You look at him and think he's not so strong, right? He's a nice guy and calm, right? Well, you don't know what's inside him. He is strong to survive what happened that night. Yeah, I was there. It was like ten years ago, but I remember it so clearly. We were all in the disco. This guy, Juan, he was an older guy, about ten years older than us, and he really liked Leo. He would buy beers for him, invite him to his house, take him out to dinner. Leo played along, probably liked the attention. I don't know if they did anything like, you know, sex. Maybe Leo let him suck him off. Anyway, that night Juan was pretty drunk and kept insisting that Leo go home with him. Leo said no, that he was going to his own house. They started arguing and Juan said to Leo, 'I don't know why you hang around with that *maricón.*' He was referring to Pepe, who was standing next to Leo. Pepe was like Leo's shadow. He was a thin and kind of effeminate guy that I think was in love with Leo, too. So Leo just told him to stop talking shit and turned his back on him. Juan grabbed him from behind and Leo turned around and pushed him so hard that he fell down. Then everybody started laughing and somebody said, 'Who's the *maricón* now?' But we all stopped laughing when we saw the look in Juan's eyes, lying there on the ground, and we knew he was crazy anyway. He had done some crazy stuff, mean stuff. He got up and walked away, but there was something spooky about it. People started talking again, but in hushed voices. Leo was quiet, but seemed okay.

After a while Leo said that he was going home and Pepe said he would accompany him since they lived near each other. Juan was waiting outside. When he saw Leo and Pepe leaving together, he went crazy and started following them. Leo realized someone was behind them and turned around just as Juan pulled out a knife and slashed him across the left side of his neck. Pepe screamed and ran back toward the disco for help. Leo put his hand on his neck and blocked a second blow that grazed his shoulder. Juan kept lunging at Leo, and Leo fell forward to his knees." Osmani stood up, acting out the scene as if he was Juan. He jabbed the air with his imaginary knife.

"The doors of the disco burst open and people came streaming out, yelling. In the light from the open doors you could see the glint of the knife and Juan on top of him, stabbing him in the back before anybody could do anything. Juan was shouting, 'You little shit, son of a bitch, faggot. Don't you know? Don't you know? I love you.' He was crying and looking at the people running toward him. His eyes in the flashing disco light looked like the devil's. Everybody was screaming, and Juan jumped up and ran away. A few guys chased after him. Leo was on the ground face down with pools of blood forming around him. We thought he was dead. When we saw he was still breathing, some of us took off our shirts and put them on the wounds to stop the bleeding. Shit, it was terrible."

I was horrified by the story and felt nauseous.

"Hey, don't worry," Osmani said. "He's okay now. That was a long time ago. They got him to the hospital, but it was touch and go there for a while. They had to operate because of internal injuries. That's why he's got that big scar up the middle. I felt so sorry for his mom. She sat there in the hospital sobbing and rocking. I don't know what she would have done if he hadn't made it. For fifteen days, I don't think she left the hospital. He came through all right. Look at him now, scarred but beautiful."

"What…what happened to…that guy?"

"He ran to his house and locked himself inside. A bunch of people surrounded the house and shouted that they were going to kill him. Everybody loved Leo and was mad as hell. The police arrived and formed a barricade between the people and the house. Then they broke in and took him. He went to prison for ten years. He got out last year, but he had to move to another town. Everybody hated him so much."

I sat frozen, disgusted and troubled.

Then he started talking about leaving again, saying that he would miss me, but I only half heard him. "By the way, do you have any clothes that you could give me, a T-shirt or something you don't want?"

I looked at him strangely. "What? No, I'll need all of my clothes."

"No problem." We hugged loosely, and I walked in a daze the half-block back to my place. I couldn't get the image out of my head of the cold steel plunging into the tender flesh of Leo's fifteen-year-old body. It seemed like an event that would leave scars far beyond the physical, a deep set of complexes and paranoia, yet he appeared so open and loving. And what was it about him that made people go crazy, like that man years ago, and just recently his wife?

Rosa must have heard me come in because she was at the door in a minute. This time she knocked and I told her to come in. She cradled a bowl of black bean soup in her weathered hands. "I just made it. I want you to try it." And in the next breath she said, "Has Leo called yet?" She appeared more anxious about it than I was.

"No."

"Don't worry. He will. Then you'll go to Holguín and have a good time. And I'll have to find someone else to rent the apartment," she said as if I had already abandoned her.

"I don't even know if I'm going. It's been three days."

She patted my arm on the way out. "He'll call."

I sat hunched over the bowl and stared into the black depths of the soup, wishing that it held the answer to my dilemma. It would be better if he didn't call. Did I want to take this any further? Even a friendship with a much younger Cuban man who lived thousands of miles away didn't make much sense. Then I pictured his smile and remembered that I wasn't talking about just any young Cuban. It was Leo with his sweet manner, his loving touch. The time we shared was something simple and pure, though I hated being so vulnerable, having my emotions exposed. I had always been perplexed by a verse of Martí's that glorified the heartfelt, and I wondered if it was his strength of character that allowed him to be open to painful feelings.

For, twisted soul, I have found
In my miraculous heart
While more deeper is the wound
The more beautiful the art

Then the phone rang. I let Rosa answer as she had a bell system rigged up that would let me know if it was for me. There was an interminable delay and then the sharp ring shook me.

"Martin, how are you? Know who this is?"

"There is only one voice like that in the world." A smile blossomed on my face. Leo sounded like he just woke up, yet it was late in the afternoon.

"Do you have your ticket yet?"

"I was waiting for your call."

"The trip was hell and I slept for a whole day. When are you coming?"

"I could come Wednesday if you still want me."

"Don't be silly. Of course I want you to come. Call me on Tuesday and tell me the exact times and everything." He seemed to be in a hurry and I guessed that his time was running out on the pay phone.

"Is that all?" I said.

"What?"

"Do you miss me?"

"Sure."

"Me, too. I'll see you soon."

As soon as I hung up the phone I felt sick. Did I really say, "Do you miss me?" I imagined that I was trying to imitate his free expression of feelings. The words seemed false coming out of my mouth.

The bus ticket office was jammed with foreigners trying to get out
of the city, but after a long wait I got a bus to Holguín, which would
arrive after 10:00 p.m. I took out my Viajero Card to pay, but she
shook her head. It was a debit card offered through Canada, good at
over 6000 locations in Cuba—the promotional literature claimed—
but this was not one of them. She directed me to a bank in the post
office across the street.

There was no teller at either of the two brightly lit glass-enclosed
booths of Banco Central in a dark corner of the vast and mostly empty
post office lobby. After a few minutes, a large woman in her sixties with
chocolate skin and copper-colored straightened hair returned from
her smoke break. She put the key in the lock and slowly opened the
door as if it was to the vault and weighed 300 pounds, then stopped
to talk to one of her co-workers passing by. The news of how her aunt
was doing with the swelling in her ankles dragged on, as did the sec-
ondary discussion of the day's heat. Then she fully entered the booth,
opened a drawer and languidly stored her cigarettes. On her chair
were a number of files and she picked them up before she actually
knew where she was going to put them; there appeared to be no open
space and she spent an inordinate amount of time looking around
the tiny booth. She leaned them against the glass, grabbed a stapler to
prop them up, and then set her attention on the computer, which had
to be turned on, the sign-in screen waited for, the password put in,
and the home screen brought up, all before she deigned to recognize
my presence. I stood with my elbows on the counter and my chin
in my fists, completely fascinated by her motions, as if each one was
calculated to take up the maximum amount of time, stretching them
until closing when she could go home.

Three and a half hours after leaving the apartment I had the ticket
for Holguín in hand, and it felt like a great accomplishment. Luka
didn't have such good luck. I had given him money for his ticket, but
there was nothing available on my bus or any other the same day. He
said he would keep trying, though he might not get there until a day
or two later.

9

After a twelve-hour trip across three-quarters of the island, the bus pulled up in front of the sparsely fluorescent-lit Holguín bus terminal. I had spent the time reading, dozing, and looking out the window at the sugar cane fields, royal palms and small, orderly but impoverished towns. My legs were heavy from the long trip, and my steps uncertain, as I got off the bus amidst a sea of passengers and their bags and boxes. I didn't see Leo and became distressed at the thought of having to take a taxi to his mother's house—the only address I had—and having to explain who I was.

Then from the shadows at the corner of the building, Leo made an entrance, a dark angel dressed in a white shirt and slacks. His eyes were dancing over my face as if I had arrived from another planet, and for my part I had a symphony going on in my head that was played out on my face as an unstoppable grin. He took my hand, then was moved to hug me tight and kiss my cheek all in a moment. He didn't seem to care who in his hometown saw us. Over his shoulder I examined the reactions of the other passengers as I inhaled the fruity essence of his hair gel. They didn't seem to care, either.

On the short taxi ride he sat close and asked me about the trip in a relaxed tone that soothed my tension from the long bus ride. When we arrived at the apartment he had rented for me just a block from the central square, Alfonso, the solidly built, middle-aged owner of the place, waited at the door. He didn't act as if there was anything strange about the arrangement as he led us up the narrow stairway to the second-floor apartment.

The air conditioning was on, but it hadn't succeeded in diminishing the heat. After a brief explanation of the facilities, and my hurried inspection of the balcony and bathroom, Alfonso took my passport and asked for Leo's ID—in case he was planning to spend the night. "The rules, you know," he said in a businesslike way. With the documents in hand, he let himself out.

Leo immediately grabbed me and kissed me as though our four days of separation meant something to him. We held each other for a long time, and then he stepped back to take off the white V-neck T-shirt I had given him for the trip to Holguín. We fell on the bed. "I can't stay tonight. My mom is expecting me home. But tomorrow night I can stay. I'll just say that we went out drinking, and it was too late to come home."

"You don't have to go right away?"

"Of course not," he said with a wink. "Tomorrow I'll get here early and we'll spend the whole day together." He helped me take off my shirt so that our chests could touch, mine covered with a mat of golden hair and his smooth. I started to undo his belt, but he took my hand. "We're gonna wait until tomorrow for that. I don't want to rush."

"Just to get comfortable. I wasn't expecting anything."

"Liar," he teased. "I know you."

The touch of his hands, the softness of his lips, the hardness of his body were all mesmerizing, but did not seem real. Yet the promise of his affection had been what made me decide to come. And now that I was next to him, I knew how much I needed his touch. In small increments my body settled into his embrace. Sleep tugged at us both.

"I've got to go or I'll fall asleep," he said. "Tomorrow."

"Tomorrow what?"

"You know."

I laughed stupidly, and we stumbled to the door, drunk with something that wasn't quite love, but more than lust, something mysterious, undefined, that like a puff of air, could be gone in a second.

The compressor of the air conditioner groaned to life while the sunlight streamed into the room through the gaps in the louvered terrace doors. I shifted my weight on the lumpy bed and marveled that I had managed to sleep so well. I got up, pushed open the doors and stepped out onto the terrace, finding myself in a cage, the security bars separating me from the world. With the sun full in my eyes I didn't realize at first that I was nearly face to face with the neighbor in her flower-print housedress across the narrow street. She was leaning on the wall of her balcony looking down at the traffic—mostly pedestrians and bicycles—on Martí Street. She glanced my way, and seeing that I was in my underwear, looked quickly back at the street.

Leo arrived an hour late—within the confines of acceptable Cuban etiquette—and immediately removed his shirt and stretched out on the bed.

"How's your mother?" I asked.

"Fine. She wants me to bring you over."

"You told her about me?"

"Of course. She knows all about you. Well, I didn't tell her everything," he said with a devilish smile. I tried to imagine what she thought when her only son arrived home with money in his pocket, a couple of new shirts, and the announcement that an older foreign gentleman would be dropping in for a visit. She would be happy of course to see her son in nice clothes, and able, at least for a short time, to mask the poverty. But did she see something else in her boy's eye? And did her imagination take her to what we might do when we were alone together?

He rubbed my chest in a distracted rather than sexy way. It seemed impossible for him to be near me and not touch me: rubbing my elbow, moving his foot on top of mine, or running his finger along my arm.

"Did you meet any other boys in Havana?" His tone was not challenging, but curious.

"I met some friends of Luka's, but I didn't sleep with any of them if that is what you're asking. It's not my thing. I don't think you realize—"

"Forget it. I just wondered."

"You're enough for me," I said with the feeling that I was jumping off a ledge.

I was desperate for him to react and searched his eyes for a sign that he heard me, but he was unreadable. After a lackluster hug acknowledging my statement he said, "Come on, the Burro de Mayabe is waiting."

Out on the street we found a pay phone and called Luka. His sister told us that he still hadn't been able to get a ticket. We had the day free without worrying about meeting him at the bus.

Leo sat in the front seat with the taxi driver, and I was in the back. We headed southeast out of the city under a partly blue sky, and I watched the shadows of large billowy clouds creep over the Mayabe Valley floor. About five miles from the center of town the cab climbed up a steep hill and let us out in a parking lot next to the reception building of the Villa Mirador de Mayabe Hotel. The lot was nearly empty and we were told at the reception desk that the resort was undergoing reconstruction though we could still visit the grounds and, of course, El Burro. While Leo talked to the woman behind the counter, I inspected the lobby of the reception building. It was trimmed in fine polished wood in curvy organic shapes. There was a bar of the same mahogany, large windows looking out over the valley, rattan furniture with tropical print cushions, and a pool table. In the center of the room, there was a square porch swing with four double-seats, magnificently carved in the same undulating shapes as the bar and trim around the windows.

A few hotel employees talked quietly at one end of the bar while a Cuban-American family stood near the entrance to the grounds, debating whether to enter or go on to the next tourist site on their list. I knew they were Cuban by their accents, though they had become a stereotypical, overweight American family. The teenage boy in baggy shorts and an oversized T-shirt was bobbing his head to the music of his Discman and seemed unappreciative of the surroundings. I overheard the girl whine, "Why didn't we just go to Cancún? There's nothing to do here." I smiled in sympathy with the parents trying to show the kids their roots, but it was hopeless. The parents even looked doubtful why they had come.

We descended the steps to the area where the cabins were being transformed from minimal wood structures to upscale *cabañas* with new tile floors, updated bathrooms and air conditioning. Huge red hibiscus burst forth from the area around the *cabañas* and reached out to welcome us. Bougainvillea tumbled over walls, and birds of paradise peeked around corners, in almost a parody of a tropical resort.

We emerged from the pleasing coolness of the shady cabin area to the empty terrace pool, which was bordered on one side by a white railing that separated us from a steep drop-off, providing a magnificent view of the valley and its tidy rows of fruit trees. Even further in the distance was the hazy cluster of low buildings that was the city of Holguín. It was easy to see how this place had become popular as a honeymoon spot, though with the renovations it would move into the dollar economy and become inaccessible for Cuban newlyweds. "I would like to come back some day and get a *cabaña*," I said.

"Sure, on our honeymoon," he said with a smile.

I scoffed, but for a split-second pictured us arm-in-arm at the window of one of the cabins, watching the sun dip into a multicolored horizon. As if in the same dream, he took hold of my arm and led me to the other side of the pool, where steps went up to a thatch-roofed outdoor bar.

The star of the day, Panchito, stuck his head out of his corral alongside the bar. We approached him, and he backed up into the shadows. It seemed he didn't want anything to do with us, empty-handed as we were. I bought three draft beers at twenty-five cents each—one for me, one for Leo, and one for Panchito. Leo was able to coax Pancho out into the daylight and stuck the little plastic cup under his snout, but this "beer-guzzling burro," as he was referred to in tourist brochures, only turned his head to the side and gave us a bored look. Leo stroked his mane and talked to him gently, again trying to get him to lap up the beer. Panchito was not to be won over so easily, and shook his head.

The bartender came over and admitted that this was the grandson of the original Pancho and was still "in training." He put some salty pretzels on the ledge for the donkey to munch on. Leo continued to pet him while I snapped pictures. With a quick motion the bartender grabbed the donkey's head, making Panchito lurch back. With his other hand he took the beer and poured the whole cup into his mouth from the side. It made the poor creature shake his head violently and snort, sending most of the beer and the empty cup to the ground. Leo and I stared at the puddle of beer as the bartender went back to his post.

We shrugged and sat down at a table to drink our beers. "Do you play pool?" Leo said.

"I used to, but haven't for years."

"Now, it's like one person has the stripes and the other the solids, right? And then you have to hit the eight ball last or something like that." I nodded, half-interested. "Did you see that table when we came in?"

"You want to play? Is that what you're getting at?"

"How did you guess?"

It was obvious from the first game that he was no novice at pool, and I accused him of being a hustler. He lifted his eyes from along the length of the cue and gave me a twisted smile, a grunt, and then continued with his shot, which he drilled into the pocket. He won the first game easily. I took the next with a lucky shot. He finished me off in the next two games as I stood to the side, fascinated by his bare arms stretched out over the table and the way the fabric of his jeans tightened over his behind when he bent over. He caught me staring at him.

"You shouldn't be looking at my butt," he whispered with a wink, brushing up against my arm, as he passed to the other side of the table.

Back at the apartment, we stripped off our clothes.

"Let's take a shower," he said.

"Together?"

"Why not? But first I have to sit on the throne."

"You are such a country boy."

"*Si, soy guajiro.*" He went into the bathroom, took off his underwear and threw them out the door, hitting me in the face.

After a few minutes, he stuck his head out. "Aren't you coming?"

The lime-green tiled shower stall easily accommodated two people, and from the open window you could look out onto the rooftops of the neighboring buildings, where fresh laundry whipped in the breeze. I slipped off my briefs and pulled back the plastic curtain to see him standing with his arms across his chest letting the water cascade over his cinnamon skin, through his pubic hair and down his hairy legs. I slipped into the shower like a ghost. The water splashed off his shoulders into my face. He turned around quickly, uncrossed his arms, and put them on my shoulders. "Turn around," he said. "I want to wash your back."

With the flowery soap he worked up a lather on my shoulders, neck and back, massaging as he went. Reaching around to my chest, he spread the excess soap up and down my torso, but stopped at my waist. He ran his hands back up to my nipples and began to play with them.

"Wait. Let me do your back," I said.

I kneaded the tenseness out of his shoulders and neck. But when I got to his back, I suffered tingling cringes as I worked around the scars, feeling how the skin bunched up strangely, noting the lumpiness of the scar tissue underneath. I moved down his legs, surprisingly thick compared to his upper torso, and then went around to the front where he was coming to life, curving to one side. I stood up. Our bodies pressed together and our mouths met under the warm water sliding down our faces. I tasted the chlorine in our kiss.

"I don't suppose you have any…you know, close by," he said.

I reached for my toiletry kit hanging from a nail by the sink. When I had said goodbye to Luka, he had stuffed some condoms in my pocket, saying that I might need them. I turned a bright shade of red, and he laughed.

As we were drying off, I asked, "Have you ever done that before, I mean, in the shower?"

"Well, with girls, but never with a guy."

"It was a first for me."

"You're gonna have a lot of firsts with me," he said. "Are you ready to go to my house?"

"As ready as I'll ever be."

In truth I was reluctant to be a curiosity in front of his family. I wondered if they would be thinking about the crazy *maricón* that knifed Leo in a fit of passion ten years before. People would have a lot of reasons to be doubtful, especially his mother.

Dusk fell on the city, and the air was heavy though we had been spared the regular afternoon deluge. Around the Parque Calixto Garcia most businesses were still open, and we checked out the car rental places for the following day. We wanted to go to Gibara, a small fishing village about twenty miles from Holguín, and Guardalavaca, a beach resort fifteen miles further to the east along the coast. In front of one of the offices were several motor scooters, and Leo had the idea to rent one. Scooters were a much cheaper option at only twenty dollars a day, so we reserved one for the following day.

By the time the taxi got to his street, it was dark. The road was full of ruts and potholes where heavy rains had carried the gravel away. About halfway down the block the driver started complaining about the conditions, so we got out and walked the rest of the way. It was a neighborhood of small, boxy homes, most of them of bare brick, and many with second stories or side rooms in various stages of construction; there were only three or four houses on the street that look finished. Despite the poverty, most of the houses emanated the bluish light from television screens, around which groups of shadowy figures huddled. I heard characters on the nightly soap opera drama-tizing their quandaries at high volume, and with everyone watching the same channel, the overwrought voices echoed throughout the neighborhood.

In front of one home, the TV had been brought out on the street with a long cord snaking into the dimly lit interior. Several people of mixed colors and ages sat on rickety chairs, frozen in front of the tiny ten-inch screen.

When we got close enough for them to recognize Leo, several called out a greeting. They looked at me with interest, though not surprise. He introduced me as his friend from the United States, and they offered me a drink of rum. A young man jumped up to get me a glass from the house while a sexy blonde in a halter-top showing her tattooed belly button approached Leo and gave him a big kiss and a hug. She held on to him tightly with her painted nails.

"This is Sulyn," he said with a big smile.

The rest of the group stayed focused on the soap opera. It was through these shows Cubans got their impression of the outside world, the impression that the world was one of constant emotional trauma—not dissimilar to their own—but where people got to live in fancy houses, wear designer clothes, and drive nice cars.

We walked to a side street and turned onto an even rougher dead-end road that went up a small incline. Near the end of the street was Leo's house, a light-blue, two-story structure with an unfinished second level. Sulyn had her arm wrapped in Leo's and I followed behind, my position usurped by the rightful consort. His mother, Lisbeth, came out on the porch to greet us and kissed me warmly. She was pretty with thick, dark hair swept back and held with a clip, and her body was soft and plump. She apologized for the conditions of the house, but when I said it was one of the nicest homes in the area, she laughed, a joyful, uninhibited schoolgirl laugh.

A number of relatives and neighbors had gathered inside, and Leo's grandmother jumped up and offered me the best chair, a large wooden rocker with cane seating. I tried to get her to sit back down, but everyone insisted that I take the seat. Leo sat on the floor with his arm around Sulyn, and they talked softly while the others asked me about my day in Holguín. I related the story of the *burro que no quería tomar cerveza,* the donkey that didn't want to drink beer, which made everyone laugh. With Leo all cuddled up with Sulyn, I was tempted to tell about the shower, but I kept the memory tucked behind my grimace.

"Leo, don't you want to get Martin a drink?" Lisbeth said. She had caught me staring at Leo and Sulyn.

He got up and went into the kitchen. Sulyn glared at me.

From where I sat, I could see Leo in the kitchen, and when no one else was looking, he shrugged his shoulders and mouthed, "What can I do?" It was a charade that he had to play, but I wondered which was the real charade, what he was doing with me or how he was with her, or neither, or both. I feigned disinterest as he pointed to his watch and made a sign for half an hour, before coming out and handing me a sugary red drink that looked like Kool-Aid.

"Here, let me take you on a tour of the house," Leo said.

The room we were in was painted white and was clean and orderly though sparsely furnished: there were several chairs and a small table with a vase of red plastic roses. Off the living room was his mother's bedroom, which had a large bed, an old wardrobe with the wood veneer chipping off, and under the one window was a table with a sewing machine and piles of material. Leo explained that she did sewing to earn extra money. On the opposite wall there was a small table loaded with creams and half-full, dusty perfume bottles.

The only other room was the kitchen, which on one wall had a counter, a sink, a double gas burner, and a refrigerator that hummed loudly. Against the opposite wall was Leo's bed and a bulky wardrobe. He opened the creaky door and pulled out a beautifully polished sculpture of dark wood. It was a foot high, a miniature gazebo with leaved stems rising up to rose buds at the top, something that might be kitsch if it hadn't been rendered so delicately. "This is for you," he said, "an early birthday present." I held the smooth wood in my hands, and felt the anger of before suddenly dissipate. "We'll keep it here for now," he said and put it back in the cabinet.

"Where did you get it? It's beautiful."

"A friend of mine made it, a guy I used to sell paintings with."

"What kind of paintings"

"Just some little things I did."

"You paint?"

"Some. You know, for tourists."

"Let me see something."

"I don't have anything here. It's all at Yudith's house."

"God, I hope she didn't burn them, too."

"She's not that crazy. I'll show you them one day."

"Why didn't you tell me you painted?"

"It's no big deal, really."

We sat in Parque Calixto Garcia on an old curlicue metal bench layered with multiple coats of paint and in need of a new one. The thick foliage and flaming blooms of the *framboyan* trees fanned out above us.

"That was your girlfriend, huh?"

"Do you like her?"

"She's cute, on the thin side."

"I've known her since she was a little girl. She used to follow me around and say that she was my girlfriend, you know, kid's stuff. She lived down the street. When I came home after a couple of years in Havana, she was a woman. Things weren't going well with Yudith, so I started up with her. Then Yudith came after me and took me back to Havana. Sulyn was so mad. I don't know if I'm ready to get married again."

"Give yourself a break. It wouldn't kill you to be alone for a while."

"Who wants to be alone? Are you crazy?"

"Not everybody is supposed to get married and have a family."

"You did. Why shouldn't I? Like I told you, my mom wants grandchildren, but I don't know if I'm ready. I think I should wait, maybe until I'm thirty."

"If you survive," I reminded him. "Isn't it strange for you to introduce me to your family and neighbors? Don't people think something funny is going on?"

"Everybody knows I have a girlfriend here and a wife in Havana.

What can they say?"

To our right was a row of benches that were filled with young men. "That's where the gays hang out," Leo announced. The way young Cubans dressed—as trendy as possible within their financial constraints—it made it difficult to tell who was gay or straight. It was also becoming common for teenagers and young twenties to experiment, so Luka told me, further smudging the lines. He had told me about his 16-year-old niece who bragged about her boyfriend being "complete," meaning he had experience with guys as well as girls.

"Were you always comfortable around gays?"

"It used to bother me seeing guys act like girls, you know, growing up here in the country."

"Is that your impression of gay men, that they act like girls?"

"No, man. The other kind aren't so easy to spot because they just act like guys. I learned about them when I went to Havana."

"And why did you go to Havana?"

"Things were getting bad here, no work. I thought there had to be a better life. Ricardo and Humberto would come back from Havana with new clothes, watches, and money in their pockets. I felt bad that I didn't have anything. They told me that with my looks I could find people who would help me have a better life." I was amazed at the casualness with which he talked about his experiences and the innocent way he framed them.

"How did you start with men?"

"There were only two before you. One night I was sitting on the wall near the Cine Yara, waiting for Ricardo, and this guy walked by a couple of times, staring at me. It made me feel sick to my stomach because I had decided to do something. I stood up and started walking. The guy followed me, and we talked. He was Mexican, so there was no problem with the language. He invited me to his place. We drank some more and I let him, you know, suck me. That's all we did. We saw each other a few times."

"And the other one?"

"He was the Italian guy I told you about that night with Luka. I met him several months later. Humberto introduced me to him because he had seen me and wanted to know me. I was already living with Yudith by that time. The Italian had a lot of money and took me to nice places."

"Do you still see him?"

"I told you the other night. He stopped calling. I thought maybe he didn't come to Cuba anymore. Then one night I saw him on the Malecón with another guy."

"Do you consider yourself a bisexual, or what?"

"I don't consider myself anything. I do what I do with certain people. Why do people always have to put a label on it?"

"You just put a label on those gays sitting over on the other bench."

"That's different."

"How?"

"Because they are acting in a way that they seem to want labels. I don't do that. You don't do that."

"Maybe they can't help it. That's just the way they are."

"I suppose. I don't care. I don't interfere with their lives, and I don't want anybody to interfere with mine."

"Are you ashamed of what we do?"

"Are you kidding? Do I act ashamed when we are doing it?"

"I mean later. There must be times that you are mixed-up."

"Just accept it. That's the way I am."

His words hung in the heavy night air as the cackling from the benches across the way reached a high pitch, like birds in the jungle announcing an intruder. "What about you, I mean, with men? When did you start?"

"Last week.

"*No jodas!* Come on, don't tell me that shit."

"You were the first."

He leaned over to search my eyes. "Man, you're serious, aren't you? I hope I didn't hurt you too much."

"At first it did. But I'm not just saying the first time for *that*. I mean for everything, being with a man, holding, kissing, all of it."

"You could have fooled me. I thought you were faking being scared just to get me hot." He put his arm around my shoulder.

"You seem pretty natural, too, at least in the things you do."

"Come on, let's go home. You're getting me excited."

When we arrived back at the apartment, Alfonso heard us come in. He stuck his head out the first-floor door and asked Leo for his ID. As we were going up the narrow stairs to the second floor, Leo grabbed my ass. "Can't you wait?" I said.

"Sure, I can wait. Can you?"

10

I straddled the bike and cautiously twisted the handgrip only to have it jerk and come to a halt as the motor sputtered and died. The rental agent, who had just given me a two-minute lesson on how to drive it in a jumble of English and Spanish, glanced at Leo with an uncertain benevolence. I saw the alarm in his eyes that he would have to return the forty dollars we had just paid. When we originally talked about renting the bike, I had imagined that Leo was going to drive. Then I found out that he didn't have a license.

I managed the bike out of the lot and through the streets. It was a simple contraption, but it still took getting used to, and the streets were teeming with pedestrians, bicycles, other motorbikes, and cars. And then I had Leo's nervous hands on my waist while he gave me directions in his off-the-cuff manner that I could barely hear above the din. By some miracle we managed to reach the outskirts without plowing into anybody.

"Let's go by my place," said Leo. "I want to tell my mom what we're doing today." We headed out of town on the Gibara Road, and just as we turned into his street, we saw Lisbeth and Sulyn with empty mesh shopping bags dangling from their wrists, walking our way. I stopped the bike and leaned over to kiss Lisbeth, but Sulyn held back. Leo got off, kissed them both, and told them about our trip to Gibara and Guardalavaca. Lisbeth smiled and nodded with an occasional supportive *ooh* or *ah*. Sulyn stood with one hand on her hip and stared at me, fingering a gold crucifix around her neck as if she were invoking the good Lord to punish me. I began to fear for my life.

Lisbeth put her hand on my arm. "Now you boys be careful and come back for dinner. I'll fix something." Leo pulled out a few dollars from his wallet and stuffed them in the pocket of her red-checked shorts. Her face had taken on a half-worried, half-pleased motherly expression as she kissed us goodbye.

When we got back on the bike, I told Leo to go in front and drive. He adeptly edged out into the heavy traffic of the Gibara road.

"What is the fine for driving without a license?" I asked.

"Thirty pesos, I think." That translated into just over a dollar, so it seemed that we had little to worry about. I relaxed, squeezed my knees against his thighs, and turned my cap around so that it wouldn't blow off in the wind.

We cruised along the dappled country road, in and out of the shade from trees, until, less than a mile outside of town, we heard the chilling screech of a whistle. A cop motioned from the other side of the road for us to pull over. Leo crossed to talk to the officer while I stood by the scooter and watched the scene through waves of rippling heat. He pulled out his ID, said something, and the cop shook his head. He looked down and kicked the dirt as the officer lectured him for what seemed like a long time, and then went to his motorcycle to radio in. There was another long wait, and I leaned against the bike with the sun burning into the back of my neck. The roar of another motorcycle cop came up behind me. He called me over.

Leo crossed back to my side and stood ghostlike next to me. After looking at my driver's license, the officer started in. "I don't know what the laws are in your country, but here in Cuba you need a license to drive even a small motorbike like that. Your friend does not have a license, and we have given him a fine." He cut an intimidating figure, a large, dark-skinned man wearing tall black boots and aviator sunglasses. His unhitched helmet strap bobbed under his chin as he spoke with a half-grin on his face. "But you are responsible for the bike and you let him drive. Now I have to give you a fine as well. Can I have your contract, please? Your fine will be forty dollars U.S. to be paid to the rental company when you turn in the bike." He took out a pen and scratched something on my copy of the contract.

"How am I supposed to know what the laws are about motor bikes? No one explained them to me."

The cop glared at me and said, "It's your responsibility to know the rules. Don't let me see your friend driving again." As an afterthought he added, "Enjoy your day."

I started out slowly, but after a couple of minutes gained confidence and got the bike up to speed. The narrow two-lane Gibara road was hilly and snaked through the small towns of Aguas Claras and Floro Pérez. We came over a hill and looked down on a valley of green pastures with a few scrawny cows grazing on the summer grass. The sun radiated in the sky, slightly diffused by the haze, but it still felt like a big angry ball of fire. Coming down the hill we picked up speed, and a curve lay ahead as the road started to level out. I squeezed the brakes, but saw that our momentum was going to make it difficult to lean into the curve and make it round the bend.

In an instant we were off the road. Time became sluggish and the scenery began to blur. Frame by frame we moved closer to the guardrail. The wheels skidded and just as we banged into the hard metal, Leo shouted into the back of my head, "Hey!"

Instead of just jumping off and scuttling the thing, I held on tight to the handlebars. The bike tipped over and my shoulder landed with a hard thump against the edge of the road, the left side of my body scraping along the pavement and gravel. Leo had fallen forward on top of me, and his weight pushed me harder into the asphalt, before we came to a stop yards from where we went off the road.

Leo jumped up. "What happened?" His voice had gone up into its high range. He lifted the bike off me and helped me stand up. "Shit, you're bleeding!" I stood a second on wobbly legs wondering why I couldn't see. I hadn't noticed any pain yet, only that everything was black. My open eyes refused to bring in any light.

"I can't see," I said in a low, frightened voice.

"What?"

"I can't see. I can't see."

"Did you lose your contacts?"

"No, it's black. Everything black." My voice cracked and I began to teeter. Then I felt Leo take my arm on one side, and there was someone else on the other who took my left arm. I screamed in pain. "Sorry," he said. They lifted me up and carried me a short distance. Every jostling movement was now excruciating, and I gasped for breath. My blindness caused me to panic, and I grabbed Leo's arm in a death-grip, imagining that if I kept holding on to him everything might be all right. I heard the door of an old car creak open. They put me down on the seat, and a surge of pain shot up my left side. I let out a protracted groan.

"What is it?" said Leo.

"I...I ...my..." I couldn't answer, but my vision was slowly coming back, and as if emerging from a dense fog, I discerned color and form, the dashboard of a small car, and I smelled old sun-baked plastic.

"Don't worry. We're taking you to a hospital." It was a voice that I didn't recognize. I could hear other voices all around me, though I couldn't focus on what they were saying. My hearing, too, seemed to be affected, sounds muffled as my vision continued to go in and out.

Then the car moved onto the road with a bump, and pain seared through me, but my only thought was: Where is Leo? I tried to turn my head to look in the back seat, but it hurt too much. I knew there were people behind me; I could feel their eyes upon me. "Leo?" I groaned.

"We'll be there soon. Just hold on," the driver said. I had no idea where they were taking me, and it was clear that Leo was not in the car. Though dizzy, I focused my eyes on my leg wound. I had a big scrape on my knee, and blood ran down my leg. Nausea hit me, and I gripped the dash with my right hand to stabilize myself. At the same moment the car rattled over a bump and sent another stab of pain through my arm and shoulder. Tears filled my eyes. I held my left arm tightly against my body with a strange fear that it might fall off.

The car was a *colectivo*, a group taxi that ran between Holguín and Gibara, stopping along the way to pick up and let out the passengers. As we got near Gibara, the car stopped to drop off and even take on a few new passengers—each time causing me unbearable pain as the car jerked to a stop, and then lurched into motion with a shudder. I was angry that we didn't just go directly to the hospital, but the driver must have figured that the business of transportation had to go on.

With my sight almost back to normal, I looked out the window at the distant hills. Gibara was where Christopher Columbus reportedly first landed in 1492 after almost three months at sea. He wrote in his journal that it was "the most beautiful land human eyes have ever seen." The claim that he, in fact, had landed in present-day Gibara was based on his description of the mountain in the distance, shaped like a saddle—the people of the area call it *Silla*.

We pulled into town, and the whitewashed buildings, the colonial architecture, the cozy little square all went by in a pastel blur. The only sight that impressed me was Leo standing in front of the hospital door. But my joy was short-lived as I took in the miserable hospital behind him. It was a characterless two-storied building in the process of shedding its white paint. Mold grew in large dark patches on its facade. Several of the windows were broken, and the frames covered with planks of wood. The sidewalk leading to the front door was bordered by brown dirt plugged with a few scrawny weeds.

Next to Leo was a mustachioed, hefty man in his forties who I guessed to be the man who had helped carry me. They got me out of the car and into the building. "How are you doing, boy? You really scared me," said Leo softly.

"Hi, I'm Tony," the other man said. He was on my left and very gentle. "You took my seat in the taxi, and I had to ride on that little shit of a scooter." He laughed. "We were right behind you in the taxi and saw it all happen."

"Thanks for stopping," I said in a weak voice.

"It was nothing. The driver didn't want to stop, but I made him. You can't leave a human being lying there in the road."

We entered a stark receiving room where a man in a white coat sat at a beat-up wooden table piled high with files and papers while several people stood around him all chattering like schoolchildren at recess. At our entrance the noise died and everybody turned to look. Leo held my good arm and asked if I wanted to sit down. I declined. Even the thought of lowering myself into a chair was painful. I leaned against a table.

A nurse walked in and Tony nearly assaulted her. "Can't someone clean off his wounds? He's bleeding all over the place." I wasn't bleeding that much any more, but I had several open sores encrusted with gravel.

"And what am I supposed to clean them with? We have nothing. We'll have to use his shirt," said the irritated nurse. They gingerly peeled off the bloody and gritty tank top, first over my right arm, then over my head, finally sliding it over my shoulder and down my left arm.

"Wow," said Leo. "He's got a big bump on his clavicle."

"Let's get him cleaned off. The doctor is almost ready for him." She took me into an alcove where there was a sink, and ran the shirt under the water. I watched in astonishment as she rubbed the dirty shirt over the scrapes. She roughly cleaned off the grit and the worst of the dried blood from my leg, side and shoulder; Leo or Tony could have done a much better job, and with a lot more gentleness.

Shirtless and with my nylon shorts, which had come untied at the waist, creeping down, showing my underwear like a homeboy in East L.A., I stood in front of the doctor. He asked me a lot of questions, but I was weak and still confused. It was hard for me to speak Spanish, and Tony filled in the words. I motioned for Leo to retie the waist of my shorts. I noticed that Leo, too, had a bloody scrape on his leg. I stared at it.

"Don't worry. It's nothing," he said.

Everyone treated me as a slightly shaken-up person with a few scrapes and bruises; they weren't ready to take my injuries seriously until they had test results. The doctor scribbled on small scraps of brown paper, stamped them, put them in my hand, and waved me away. Tony took the scraps and they helped me shuffle to the first nurses' station where, for a urine sample, they gave me a tiny glass vial that looked like the container that contact lenses come in. I stared at it in disbelief.

There was a toilet off the main lobby, and the stench hit me before I even entered the phone-booth-sized room. There were scraps of soiled newspaper—Cuban toilet paper—on the floor, and the toilet was full of excrement. There was no glass in the small window frame and I looked out at the blue sky filled with fluffy white clouds, held my breath to control the nausea, and took aim at the tiny opening of the vial. Of course I made a mess of things, and there was no water in the faucet of the miniscule sink to wash my hands. When I came out, Leo had to tie up my shorts again.

"Baby, you peed all over yourself."

"I know," I whined. He found an unused corner of paper and wiped off my shorts and hands. I took my golden offering back to the nurse's station where they pricked my finger and put a drop of blood on a slide to determine my blood type.

Tony called the nurse over again. "You need to clean off his wounds better than that. You must have some kind of disinfectant." She stared at him with dagger eyes, and then went off to another room. "You have to beg for everything," Tony explained. "They hoard things and won't give it to you unless you insist." In a few minutes she came back with a bottle and a tiny piece of gauze, which she used to paint my abrasions a gorgeous deep red. It reminded me of when I was a little kid, and my mom would put mercurochrome on my cuts, making them all red and stingy, after which she would send me off with a kiss, saying I was a good little soldier. Instead of a kiss and words of encouragement from the nurse, I sensed a resentment that I was a foreigner using up their supplies.

The X-rays were taken in another location a few blocks away. It was torturous getting into the dented white van—a big step up, and then a laborious fold of the body. I shared the vehicle with a young mother, who avoided looking at me, and instead focused her worried gaze on the tiny baby in her arms. We had to wait about ten minutes, and I sat almost delirious while Leo stood at the open van door, smoking a cigarette and giving me reassuring looks. In the suffocating air of the van I detected a urine smell. I thought it must be the baby's diaper, and then I realized that it was probably me. I added embarrassment to my list of negative emotions. Leo's bare leg was just a few inches from my hand on the door handle. I was desperate to bridge the gap, touch the hair on his leg, make contact with him, have him turn and give me his boundless smile. But I sat frozen in pain, wondering why he even bothered to stay with me.

At the other building they took the young mother first, while I stood propped up against a wall. Leo and Tony, who had ridden over on the bike, formed two pillars on either side of me.

After the radiologist finished with the baby, he came out to get me. He was a short, solidly built, good-looking man with dark curly hair escaping out the neck of his white hospital jacket. We went into the room with its equipment—all chipped, off-color enamel with the bulky, curvy style of the fifties. It was like walking into an old movie set, and I expected the good doctor, who had disappeared into the back, to emerge with a hunchbacked, beady-eyed assistant. Instead he returned shirtless, his well-formed chest covered with dark curly hair, dotted with glistening beads of sweat.

"I hope you don't mind. It is so hot. Can you lie on the table?" I tried to imagine where else in the world you might be attended by a bare-chested doctor, and wondered if I was hallucinating on top of everything else.

"I don't think so."

"Come on. We'll help you." They backed me up to the table and the three of them make a cursory attempt at lifting me, but I stopped them almost as soon as they started.

"No, no, no. This is not going to work." They could lift me up, but I was convinced that lying down—and getting back up—would kill me.

"Okay," said the doc. "We'll have to do it standing up."

"Standing up, definitely." Leo arched his eyebrows and gave me a silly look.

Back at the other building the admitting doctor studied the X-rays and furrowed his brows over bloodshot eyes. "Hmm, you've got a few broken bones here, your clavicle and at least four ribs. We're sending you to Hospital Lenin in Holguín, where you'll get better care. We should have an ambulance in a few minutes." Leo and Tony leaned over to look at the X-rays and the doctor traced the fractures on the over-sized negatives with his finger.

In the time waiting for the ambulance, we decided that Tony would ride with me to Holguín, and Leo would ride the bike back to the rental place, and then meet us at the hospital. I gave him my wallet with over $200 in it and didn't even think about whether I should trust him or not. He patted my good shoulder and left.

A short time later they put me on a stretcher—I nearly blacked out with the movement—and stuck an IV in my arm. They loaded me in the back of an ambulance, and Tony crawled in to sit beside me.

Hospital Lenin was an improvement over the one in Gibara, but as they wheeled me in, I noticed a number of missing ceiling tiles and broken light fixtures, peeling paint, and scuff marks where hundreds of trolleys like mine had bumped against the walls. Then I was in an admitting area that bustled with doctors, other patients, nurses, police officers, and people in military uniforms. It was like a bad dream. I heard voices whispering, "*Extranjero*," and then someone would come over and peer at me as if I were an exotic specimen; some of the gawkers look like they had just walked in off the street.

A nurse with a huge needle in her hand arrived at my side, accompanied by a policeman. It was an old-fashioned syringe, hopefully sterilized, and I again pictured myself in a 1950s horror film. She drew blood, and I concentrated on the farthest wall while Tony pressed his fingers lightly on my other arm.

"They're looking for alcohol in the blood," Tony said after they went away. "You weren't drinking, were you?"

"Come on, it was like 10:30 in the morning."

"That's a perfect time to have a *trago*," he joked.

A man in a military uniform, sitting in a chair against the wall on the opposite side of the room, started throwing questions at me in a monotonous voice. The room was still full of people, and I was annoyed by the lack of privacy, though it seemed the norm in Cuba.

He asked about my medical history, everything from broken bones to sexually transmitted diseases. I told him that I had broken the same collarbone when I was a baby and tried to climb out of my crib. Hospitalized? No. Medications? No. Diseases? No. Answering no to everything seemed easiest.

A second nurse approached me with a urine bag attached to a long tube, which she jammed into a place where nothing should ever go. I yelled, but it made me forget all my other pains for a moment. Still, it was cruel.

They took me, in my weakened state, away from the crowds into a side room where I met Jonni, the administrator in charge of foreign patients. They appeared to have no problem applying delicate medical procedures in public, but the financial arrangements had to be discussed in private. He explained in a business-like manner that I would be taken care of and admitted into a private room that was reserved for foreigners. He itemized my expenses so far, which amounted to $420, and explained that each additional day would be sixty dollars. "Special meals are brought in from outside," he added with a bit of excitement. Since I was an American and couldn't use a credit card, he informed me that I would have to pay my bill in cash before leaving the hospital. Though it was incredibly cheap compared to the States, I hadn't budgeted for a stay in the hospital, plus I questioned all I had heard about free medical care in Cuba. I told him I would pay the bill with a Viajero Card. He seemed satisfied, and they took me up to my room.

There were two rooms reserved for foreigners. Mine had air conditioning, a TV, a VCR, but no videos to watch, and a mechanical bed with a remote control. On one side of the bed was a hospital-issue side table, and on the other a plastic patio chair for visitors. They got me and all my tubes onto the bed. Tony was still with me, and Jonni hovered outside the door at his station, a small desk with a phone. In addition to my discomfort—no one had as yet offered me any painkillers—I was hungry, thirsty, and in need of a bath, but at least I wasn't surrounded by crowds of people and I could lie down.

Leo arrived and told me he had returned the bike and everything had been taken care of. They only charged a rental fee of six dollars for one hour and ten dollars for the damaged mirror; I was a mangled wreck, but I had saved the bike. They kept the forty dollars I already paid for the two days to take care of the fine the cop gave me.

We sent Tony on his way. He took my hand and held it. "I'm glad it was me that came along."

"Me, too. Thanks for everything."

"Here's my number and address in Gibara. Don't hesitate to call if you need anything." He squeezed my hand and patted my arm.

Jonni shouted in from the hall, "What would you like to eat? The doctor hasn't cleared you for food yet, but I have to order from across the street and they close soon." The IV had taken the edge off the hunger, and even though I hadn't put anything in my stomach since a muffin in the morning, I couldn't think of a thing I wanted to eat.

"What do they have?"

"I'll order you some ham and cheese sandwiches. Do you like yogurt?"

"That's fine."

Leo nodded his head enthusiastically.

"Didn't you eat anything when you were out?" I asked.

"I wanted to get back here as soon as I could. I forgot."

A doctor came in, the third one I had seen since I got to Hospital Lenin. He was a soft-spoken man in his fifties and was the first to attend me since the accident who seemed to care. He studied my chart and examined my eyes and clavicle.

"Can you take out this catheter?" I pleaded. "It's driving me crazy. My friend can help me go to the bathroom."

"Catheter?" He looked surprised. "Oh, of course. You don't need that. But I don't want you to eat or drink anything until tomorrow. If you get nauseous and have to vomit, you could hurt your ribs, even puncture a lung, and that could be very serious. Try to relax, and someone will see you in the morning."

"How can I relax when I am in such pain?"

"Nobody gave you anything? Oh, dear, we aren't being very good to our foreign guest. I'll tell Jonni to get you something."

A few minutes later Jonni came in with a couple pills that looked like Tylenol. I stared at them with a smirk, thinking of the Vicodin I had brought in with the donations. I had snagged a couple for myself, but they were with my things at the apartment.

The food deliveryman arrived with sandwiches in styrofoam trays, fruit salad, yogurt, and two of bottles of mineral water. Jonni reminded me that I was not supposed to eat and took the fruit, yogurt, and water to the refrigerator in the hall, though he left the sandwiches on the bedside table. Leo stared at them.

"Go ahead," I said. "They'll go bad by tomorrow anyway."

"Thanks, baby."

After they took the catheter out and what felt like half of my insides with it, I lay in a post-trauma stupor. Leo turned on the TV. With the curtains closed, I only knew it was dark because the evening movie was on, Spencer Tracey in *The Old Man and the Sea*. The Cuban authorities, who controlled all programming, never tired of promoting the Hemingway-Cuba connection. It was a dubbed version and hard for me to follow, though I stared at the screen. Leo became engrossed in the movie, and I asked if he had ever read the book.

"Me?" he laughed. "I've never read a book in my life. I dropped out of high school to go to work. I suppose it was a mistake, but too late to do anything about it now."

Near the end of the movie, Leo got called downstairs. When he returned, he said it was his mom. She didn't believe he was all right until she could gaze on him with her own eyes, touch him. She wanted to see me, too, but they wouldn't let her come up.

"Can you help me up? I need to go to the bathroom."

He heard the weariness in my voice. "Here, just use the bedpan."

He positioned the little plastic pitcher between my legs.

"Don't look," I said.

"I've already seen it," he laughed.

"I know. I hate this." With his other hand he tousled my hair. After a long pause, a pathetic stream trickled down the side of the container.

"Is that all?"

"It's mostly just the urge."

Leo stayed the night, trying to sleep in the lawn chair, and I couldn't find a comfortable position in the bed. We passed a horrible night. Very early in the morning, I asked him to find the night nurse and get me something for the pain. The Tylenol had done nothing.

The nurse was a sleepy-eyed young man who smiled sweetly when he caught Leo and me holding hands. He injected something into the IV bag and said that it should help alleviate the pain. It worked because I slept almost three hours.

In the morning Leo left to collect our things from the apartment, shower, and change clothes. He told Jonni that he might need a pass to come back up. The night before he had to fight with the guard to let him back in after meeting with his mother outside. Jonni tore off a square of natural-colored recycled paper and wrote out "*Pase de Acompañante Permanente*" and put a Ministry of Public Health stamp on it. Leo came over to say goodbye and showed it to me. "I guess this officially makes me your permanent companion," he said with a big smile. His playfulness sweetened the morning, but watching him go out the door sent me into despair.

I heard a noise and opened my eyes. Again I thought I was hallucinating when I saw Sulyn and a man in medical garb standing in the room. She introduced him as her father, a radiologist at the hospital. There was still the look of suspicion in her eye, and I was convinced that she had come by to make sure that the spell she put on me had worked. Maybe the man with her was here to deliver the *coup de grâce*, though he looked professional in the way he held the large wobbly X-rays up to the light.

"You actually have six broken ribs." He pointed them out and counted.

"They told me four."

"A couple of them are very small fractures, but it's six."

Sulyn stood over by the door like an understudy waiting in the wings. "Where's Leo?" she said.

"Oh, he spent the night," I said with pleasure, "but he just left to change clothes."

They only stayed a few minutes, and she wished me well with a false grin.

Later the surgeon came in and asked if I wanted them to operate on my collarbone. "It's a very simple half-hour operation," he said. "We make a two-inch cut right here," he sliced his finger across the bump in my clavicle, "put in a pin and you're as good as new."

"Does it have to be done right away?"

"No," he answered hesitantly. "But I wouldn't wait too long. If you feel more comfortable doing the surgery in your country, you could wait long enough to get back there. We would be happy to do it for you though."

"What about the recuperation time?"

"You would have to stay here a while, say a couple of weeks before traveling."

Cuba had a good reputation in the world for its healthcare, and many foreigners came here for procedures they couldn't have done, or couldn't afford to do at home. But this hospital was not one of the upscale clinics that catered to foreigners, and I hadn't been impressed with my care so far. Once I paid my hospital bill for the expenses I had already accumulated, I wouldn't have the money for the operation or to stay in Cuba.

"I feel better about doing the surgery at home in Los Angeles, but thanks for your care."

"As you wish. You can eat now, but I want you to stay in the hospital another twenty-four hours. I'll come to see you again tomorrow."

11

Leo got back to the hospital, the half-moons under his eyes looking even darker than normal, while our backpacks, one slung over each shoulder, seemed to weigh him down. There was no one around, so he came over to the bed and pecked me lightly on the mouth. His jaw hung low as he paced around the room putting the backpacks in one corner, and then moving them to another.

"Alfonso wanted me to pay for four days," he muttered.

"We were only there two nights."

"Our things were there last night. He said that we promised to stay four, so we should pay four. I bargained with him, paid him three and an extra ten dollars." I shook my head and thought of the money in my wallet—which Leo still had control of—rapidly dwindling. "I got all our clothes and things." The tone in his voice was flat, and he continued to stir the air in the room with his restlessness.

"That's good. I'm dying to take a shower and change clothes."

He stopped at the side of the bed, just out of reach, distant and unapproachable. "You, uh, sure have a lot of pills," Leo said.

His comment depleted what was left of the good air in the room and I fought for the next breath. I had just begun to climb out of the dark pit of my accident, and then I was sliding back down with my muddy secret falling on top of me. I grabbed the remote and turned off the afternoon soap opera. The room was very quiet. I started to speak several times, but nothing came out. I looked up and his eyes, more open than usual, were upon me. "Well?" he said.

"I take a lot of vitamins. Most of the pills are, you know, vitamins." I was buying myself time. I could have lied and kept it hidden, but what was the use?

"It's funny I never saw you take them," he said calmly.

"There's something else. Shit. I should know how to do this, but I don't. I'm positive. I have HIV."

He went to the window, threw the curtains open, and looked down at the busy street. His eyes narrowed on something below, and he lifted his hand to shade them from the sun pouring in through the glass. I tapped the remote on the mattress.

"You weren't going to tell me?'

"Of course, I mean, I don't know. I was afraid. I didn't want you to run away."

He turned away from the window and his eyes burned into me. "You think I'm a stupid country boy? I know about AIDS. I know how to take care of myself."

"I don't have AIDS. I have the virus."

"I know the difference." He was staring at me, half sitting on the ledge of the window. The muscles in his face were taut. He took out a cigarette and lit it. "So that was all a big lie about me being the first one," he spit out.

"No. Sex isn't the only way to get HIV. I got it from a blood transfusion a long time ago. I had a serious car accident in 1985. It was a month before they started screening the blood supply and later that year they recommended that everyone who had a transfusion prior to March 1985 get tested. When I got the results, I thought my life was over. My daughter was just eight years old. I could barely look at her without crying. Lizzie and I weren't doing too well back then, but she was great. She kept the family together and gave me the strength to go on. We didn't tell anybody and just hoped for the best."

"I'm sorry." He came over to the bed and kissed me on the top of my head.

"You know, we haven't done anything that even falls in the category of 'possibly risky.'"

He shrugged, but still looked concerned. I felt the guilt of deceiving the person I most needed at the moment, someone who might help me get through this and be my friend. My mind went straight into defense mode. The last thing I wanted was to be left alone, but I had to start preparing myself. Maybe the night nurse could help me shower. Maybe Gerard could take a few days off work and come and get me. I would get by.

"Leo, I'm sorry. I understand if you want to leave now. I won't blame you. You can go."

There was a long silence. My mind in panic was racing, thinking, gauging, planning. I stared at the blank TV set, the remote sweaty in my hand.

"I can't now. You need me." He started grinning as if nothing had happened. "Come on. We should get you cleaned up. To be honest, you're beginning to smell." His grin spread into a smile. "Hold on to me. I'll lift you up."

I was in his arms and a choking sound escaped from my throat as my eyes welled up. "None of that, now. It's okay." He had a cigarette hanging from his lips as he held me up. The smoke curled around and went up my nose. I snorted.

"Come on. Stop that." Then he realized about the smoke. "Sorry." He dropped the cigarette into the ashtray on the floor next to his chair. "They keep telling me not to smoke here." He giggled.

"You shouldn't. It's a hospital for Christ's sake."

He got me into the shower and pulled my shorts and underwear down. I stood before him like a naked, helpless child, and he emitted a high funny laugh. "Don't worry, baby. I'll take care of you."

He wet the washcloth under the cold water of the showerhead, soaped it up and then began gently scrubbing me, starting with my upper body while I held on to the wall with my good arm. He tenderly cleaned my scrapes, and then started on my left arm and shoulder, which I held plastered to my body in fear of moving it.

"Can I move it just a little out from your side to get to that pit? Come on, do it for me. That's right. Good boy." He was a natural at this.

Then he looked at my crotch, shrugged a bit, took a deep breath and began applying the same gentle wash that he had on my upper body. He held my shriveled penis as if it was a wounded bird he had picked up off the ground and self-consciously dabbed at it with the soapy cloth. I chuckled and he looked up at me with pursed lips. "You're touching it," I said in a kid's voice.

"I was just thinking the same thing."

"Touching it doesn't make you a *maricón*."

"Maybe a little." He sighed good-naturedly. We laughed, and he continued his work until he had bathed my whole body.

Back in bed I felt clean, and lighter after my confession. Leo slumped into his chair. "Martin, why didn't you just tell me?"

"I swear to God I wouldn't put you at risk. Remember that time I didn't let you use my razor?"

"I'm not worried about that. Why didn't you trust me with something that is so important? Something about you?"

"That's the tricky part. When you feel something for another person, you want to tell them, but at the same time it's when you most want *not* to tell them for fear that they will run away. I want people to know me for who I am first and not think of me as a person with a disease. Leo, we've had a good time together. You've been great through all this. I am feeling something, you know, for you, but I don't trust it yet. We hardly know each other."

He nodded his head. "Ten days," he said.

"We've been through a lot. Seems like more."

"What are we going to do now? What did the doctor say?"

"Probably they will release me tomorrow. I told him I didn't want to have the operation here, so there's not much they can do. I need to go back to Havana and then change my ticket to go back home. I hope you can go with me because traveling alone would be very difficult."

"To Los Angeles?"

"Ha! I wish it were that simple."

"You mean you would take me if you could?" He was excited, and

I was struck by the serious look in his eyes.

"Slow down, boy. Ten days, remember?"

"I know. Of course I'll go with you to Havana."

"*Hola,* Lisbeth. Come in." She came over to the bed and kissed me.

"And Leo?"

"You just missed him. He is on his way home to change clothes and eat."

"I'll see him later." Her shoulders slumped and her fingers were entwined in an awkward embrace. It was the first time I had seen her without Leo nearby, and the glow about her was missing. "I tried to see you last night, but it was too late." She was almost whispering.

"Leo told me. Thanks for coming. That was sweet."

"I feel so bad for you. You'll probably never want to come back to Holguín now." I wondered if it was wishful thinking. "It could have happened anywhere. Sulyn and I were so worried when we heard the news. You know, I had a bad feeling about that trip. A mother has these feelings, but when I express them, it bothers Leo. So I just keep quiet. That's a bad road, that road to Gibara. I also hate it when he goes to Havana. That's a bad road, too. And then he stays so long there. He's all I have, so you can imagine how I felt when the neighbor told me about the accident."

"He's fine. Just a scrape."

"But look at you. I'm so sorry. Are you eating anything?"

"I just finished some fruit and yogurt."

"I mean real food. Don't they give you anything? I'm going to send some food with Leo when he comes back. I had better go, so I can catch him. He said he is going to spend the night with you again, and I think that's fine. You need somebody here with you."

When she got up to leave, I searched her eyes to see if she knew. There wasn't a glimmer of suspicion; the only readable emotion was a true concern for me, and I knew right then where Leo got his loving nature. I was overcome with a peculiar emotion, wanting her to hold me and be my mother for a moment. I wanted to say something grand and poignant, confess to her, lay my head on her breast, and ask her forgiveness. If she had any inkling of the random sentiments inside me, she didn't let on. She just wagged her finger and said, "No more motor bikes." One of her sparkling laughs escaped from her painted mouth, and then she was gone.

Later, I confided on the phone to Gerard, "It was so strange. I had this compelling urge to confess to her everything Leo and I had done."

"Confess, my dear? You think she doesn't know?"

"Either she doesn't know or she has complete confidence that whatever Leo does is good."

"Most likely the latter. I just hope he doesn't decide to dump you in a ditch somewhere on the way back to Havana. She'd probably be fine with that, too."

"You've lived here too long."

"Maybe I have. I can measure my time in Cuba by the men, and their overprotective mothers. Anyway, I'll look into changing your flights. Get back here as soon as you can. I'll also tell Rosa you'll need to stay another night or so at her place. If you need money, don't worry. I can lend you some."

"*Gracias, amigo.*"

Leo sauntered in a couple of hours later carrying a plastic container of food his mother had sent. I wasn't hungry, but I tried to eat a few bites so as not to seem ungrateful. Leo was restless, and every hour went down to the lobby for a cigarette; the night nurse had laid down the law about smoking.

We spent another restless night, and in the morning he said he was going out to make a phone call, but didn't come back.

Mid-morning a woman came in to clean. She had heavily painted eyes and her hair was in disarray, dyed so many times it had the texture of a dimestore wig. I guessed that she was in her late twenties, but she moved around the room with the weight of someone much older. A loose tank top showed her thin breasts when she leaned over, and tight cutoffs were molded to her slim hips. She glanced at me, but didn't say anything as she dipped a dingy, shredded rag into dirty water, wrung it out with her bare hands over the bucket, wrapped it over a T-shaped pole, and passed it over the floor. A couple of times as she slopped the mop around the bed, her ass was in my face, and she twisted her head around to watch my reaction. Later her friend came to the door, and they stood talking about me as if I were an alien creature.

The friend was everything that the mop girl was not—voluptuous, intriguing, a raven-haired beauty. Her bronze skin glistened, her sable eyes questioned, her simple clothes appeared stylish. With soft arms crossed in front of her bosom, she leaned against the doorjamb, a bit aloof, sultry and enchanting. She was very close to what I had always imagined as my ideal in feminine beauty, and yet I looked at her and felt nothing. If I had seen her a couple of weeks before, would it have made any difference, or had my desire for women faded long ago? The blonde caught me staring at her friend and gave her a piercing look.

"I'm sure he's Italian," said the mop girl in Spanish.

"No, I heard he was American."

"He's a little ugly. Don't you think?"

"I think he's cute. Look at those eyes. A little sad though."

"He just needs some good loving." They both giggled.

I ignored them and didn't let on that I understood. Then the surgeon rounded the corner and scowled at the girls, which sent them scurrying. In a cheery voice he explained that I could travel, and ordered that I be sent down to Orthopedics to have them gauze and tape my arm so it wouldn't bounce around. "You're free to go," he said. "Have a good trip home."

Jonni came in with my bill, but when he swiped my Viajero Card, the transaction came back denied. It must have been a system failure, but the Viajero office was closed until Monday. Jonni informed me that I couldn't leave Holguín until I had paid. If I didn't want to stay in the hospital, he could arrange a private home for the night, but the bill had to be paid.

The cleaning woman and her friend showed up in their new roles as aides to take me down to Orthopedics. They parked the wheelchair by the side of the bed and launched into the same chatter about how I needed a *novia,* girlfriend. Neither of them looked particularly strong and I was afraid they wouldn't be able to support me as I moved from the high bed to the chair. I got my good arm on the armrest and eased myself down, but the chair started rolling backwards. I nearly ended up on the floor. "*¡Coño! No pusieron el freno.* You didn't put on the fucking brake!" I shouted. The girls looked at each other, as though each thought it was the other's fault.

"*Dios mío, habla español,*" said the blonde. "*Señor,* me sorry. Me sorry. No work chair." Ironically, now she was trying to speak English.

"*Habla español, tonta.* He speaks Spanish, silly," said the dark one to her friend.

On the way to Orthopedics they began a barrage of questions about where I was from and what life was like in California. The blonde said she had a boyfriend in Denver and wondered if it was near my state. In the end they weren't so bad, struggling like everybody else, working a crummy job for pesos and looking for a way out of their miserable lives that had made them old before their time, their eyes painted with a thin layer of desperation.

Leo was waiting when I got back to the room all wrapped in gauze and tape from my shoulder to my waist. I gave him a cool reception. "We can leave the hospital," I told him, "but not Holguín. My card didn't go through."

Jonni came in and teased Leo for being gone so long. "Well, you know, *la novia,*" he said.

"I just tried the card again and got the same message," Jonni said. "I have some friends who can rent you a room for tonight. In the morning I'll come over with the credit card machine and try again. I'll keep your passport here at the hospital."

"You know I'm screwed if my passport gets lost."

"Don't worry. I'll lock it in a drawer."

Jonni's friends Lucy and Paco had a room to rent over their garage on a side street not far from the hospital. It was minimal: a bed, table, chair, refrigerator, and small bathroom. There was no TV or telephone. It was painted an adventurous orange color, which they probably thought was cozy, but to me it just made the room hotter.

The owners hardly seemed likely friends of the dour and uptight Jonni. Lucy, with her bangled wrists, loose clothing, and herbal scent, and Paco, with his long dark hair, faded jeans, and sandals, looked like holdovers from the sixties. But the way they kept looking at Leo, I could tell they weren't comfortable with him staying with me, even as my caretaker.

After another gentle bath, we stretched out on the bed and discussed options. It was hard to make transportation plans when we didn't know when the card would go through. I suggested we start looking for a private taxi to Havana, though I knew it would be expensive. Leo massaged the top of my head, and I felt like a hypnotized cat; my thoughts turned to mush, and my mouth stopped working. We tumbled into a dreamy nap.

When I woke up I was alone, but spied him in front of the bathroom mirror, messing with his hair, which had gone out of shape from the pillow.

"You going out?"

"I thought I would start asking around about a car. Then I'll go pick up some food from home. Are you hungry?"

"Not really."

"You've got to eat. I'll be back in a couple of hours."

"You'd better help me up and put me in a chair." I was afraid I wouldn't be able to get up to go to the bathroom. He took the pillows and cushioned the chair for me, and then kissed me goodbye. Each time he left I felt like a Motown singer, crooning that this time out the door would be his last, and there wasn't any reason for him to come back. Cuba was all about drama, and I had caught the tragedy bug bad.

While Leo was away I hobbled down the stairs in a series of step, rest; step, rest; and got Gerard on the line.

"I called the hospital and when they told me you'd left, I assumed that you were on the way back to Havana."

"My Viajero Card isn't working and I don't have cash. They said

I can't leave Holguín until the bill is paid."

"Just leave. Leo will help you, won't he?"

"They've got my passport. But that's not the worst of it. I'm running out of the medicine I need to take. I have about two doses left." I stopped short of telling him what the meds were for. Missing one dose of the cocktail was not that bad; I had already done that the first night I was in the hospital. Missing several was bad.

"What are the meds for?"

"Well, shock number two. I've got HIV. Not sexually transmitted, though it doesn't make any difference at this point. But in light of our earlier conversation, it was from a blood transfusion." After telling Leo, Gerard was easy. I knew he would be sympathetic because of his volunteer work, but I doubt I would have told him if it weren't for the mess I was in.

There was a brief silence on the line. He came back in an even voice. "Don't panic. We'll figure something out. You have more medicine back here, right?"

"I thought I would be gone about three days, four days max."

"It's not like those pills add extra weight. I don't want to make you feel any worse, but you should know by now Cuba is the land of the unexpected."

Then he started getting fired up about the way they were treating me. He asked for Jonni's full name and said that he was going to make some calls. He would also try to find out what was happening with my Viajero Card. I pulled myself back up the rickety stairs, feeling that with Gerard as my crusader, my downward spiral would surely cease.

Jonni arrived in the morning with my X-rays, an itemized bill that had been hand-written and stamped, and his credit card machine. He plugged the machine into the phone line down in Lucy and Paco's enclosed sun porch with its large wooden rockers, artificial flowers, and vinyl curtains stamped with giant daisies. Everyone leaned over in anticipation as he slid the card through. I fell back in my chair when a small two-inch stub poked its head out of the machine—transaction denied. Jonni looked at me like I had put a hoax on it. He reiterated that he would hold my passport until the bill was paid, and marched out the door exhaling an exaggerated puff of air. We watched his shoulders, looking like a tensed rocking bow, descending the narrow staircase.

We told Lucy that we might have to stay another night and went back up to the room. I fell back into my black mood.

"I'm going out for a bit." But before he got to the door, Lucy called from downstairs that there was a visitor.

"Can't they come up?" said Leo.

"No visitors in the rooms," Lucy shouted back.

"Who is it?"

"You'll have to come down and see."

Leo convinced me to go down with him. Before we even got to the street I felt the sun prickling my scalp and the white light of mid-afternoon blinding my vision. I was almost at the bottom of the stairs before I recognized Humberto. I hadn't seen him since the night when he and Ricardo were after the Spanish guy in Havana, but Leo had told me he was back in Holguín. Clumsily we hugged and then stood on the hot, shadeless sidewalk. At first he acted interested in the story of the accident, but as I got into the telling of it, he started looking around, taking out another cigarette, his eyes going cloudy. In mid-sentence I stopped, and he didn't seem to notice as he examined the cigarette ash. I looked at Leo and smiled, thinking he had so much more to offer than his buddy. I wondered why they were friends.

And then Leo looked over my shoulder down the street, and I turned to follow his gaze. Jonni steamrolled along the sidewalk and appeared to be out of patience. He didn't bother with the usual pleas-antries when he caught up to us, and we all went upstairs. He pulled out a receipt from his notebook. "Please sign," he said gruffly.

"It went through," I said, still confused as to why he was flushed and his eyes so hard. I signed it and he handed me my passport. There was a disturbing silence, and I could hear Lucy rummaging around in the kitchen.

"I don't appreciate the way your friend in Havana talked to me on the phone," he spit out. "He has a lot of nerve threatening me. He also told me that you are seropositive and that you are running out of medication. Well, my friend, that is your problem and it doesn't concern me in the least. We gave you the best care available in the hospital and for that we are obliged to charge. Your obligations to us are now fulfilled." He turned around and stormed out.

The silence of before was now deafening, and I reddened. He might as well have grabbed a bullhorn and announced my condition to the whole town, the secret that I had managed to hide for years from all but a few of my closest friends and family was out in Holguín within a couple of days. Humberto stared at his shoes, and Leo lit a cigarette. I walked out without a word and trudged up the stairs.

Leo came up after a few minutes and squeezed through the half-open door. He tried to act casual, but looked embarrassed. "Let's pack up."

"What for?"

"Lucy told me they have the place rented for tonight and she needs to clean."

"And when did she realize that? About 10 minutes ago?"

"She said Paco forgot to tell her someone called earlier."

"Where are we going?"

"To my house. Humberto thinks he knows someone who can drive us to Havana and went to find out about it. It'll probably be about $200."

"I don't care. I just want to get as far away from here as possible."

Leo's house was full of people and everyone was nice not to stare as Lisbeth settled me into the big rocking chair padded with pillows from her bed. Sulyn sat in the corner and talked to a heavy, half-drunk man that Lisbeth introduced as her boyfriend, Ramón. Humberto arrived a few minutes later. The aunt from upstairs and her kids were in and out, as well as various neighbors. Leo and Humberto drank rum, and then Leo sat down to a game of chess with Ramón while Lisbeth busied herself in the kitchen. Despite Lisbeth's efforts to make the chair comfortable, I couldn't get my body settled into a position that didn't put pressure on my cracked ribs.

Everyone seemed to have forgotten the car to Havana. From the kitchen door Lisbeth caught sight of me squirming in the chair and suggested I move into her room. They stopped the chess game and helped me re-situate myself on Lisbeth's bed, propped up into a sitting position with the pillows. She gathered a stack of outdated *Holas* and *Lecturas*—fat, glossy gossip magazines from Spain—and put them in my lap. The pages had been leafed through by so many wishful hands that they were wrinkled and creased and had lost their shine. They were full of stories about the royal families of Europe and the latest scandals involving people who, either through birth or money, had made a name for themselves and didn't mind having it splashed all over the pages in splendid color. I thumbed through them, but every few minutes I looked toward the living room to see if anything was happening besides chess and rum.

Leo's ten-year old niece, Adita, came into the bedroom, went to the far side of the bed, and idled there until I looked up.

"Leo's very nice, isn't he?" she said dreamily.

"Yes, he's been very nice to me."

"He's good to help around the house. My mom said a lot of men don't do that. Do you help your wife around the house?"

"I certainly do. I do most of the cooking."

"Oh, that's wonderful," she said like she had an adult's understanding of these things. "We had some visitors last summer from Switzerland. We killed a pig and had a big party. Now I have a pen pal. Her name is Gilda."

"Where does she live?"

"In Geneva. She invited me to visit her, but I can't go this year. Does your shoulder hurt a lot?"

"Yes, it does." She ran out of the room and came back a few minutes later with her mom, who had several small boxes of medicine from Europe. I didn't want to use up their painkillers, but they insisted I take them. Adita went to get me a glass of water and had to squeeze by Humberto hovering in the doorway. Beyond him Leo was deep in thought about his next move on the board.

"Aren't you hot in those jeans?" said Humberto.

"I'm dying. Could you get me some shorts out of my backpack?"

He pulled out a pair of baggy khaki shorts, helped me stand and change into them. Adita and her mother fled the room, but I hardly cared.

Lisbeth brought in a plate of rice and chicken still on the bone. She looked down at the plate. "Leo, get in here and help Martin eat."

"In a minute," he said, reluctant to leave the game.

"*Vete.* Go on," said Ramon. "Your mom is calling you."

Lisbeth went in and sat on Ramon's lap. "Now, go on, Leo. Your friend needs you."

He had been drinking for some time, but the only sign of it was a silly smile distorting his face.

"You remember me?" I said with a smirk.

He remained silent as he started cutting the chicken off the bone. Then he said softly, "Are you okay?"

"No, I'm not. Maybe you remember that I had an accident and my fucking body hurts like hell and I am trying to get to Havana so I can go home."

"What do you want me to do?"

"I thought you were getting a car."

"You can't just snap your fingers and make it happen. You have to be patient. The guy has the address here. He'll come when he comes. If you want, I'll go out in a little bit and call him."

I woke up when the headlights streamed through the thin curtains and a rumbling motor cut off. Leo came in and announced that the car had arrived.

"Thanks," I said as he helped me get up. His gentle touch made me feel guilty.

"I'm sorry I've been so bitchy. Forgive me?"

"Don't worry about it. You're just being normal," he teased. I slapped him playfully on the butt and then noticed Humberto staring at us from the living room. He was sitting in a chair by the door with a large, black, half-filled duffle bag that looked sad and deflated at his feet. As we crossed into the living room, Humberto jumped up as if at attention, but then teetered from too much rum.

I went to the doorway of the kitchen and in the low light viewed a dispirited Sulyn packing Leo's clothes for the trip. Lisbeth stood watching, biting her lower lip. When she saw me, she dropped her shoulders, came out, and took my hand.

"Please, send Leo back home as soon as you leave. I don't want him to stay in Havana. I'm counting on you. He won't listen to me. I don't want him staying one more day after you leave. Please, Martin." I promised her I would do the best I could, but without the least confidence that I, or anyone, could make Leo do anything he didn't want to do. We headed to the front porch to say our goodbyes, and Humberto picked up his bag. I cringed at the realization that he was going with us. Of course no one had bothered to ask me.

Leo half-carried me to the car and helped me fold into the back seat before getting in the front next to the driver. I was stuck with Humberto. I grabbed my toiletry bag and found my last Vicodin to knock me out for the trip.

The ten-year-old Toyota ran well, but the shocks were gone, and just getting out to the main road jostled me so badly I was sure that any mending my bones had done was shaken loose. Then the driver got on the almost-deserted road and stomped on the gas, at times going 130 to 140 kilometers an hour, none of us with a seatbelt. Leo and the driver chattered away in the front seat, and I heard the driver say he had worked all day and was tired. Leo was in the front to keep him awake. Humberto, who had a hard time putting three intelligible sentences together, would probably have so bored the driver that we would have all been in jeopardy.

I put my hand on Leo's shoulder. "*Dime, corazón,*" he said. The driver gave him a sideways glance. Leo probably didn't even realize he was calling me sweetheart. Dear words flew out of his mouth without thinking. It was one of the things I loved about him.

"We forgot my birthday present."

"Damn. I'll have to send it to you."

"Send it to me? How?"

"We've got DHL here."

"Ha!" I said with a snort. "Maybe to anywhere else in the known world. The package would probably end up in Timbuktu."

"Where?"

"Never mind. I just don't think it would get to L.A. I'll get it next time."

He turned around in his seat. "You're coming back?" He sounded a little too excited, and the driver looked over at him again.

"I have to finish my book research. Oh, and my X-rays. We forgot them, too."

"Sorry. We left so quickly."

"You can keep them as a souvenir, frame them, put them up on your wall."

"Better you send me a picture."

We passed through Las Tunas, Camaguey, and Ciego de Avila under the cooler blanket of darkness, but it was still muggy. Hundreds of insects ended their lives on the windshield, and when I chanced a look at the road ahead, a small animal was splayed out on the asphalt, its lifeless eyes shining in the headlights. My bandages were beginning to emanate a rank smell, and I had a strange metallic taste in my mouth. The annoying hum of the motor and the wind whipping through the windows was a relentless soundtrack to this horror film where my clouded brain imagined that I had been kidnapped and was on the road to hell.

Past Ciego de Ávila, the wide and almost empty *autopista* that would take us all the way to Havana, spread out before us. I dozed off, but my eyes popped open when I felt the car jerk and move back to the center of the road. Leo had gone silent and his head had slumped against the window.

"You okay?" I said to the driver.

"Everything's cool."

"What?" said Leo in a groggy voice. "Oh, shit. I fell asleep. What's going on?"

"We should stop. I've got to pee anyway," I said.

He veered the car to the side of the road, turned off the engine, and cut the lights, leaving us in total darkness, surrounded by a wall of humidity and buzzing insects. Leo helped me step out into the foot-tall grass that wet my ankles. I stepped away from the car and sent out a burning stream. The irritation from the catheter was still with me. We got back in the car and tried to sleep. My ribs and shoulder were throbbing; the Vicodin had done little more than take the edge off the pain. I folded my legs one way and then the other, and resettled myself on the hard seat several times without finding a suitable position. I sighed and listened to the chitter of the cicadas, the males of the species doing all the singing, trying to get a mate.

I managed to drift off for a time, and when I woke up we were moving again. It was light out, and the hazy sun hanging low on the horizon brought me a guarded hope as it shined on the green fields and stately palm trees. Hawkers selling their homemade goods were already on the side of the road, and some held out huge slabs of cheese and mounds of *guayaba* paste for our inspection as we flew by. A few went so far out onto the road that we had to swerve to miss hitting them. There was more traffic now, trucks loaded with mangoes, and others loaded with people traveling to work, standing and swaying, holding onto the rails of the truck bed. In the stoic jaws and unflinching eyes of these Cubans was resignation as they began another day of hard work in an unending struggle to feed their families. Yet there was a dignity, too, in their heads held high looking out towards the hills, the fields, and the road falling away behind them.

12

June 2006

Anabela and I sat on the cool tile floor painting pictures on large pieces of brown paper. We had one brush with good bristles, but the shaft was broken in half. The other had bristles that stuck out in all directions like a fright wig. I kept moving the glass of muddy water just as she was about to tip it over. Most of the ten watercolors in the metal tray had been sullied by neighboring hues. The picture we were working on had a yellow-green house surrounded by purplish grass and a brownish sun in the sky.

For the third time in the last half-hour she asked, "*Dónde està Papi?*"

There was a smell of frying chicken coming from the kitchen, and Lisbeth poked her head out to smile down on us. "He's at work, *mi amor*. He'll be home soon."

"¡*Tío, no*. I want to do it!" shouted Anabela. I was trying to clean the little square of yellow.

Her great-grandmother, Lola, was at the table playing war with Adita. "Ana, be nice to your *Tío*, who came so far to see you."

"No, he's waiting for *Papi*."

"I'm here to see you, too, *mi vida*. I'm here to see everybody."

"*Mami*, too?"

Lisbeth shook her head and went back to the stove. Lola slammed down a card and said, "Oh, the suffering that woman has brought on this house. She was no good when she was here, and then she runs off to Argentina with Leo's daughter."

"Mother, hush," said Lisbeth, back at the doorway.

"I'm so glad you're here," Lola said to me. "This past year has been hard on Leo."

Lola had never liked Sulyn, and always seemed to be on my side. She would tell me what a good boy Leo was, and then whisper in my ear disparaging remarks about Sulyn. "She can't cook. She is a terrible housekeeper. Leo has to bring his laundry over to have Lisbeth do it." It was as if the fact that I was a man had no bearing on the issue for Lola and Lisbeth, that being small-town folks on an island cut off from the rest of the world somehow allowed them a clarity of vision. Love was love, and they could recognize it no matter what form it took.

When Lola had heard Lisbeth yelling my name and carrying on at my arrival a couple of hours before, she had run down from her house two doors up the street. She beamed as if I were the prodigal son, kissed me, and wouldn't let go of my hand. Lisbeth, teary-eyed, had told me she never expected to see me again. When Leo announced he had run into me in Havana, she was at first excited, and then disappointed that I wasn't coming to Holguin. I told her that I had changed my mind and that Leo didn't know.

"Come on, *Tío*. We have to finish this picture for *Papi*," said Anabela.

I put my hand on her dark silky head and bent down to kiss it. I loved her like my own daughter, her almond eyes and the grave contortions of her face so like Leo's. I wanted her to love me, too, though I knew there was only one man in her life.

We heard the crunching gravel of someone walking up the street, and Lisbeth ran to the door. "Come, *mijo,* quickly." She was so excited her round body was shaking.

He walked in with dusty jeans and a grease-stained T-shirt, acting as though he was not even surprised to see me. But he grabbed me and squeezed me so hard I thought he was going to break my ribs.

"*Mi vida,*" he whispered in my ear. I looked over his shoulder at a pool forming in Lola's eyes.

There was a crash, and we looked down at the glass on its side with brown water spreading over the floor. Anabela started to wail. We separated, and he bent down to pick her up.

"It's okay, *mi tesoro.* Don't worry. *Papi* is home." He gave her big smacking kisses and held her tightly.

Leo was able to calm Anabela down, but she clung to him even as he washed his hands for dinner. When we sat down, she insisted on being in his lap and looked at me across the table with a mixture of amusement and suspicion. I made funny faces at her and almost got a smile, but she turned and buried it in her father's chest.

"Come with me and let your daddy eat," said Lisbeth.

"No," Anabela shouted with dark burning eyes that silenced Lisbeth.

"She's no problem," he said, reaching around her to cut a chunk of pork off the bone. She played with his mouth, pinching his lips closed with her little hands. "Ana, let your *Papi* eat. Don't you want me to be strong so I can work and take care of you? Come on, turn around and look at your *Tío.* He looks just like the pictures, doesn't he?"

"*Papi,* are you going on the plane with us?"

Leo gave Lisbeth a worried glance.

"*Mi cielo,* let's not talk about leaving," said Lisbeth. "It makes me sad. You have two more weeks and you are going to be with your daddy every day."

"Is he going on the plane with us or not?" she asked louder and more forcefully. Her jaws were reined in tight.

"*Si, mi vida,* I'm going to come live with you."

"Is *Tío* Martin coming, too?"

"No. He has to go back to his home in Los Angeles."

"I'll visit you in Argentina," I said with a nervous smile, not sure if that would make her happy or sad.

After the dinner, Leo, still holding his daughter, told her he was going to take me back to Roberto's house where I was renting a room.

"No, *Papi,* no."

"I'll be right back, *mi vida*. Don't worry. I think *abuela* has some ice cream for you."

"I don't want ice cream." She tightened her grip on him.

"Come, Ana, come." Lisbeth tried to take her from Leo's arms.

"No!" screamed Anabela, smacking Lisbeth's hand with surprising force. "No, no, no!"

"She was never like this before," said Lola from the rocker in front of the TV. "Always so happy before they took her away."

"Mother, hush. You're not helping."

Leo managed to pry her hands from his neck and put her down.

"Don't go, *Papi*. Don't go." She stomped and her face became beet red.

Lisbeth made a sign for us to go. As we shuffled out the door, her screaming reached a frightening pitch. I felt like a criminal as we started down the street with slow anxious steps. Her tortured wailing seemed to get louder with each pace, and I stopped. "Leo, go back."

He looked relieved. "I'll come over later. Wait for me." He embraced me under a dim street lamp and rushed back to the house. I stared up into the starry sky until her sobbing was quieted, and then I walked on.

13

It was mid-morning when we arrived in Havana after our all-night drive. The four of us traipsed into Rosa's small kitchen and she smothered me with sympathetic looks, shaking her head at my misfortune, yet she was reticent about looking me in the eye. I wondered why she had brought us into her apartment rather than directly to the rental. She bustled about gathering up the things I had left behind: a bag of clothes, some food, and a bottle of rum. Then she broke the news that she had rented the apartment to a nice young couple from Canada. The hope of resting my bones in familiar surroundings turned to exasperation on my face, and she became defensive. "I didn't know when you were coming. Gerard told me you would be here yesterday. But don't worry. I have a place for you in the building. My friend, Leonor, has a room with a private bath and there is no problem if Leo stays with you."

"I don't have much choice," I mumbled in resignation, but I felt betrayed. "Can I use your phone to call Gerard?"

"Oh, I forgot. Gerard left this for you."

I opened up the envelope and counted the money. It was just enough to pay off the driver, and I handed it over to him so that he could be on his way. Humberto watched the transaction with wide eyes, as if he were viewing a dessert tray passing in front of his face. I had no doubt that some of that money was going to end up in his pocket as a commission, and I hoped that we would be saying goodbye to him, too.

But Humberto continued to tag along with us. I knew the owner of the apartment wouldn't appreciate another person being in her home, and Rosa confirmed my worry. "The room is for you and Martin only," she said to Leo, slanting her eyebrows toward Humberto.

"Of course. He just needs to call the people where he is going to stay," Leo explained.

Leonor was a tall, attractive woman in her forties with thick, sandy-blonde hair and green eyes. She was wearing a beige linen pant-suit, sleeveless and slightly wrinkled so that it could serve as casual or dressy. The amber-colored beads around her neck with bracelet to match gave the impression she was going out to a casual lunch, yet her kind face couldn't quite hide her worry at allowing three strange men in the door. Rosa gave her a reassuring look as we filed into the hallway, and explained that Humberto would be leaving soon.

The two-bedroom apartment was well kept up and the large living room gave onto an expansive terrace. The bedroom I was to take had a smaller terrace and the bathroom across the hall was mine exclusively. I ducked into the bathroom and closed the door. I stood over the spotless toilet and watched a stream of bloody urine color the water with crimson spirals. Oh God, I was dying. Tears came into my eyes as I cleaned off the reddish spots on the rim with a wad of toilet paper and quickly flushed. I splashed some water on my pale face and smoothed back my hair. When I exited the bathroom, Rosa had gone, Leonor was in her room, and Leo and Humberto were conversing in low voices in my room.

Humberto had found the bottle of rum and was taking neat little swigs. He held my gaze without flinching and said, "Just a little, you know, to start the day." He giggled like a child. I gave Leo an accusing look, but he smiled sweetly as if unaware of any problem.

I lay down on the bed and Leo fixed the pillows to get me comfort-able before going in the other room to make a phone call. Humberto stretched out beside me, bottle in one hand, and spoke soothingly. "Don't be mad. Maybe you should have some. You've had a rough time and I'm sorry." He put his hand on mine. The jerk was flirting with me and even when Leo came back in the room he kept it up. "Your skin is so smooth." He moved his hand up my forearm. I pulled my arm away. "So tell me about Gerard. Does he have a boyfriend?" he asked.

"Yes, and they live together."

"I would still like to meet him." He took another drink and offered the bottle to Leo, who tossed the cordless phone on the bed next to Humberto and upended the rum, ignoring my dagger eyes. After a lengthy swill, he started emptying out my backpack, putting things away—his underwear mixed with mine in the drawer, his toothbrush on the dresser next to mine, our shoes side-by-side in the closet.

Humberto chatted with Ricardo on the phone and took sips of rum. He told him he was in bed with me and laughed as if it were the funniest thing in the world. Leo walked by the end of the bed and kissed my big toe. I wanted to shake him and say, "Don't you see what your friend is doing?"

Humberto got off the phone and started preparing his things to leave. Leo pulled my backpack from the closet floor, and they began folding Humberto's half-empty duffle so that it would fit inside the backpack. "What are you doing?" I said in an annoyed voice.

"It looks bad to be carrying a big bag on the street. The police stop you. Looks like you just arrived from out of town," Humberto said.

"But I need that backpack."

"Don't worry. I'll bring it back later this afternoon," said Leo.

"You are going, too?" I sounded whiny, afraid of being left alone.

"I'm just going over to say hi to Ricardo and Miguel."

"Who is Miguel?"

"Ricardo's partner."

"Ricardo has a partner?"

"Yeah."

"It didn't look like it last week." I remembered his flirtatious behavior on the Malecón. "Come back soon. I have nothing to do here."

"In a couple of hours," Leo said as he kissed me. "Try to get some sleep."

They went out the door and Humberto held up the bottle with a questioning look. "Go ahead," I said.

In a dream, Leo and I were in a supermarket in my hometown, and I showed him the variety of things to buy, but he didn't seem impressed. We looked at a box of colored baby chickens that chirped loudly. Then he went off to another aisle, and I searched for him though I only found my college English professor pushing an empty cart. He didn't recognize me. As I went to the next aisle the store changed to dark and empty. I was afraid that people were going to see me inside the store and think I was trying to rob it. There was a knocking sound and Leo was outside looking into the store with cupped hands against the plate glass; he couldn't see me. I shouted, but no sound came out of my mouth, and there was no way to get to the window because all the shopping carts had been lined up to form a barricade between me and the windows on the other side of the checkout counters. Then a buzzer went off, and from the depths of my dream I thought it was the store's burglar alarm.

It was the doorbell, and I struggled to get up. At first I thought it was Leo until I remembered he had taken the key. I heard Gerard's voice and threw the door open. "I brought you some water and cookies. Sorry for the paltry supplies, but as usual the gang has eaten up almost everything in the house. Leo's *mujer* called my place looking for him," he said, wrinkling up his nose. "I gave her the number over here."

"God, we've only been gone half a day." The same moment, the phone rang.

I recognized Sulyn's voice, but I had learned the trick of forcing people to identify themselves by using "*¿De parte de quién?*" in a cold, distant voice. She said she was Leo's wife. I told her he had gone out and I didn't know when he would be back. As soon as she hung up, the phone rang again. It was Leo calling from Ricardo's. He sounded drunk and asked me not to get mad, but he was going to stay for dinner and wouldn't be back for a while. I told him about Sulyn calling, and he signed off with a kiss.

Gerard shook his head. "How do you get yourself into these situations?"

"I'm not in a *situation*. He's free to do what he wants. He's just a friend."

"A friend would stay around and take care of you."

"He has. He's taken good care of me."

"I still say he shouldn't have run off like that, and I can't stay. I have to go to a meeting. The CDR is on my case again."

"Luka is supposed to come over in a while. I'll be okay."

After he left, I watched the news. Spanish investment in Cuba's tourism industry was up and the price of sugar down. Fidel attended the opening of a new hotel in Varadero and the Jamaican Minister of Foreign Affairs was arriving the next day to discuss issues of common interest. I turned off the TV and the apartment was cast into darkness. I lay in the gloom until I heard the door again and had to fumble for the light switch.

"*Muchacho,* look at you. Your gauze doesn't even match your shorts," Luka said as he embraced the right side of my body. "I hope you're not planning to go out on the street like that."

"I don't think I'm going anywhere for a while."

"Where's Leo? Not back yet?"

"He's getting drunk with those lowlife friends of his."

We sat on the bed and I recounted the story of Holguín, the accident, and my time in the hospital. When I got to the part about the pills, I revealed my status to him, too.

Luka stared at me with his mouth hanging open. "I expected you to make a confession at some point, but that's not the one I was waiting for. I've never met anyone who got it that way. In Cuba they started screening the blood early on. But you're healthy, right?"

"I'm doing all right."

"How did Leo take it?"

"He was weird at first, but then he acted like it didn't make any difference. Still I wonder what is going on in his head."

"You're lucky. A lot of guys freak out about it."

"It remains to be seen what will happen with Leo. Obviously we haven't done anything since he found out."

"I guess you'll just have to come back when you're all healed and see how he reacts."

I shook my head. "I have to come back and do more research for my book, but that's it. I can't continue this. And if that jerk doesn't get back here in the next hour, I won't even bother to call him and say hello. What an asshole!"

"You're talking like somebody in love, waiting for *papi*."

"Oh, shut up. You're out of your mind if you think... I'm only angry because it's his fault that I got in this mess in the first place. I admit he took good care of me in Holguín, but does that give him the right to just take off?"

We settled in to watch the evening *telenovela* and I tried not to think about the absence of Leo. The idea that he would leave saying he would be back in a couple of hours—it was already eight hours later—burned me.

Luka saw me looking at the clock again. "Do you have Ricardo's number?" he said. "I could call and say that I'm over here and hope that I can see him before I leave."

"You know, it's strange. Humberto left his ID on the table. It's in a little plastic sleeve that also has some phone numbers written on a scrap of paper. Maybe one of them is Ricardo's."

"It's not that strange. Guys from other provinces often walk around without their IDs. If the police stop them, they say they lost it or left it at home."

We found Ricardo's number, and Luka called.

"I guess I won't be seeing Leo tonight," he said as he got off the phone. "They still haven't eaten dinner yet and are drinking a lot."

"I'm going to bed," I said.

Shortly after Luka left, Leonor came home and passed by my open door to say goodnight. I felt as though I should tell her something in case she heard Leo coming in. "Leo went out with some friends. He'll probably be coming back late."

"Does he have the keys?"

I hesitated a minute. "Yeah, he does."

Her expression changed and her eyes fluttered a bit. "Hmm," she said with pursed lips. "Goodnight." She turned and went to her room.

I settled into the half-sitting, half-lying position that I had adopted for sleep; the bed felt desolate without Leo, and with its crisp, line-dried sheets, institutional. I lay awake and watched the shadows move across the room.

It was early in the morning, and a groggy Ricardo didn't recognize my voice. When I asked for Leo, he said he wasn't there, then hung up. I was sitting on the living room couch with the phone still in my hand when Leonor came through on her way to the kitchen.

"Would you like some coffee?" she said.

"Sure."

"Should I make some for your friend, too?"

"He's not back yet," I admitted.

"And he still has the keys?"

"I had no idea he would be gone this long."

"I never allow Cubans to take the keys."

"Sorry. It's my fault." Then I thought I should defend him. "He took them because he thought I would be sleeping when he came back. He hasn't given me any reason not to trust him."

"What about the other one?"

"I am wondering about him myself."

Over coffee we talked about Mexico, where she had lived for a few years. In the middle of our conversation, Humberto called and asked if Leo was back yet.

"You mean he's not with you," I said.

"He spent the night on the couch, but got up early. I think he had to file some papers for his divorce."

It sounded as if he was covering for him, but I didn't care anymore. I just wanted to go home and end this nightmare. "You know you left your ID here," I told him.

"I'll pick it up later. Tell Leo to call me when he gets back."

In the early afternoon Leo waltzed in with his casual demeanor and a half-smile on his face; my empty backpack was slung over one shoulder. I was propped up with pillows on the bed and had been staring at his clothes hanging in the closet, wondering if I had the resolve to pack them all in a bag and put them outside the door. My plan was to say goodbye as soon as he came back, and I imagined how the scene would play out with his begging me to forgive him. Of course, he was too smooth for that. The first thing he did was come over to the bed and disarm me with a kiss. Then he mumbled, "I'm sorry I didn't spend the night with you. I got too drunk."

"And all morning?"

"I had to go deal with some papers. Don't be mad. I thought you were tired and would just be sleeping anyway."

"For twenty-four hours?"

"You know how those guys are. They wouldn't let me go." He put his arm around me. I didn't have the strength to shake it off.

"You left me here without anything to eat and not even bottled water to drink. Leonor is very upset that you took the keys."

He had no response, but leaned back with a sigh and bumped his head against the wall.

"Do you want a pillow?" I said softly. He took his arm from my shoulder and took hold of my hand.

"Want me to go out and get you something to eat?"

I was afraid that if he went out again he wouldn't come back. "I can go out, I think. I need to go to the bank anyway and get what's left on my Viajero Card. We could get a sandwich or something."

"Are you sure you want to do that? The bank is several blocks away."

"It would be good for me to get out. But I've got to shower and wash the grease out of my hair."

"Let's do it."

In the bathroom he gently pulled down my shorts and got the water running at a good temperature. Everything was back to normal as he made little jokes, kissing me between actions. I resented his power over me, but it was hard to be angry when he washed me tenderly, careful not to get my bandages wet. Then he shampooed my hair while I sat on a stool and leaned my head back over the sink. He massaged my head as he soaped it, and I felt tears coming to my eyes.

"What's wrong?" he said.

"Nothing. I got some soap in my eyes."

"Liar," he said with a satisfied grin.

He dried me off and helped me get dressed in a pair of shorts and the only shirt that I could wear over my mummified left side, a long-sleeved white western shirt with pearl snaps. Then we headed for the door, but Leonor stepped out of her room when we were halfway down the hall. "Do you have the keys?" she said sternly to Leo.

"I have them," I said and pulled them out of my pocket to show her.

"If you go out alone again, you will leave the keys with Martin. Do you understand?" She looked Leo right in the eye. They were about the same height.

"Of course," he said in a way that was polite, but not backing down.

"We'll be back shortly," I said. "In case anyone calls." I kept moving toward the door to break the tension.

Down on the street I questioned my decision to go out. Just getting to the elevator and out the front door was exhausting, and then the heat rising off the pavement nearly choked me. We had to move slowly, and each time I set my left foot down it sent a jab of pain up that side. I began to sweat immediately and a foul odor drifted up from under my bandages. Leo kept looking over at me in sympathy, and when we got to an uneven surface—a cracked slab of concrete with an exposed root of a large tree sticking up—he took my arm.

I got the rest of my money out of the bank, and we walked across the street to the Pain de Paris bakery, where I ordered a soda and a ham-and-cheese sandwich on a croissant. Leo got a chocolate éclair, a malta, and cigarettes. We sat outside under a big, red umbrella that advertised Bucanero, and seemed to hold in as much heat as it deflected. I told Leo that I was leaving the next morning, and he took it in stride, without the slightest emotion in his face.

"When are you coming back?" he said.

I wanted to say never. I wanted to get a reaction out of him, even hurt him. But I heard myself saying, "I guess when I get all my pieces put back together. You want me to come back?"

"Why wouldn't I?"

"Don't answer a question with a question."

"I know. Yes, I want you to come back."

"What are you going to do?"

"What do you mean?"

"When I leave."

"I'll go back to Holguín."

"Are you going to marry Sulyn?"

"I don't have to marry her to be with her. What do you think?"

"Does it matter what I think?"

"It matters."

"If I told you to dump her, would you?"

"No."

"See. If you love her, that's your business. Do you love her?"

He thought about it a minute. "I like her a lot."

Back at the apartment we lay on the bed with the cool of the air conditioner blowing over us. Compared to the last few days, it was a bit of heaven with Leo running his hand up and down my arm, his head touching mine on the pillow. He was tired and fell asleep. I took in his smell.

Gerard called with a confirmation on my flight for 7:30 a.m. He also said he was bringing over some food. When the doorbell rang a few minutes later, I was surprised to see Humberto instead of Gerard. He had come to collect his ID, which I had hidden until Leo returned my backpack.

Humberto was subdued and sat back on the bed as if he was planning to stay a while. A few minutes later Gerard arrived, and Humberto got his wish to meet him, though Gerard sized up his vapid, bad-boy personality in a second, and ignored him. He had brought some vegetable soup, hard-boiled eggs, and crackers. He lured me into the kitchen. "I don't have enough food for everybody. And what is he doing here anyway?"

"He came to get his ID, but I wish he would go. I don't trust him."

We set up the food on the small, white, wrought-iron table on the terrace off the bedroom. There were only two chairs, so Leo, with his shirt off, sat on the floor in the doorway with the double doors swung open. Through the opening I had the disturbing view of Humberto lying on the bed smoking. After staring at Leo's scars for a time, Gerard asked about them. Leo answered casually that a guy attacked him with a fishing knife at a discothèque and that he was in the hospital for fifteen days. "I almost died," he said without emotion. It was a very short version of what Osmani had told me, but it was the first time I had heard him talk about it. And though calm, he didn't appear to want to go any deeper into the story. Gerard didn't pursue it. We fell into silence, and then Leo picked up our plates, took them into the kitchen, and washed them.

Gerard stood up to leave and dragged Humberto out with him. Leo and I were alone. I packed my things with a mixture of relief and sadness. To lighten my load, Leo ended up with my flip-flops, black gym shorts, a few T-shirts, a guidebook on Cuba, and a key chain with a tiny blue flashlight on it, in addition to the shirts I had already given him. He took off my watch, which he had been wearing since the accident and put it back on my wrist without asking for it. We went to sleep early, and he held me through the night.

Leonor woke us up at 5 o'clock in the morning. I splashed some water on my face and looked for the small bottle of cologne I had brought, but barely used. Each day my bandages were stinkier, and I didn't want to disgust the person sitting next to me on the plane. The cologne was nowhere to be found, and Leo said he didn't know where it was. Before we left the room, he kissed me long and hard on the lips. In the pit of my stomach, I felt I would never see him again.

In a friend's car Gerard drove us to the airport, a quick trip as there was almost no traffic. I said goodbye to Gerard at the door, but Leo came in with me.

"Will you write to me?" he said.

"Only if you write back. See if you can find that guy who has access to email."

"I'll also send you a number where you can call me." His eyes were sad, but there were nothing like tears in them. "I can't stand long goodbyes, so I'm going."

"Okay." Those were my final words as we hugged. It seemed so inadequate, so far from what I wanted to say. Okay isn't even a real word. And then he was walking away, and I turned to go through security. I didn't look back. It was all over, an adventure that couldn't be repeated. I was going home.

14

The short flight from Cuba to Cancun was a giant leap toward home, and though I was anxious for the comforts of my culture—air conditioning, restaurants with varied menus and good service, cash machines, and clean public restrooms—I felt I had left something simple and genuine behind. In contrast to the dreamy decadence of Cuba, the Cancún airport was a temple to tourism where young workers, uniformed and labeled, stripped of their Mayan heritage, pandered to tourists. Hordes of Americans and Canadians stumbled over the polished floors, wearing message T-shirts that proclaimed their willingness to pass their vacation drunk on tequila and fall down a lot. In horror I watched a young, overweight, pimply-faced college student in baggy shorts and flip flops pass by wearing a shirt emblazoned with "Fuck you, you fucking fuck." He caught my look of disgust and sneered back at me.

In the VIP lounge with its brown plush sofas and matching chairs, computer access, and drinks in a climate-controlled atmosphere, I sat down to write an email to Lizzie and Jenny. I stared at the blank screen for a long time and agonized over what to say. Gerard had sent Tomás a watered-down version of what happened, so that he could convey the message to Lizzie. I told him to say I had fallen off a bike

and broken my collarbone, but I was fine. No details. I didn't want
to worry her. No mention of the six ribs. After the news of my HIV
infection, it took years to get Lizzie, and later Jenny, to stop treating
me as a person about to keel over any minute. But now I needed their
attention for my body and my soul.

> *Dear Lizzie and Jen,*
> *Sorry your Pops is such a doofus. Took a spill on a moped. How bad*
> *is that? Arriving on the 3:45 p.m. flight from Dallas. I guess I won't be*
> *able to drive for a while. Can you make an appointment with Dr. Broder*
> *ASAP? Can't wait to see you. I'm okay. Just a little busted up. Love, M*

I stretched out on one of the sofas and thought about what stories
I would tell, and what secrets I would have to keep. Still, I began to
anticipate the comfort of being home, of being with loved ones who
would take care of me and hopefully wouldn't ask too many questions.
The painkillers I bought at the airport pharmacy helped me fall into a
dreamless sleep until the attendant woke me up to say they had called
for my flight. She also managed to get me a first class seat on the leg
to Dallas—the prime seat closest to the door.

I had just one more hurdle to clear: coming back into the U.S. I
remembered Tomás' words. "Just say you have been to Mexico. Don't
be nervous. There is no reason for them to suspect." I felt like a criminal
in my own land, forced to lie about something as mundane as visiting
a neighboring country. Then I was thrown into panic that I might have
forgotten to remove that one plastic bag from the supermarket with
Cuba written on it from my luggage. If they searched my bags, I was
dead. It would be a fitting end to this trip. But the flight attendant had
requested a wheelchair for me, and I was soon to discover the joys of
traveling incapacitated. The wheelchair people are anxious to avoid
delays, and they know the ropes. The young man that wheeled me had
the expertise of a race car driver with little patience for lollygagging
travelers blocking the terminal paths with their teetering roller bags.
And then we whipped through customs in record time with the officer glancing at my passport and waving me on. I could have loaded

my bags with Cuban cigars and rum, and financed my trip by selling them on eBay.

Jenny was at LAX, and I was glad to be facing her first. I feared that her mother would see through me in a minute. At least I had my injuries to hide behind until I got my strength back.

I forced myself up out of the wheel chair. "Oh God, Dad. Don't get up." I hugged her with my good arm. "Now sit down in that chair."

"I don't need it."

"Of course you don't need it, but it's a lot more comfortable, right? At least until we get to the baggage claim. How do you feel, really?"

"I'm much better now," I tried to smile. I wanted so much to feel good about seeing her, my beautiful, loving daughter, but I felt sick, as if I had let her down in some way. Jenny held on to my arm as the service person pushed me along. I felt undeserving of her touch.

"Mom is at the Grans. GD fell again, but he's okay, just bruised. She'll be back this evening."

"Everybody's falling," I said with an awkward laugh. "At least GD has an excuse. Mine was just idiotic."

"Don't be so hard on yourself, Dad. Everybody has accidents. The important thing is that you're all right. You look a little thin. Were you eating enough over there?"

"These last few days I haven't had much of an appetite."

"Well, you're going to do nothing for the next month but rest and get fat. Oh, you have an appointment with Broder tomorrow at ten. He was very concerned and wanted to know if you missed any doses of your meds."

"No, I didn't," I lied. I hated that she brought that up in public. The wheel chair attendant was within earshot as well as several passengers. I imagined that everyone was clearing a wide path around me. Despite the many years of being HIV positive, I felt that I would never get used to being a person with a disease and permanently on drugs.

Jenny had the agent deposit me on a bench while she went to get the luggage. After taking a few steps, she turned around to look at me. "Daddy, you look so sad."

"I'm just tired, honey." But I wondered how long it would take them to figure out I had changed… or had I?

When we opened the front door, our little mutt, Yuni, ran to greet me, not noticing in his unconditional love that anything was different. "He missed you," Jen said. He ran around my feet, expecting me to lift him up and let him lick my face, giving me a funny look when I didn't. It was not until Jenny had set me up on my bed with lots of pillows that Yuni jumped up on the covers and got his licks in. "There's just no denying him," Jenny laughed. She was stretched out with her long limbs across the rest of the bed, her chin resting on her hands. "I want to hear all about it." She had her blonde hair cut short like a boy's, which I didn't care for, and she had on faded jeans and a scoop neck T-shirt that showed a bit of the tattoo on the upper part of her left breast.

"Not tonight. You're going to be around until Monday, right? We've got time." Then I heard the slow, muffled grind of the garage door and found myself gasping for air.

"Mom's home," Jen said with an exaggerated sense of cheer.

In a moment her mother was at the door, and I moved as if to get up.

"Don't you dare move," she said, coming over to the bed. She put her hand on my cheek like a mother and kissed me. "My wandering boy, what have you done?"

"Mom, he refuses to tell me anything," Jen said and took her mother's arm.

"I don't refuse. I'm just tired."

"And he's kind of cranky, too." They both laughed.

"You're ganging up on me. You always do that."

"Come on, Jen-Jen, let's let Grumpy have his rest while we make dinner. And you *are* having dinner," she said to me. "You look much too thin."

I was home. This was my bed and this was my family. In a few days everything would be back to normal. I was tired, that was all.

Instead of planning how I was going to celebrate my birthday, I had to think about doctor's appointments. Lizzie went back to take care of the Grans, but Jen had taken a couple of days off from work so that she could accompany me to the hospital and do the rounds: my primary care physician, more X-rays, and the orthopedic surgeon. The surgeon told me that they didn't operate on broken collarbones and drew me a neat diagram showing how it would heal. She wanted me to start physical therapy right away so that I wouldn't get a frozen shoulder. The ribs also would heal on their own. The nurse cut off all the tape and gauze from Cuba, gave me a sling for my arm, and sent me home.

Jenny hummed along to a song on the radio by the Red Hot Chili Peppers as we wound through Laurel Canyon to the house nestled in the trees, the property that Lizzie and I had fallen in love with so long ago. It was not convenient to anything, halfway between the Valley and L.A. proper, but it was a refuge—and when you live in L.A., you need a refuge.

"The house could use a paint job," I said as we pulled Lizzie's old Volvo station wagon into the garage. "Where's the Mazda?"

"Uh... Mom has it." She looked at me strangely.

"Right... of course."

"She'll be back this evening for your party."

In the bedroom I viewed with little enthusiasm my bags still sitting in the corner. I began a one-arm unpacking job, most of it going straight to the laundry basket. Yuni scampered off with a dirty sock in his mouth. Each thing I took out of my bag was attached to a memory of Leo and then I shuddered, thinking of the digital camera. I needed to erase the pictures. In a panic I dug through everything in my roller bag, but didn't find it. I went to the backpack, emptied the contents on the bed, and still didn't see it. I returned to the roller bag and rechecked every pocket and corner; I did the same with my backpack. No camera.

"What's going on in there?" said Jen. She stood tall and lanky in the doorframe. "Do you need help?"

"No, I'm fine." I remembered that I wasn't able to find the cologne the morning I left Havana. I looked through my clothes again and discovered that I was also missing a new pair of swimming trunks that I never got to wear because my accident had interrupted our trip to the beach. I stopped the search and sat down on the bed. Suspicion fell on the one person who had had complete access to all my things. I had thoroughly trusted him and this was how he repaid me? Yet it didn't fit into Leo's style. He was smarter than that. To rob me would be jeopardizing his chance for the big fish—a trip to Gringoland—a subject that he had touched on a few times though we never discussed it seriously. Now it seemed completely ridiculous. Had I for a moment, in some crazy fit of passion, imagined that I might bring him to live with me? As I sat picking at the bedspread, I thought about one day back in Havana when Leo and I were in Rosa's apartment and he watched me unlock the suitcase. It was shortly after meeting him and I still wasn't sure if I could trust him. Feeling that I should offer some sort of explanation, I said, "I've had things stolen before, traveling in Mexico, so I just want to be safe."

"You don't have to worry about me. I prefer to ask you for things rather than steal them."

My face went blank. I imagined his statement was supposed to make me feel reassured, though that was far from what I felt. First, the assumption was that he deserved things from me. And second, if I didn't give him what he asked for, did that mean he was justified in taking it? Simply by using the word 'prefer' it sounded as though stealing was something he was capable of.

Jen came back to the door and caught me staring at the floor. Yuni had lost interest in the sock and was curled up at my feet. "Everything okay?"

"I think someone stole my camera." The dog lifted his head and looked up at me in an appropriately serious manner. To make matters worse, the camera had been a gift the previous Christmas from Lizzie and Jen.

"Do you think it happened in Cuba?"

"I guess."

"Maybe it was the baggage handlers at the airport. I saw this special on TV where hidden cameras picked up these guys stealing all kinds of stuff. When was the last time you remember seeing it?"

"I had it in the last apartment where I stayed in Havana." In truth, I didn't remember seeing it there, but I did remember Leo taking some horrendous pictures of me in the apartment in Holguín. With a glimmer of hope I went to my computer and tapped out an email to Gerard. I asked him to check with Rosa and Leonor to see if either of them had come across my camera.

Jen stood behind me and said, "Don't worry about it, Dad. It's just a camera. We can get you another one. The important thing is that you're safe at home."

"If I left it somewhere, I can pick it up when I go back down there."

"You're going back?" The strain in her voice made it obvious she thought it was a horrifying thought.

"I have to finish my work. I'm not going to sit around the house for the rest of my sabbatical."

"It just seems like you could do the research from here."

"It's not the same. Plus, when I write I want to be in the place he was, breathing the same air, you know, looking at the same sea."

"Like everything is the same as a hundred years ago."

"I support some of your crazy ideas, you can at least support mine. I want to do this. And you shouldn't worry about my health. I'll be fine."

"Just take a few months to recuperate first."

Lizzie had thrown together a party to celebrate my birthday. Tomás and his partner, Jim, were there, along with a few of my colleagues, Jen with her tattooed bartender boyfriend, and my brother and his wife, who drove up from Long Beach. Maybe it was my imagination, but I swore that Tomás had given me a funny look when we greeted each other. I was ready to kill Gerard if he said anything to him.

By the time we got to the dinner table, the Percocet the doctor had given me kicked in, and I started losing track of what was going on.

People took digital photos, then forced me to look at my zombie-like image. Other people asked me questions about Cuba, and the painkiller acted like a truth serum. I started talking about the sensuality of the people, how they may not have political freedom, but their bodies were sure free. At one point I looked up and Lizzie was staring at me from across the table. Joanie, my brother's wife, was fascinated and wanted to hear more, but I changed the subject and started talking about the classic old cars, Cuba's rolling museum. By cake time I was in a fog, and for a second I wondered whose birthday it was when all the twinkling flames came through the doorway. Jen had to help me blow out the candles.

A fly crawled across the counter. It took flight and landed on the dirty breakfast plates in the sink, the dishes that were normally my job to wash. Lizzie hated housework and I was incapable of doing it, so we sat in a dirty kitchen, a situation hard for me to ignore as we had coffee at the white birch dinette set. The sun streamed in the window while she told me the latest about her parents, how complicated it was to make a decision concerning their care. Her father had absolutely refused to go to an "old folks home."

The streaks of gray in her dark hair shined in the rays of light, while the same light accentuated her laugh lines, the developing double chin. I wanted to burn the AIDS Walk sweatshirt she constantly wore around the house, stained, faded, the letters cracking. There were so many things bothering me at the moment that focusing on what she said was next to impossible. The more anger I felt, the more guilt arose until I was caught in a vicious circle of annoyance, anger, guilt, and then back to annoyance.

The phone rang and she jumped up to answer it by the second ring as people with elderly parents in crisis do. She listened, furrowed her brow, and said, "Just a minute."

"What?"

"It's a collect call from Cuba," she said, holding the receiver against her stomach, nestled in the old sweatshirt.

"Don't accept it," I hissed.

"Maybe it's Gerard calling with news about the camera," she hissed back.

"He wouldn't call collect. He would just email." In fact Gerard had already answered my email that morning saying that no one had found a camera. At the end of the message he mentioned that Leo had called asking about me and denied knowing the whereabouts of the camera. I could tell that he thought Leo was guilty one way or the other, but the part about Leo asking about me lifted my spirits. So I had a smile on my face when I had come down to the kitchen, at least until I saw Lizzie standing over the stove with a spatula in her hand, trying to make pancakes. And then the guilt had come back.

"Oh, shoot," she said when I walked in. "I was going to bring you breakfast in bed."

During the breakfast conversation about her parents, I was only half there, using the excuse of the painkillers when she commented on my distractedness. I kept thinking about Leo, seeing his face, feeling the touch of his hands.

Lizzie still stared at me with the phone against her stomach. I couldn't talk to him, certainly not in front of Lizzie. If I took the receiver, I would be discovered immediately, so bad was I at hiding things. What had protected me so far from Lizzie's perceptive eyes was her preoccupation with her parent's declining health, and my insistence that my moodiness was only a result of the pain from my injuries. I shook my head.

"No, I don't accept the call," she said and hung up. She sat back down and muttered, "I guess we'll never know, will we?"

"I shouldn't have given out so many of my cards, you know, to people on the meds project, and Martí scholars. I *told* them to email me." She stared at me with a hint of the old clairvoyance around the edge of her eyes. "People there don't realize how expensive collect calls are."

"I see," she said.

"What will you have for lunch?" said Tomás. He had taken over for Lizzie who was spending the day in Santa Barbara with the Grans.

"We could go to Burger King."

"Ha ha." He was standing at the cupboard with the doors open. "How about some soup, and I'll make a salad?"

"I'm sick of healthy. I want junk food—chocolate cake and a cherry coke."

Tomás turned around and gave me his scrunched-up, bushy-eyebrow look. "You know you need a healthy diet."

"What do you mean?"

We stared at each other for a long time.

"Why didn't you tell me?" he said.

"What are you talking about?"

"Your health situation." He eased the words out in a soft voice: "Your HIV."

"Oh, that." I hoped that was all Gerard had told him.

"Yes, Gerard let it slip. He thought I knew, with you bringing the meds and everything. You could have told me. I thought I was your friend." He leaned back against the kitchen sink.

There was another long pause.

"Gerard didn't say what I was doing when I had the accident, where I was, who I was with?"

"No, but that does seem to be the big mystery."

"I was visiting a young Cuban guy in Holguín."

"So?"

"Don't you think that's strange?"

"Did it have something to do with your Martí research?"

"The very opposite of it." The need to confess was a burning fire in my gut, and I had to put it out.

"Meaning?"

"I had sex with him."

"Is that supposed to shock me?"

"I've been married to Lizzie for twenty-two years. I have a daughter just out of college. I never had sex with a man before and I'm HIV-positive. Within my first few days in Cuba, I am in bed with a man.

That doesn't shock you?"

"Nope."

"It shocks the hell out of me."

"Martin, you can talk to me. Nothing will go outside this room. I won't even tell Jim. You seem like you want to talk, so let's have it."

I told him the story of meeting Leo, the accident, meeting his mother, the trip back, even the missing camera, and I felt better for it. Tomás knew Cuba and the culture. He knew my family. I had always liked him, but held back as I had with all the openly gay men I had met. It was only because of Lizzie that we became friends. She made it safe. I found myself confessing to him in the hope that he could help me.

"First, let me talk like a doctor," he began. "The worst thing for people with the virus is stress. I see you beating yourself up. I've noticed it in your face since you got back, something more than the pain in your body. You need to talk to somebody. It doesn't have to be me if you don't feel comfortable, but you can't hold all that inside. Now, as a friend, I love Lizzie, and Jenny is a super girl, mostly because she has great parents. I would hate to see them hurt—"

"I have absolutely no intention of hurting them. This thing is over!"

"Wait, Martin. I didn't finish. You didn't do anything wrong. You're my friend, too, and you need to be the person you need to be."

"Don't give me that crap. Sometimes you just can't be the person you 'need to be.' You get into life situations. You have responsibilities and people depend on you. You can't go off and play with fire just because you are excited by it."

"It looks like you already have."

"I did, but it's over."

"Is that what you want?"

"What I want doesn't matter."

"Martin, you're not a sixteen-year-old kid that went out on a wild and crazy night and experimented, thinking you might be bisexual. You're forty-six, and if you ask me, you did something you've wanted to do for a long time."

"I didn't ask you."

"Did you know that I was married before I met Jim? I forced myself into a marriage to please my parents, and for all the reasons you can probably imagine. I knew it was wrong, and eventually my wife knew it was wrong, too. It was a terrible time, but everybody got over it, even my father."

"Are you saying I should dump my family and run off with Leo?"

"It's not about Leo or Lizzie or Jenny. It's about you. It's about a part of you that has been held down all these years, locked up."

At first I had been relieved to tell him my story, but then I wished he would leave. I wished I had never said anything. I had to do what was right, and that was to not hurt the ones I loved. "I need time to think."

"Sorry if I overstepped. We better get your lunch or we'll be late to your physical therapy."

My physical therapist told me I already had a frozen shoulder, and it would take a long time to get it back to normal; she admitted that it might never be the same. The exercises she gave me were torturous at first, and just lifting my left arm ever so slightly seemed impossible. I had a stretchy red plastic band that I twisted around my hand while I stepped on the other end. Then I tried to lift up my arm. It had gotten so terribly weak in such a short time that a giant rubber band forced me to cry.

A few times, when I was home alone, the phone rang and the operator said that it was a collect call from Cuba. I hung up without saying anything. But rather than forget about him, I spent more time than ever in fantasies that included him. Tomás's suggestion that I call a therapist went unheeded; I couldn't bring myself to dial the number he gave me. My papers collected dust on my desk while I sat like a vegetable through Oprah after Oprah and lots of B-movies. Lizzie and I didn't talk much, but sometimes I caught her looking at me from across the room as though I was a person that she didn't know. Then one afternoon when I was trying to nap in my darkened room, she came in and dropped a letter on the bed.

"You got a fan letter." Her tone of voice disturbed me. I stared at the letter as though it might bite me. She let out a big puff of air and struck a pose like a lawyer readying to interrogate. "Did you have an affair in Cuba?"

"Me? An affair?"

"I've heard it is quite common for men who travel to Cuba alone."

"You know why I went to Cuba. It's true that a lot of women make themselves available. I wasn't interested."

"I've also heard that it is not only women who make themselves available."

The walls of the room thumped in and out with the beat of my heart. Her eyes were on me, waiting, while mine were fixed on the geometric pattern of the spread. Lizzie had always been gutsy, and she hadn't lost that. It was one of the things that had attracted me to her that day on the quad when she raced up to me on roller skates with a beer in her hand and offered me a swig. She had a winning smile and soft brown eyes. Then she did a fake fall, and I had to catch her.

I had shared everything with her over the years, and she stood by me. Her needs and aspirations had become mine. An interdependency of her making, a transparency at her insistence, made me want to blurt out the truth. But I pressed my teeth down on my tongue. Not this time. I couldn't share this with her. I couldn't. Which meant that I had to summon up all my powers to deflect, and at a time when I felt at my weakest. I patted the edge of the bed for her to sit down.

"I know I have been difficult these last couple of weeks. The accident shook me up, but even before that I wasn't myself. I couldn't work. I didn't know how to start my book. Now I use my banged-up body as an excuse not to work, but that's not it. I feel so useless. This was supposed to be my big moment, what I've waited for all these years, the sabbatical and my chance to write my book. Now it all seems like a lost cause. Who would even want to read it?"

Her face changed, and she seemed willing to let the other matter go for something she could better understand. "You know what? I bet Martí had this very same conversation with his wife before he wrote

Versos Sencillos."

"Don't even put me in the same sentence as Martí. I can't believe he ever had a moment of doubt in his life."

"I think you're wrong. In his poetry there is a lot of reflection, and in reflection there is always doubt. He was human just like you and me. That should be the angle of your book. Find the doubt in his life and show how he overcame it. Show his humanness."

A few minutes before I had wanted to hate her, and now I could do nothing but love her. The idea was brilliant, simple and brilliant. This was the woman I had chosen to be with—or better said, she chose me—and I was reminded once again why. She deserved better of me. I knew she had probably expected more of me in my career, more than a professor at an unimportant college with only a few published articles to his credit. If I could just get working again, if I could put her idea into play, if I could finish my book, it could turn my life around. I still had a chance of making my mark, albeit small, on my field. And I still had a chance of getting back to my life as it had been before.

I took her hand in mine and said, "That was utterly brilliant."

She kissed me and got up. "I'd better think of something brilliant for dinner because right now I don't have a clue."

"Order Chinese. You don't have to cook."

She gave me a smile, not a totally confident-that-we-had-talked-about-everything smile, but an all-right-for-now one. I had weaseled my way out of near disaster without lying. Though I shouldn't have felt good about it, I did because I knew I had the strength to go forward, to leave my deviant behavior behind and concentrate on what mattered. Chasing after a young guy for gratuitous sex appeared to me as something vile. I swung my legs over the side of the bed and planted them firmly on the floor, but at the same moment something fell at my feet, a dingy envelope that had traveled a great distance. For a few minutes I had forgotten all about it, managed to put it out of my head. Now I had to do something. Throw it away? I was afraid if I merely touched it, I was lost. The sharp pain that I suffered when I reached over to pick it up didn't stop me. It was like trying not to read the scrawl on a bathroom wall. Forgive me, Lizzie.

2 August
Havana

I begin by telling you Happy Birthday and I am sorry you couldn't spend it here. Also I must tell you that I didn't go to Holguín, but rather I went back with my wife, the one I told you all those stories about. I want to begin my life here simply because for people who aspire to a better life there are many more possibilities. I always think about having a house with all the comforts and maybe I'm selfish, but I don't want to go to the grave with nothing.

I hope my words don't bother you, but that's the reality. At the same time I have a lot of affection for you and I don't know if it is because of what we lived through or just because you deserve it. Anyway, I'm going to change the subject.

I want you to tell me everything when you write me, even the smallest things as this will be our means of communication until later when I figure out how I can talk to you. You don't accept my calls and I wonder why. Maybe you can't talk from your home. I don't want to bother you, but I want to talk to you.

So I will close and wish you all the best in the world and I hope you get better soon because health is the most fundamental thing. Keep fighting for it.

Nothing more, your friend,
Leo

The tone of the letter was cool, nothing that I felt compelled to respond to. I could easily forget about it, though I had to laugh at his staying in Havana, exactly what his mother had been afraid of, and he had gone back with the hysterical wife, which he swore he would never do. It seemed that the temptations of the comfortable life were too great. There was no mention of the camera, as if it were insignificant. I read it a couple more times, and then I heard Lizzie calling me down to dinner.

"What was the letter about?" asked Lizzie.

"It was just a thank-you letter from the person I handed the meds over to."

"You mean the doctor, Tomás's friend?"

"No, someone who works with the doctor."

"You just handed all those drugs over to someone who wasn't a doctor? He could be selling them on the street right now."

"He seemed like a very reliable person. Anyway, nobody has the money to buy them on the street. They're used to getting their medicine for free."

"I just hope it gets to the right people."

"It will," I sighed, sticking my fork into the micro-waved supermarket lasagna. I didn't have much of an appetite, but if I didn't eat it, Lizzie would get upset. She stared at my fork, and I smiled as I looked up and put a hunk of the gooey mess in my mouth. A strand of her dark hair has fallen out of the clasp and she scooped it back and cupped it behind her ear. Preoccupation pinched her face as she poked her fork around in the food.

"It's pretty awful, isn't it?" she said.

"It's not that bad. I'm just not very hungry."

"Next time I'll get the Costco lasagna. It's a lot better. I can't wait until your shoulder heals and you can fix us a decent meal again."

"Me, too," I laughed, and she threw her napkin at me.

15

An email from Alfredo Limón popped up on my list. I didn't recognize the name and figured it was probably an ad for Viagra that slipped through the spam filter. I was about to delete it when my curiosity got the better of me. I scrolled down to see it was signed by Leo, and I was paralyzed by the three letters staring at me, eyes from the screen looking through me.

Hello my friend Martin,

I hope you are in good health and recuperating well from the accident, and that your whole family is enjoying good health. My uncle is sending this email for me. I am here in Holguin with my mother, and I have begun studying a new course. Next month I am thinking about taking a course so I can get my driver's license. I want to forget about Havana, at least until you come next time, and I need your help so that I don't have to go back there.

A big hug and kiss from me and everybody here.

Leo

Please call me at 024 42 8736. It's a neighbor's house.

The letter that I got from him sat in the back of my desk drawer while the work on the book had been going well, thanks to Lizzie's encouragement and large amounts of coffee. I had gotten into a morning routine, starting with my rubber-band exercises to unlock my frozen shoulder, and then sitting down to write. The phone number jumped off the screen and beckoned me. Lizzie was not home, and my cell phone sat in the palm of my hand, absorbing its warmth.

My trembling fingers labored over each digit, and I felt crouched on the edge of a great abyss, ready to leap. In a scratchy voice I explained myself to the neighbor who told me to call back in a half hour, as they had to run and get him. I had another chance to save my life. Don't call back, I simply said to myself, but redial was just a single button. He answered on the first ring.

"I talked to Gerard and he told me about the camera. I don't want you to think it was me. I would never do that. I called every place we were, and nobody has seen it. Someone saw Humberto with a camera that he was trying to sell back here in Holguín. I went to his house, but he is avoiding me. I'm going to get that camera back. I'll have it for you when you come next time." It all came out in a rapid string of words. I knew the camera was gone, but I let him say what he thought he had to say.

"I didn't really suspect you. But you should keep better company."

"He is no longer my friend. That's for sure."

"I still don't understand how it happened. When was Humberto alone with my things?"

"That's what I was trying to figure out, too. Did you write me a letter yet?"

"I have been meaning to."

"How was your birthday celebration?"

"Not one of my best."

"Next one will be better. We'll celebrate it together."

"Sure, but—"

"And what about your broken bones? Are they healing all right?"

"It's still hard to sleep at night."

"I guess you miss me," he said with a laugh. "Will you call me next week?"

"I guess. Sure. When?"

"Whenever you want. I'll run to the phone to talk to you."

I laughed nervously.

"Take care of yourself and don't forget to take your medicine."

"Thanks for remembering. *Besos.*"

I felt a combination of nausea and giddiness when I got off the phone. Why was I compelled to throw in "*Besos*" at the end, sweet words that Cubans thrive on and self-conscious foreigners are so titillated by? They are magic words that ring of the forbidden. I also felt I was only prolonging my agony and giving him hope—for what I wasn't sure exactly.

I tried to get back to my work in front of the pale blue screen, my notes nearly unreadable as I stared at them with blurry, forlorn vision. Instead of working on my notes, I tapped out a letter. It was firm without being overly judgmental. I suggested he find better friends than Humberto, but I also wanted to thank him sincerely for taking care of me, at least most of the time, and for the kindness of his mother. I told him to open a Viajero card account so that I could send him some money. He hadn't asked me for it, but I knew the realities of life in Cuba, and *ayuda* was always appreciated.

When I reread the letter, it sounded like something I might write to Jenny. It gave me a queasy feeling, but I sent it anyway. I didn't call the next week as I had promised, but waited until I thought he had gotten the letter.

"I'm so happy to hear from you," he said in a bubbly voice that was uncharacteristic of him and I wondered if he had been drinking. "It has been so long."

"Sorry I haven't called. I've been working hard on my book."

"I'm working hard, too. I'm studying."

"What are you studying?"

"I am trying to finish my high school diploma. And I'm going to get my license so I can drive next time."

"Good idea. How's your mom?"

"She sends you hugs. I got your letter. Next week I'll go open a Viajero Card account. I don't like to ask you for things, but you know how it is here. I want to improve myself and finish school. When are you coming again?"

"I've got a lot of healing to do first."

"You have to come back and finish your research, don't you?"

"Yes, but, I don't know."

"I want to see you again." His casual ease stabbed me.

In a moment I forgot all the negatives, how unstable his life was, how ordered mine was, how the chaos of his life had spilled over into mine. I wondered if his emotions were true and what had led to his sudden change of heart about his Havana wife and then change again. In his letters and on the phone he was vague about his other life, while at the same time he was openly affectionate with me. None of it fit into my way of thinking, and yet I tried to make sense of it.

The next communication I had from Cuba was from his mother, an email sent through her brother, Alfredo.

Hello my dear friend Martin,

I hope you are in good health. Martin, I need to ask you a big favor. What happened is that Leo is crazy in love with a woman of the street, a little bandit who is only waiting for you to send money to Leo in order to spend it on parties and expensive clothes for him. The favor I have to ask is that if you are going to send money, please don't do it now, but only when I tell you. In addition I plead that Leo never finds out about this. I am doing this as a mother who knows what is good for him. I will write you a letter and explain more.

Thanks again, my friend.

Please accept a kiss and a hug from one who regards you with esteem.

Lisbeth Amaya Gonzalez

The email left me with a lot more questions than it answered. Was she referring to Sulyn? I remembered them being good friends, always together. Now she was calling her a bandit. And though I had witnessed Leo being affectionate with her, it didn't seem that he was crazy in love. Why would he spend more than a month in Havana with his ex-wife if he was so in love with Sulyn?

This message also undermined my trust in Leo, making me think that he was easily influenced and maybe he couldn't be trusted with money. It even put in doubt my letting him off the hook so easily about the camera. What was he capable of to impress his girlfriends?

Two weeks later I received another email from Lisbeth, saying I might as well go ahead and send the money. Against her wishes Leo had moved in with Sulyn.

"Did you get all the account information?" Leo said, the next time we talked.

"Yes, I sent you some money. But I just want you to understand that this money is only for you and your mom."

"Don't worry. I understand how you feel. I will only use the money for necessities. I promise." He was almost whispering into the telephone. "But I can't talk about that now. I'll write you a letter. Anyway, you should know how I feel about you by now."

"I should?"

"Come on. We talk and email. We have good feelings. And when you come back in December, it will be even better. You'll see."

"I didn't say I was coming back in December."

"You have to. Aren't you ready for a vacation?"

"If I go to Cuba, it is to do more work on my book."

"Maybe I could help you."

"How could you help me?"

"Help you relax," he said in a sexy voice. "But then, of course, if you don't want to see me…"

"Your life is confusing for me."

"Not for me, and I'm the one that has to live it."

"Let me think about it."

9 October
Holguin
Hello Martin,
I hope you are recuperating like you said in your emails. I'm sorry the physical therapy causes you a lot of pain, but you know it is necessary. You want to be strong for your next visit, right?

I want to tell you that when I think about making someone part of my life, I do it because I want to. In thinking about my 25 years I never regretted anything, even the wasted time and not finishing my studies when I should have. But now I think differently because I think about myself, the future, and I don't want time to pass me by, rather I want to pass it by. If I have big ideas to leave here, I have to study if I want to be somebody in another true land.

With that I give you a little answer to your worries though I'm sure not all. I ask you that if you want to know something, you can ask me without having hairs on the tongue as we say here.

That's all from your friend that loves you and respects you a lot. Greetings from my mom.
Leo

I arrived home after a frustrating physical therapy session where my therapist expressed some concern about the slow progress in the healing of my frozen shoulder and found another letter from Holguín in my mailbox. Though the return address said Leo, upon opening it, I noted a script that was very similar to Leo's, but flowed more evenly across the page and was slanted a bit more to the right. The language was also more circuitous and seasoned with God-expressions.

20 October, Holguin
Hello dear Martin,
I pray to God that you are in good health. We're fine here. Thank you so much for the help that you sent Leo. Today we are working on the room that Leo is constructing. We are putting up the beams that sup-

port the roof, but the roof will be later. We have to go little by little. Leo is very happy studying and calm for the most part, thank God. Today he told me that he is going to the telephone to call you. He bought me a television so that when you come to visit, you will be more comfortable and even though there isn't much to watch, at least you can entertain yourself a little. I hope that when you come back to Holguín I can offer you our house so that you can be with us and you don't have to rent a place. Little by little Leo is planning to finish the room for you.

I hope that when you come back, you will have a better time going to Guardalavaca beach, Gibara and other places.

Leo and Humberto had a fight. I don't know why that boy is such an ingrate and Leo is so noble.

I hope that you write us. With affection and respect, a hug and a kiss.

Lisbeth and family

I read the letter a second and a third time, and tried to decipher the Cuban mind, in this case a mother caught in a struggle to both protect her son and give him advantages in a society that keeps people on a short leash. I had learned that you always had to look beyond the words, that the gap between what they say and what they mean is often great. Did she know why Leo and Humberto fought? Or did she know the true story, but was lending support to Leo's innocence? Why all this talk of me coming back to their house and staying with them? Was she giving her blessing to my friendship with her son or simply helping to keep Leo's options open? Was she hinting that I needed to send more money to finish the house?

The book moved forward at a snail's pace, and I gave up trying to resist the temptation of Leo, who slipped into my thoughts, haunted my dreams, and became a good-natured, imaginary audience to my silent monologues. After one of them I decided to call him.

"I made a plane reservation today."

"Where to?"

"The pearl of the Caribbean."

"I knew you would. When do you get here?"

"I'll be there for New Year's."

"Great! I'll meet you in Havana and stay with you. Or do you want to come to Holguín?"

"Not on this trip."

"Bad memories, huh?"

"Not all bad. I would rather spend New Year's in Havana. It would be nice to see you, but remember I am there to work on my book."

"I'll get a doctor's excuse to miss school. We have exams in the middle of January, so I'll have to go back by then."

"How is school going?"

"It's boring sometimes, but I've got to do it. I'm very bad in English."

"We can practice when I'm there."

"And bring your tennis racket and one for me."

"You want to play?"

"I'm crazy to play tennis. I'll go to Havana a day early and meet you at the airport."

I had settled into a cozy anticipation of my rendezvous with Leo, letting my emotions carry me. Then, the day that I was supposed to leave, within hours of my actual departure, the whole puzzle with each piece neatly in place was thrown up into the air by an email I received from him. In a way, I felt it was what I deserved for my weakness.

29 December

Hello my friend Martin,

I hope you are in good health. Everybody here is fine except that my mom almost broke her foot and is in bed. I didn't write you before because I was waiting to tell you if the money arrived or not and I can tell you that it did. Also I have to tell you that I can't go to meet you because my exams begin on the 20ᵗʰ and I have to study to get good grades. I hope you will come and see us. Anyway I have the number where you will be staying in Havana.

Best wishes,
Leo

Though my bags were already packed with gifts for him and his family, part of me was relieved, the part of me that wanted to work, the rational me. Then anger crept in, the emotional me feeling rejected.

16

A thunderstorm beat down on Cancun and caused my flight to arrive in Havana two hours late. It was close to the high holidays of New Year's and the anniversary of the revolution, so the customs and immigration people were efficient and uncharacteristically pleasant. I exited immigration quickly, knowing I had to show resolve or the taxi vultures that I remembered from my last trip would be upon me in seconds. I walked straight out and headed for the nearest Panataxi— the cheapest of the official taxis. But I faltered ever so slightly, slowing down for mere seconds to scan the waiting crowd with the thin hope that Leo had changed his mind and was going to surprise me. As I started to get up speed again, I had a man to my right and one to my left. The one on my right had better positioned himself and grabbed at the handle of my rolling bag as they both shouted, "Taxi, taxi." They kept repeating it as if they thought I was deaf, or I might imagine they were there for some other reason.

I still had control of my bag, but I stopped and looked at the skinny, dark-skinned youth with tight curly hair and slightly crossed eyes.

"Only ten dollars," he said in English.

"Let's go," I said.

We got to a splotchy red sedan, obviously not an official taxi, and there was a second man leaning against the door, picking his teeth. He was large-framed and menacing, his shirt dampened with patches of sweat. They threw my bags in the trunk and the mean-looking one took the wheel, pointing to the front seat with his chin.

As soon as we passed through an airport checkpoint and got out on the road, they stopped and picked up a third shadowy figure, who got in the back without a word. It appeared prearranged. The air of the car was dense, and mixed with the musty odor of weathered upholstery and unwashed bodies, the smell of misadventure. "We've got a good place for you to stay, man. Really cheap," the driver began in a Spanish measured for foreigners.

"No, I've got a place, thanks." I gave him the address in Vedado. While my bones were healing, I had plenty of time to surf the Internet and discover a new innovation in travel to Cuba: web sites where you could book private apartments. A local agent made a reservation for me, though there was no way to make a deposit because of the problem of sending money to Cuba.

"What kind of girls do you like? *Negras? Mulatas? Blancas?*"

"I've already got a girlfriend." It seemed like the easiest answer.

"Where is she? She didn't even come to meet you?"

"She works in a hotel. They wouldn't let her off."

"You and your girlfriend want to go to Varadero? Only fifty dollars."

"No, we're going to stay around Havana." He stared at the road, calculating his next offer. He hadn't tried to sell me cigars yet, and I expected that he was going to bring it up at any minute. In the momentary silence, I sensed something much more troubling. I didn't recognize the poorly lit road we were on.

The week before I left, I had read a story on the Internet about a Mexican-American who was found murdered in some bushes off Calle 23. He was a director attending the Havana Film Festival and was robbed of $850. That was less than I had in my money pouch. The murder was shocking because violent crime was rare in Cuba. I got a strong feeling that I was the next victim and wondered if I should jump out of the car at a light, at least saving my life. But there were no traffic lights or even stop signs.

The car slowed, and then veered off on a smaller road that had no streetlights at all. I swallowed hard and my legs began to shake. The car was extremely quiet except for the grind of the engine and the rattle of the frame when we hit the potholes; every time the driver slowed down to avoid one, I thought my time had come. They were going to pull into a dark alley and murder me. I could offer them what I had in my wallet—about forty dollars—and hope they wouldn't go searching for my money pouch. I glanced at the driver, and in the pale green light of the speedometer, he looked like the devil. In the same article I had read that crimes against tourists were punished severely, so they would be better off murdering me and dumping the body out in one of the fields I saw out the window. With my hand on the door handle I again imagined how I could jump out of the car.

We bumped along on the dark road, but up ahead was an entrance ramp and we took it. The sign overhead said Vedado and I breathed, it seemed, for the first time in ten or fifteen eternally long minutes. Soon there were lights, other cars, and people on the streets. A few minutes later we pulled up in front of the address on M Street behind the Hotel Habana Libre.

A young man in baggy shorts and a tank top ran over to the driver's side window, calling my name. The two guys in back jumped out and unloaded my bags. "Martin, I'm Tony. We have a problem with the apartment. We're very sorry." As he talked through the driver-side window, a young woman came up to stand next to him. In the confusion, all I wanted to do was pay the taxi and be rid of them. In the near darkness inside the car I tried to search for ten dollars; I had no small bills in my wallet. I reached down and unzipped the pouch wedged between my underwear and jeans. The young man who originally had picked me up was now at my window insisting I pay before I get out of the car so that I wouldn't be seen giving them money on the street. He reached in the window and tried to grab the bills from my hand. With the uncertainty of the surroundings pushing in on me, I shoved the door open, nearly knocking the youth down.

"Hey, *tranquilo*," he said testily.

"I can't see what I'm doing in the car." I stepped out into the street and came up with ten ones, which I pushed—slightly crumpled and one even torn on the pouch zipper—into his insistent hand.

My bags sat on the sidewalk a few feet from the car near a dumpster piled high with plastic supermarket bags of garbage that gave off a putrid odor. Tony continued talking to me in heavily accented English while I moved toward securing my bags.

"Martin, we have to go to other location, but is anyway more better apartment."

"What?" I now understood that something was wrong.

"Problem with this apartment."

"I shouldn't have taken an unofficial taxi," I mumbled in Spanish.

"You speak Spanish," said the woman, relieved. The conversation shifted to their language. "We're sorry, but the woman decided to rent to someone who is going to stay longer."

"So the reservation didn't mean anything."

"We guaranteed we would find you a place and we have. In truth, I think you'll like this new one better."

"I've already given the phone number and address to several people."

"As soon as we get to the place, I'll call the woman here and have all your calls forwarded. Don't worry."

The new apartment owner, Victor, greeted us at the door and seemed befuddled by our arrival, as if he had only gotten word a short time before. He was tall and thin, and gave the impression of a person who wanted to drift back into the shadows. As I moved close to shake his hand, I smelled alcohol and his eyes held a sadness that made them retreat into his head. His speech was slurred, and he insisted on speaking English, though his vocabulary was limited and his pronunciation poor.

In the living room Victor rocked back and forth on his feet in an awkward silence until he remembered to ask us to sit down.

"Why don't we show him around?" said Tony before we had a chance to be seated.

Victor led the way toward the kitchen. The counter around the sink was of green tile that was chipped and cracked, and needed to be regrouted. The avocado green refrigerator was at least twenty-five years old. The motor rumbled and shook, belched, then went quiet.

"Don't worry. She run good." The three of us stared at the green hulk, a faded relic that had a latch on it to keep it closed, and was dotted with faded plastic fruit magnets. The gas stove was also from another era, marked with baked-on grease, a testament to Cuba's love of fried food.

The bedroom was simple, marginally tasteful. There was a colorful tropical lagoon painting above the bed, and a lamp of red-and-white stained glass hanging above one of the two bedside tables that were affixed to the wall. I pictured Leo stretched out on the bed and quickly moved to inspect the bathroom.

The place would do, and though I was put off at first by Victor's inebriated state, I began to warm to him, seeing him as a gloomy but sympathetic character.

Once alone in the apartment, I started unpacking and discovered that my favorite gray fleece shirt—the only warm thing that I had brought—and a magazine were missing from my backpack. My taxi friends had at some point snatched the top two things from the bag. The loss of the shirt was a pain. The magazine would no doubt end up as toilet paper.

I abandoned the unpacking and called Luka. He said he had been trying to call the other place, but no one knew who I was. So much for forwarding my calls. I filled him in on what had happened with the apartment as well as Leo's reversal on coming to Havana. "Not a very good start for the trip," I said.

"Forget about it, my friend. You're in Cuba. You're going to have a good time. Some Colombian friends of mine are in town and are crazy to go to a drag show. They have a rented car, so we'll pick you up about 10 o'clock."

"Thanks for the offer, but drag shows aren't my thing."

"Have you ever been to one?"

"No."

"We'll pick you up at ten."

"But—"

"Don't be difficult your first night here. See ya."

Luka and the Colombians, Freddy and Juan, picked me up about 10:15, and were on edge because we were running late. They had made a reservation for a table at 10:30, and it was a long drive deep into the Havana sprawl to get there.

"You need a reservation for a table at a drag show in Cuba?"

"Once the place is full they close the doors and won't let anybody else in," said Freddy, drumming his fingers on the dashboard. I arched my eyebrows at Luka and he shrugged. I was annoyed with myself for accepting the invitation, and the drive there was further taxing my nerves. It seemed that we had already bumped our way over bad roads through half of Havana's 15 municipalities and still weren't there. Some of the potholes could have swallowed a small vehicle and mammoth piles of debris made it look like the city was crumbling block by block.

La Casa de Rogelio was clearly distinguishable from the other cinderblock houses by its dazzling display of Christmas lights, which blanketed the facade. Despite the late arrival, they let us in and we climbed up to the rooftop terrace, enclosed with a makeshift construction of clear plastic walls topped with a corrugated plastic roof. I imagined a hurricane lifting the flimsy cabaret, clients and all, halfway across town before depositing it in the patio of an unsuspecting family glued to the nightly soap opera.

There was a large crowd around the stage set off by bamboo fencing at the back, more twinkling Christmas lights, and several large potted palms on either side. Two spotlights, currently bathing the stage area with a soft rosy light, were precariously attached to piping that was holding up the roof. A drag queen in a floor-length gold lamé gown, a bouffant hairdo, and pointy heels that could take out an eye, was in the middle of her number, so we waited until she finished the song before going to our table with its set-up of a bottle of rum, mixer, and snacks.

The audience was a mix of men dressed like women, straight

tourists, and Cubans with their foreign boyfriends or girlfriends. We settled in and listened to a string of impersonations of Latin chanteuses, most of the songs about wallowing in the tragedy of lost love. I recognized almost none of them—except for a few Celia Cruz numbers that one of the performers had in his repertoire—but I watched others, including Freddy and Juan, mouthing the words along with each singer. After every number the audience broke into wild applause, and when the clapping died down the performer bantered with the crowd in Cuban slang.

"Hey, you in the front row. Did your cat just die or did you accidentally sit on your boyfriend's beer bottle? My lord, live a little. Not that I'm trying to give you any ideas what to do with your bottles. And you over there. Oh God, not the rum bottle. You are shameless, girl. " The music started up and the entertainer launched into Rocio Dúrcal's "Quédate conmigo esta noche."

She came to the edge of the stage and stared into my eyes. As her thick lips moved in sync with the music, she struggled to hold back a flood of tears. Every muscle of her face was taut with passion and I sensed that her mischievous brain contemplated dragging me on stage. I silently pleaded, "Don't do it, please."

Without breaking eye contact, she bent down and lifted my hand off the table, pulling with a relentless force that gave me no option but to join her on stage. With the mike in her right hand, she hooked me with her left arm, pressing me tight against her. The sequins of her dress scratched my arm. Her platform heels elevated her so that I had to look up at her. I breathed cautiously and caught a flat but fragrant whiff of powdery makeup, overpowered by an intoxicating scent of Jungle Gardenia. It catapulted me back to an afternoon when I was nine years old.

That morning the student body of St. Vincent's School had been subjected to a zealous sermon by the parish priest, encouraging us to consider a vocation to serve God. The discourse so melded with our tender brain cells that my sister—one year younger—and I decided to play "nun and priest" as soon as we got home. Mother was out, so we swung open the mammoth doors of her closet, perusing her wardrobe for black frocks. Margaret found a sack-like dress that mother had gotten for my grandfather's funeral when she was pregnant with our youngest sister. I slipped a satiny gown with a full skirt over my head backwards so that the zipper would be in the front. From the built-in closet drawers we took out white, lace-trimmed handkerchiefs, and I tied one around my neck, while Margaret put one around her forehead. She then lifted a black silk scarf into the air and let it float down over her head in a serene gesture.

While Margaret religiously pondered the effect in the mirror, I spotted the furry edge of a mink stole wedged between two wool coats in the far reaches of the closet. I only remembered seeing my mother wear the stole on one occasion. I let my fingers dance over the silky, luxurious pelt. Like a snake, the stole slipped off the wooden hanger and landed in a heap at my feet, causing Margaret to swing around in surprise. We both looked down in horror, as if we had shattered a priceless vase. I snatched it up, anxious to return it to its place, but once I had it in my hands, I was captured by its softness. In a moment, I had it wrapped around my shoulders and buried my cheek in the fur, igniting a newfound excitement.

Margaret gasped at my sacrilegious image. "That's not for a priest!"

"I know," I snapped at her and wrapped it tighter around me in a fit of wicked indulgence. I started to laugh, but it was cut short by a cloud of Jungle Gardenia hovering over us.

"Children, what in the world are you doing?" said my mother. Her eyes were locked on mine in utter bewilderment and fear, a look I can still recall as clearly as if it were yesterday. "Take that off this instant," she shouted at me, completely ignoring Margaret.

The shame was a burning hot iron that began in my chest and fell in slow increments to my stomach. It made me feel that if God had struck me dead at that moment it would have been better than standing in the burning gaze of my mother's disappointment. That was my one and only experience with women's clothes.

The performer took my hand in her large, slightly calloused paw, the thick fingers capped with long red nails. Her mouth was stretched to the limit as she imitated the long vibrato of the final note. The crowd rose to its feet, applauded and whistled. She bowed and waited for me to join her, but by the time I realized what I was supposed to do, she was coming up, and I was going down. Then she bowed down again as I came up, provoking raucous laughter from the audience. Sweat ran down my cheeks from the heat of the lights, and when I bowed a second time drops fell to the floor.

The applause revved up again as she kissed my cheek, released my hand, and allowed me to return to my seat.

With twelve beers loading down a plastic bag in my hand, I stood dwarfed by the giant socialist-style housing project, watching the taxi pull away. The driver, who was white, was reticent about dropping me off in this neighborhood where most everyone was black. I assured him that a friend of mine lived there, and that I would be all right.

The intimidating concrete structure had water stains running down the sides, broken windows, and chunks of balconies missing. I took a deep breath and approached a bluish light that spilled out on piles of garbage and broken-down furniture piled beside an open door. An extended family crowded around a TV at full volume, and I shouted, "Excuse me. Where can I find number 18?" A shirtless youth sat so slack on the upright chair that he looked as though he was going to slide onto the floor. He pointed to a dim stairwell and held up four fingers.

I trudged up the four flights, and Luka's sister, Olga, answered the door and embraced me. She was 15 years older than Luka, darker-skinned, the same height, but 80 pounds heavier. Her plump cheeks gave her a cheery image, but when she talked you heard the words being drawn out from somber depths and laid out hesitantly in front of her. Luka had told me about her unhappy life and how she had taken over the role of matriarch since their mother had died a few years before.

Their father sat at the dining table close to the entrance hunched over a plate of food. He looked more like a beggar who happened in off the street than the lord of the house. He appeared quite old, with leathery skin stretched over a small frame, but he still had a full head of cottony white hair. "*Buenas noches, señor*," I said to him. He raised his head in surprise, muttered a greeting, and then went back to his food. I had no idea if he knew who I was.

With the cordless phone to his ear, Luka came out of a bedroom and waved to me. Olga invited me to sit down in a rickety cane-bottomed chair situated in front of the small black-and-white television. The TV was atop a crate that sat on a broken armchair. In the corner was a single bed topped with a worn brown blanket.

Olga went off to the kitchen to finish cooking, and I watched the end of the year variety show, which alternated between comedy and music. The premise was that a large, bosomy *mulata* sat at home playing hostess while a variety of famous figures from Cuba's entertainment world stopped by to visit her. There were a few jokes, and then it cut to musical groups that were performing at venues around the country. Most of the music was salsa, but there were also some Cuban hip-hop and rap groups, as well as great dance routines.

When his father finished eating, Luka helped him up and deposited him in a rocker before taking one of the chairs from the Formica dining set for himself. We sat in silence while Isaac Delgado performed "*El año que viene*" in a silky voice on the fuzzy screen. Luka asked his father if he knew who was singing and he said no. Luka explained that his father could barely see the images, mostly just the light.

Around 11:30 they brought out the food and set up the table. Luka's nephew, Adrian, arrived from his job at the hospital and we opened the beers. The father had gone over to the bed, covered himself with the blanket, and was staring at the ceiling. Just as we sat down to eat, laughter came from the TV, and we all turned to watch one of the characters cleverly trying to steal the food the host had prepared for her party in order to take to his party next door. We all laughed, too, knowing the importance of food in Cuba, but especially being able to provide food for one's guests and family at New Year's.

Our meal was the traditional pork, rice and black beans, lettuce, tomatoes, and some garlicky yucca. The dinner conversation was subdued with Adrian and Luka doing most of the talking while Olga kept trying to get me to eat more. When I convinced her I was full, she went to make coffee. It was getting close to midnight, but no one appeared in the least excited, and the television droned on.

Out the window fireworks burst against the inky distant sky and everybody jumped up and began hugging each other. Even Luka's father threw off the blanket and rose up with startling energy to come over and greet everyone. He held my hand in his warm bony palms and with a clear and formal voice said, "*Feliz año*."

Then the door swung open, and I heard people up and down the stairwell wishing each other a happy new year. Neighbors came in and out with their greetings, while Luka and I went to the window to watch the fireworks. After a few impressive bursts in the sky, the show fizzled, lending to the cheerless atmosphere of people going through the motions without any real hope for the coming year. The commotion in the stairwell, too, died down quickly, and Olga cleared the dinner dishes.

17

Luka and I arrived at Cine Yara and found a large number of people milling about in search of a way to bring in the New Year. Within a few minutes of working through the crowd, Luka had the party location, and we got in a taxi that would take us there. Locations are not usually divulged until the night of the party. A friend of Luka's, Jose Luis, had attached himself to us. He looked vaguely like Leo, though more conservatively dressed and without the tattoos. When we shook hands, he gave me that same quizzical look I remembered from Leo the night we met. He kept staring, anticipation in his eyes.

The party was in Marianao, far from the center, on an open piece of land that was part of a farm and surrounded by a high fence. The powerful sound system—geared for loudness, not quality—blasted the new arrivals. We paid our two-dollar entrance and joined the open-air party of about 300 people. There was an uneasiness not yet smoothed by alcohol in the isolated groups that stood about on the earthen floor as if they feared dancing might get their shoes dirty. We headed for the beer and rum area with Jose Luis still tagging along.

Most of the music was in English, and a few of the songs I recognized as popular with my daughter and her friends. The lights, rigged up to the various sheds on the property, were pointed at the crowd like interrogation lamps, and added to the uneasiness. Luka had convinced me that I didn't want to be alone on New Year's, and I had again allowed myself to be pressured into being part of a gathering where I didn't feel comfortable. At the same time, I believed that in traveling, you should allow yourself to be in new and possibly awkward situations, an attitude I had honed on my trips to Mexico. But this was discomfort of a slightly different kind. Most of people at the party were half my age, and the few close to being peers were other foreigners. I still struggled with an identity where people saw me as a foreigner scouring the countryside for young men. But now that Leo had unlocked that door of passion, I could no longer deny the current that shot through me when an attractive youth stared, and then smiled. I chugged my beer and went to get another round.

I made a few unsuccessful attempts to talk to Jose Luis over the loud music, though he expressed no curiosity about me at all. For him, it seemed, all he needed to know about me was that I was a foreigner, and by staying close, some small amount of what I had would eventually come to him as if by osmosis.

The music shifted to some Latin dance numbers, and the three of us edged closer to the center. We started shifting our feet, but I noticed that Jose Luis didn't automatically catch the *clave* like most Cubans. Back in Los Angeles at a neighborhood party, Tomás had explained how you felt the beat. We listened to a song, and he made me tap out the rhythm on my thigh. I wasn't very good at it and after five minutes, he sighed and gave up.

I thought about the *clave* and tried to get my feet in sync with the music. I attempted a little spin, and Jose Luis grabbed me and pulled me close in a clumsy, un-Leo-like gesture. I hurriedly moved away from him and went to get more beers.

I woke up to the New Year and became immediately aware that something was wrong. The dark-haired young man at my side was not Leo. It took me a minute to remember his name. I tried to get up with the slightest of movement so as not to wake him, but he stirred and opened his eyes. I smiled, but in my head I was already planning how to get rid of him.

"*Buenos días*," he said.

I got up and headed for the bathroom. "I'll be right back."

I hurried back into the room, remembering my wallet on the dresser. He lay on his back with his hands behind his head. An erection slightly lifted the sheet.

"I've got a terrible headache," I said.

"Me, too. It's sad when you can't be with your family on New Year's Day. My family is in Pinar del Río, but I don't have any money to get there."

I should have seen this coming, but I barely remembered allowing him to come home with me. I did remember that we had been too drunk to do anything.

He must have read the lack of enthusiasm on my face and let out a miserable groan. "I should probably go," he said.

While he got dressed, I slipped a twenty in his pocket. "Maybe this will help you get to Pinar del Río."

"Thanks."

At the door he pecked me on my dry lips. "If you see me on the street, you'll say hello, won't you?" he said.

"Of course."

The hazy noon outside reflected what was in my head. I longed to escape into sleep and wake up in a different year, back before this all began. In my months of recuperation and confusion, there were moments of clarity where I envisioned a place in my life for a man as affectionate as Leo. But not this, not the anonymous sex with strangers game. I imagined such a future stretched out in front of me like a parched and empty riverbed, and it terrified me.

I tried to force my eyes to close, but I couldn't turn off my brain. I felt I owed it to Leo to at least let him know where I was. I called the neighbor in Holguín and asked them to send a message to Leo that I had a new number.

Leo's late afternoon call woke me up, and I was wooed to consciousness by his telltale scratchy voice. "I was calling the number you gave me, but you weren't there." He sounded hurt.

"If you had been here to meet me, there wouldn't have been the mix-up."

"I'm sorry. I couldn't."

"So how was your New Year's?"

"Great. We had a party on the street and roasted a pig. My mom said you should have been here. You would have enjoyed it."

"I got your email the day that I left. Too late to change my plans and go to Holguín."

"But you can come now. For a few days?"

"Why can't you come here? That was our plan."

"The director of my school said I couldn't miss class, that they would fail me and I would have to start all over again. Don't you want to see me?"

"I have a nice place here and we could play tennis."

"You brought the rackets?" He sounded excited for the first time in the conversation.

"You asked me to bring them, and I—" the line went dead. A few minutes later the phone rang again.

"Sorry," he said. "I'm using a card and it ran out. This one only has a little left on it. I'll call you tomorrow. *Besos.* Bye."

I fell back on the daybed with the receiver still cradled in my hand. It was warm from the sun shining in through the open balcony doors. Below the balcony kids played in the street, and their shouting reached a feverish pitch. It sounded like an argument in their game. I had seen them the afternoon before playing baseball with planks of wood serving as bats and some kind of makeshift rubber-band ball. To them New Year's day was just a holiday, a day without school, a day when they could spend all day outside while their parents sat at home and watched the annual Fidel speech on TV.

I stared at my pile of books and notes on the coffee table, but felt no impulse to tackle them. What I needed was to recognize the New Year in some way that was meaningful to me. I forced myself up and went out the door, walking straight down La Rampa to the sea, and crossed over to the Malecón. I sat on the wall facing the water and remembered the New Year's Lizzie and I spent in Rio de Janeiro, where millions of Brazilians dressed in white and carrying flowers went to the beach to honor Yemaya, the Orisha goddess of the seas. I looked down where the water lapped at the rocks and saw the trash bobbing there, tangled in seaweed, a sad reminder of how we treat our planet. The sunset was beginning and a colorful constantly changing future rode up and down on the waves. Having no flowers to offer the sea, I reached into my pocket and pulled out a handful of coins, tossed them into the water. It was a sad recognition of the New Year, and I wondered what meaning it had, if any.

   The following day broke with a bit more hope. I crossed Parque Central on my way to Old Havana to view the restoration of the colonial architecture that was moving along with Spanish money, and to visit a bookstore on Obispo known to have some books by Martí. Obispo was the best people-watching street in Havana, a ten-block pedestrian thoroughfare that took you into the very heart of Habana Vieja, packed with window-shopping *habaneros*, tourists, and *jineteros*. In addition to bookstores there were shops selling clothes, art, and handicrafts; restaurants and cafes; and little doorway stands selling pizza and ice cream. My guidebook told me I could make a pilgrimage to Hemingway's old room at the Hotel Ambos Mundos where he began writing *For Whom the Bell Tolls,* or visit the ornate former headquarters of Bacardi rum.
   At El Navio Bookstore on Obispo I found a used copy of Jose Martí's *Amistad Funesta*, a novel, and a new edition of *La Edad de Oro*, a collection of short pieces for the children of America. Content with my purchases, I strolled the length of Obispo and walked past the Plaza de Armas and the Castillo de la Real Fuerza, the oldest fort in the city. Then I cut back and entered Plaza de la Catedral, where the heart of the city beat a weary rhythm. The baroque cathedral dominated the small, enclosed square, and people walked in circles as if they didn't quite know how to leave its confines. A bushy bougainvillea tumbled over a wrought-iron balcony, and the daring red flowers competed

with the brilliant blue of the balcony doors and the blue-and-white half-moon stained glass windows, *mediopuntos,* above them. It was a dream set in colonial times. The music coming from the trio at the outdoor café was a *son montanero,* and the swaying rhythms lured me deeper into the trance. The African beat of the drums and the steely sound of the *tres* guitar provided a perfect soundtrack to the Cuban experience: rhythmic, sensual, emotional.

I left the square still feeling the heat of the music and walked past a group of nicely dressed black men with athletic bodies. They concentrated intensely on their ice cream cones while long pink tongues curved around the edges, lapping up the creamy trails that were making their way down the sides. A pair of black eyes met mine and I realized my curiosity had lingered a second too long. I looked away and almost at the same moment heard, "Hello."

I started walking fast, but he came up beside me. He wore a gold silk shirt half-unbuttoned and sand-colored dress slacks that were a tight fit. "Hey, my friend. Where are you going so fast?" I stopped to shake the meaty hand that he offered me. "My name is Alberto," he said. "Wait here a second. I want to get my friend." He ran over and got another black guy who was wearing jeans and a flowery shirt. He had powerful arms and a massive chest.

They started walking with me, talking between slurps of ice cream.

"We're boxers," said Alberto. "On the national team."

"Oh," I said, hopefully with just the right amount of respect.

"Where are you staying? In a hotel or a private house?" asked the bigger guy whose name was Beny.

"In a house."

"Great. What are you doing now?" said Alberto.

"Just walking."

"We'll walk with you. You know, some of the people here have bad intentions, but they won't bother you if you're with us."

"Thanks."

"We can go with you to your place to make sure you get home alright," said Beny.

"Actually, I'm not going home. I'm supposed to meet a friend in Vedado at 4:30." I glanced at my watch to show my concern about the hour.

"Come on. We could just come to your place for a while. We would like to talk to you a little," said Alberto.

And Beny added, "We want to get to know you."

"No, there's no time. Got to meet my friend."

"Man," Alberto said with an extended exhalation. "I thought we were going to, you know, share." Their nice guy act was beginning to crack. He took what was left of his ice cream and dropped in on the street with a splat.

"Thanks, but it just can't be today." They were both shaking their heads and acting as though I had given them a raw deal. I increased my speed and said, "So long, guys."

They slowed down and I heard one of them mumble, "*Pinga!*" I kept walking without looking back.

I made my way through Parque Central, over to the Gran Teatro to look at the ballet schedule. In front of the theater I ran into Freddy, also looking for ballet tickets. They were performing *The Nutcracker*, and though I had seen it several times, I went inside with Freddy to check on tickets. The woman at the desk said that it was sold out, and then quickly added that a friend of hers might have some tickets for forty dollars; the regular price for foreigners was ten. Freddy was still interested. "Do you have to dress up for it?" he asked the woman.

"Nothing formal," she said. "Of course you have to wear a shirt with sleeves and no shorts." She looked at Freddy's cut-offs and tight tank top showing off his gym body.

"Almost all of my clothes were stolen, so I just want to be sure I have something to wear before I get the tickets."

That night Luka came over for dinner, and I asked him about Freddy's clothes.

"He got ripped off, a Discman, some CDs, a watch and a camera. A guy he met on the Malecón," Luka said matter-of-factly. "They spent several days together. One morning Freddy and Juan got up and went to the gym, but the guy stayed in sleeping. When they got back, all

Freddy's things were gone."

"Did they call the police?"

"Freddy wanted to, but Juan calmed him down. He convinced him that it would get too messy. They would have to explain what the guy was doing in their apartment."

"Does that happen a lot here?"

"It does seem worse than a few years ago. A lot of the guys out in the scene are different, more ambitious and with less scruples. Even I worry about someone stealing the few nice clothes I have." I thought again about my camera, though I knew I would probably never know the exact circumstances of how it was stolen.

I tried to forget about the dramas of Cuba and get to work on my project. I sat down to read my new Martí books. They were in Spanish, so it took me a while to get through them. Leo called one afternoon and asked when I was coming to Holguín. I told him I hadn't decided yet.

In a taxi on our way to Cesar and Monica's house in Playa where we had been invited to dinner, Luka said he didn't see the point of me going to Holguín.

"Why not?" I asked.

"If he wanted to see you, he would find a way. Cubans always do."

"You're right. I shouldn't be chasing after him."

"Stay here and enjoy your friends that really care about you."

Cesar was building a house above his mother's simple square bungalow. We climbed a piece of metal fencing with slats that, turned sideways, served as a ladder and we stepped onto the cement floor of what would be the front balcony. The cinderblock walls were up and the roof was done, but none of the interior or exterior finishing was completed, nor were the windows in yet; roll-up bamboo blinds covered the holes that were the windows. The one-bedroom apartment had appliances in the kitchen and a few essential pieces of furniture. In a large common room that was part kitchen and part living room, a new large screen TV sat in stark contrast to the bare walls.

Monica turned around when she heard us come in and approached us with a butcher knife in her hand. "Oh my God, she's going to kill us," said Luka.

She laughed and pantomimed a murderous housewife, a role she assumed well with her wild wavy black hair cascading down to her shoulders, her shadowy painted eyes, and her Cordovan skin. Though not pretty, she carried herself with the sexy confidence of a woman, who over forty, had come into her own. She was wearing low-rise tight white hip-huggers and a yellow halter top that showed a lot of cleavage. Still holding the knife, she reached up and gave Luka an embrace that showed a genuine affection. Luka introduced us, and I bent down to kiss her.

"Where's Cesar?" Luka asked.

"He went to get some beer. He'll be right back."

"How is everything going?"

She hesitated a moment and puffed out her lips in a pout. "You know he's leaving in a few days for France. He'll probably be gone a couple of months."

"I forgot it was so soon." Luka turned to me. "Cesar has a boyfriend in France." He picked up a picture off the shelf and pointed out Cesar with his arms draped over an older man's shoulders. There seemed to be no end to Cuba's sexual fluidity, which, though admirable in some ways, added to my confusion.

Cesar walked in with a plastic bag full of beer hanging from each hand, and caught us looking at the picture. He was ruggedly handsome with thick brown hair and blue-gray eyes. He was shirtless and had a carpet of hair covering his torso, a jaguar tattooed over his shoulder. Though he had a naturally well-formed body, a belly was creeping out over the top of his shorts. He was probably ten years younger than Monica, and she looked at him as a mother might, shaking her head as he talked. Her eyes were on the bags that he was still holding in the air.

"Put the bags down, Cesar," she said. He laughed self-consciously, dropped the bags, and hugged Luka. He shook my hand and held it a moment in both of his.

Two more guests arrived: a thin, dark, curly-haired Italian about forty years old, with a much younger Cuban version of him in tow. The Italian was wearing an old Hawaiian shirt and baggy jeans while the Cuban was fashionably dressed in a tight Versace T-shirt and cream-colored designer jeans. I imagined that if I ran into any of these people at a party or on the Malecón, I would have nothing to say to them, but here, sharing a meal, gathered around a table in a more relaxed environment, we were able to discuss culture and politics as well as tell jokes and personal stories.

On the unfinished terrace Cesar set up a boom box with an extension cord and put on the Beatles *Hey Jude*. It was a nostalgic soundtrack that flowed out and floated on the completely still air while we were treated to a serendipitous backdrop of an almost full moon hanging over a giant palm tree across the street. When Monica brought out a large bowl of black beans, our animated conversation stopped as the aroma of the beans teased our appetites. Then Cesar came out with plates of roasted chicken, rice, and tomato salad, and the silence was broken with applause.

It was after midnight when the meal finished, but in Cuban fashion no one wanted the party to end. We piled in two taxis and headed for the Malecón where a respectful number of revelers were keeping the party going into the night.

Shortly after we arrived a young solidly built guy sitting on the wall called Luka over, and they had a long talk. When he came back, I asked him if it was somebody he was interested in.

"That's the one who robbed Freddy. He wanted to give his side of the story. He was afraid I was going to go around and tell everybody what he did."

"What is his side?"

"He said he told Freddy that he wasn't gay. He would hang out with him, but he expected something in return. He claims that Freddy refused to give him anything, not even some clothes that he asked for. So he felt he was justified in taking what he deserved."

"What do you think, Luka?"

"Of course what he did was wrong, and I told him that. Freddy is a friend of mine and I don't like to see him hurt. But if what the guy said is true, it isn't right what Freddy did, either. He knows how things are here. When you get involved with someone like that, there are conditions."

The partying on the Malecón went on, but the brief conversation with Luka was stuck in my head and did battle with the image of Leo. Freddy's friend sitting on the wall was nothing like Leo. He moved differently and his energy was so unlike the quiet charm of Leo. The young man feigned a laugh at something said by the older man who talked to him and pawed him at the same time. I convinced myself that Leo and I didn't look anything like that when we were together.

I was in my usual late afternoon haze after a morning of poring over my books and taking notes when the phone rang. I took a deep breath to gather my resolve.

"*Hola,*" said Leo. "I found an apartment for you to stay in, only twenty-five dollars a night."

"Thanks, but I'm not going."

"What? What do you mean?"

"I'm not going to Holguín. I have a lot of work to do here."

"You could take a break for a few days."

"It doesn't seem like you want to see me."

"Of course I do. Why are you doing this?"

"Then why didn't you come to Havana like we planned? As soon as you had the money I sent, I got an email saying you weren't coming."

"No, no. It's not like that. My mother wanted me to be here for the holidays and the director of the school said he would flunk me if I missed school. Don't be mad at me. I tried."

I heard the little warning beep that we were going to be disconnected.

"I'll call you before 6. Wait for my call…" The line went dead. I didn't expect him to call back. That was it. I could put this behind me, enjoy my trip, and get some work done.

Luka came over for dinner, and then we planned to go out for a walk. I was in the kitchen heating up the food I prepared earlier while he watched TV in the living room. It was past 6 o'clock and Leo hadn't called. "Luka, do you have a watch?"

He held up his bare wrist so I could see it from the kitchen.

I went into the bedroom, dug into the bag of things I brought for Leo and pulled out a sporty Fossil watch with green glow-in-the-dark numbers. I dangled it in front of Luka and said, "You've got one now."

"Thanks," he said. I wondered if I should give him everything I had brought for Leo.

After dinner we sat at the table and drank rum. I detected a heavy ozone smell coming in from the open balcony, and a short time later it began to rain, light at first, and then continued with a steady, drenching downpour. Instead of going out, we stretched out on the sofa with our feet on the coffee table and watched two movies back-to-back. The first was Alfred Hitchcock's *North by Northwest* with Cary Grant and Eva Marie Saint. That was followed by a silly day-in-the-life movie from Puerto Rico called *12 Hours*. I fell asleep and Luka woke me up when it was over. I stumbled to my bed and Luka stayed on the sofa.

18

A phone rang from far away in the half-light of early morning. Someone called my name, and I staggered out to the sofa where Luka was sprawled out, naked except for his bikini briefs. The receiver looked foreboding, lying on the table next to the sofa, off the hook, silent in my fuzzy view.

"Hello," I said with my throat full of sleep.

"Are you awake?" said Leo.

"I'm getting there."

"Here, write down this number and call me when you wake up."

"What? Where are you?"

"At the bus station."

"In Holguín?"

"No here, silly." He gave me the number and I jotted it down. "Talk to you later."

When I got off the phone, I sat down in shock on Luka's bed. Everything was in the slow cadence of a dream.

"*Papi llegó. Papi llegó*," Luka said in a sing-song voice, and then laughed. "Is he coming over here?"

"Uh, no, I mean, I don't know. He gave me a number to call later. I should have just told him to come here."

"Calm down, boy. You're going to see your *papi* soon."

"Oh, shut up. He's not my *papi*."

I went back to my bedroom and tried to sleep. The birds chirped happily after the previous night's rain and the early morning rays of winter sun slid through the cracks of the louvered windows. There was a joyous feeling dancing around inside me while my warden brain tried to get me back in line. I hated being so mercurial, so vulnerable to his whims, but I couldn't deny the excitement I felt.

I got up, did some exercises, and puttered around, while Luka managed to sleep through it. At a respectable hour I called the number, and a sleepy voice answered. I asked for Leo.

"Is this Martin?" the voice said.

"Yes, Leo's friend."

"Ricardo here." I was not overjoyed that it was Humberto's sidekick from the summer before. "Leo dropped off his things, but went out for a while. He should be back in an hour. Why don't you come over?"

I agreed to go to his house, about a fifteen-minute walk away, and convinced Luka to go with me.

The house was in Vedado on a street of fine old homes in what was once an upper middle-class neighborhood. We opened the rusty gate and climbed the steps under an arched trellis covered with jasmine, and continued up to a large porch filled with potted plants, some of them tall palms towering over a few battered chairs from an old patio set. Large ferns fanned out as if hushing the air. We knocked on the ornately carved door with its many layers of paint.

"Leo's not back yet," Ricardo said and waved us in. "Have a seat."

I introduced him to Luka, but they seemed to know each other, at least by sight from the fiesta scene. Then Ricardo went off to make coffee. We sat down on the couch by the mantel, taking in the high ceilings, the water-stained walls, and the three framed Madonna posters spaced about the room. Ricardo brought out the espresso cups half-filled with thick sweet Cuban coffee, and we downed them like shots of whiskey. Soon after, Miguel, Ricardo's partner, arrived from his early morning warehouse job. The authority with which he moved around the house clearly showed that it belonged to him.

The conversation faltered and Luka was antsy. "I have to go," he said, and I wasn't sure I wanted to wait any longer. Then Leo sauntered in with his shoulders hunched forward and a half-smile on his lips. He greeted me last with a big kiss and hug, and we fell down on the sofa thigh to thigh. He took my hand in his and rested our joined hands on his leg. Months of uncertainty faded away.

"You look tired," I said.

"I slept very little on the bus. We'll go in a few minutes."

We all grinned at each other, and Luka stood up. "Now I really need to go," said Luka.

Leo gathered up his things and we said goodbye to Luka in front of the house.

"So you thought I wouldn't come?" Leo said as we crossed the wide boulevard of Paseo.

"I had my doubts. I'm sure your mom's not happy about this."

"No, but it's not her decision. I just said I was going and that was that."

"And what about school?"

"I told them I'd be back on Monday. It'll be okay."

As soon as we were inside the apartment, Leo dropped his backpack and kissed me hard on the lips. We held each other and stood in the middle of the room. I felt clumsy and embarrassed. I broke away. "Don't you want to see the apartment?"

"I didn't spend all night on a bus to see an apartment. But I guess you could show me the bedroom."

From the bedroom he headed straight for the bathroom. Like an idiot in a trance, I tried to control my heartbeat as I watched him slowly strip down to his lovely nakedness. After his shower, he put on clean underwear and got into bed.

"I need to sleep a bit." He winked at me. "Don't worry. After a siesta my batteries will be recharged and who knows what might happen."

I smiled at his cockiness, the ease with which he controlled the immediate world around him. I lay down next to him, and he put his arm on top of mine. All the months I had dreamed of being next to him, touching him, were in the past. It was just us, there, alone.

He slept soundly for a few hours and I dozed off for a short time, but woke up intoxicated by his presence and moved closer to him, and then drifted off again. When I could sleep no longer, I stared at the ceiling until he opened his eyes the fraction that he could manage when first waking up. "Can you make me some coffee?" he said.

When I came back with the coffee, he was smoking a cigarette, his head propped up with both pillows. I shook my head.

"It helps me wake up. You want me to be awake, don't you?"

I nodded.

He reached up and ran his finger along my collarbone feeling the big bump. "Does it hurt?"

"No, it looks worse than it is. I'll always have something to remember you by."

He flashed his surprisingly white-for-a-smoker teeth at me, and stretched open his eyes, which shined like polished black marbles.

"Can you raise your arm up?"

I showed how I could raise my arm over my head, though I couldn't reach as high as with the right arm. He snubbed out his cigarette and pulled me down on top of him. I wondered if in my fantasies, I had exaggerated his boundless affection, and I was still afraid things would be different when we had sex; it would be the first time since he found out about my status. But soon we were in a passionate kiss as if picking up where we left off nearly six months before. I was aroused quickly, but Leo junior was unresponsive. There was a moment of apprehension.

"Don't worry. He's shy and just needs a kiss."

"*Descarado!*" I said. He was shameless.

The sex was over quickly, furtive and animalistic. Yet it was a great victory, knocking down the barriers of distance, culture, society, our doubts, and any fears he might have had of HIV. We had rekindled something I had thought lost, a satisfying and uncomplicated sharing.

We cleaned up, and then lay together for a long time, touching and talking. In the golden light of late afternoon, it all seemed extraordinarily simple; all the thousands of intricate pieces of the puzzle were forgotten, and it was a solid, clear picture. I started feeling greedy. I wanted his touch all the time.

And then, as if in echo, Leo said, "I wish we had more time. Only three days. When can you come back again?"

I sighed heavily. "Summer, I guess."

I jumped up and pulled out the bag of gifts. First, I took out the tennis rackets and two cans of new balls. He sprang off the bed and began swinging the racket around as if playing a match, his dick flopping back and forth with the rhythm of his movement.

"Now that's an idea," I said. "Nude tennis."

"You wouldn't even need a racket to hit the ball," he joked.

"*You* wouldn't."

I fished out a baseball cap with Los Angeles embroidered on it and a pair of red gym shorts. There were jeans and underwear and socks and shirts, but he wasn't interested in any of that.

"Let's play tomorrow. Can I open up a can?" He pulled the tab, surprised by the whoosh of released pressure. Then he took out the yellow fuzzy balls and caressed them as though they were magic. He slipped on the red gym shorts and handed the other racket to me. We hit the ball back and forth in the air. His laughter when he or I missed was sweet and contagious. When we had played the game to the point of working up a sweat, we stopped and fell in a heap on the bed.

"I brought you something, too." He went to his bag and pulled out a rectangular object wrapped in an old issue of *Granma*. He carefully unwrapped it and put it on the bed. A silence fell on the room and a trickle of sweat edged down his right temple.

The small painting, on what looked like thick, homemade white paper, was in somber tones heavy with mystery: brown, sienna, chestnut, saffron, beige, ashen and slate. It was a narrow, secret street that drew you toward a figure in the distance. I stared in amazement. He waited for me to say something.

"You don't like it?"

"I…I love it. It's…I don't know…so dark, almost scary, but full of life at the same time. I feel like I am looking into your soul."

"Come on. *No jodas.*"

"I'm serious. It's very good. I'm not an art critic, but it's a moving scene, at least for me. You're a real painter."

"Oh, shut up. If it's so good why did I have such a hard time selling them?"

"Because you were working the wrong market, selling to tourists. People on vacation want colorful mementos, happy trinkets and garish paintings. I've seen the stuff they sell at the craft fairs. They're horrible. This is art. You've got to paint more."

"I haven't done anything for about six months. On weekends Yudith and I used to go to that outdoor market on Primera, but I was lucky if I sold one a day."

"How much did you sell them for?"

"Ten."

"They are worth so much more than that. I bet I could sell them back in L.A."

"Are you serious?"

"I can't promise anything, but I have a feeling something like this would go. I want to see more."

Each day with him brought new things. Some of them haunted me. Some of them enchanted me. All of them made me want to know him better.

"I'm hungry," he announced, and I smiled at how he brought us back to earth.

We went to dinner with Ricardo and Miguel at a café near Calle 23 and Calle 12. After we ate, Leo and Ricardo headed off with a stack of quarters to play a racecourse video game, while Miguel and I talked. Miguel was about 10 years older than Ricardo, short and skinny with bad skin. Like Ricardo he dressed in the slutty fashion of the Malecón boys: tight-fitting shiny clothes with European labels. He was not the kind of person I would normally be friends with, and I searched for a topic we could discuss. I knew he was infatuated with Madonna, so I told him that my wife once dragged me to a Madonna concert, and he practically got down to kiss my feet. I gave him an embarrassingly inaccurate description of the staging and song list, but he hung on every word.

There was an uneasy lull in the conversation, and then he launched into a self-pitying description of his relationship with Ricardo. It made me uncomfortable, but it looked as if he had been dying for someone to talk to.

"Ricardo is unbearable. He gets drunk all the time and spends all the money I give him. He sells my gifts to buy more rum or clothes. A few weeks ago I got him a cell phone, but he sold it. He'll stay out all night and I won't see him until the next day. But what am I to do? It is so hard to find someone here that you can be with."

"I imagine it's the same everywhere. But that doesn't mean you have to stay with someone you're not happy with."

"Oh, we're happy. It's just that sometimes, I mean a lot, he drinks too much. I've tried to change him, but that didn't work. I've tried to end it, but he always comes back and apologizes, and I take him back. He really can…" Miguel looked over my shoulder and quickly stopped talking.

Leo and Ricardo were back at the table, out of quarters. "Can we get some more beers?" Leo said. Everybody looked at me.

"Sure. Get another round."

"Is Miguelito telling you what a pain in the ass I am?" Ricardo said to me.

"Don't start, Ricky," Miguel said. In an instant, the cords connecting them were twisted taut.

"What's going on?" Leo was back with the beers.

"Nothing," said Miguel.

"He's always talking shit about me," Ricardo countered.

"Shut the fuck up, Ricky," Miguel shouted.

"Hey, guys, come on. Not now," Leo said quietly.

They listened to Leo, but we didn't stay much longer. It was after one in the morning and I was ready to be in bed with Leo. After a drawn-out goodnight to Ricardo and Miguel, and a long walk home, I got my wish.

Leo, Luka, and I were in a taxi on the way to a party. I had agreed to one big night out while he was in Havana. There was a huge mandarin orange full moon hanging over El Moro, the old Spanish fort on the other side of the entrance to the bay. The color was striking, so deeply orange in fact, that Leo called it *rojo*. It felt like a night of possibilities.

Leo wore a tight white T-shirt, blue jeans and a camouflage fisherman's hat.

"You look like such a *gringo*," I told him.

"Yeah, man, I'm ready for *La Yuma*." Cubans liked to refer to the U.S. as *La Yuma*, though nobody knew exactly how it got started. Some said it was a reference to the old Wild West movies set in Yuma, Arizona.

"What? You guys didn't tell me," said Luka.

Leo and I looked at each other. Then Leo winked at me and said, "Yeah, I'm going to Los Angeles. I have a boyfriend there."

"What do you think, Luka? Do I dare?"

"I would," Luka said emphatically, and then laughed. Just a few days before he had had a different opinion.

I went along with the joke, but it hardly seemed a possibility. This was my life here now, but I had another life back there. How could the two mix? And yet I had already begun to understand that every relationship between a Cuban and a foreigner came down to the question sooner or later: did the foreigner care enough about the Cuban to help him leave the country?

The party set up was similar to the New Year's location: a farm with sheds for animals and tools, hard-packed dirt to dance on, and a barnyard smell even stronger than the other place. I prayed that we wouldn't run into Jose Luis.

Shortly after arriving, Leo greeted Diego, a friend of his from Holguín. Diego's eyes lit up when he and Leo began to speak, as if he had been lost at the party until he found someone else from his hometown. Then he turned to me and asked how long we had been together.

Before I could explain that we weren't really a couple, Leo exclaimed, "Six months." In six months we had slept together a total of eleven nights and had sex five times. Despite my careful tally, I wouldn't have said we were "together."

"That's cool," said the young man. He sounded envious.

Midway through the night, Ricardo and Miguelito showed up stinking drunk. Miguelito wore a sullen expression that verged on exasperation, and Ricardo sported a nasty smile. Ricardo was the kind of drunk that didn't exhibit a lot of the outward signs, the slurred speech or staggering, but one could tell he was smashed by his vacant eyes. Miguel, on the other hand, spoke loudly and could barely stand up.

Around them the balmy air was disturbed by the little clicks of a time bomb. Ricardo grabbed the arm of a young man walking by and whispered in his ear. Miguel raised his bottle of beer and smashed it into the side of Ricardo's face. The bottle remained intact and fell to the dirt.

"*Maricón*," screamed Ricardo. He shoved Miguel so hard that he fell to the ground. With a rush of adrenaline he was up, but someone grabbed him from behind. Ricardo approached Miguel, holding his head with one hand, and slapped him hard across the face. Miguel sent his elbow back heavily into the guy who held him and broke loose. He snorted like a bull and charged with his head aimed at Ricardo's stomach. The impact sent them to the ground. They kicked and punched and rolled with most of their sloppy blows not hitting the mark. The crowd stopped dancing and surged in close.

When the fight had started, Leo moved back to the edge of the crowd and came face-to-face with Diego. They looked at each other a moment, and then pushed their way back through the gawkers. Leo dragged Ricardo away from Miguel, got him on his feet and half-carried him toward the exit, while Miguel yelled insults from the grip of the much bigger Diego.

A few minutes later Luka was back by my side. We had gotten separated when the fight began.

"Where's Leo?" I asked.

"He took Ricardo outside, and nobody knows where Miguel is."

"Oh, this is great! Leo has to babysit. So much for our special night of the orange moon."

"What?" said Luka.

"Nothing."

Leo showed up with a bottle of rum, some plastic cups, and a can of Cachito. Luka, Diego, and I formed a huddle while Leo poured a good quantity of rum and then a splash of soda into each cup. We raised our glasses and Leo said, "To love." They laughed, and in their eyes I saw the flickers of something like arousal after the fight. I, on the other hand, felt a dry lurch in my gut, which I knew the rum wouldn't soothe. Seeing Miguel and Ricardo rolling around in the dirt had disturbed me, the fact that they were supposed to be lovers made the gay experience more unsettling.

 After the second round of drinks, the music came to an abrupt stop. We looked at our watches in shock. It was 3 a.m. Leo took hold of Luka's arm. "Cool watch. I never saw that before."

In the back seat of the taxi Leo put his arm around me and started playing with my ear, stroking the ridge and pulling on my lobe. At first I ignored it, but after a time I looked over at him with a guarded smile. "Martintón," Leo said from somewhere deep inside him, as if it were an incantation. "Martintón. Where are you?"

As soon as we got to the Malecón, Luka and Diego went off on their social rounds, and I knew that Leo wanted to as well, but felt obligated to stay with me.

"Go ahead and walk around if you want."

"Are you sure?"

"Of course. I'm okay."

"I'll be back in a few minutes." He gave me a big kiss on the mouth.

The few minutes turned into twenty. Luka and Diego were the first to rejoin me, making their reports of who was with whom. Leo showed up a few minutes later, glassy-eyed, in a good mood, but sloppy. His speech was exaggerated. The bottle was almost empty.

"Ready to go home?" I asked.

He gave me a look with his jaw hanging down, and his head rolling to the right like it might fall off. "Are you kidding me?" I felt I had let him down irrevocably.

"Forget it." I moved out of his arms.

He pulled me back and nuzzled my neck. "Come on. We'll go in a little bit." Then he jumped down off the wall and had to catch himself from falling. "Wait here. I have to go talk to somebody."

It was almost 6 a.m. when Leo, Luka, and I started up La Rampa. Leo staggered a couple of times, and Luka and I positioned ourselves on either side of him.

"I've never been this drunk," said Leo, drawing out each word.

"It's the beer and rum combo," said Luka.

"I have to pee," Leo whined.

Luka nodded toward a couple of policemen on the other side of the street.

"Not here," I said. "We'll be home soon."

"Why the fuck not?" He moved toward a side street. We pulled him back.

"Keep walking," I said. I glanced across the street to see if the cops were watching.

"Don't tell me what to do." He stopped and put his face close to mine. "Who do you think you are?"

"Great. Are we going to fight now? Get down on the ground and punch each other?"

"Leo," said Luka in a calm voice, "keep it together. It's just a couple of blocks."

Leo broke away from our grip and walked alone in a silly show of bravado. He picked up the pace, but he was suffering.

As soon as we got in the apartment, he ran to the bathroom and a range of guttural sounds escaped through the door. I went in to see if he was all right; he stood over the sink trying to barf. I stroked the back of his head while he had dry heaves. Then I got him to the bed and undressed him. He passed out in a few minutes.

Leo crawled out of bed in the early afternoon, and we sat down to a meal of leftovers. The phone rang and he jumped up to answer it as if he expected a call. From the way he talked, I knew it was Sulyn. He stared at the floor and gave one-word answers. After a long time without responding, he raised his voice with, "I told you Monday." Then he stared at the silent receiver for a moment with a disgusted frown before slamming it down.

He let out a caveman grunt as he came back to the table. "Why does she have to talk that shit?" He pounded his fist on the table. "No woman is indispensable to me." We finished the meal in silence and then he picked up the dishes to wash them. On the way to the kitchen, he leaned down and kissed the top of my head, letting a fork slip to the floor.

"I wish I could stay until you go," he said, "but I should leave tomorrow. If I don't, I'll probably end up staying in Havana like last time. Ricardo and Miguel are pressuring me to come and live with them. Miguel says that I need to be more independent of my mother."

I followed him into the kitchen and leaned against the counter while he washed. "I don't think moving in with Ricardo and Miguel is a good idea. Do you want to be in the middle of their shit all the time? And what about school?"

"I should go back and finish. There's an architectural program at the university in Camaguey. I always wanted to study architecture."

"That would be good." I tried to sound enthusiastic, but had a feeling it would never happen. "You should paint more. I've only seen one of your paintings, but I'm impressed."

"Let me give you some pictures to take back. See what people think of them over there. Then I'll decide about painting more."

"You don't feel compelled to paint, only when you think you can sell something?"

"I paint all the time in my head. It costs money, you know. I can't be buying painting supplies if my mom doesn't even have food to put on the table."

"Before you leave tomorrow, I'll give you some money. Promise me that you'll take part of it and buy whatever you need to paint."

"Thanks," he said, taking my hand.

"What's going to happen with us?"

"What do you mean?"

"Do we just go on like this? I come to visit you when I can?"

"You know I would like to go to Los Angeles, but you haven't invited me."

"You make it sound so simple. I just invite you and we go."

"I know a man in Holguín who arranges things. He helped a woman on my street leave for the U.S. It's expensive, of course."

"How does he do it?"

"He finds single people who win the lottery for a visa to the States, then arranges a marriage and you go as the spouse. With those visas you can bring a spouse or child."

I was skeptical. People were always coming up with new schemes to get Cubans out of the country, but most of the time they didn't work and somebody was out a lot of money. Leo doubled over in pain with a sudden jerk and held his stomach.

"What's the matter?"

He ran to the bathroom and I could hear him retching. He came out with his face drained of the enthusiasm he had just expressed about leaving. He lay down on the bed and started shaking. "Was I horrible last night? Don't ever let me hurt you?" he said through barely parted lips. I found a blanket in the wardrobe and spread it over his noble childlike suffering. "Hold me. I'm cold."

He wasn't dragging me. I went willingly into his netherworld of raw urges where desires demanded immediate attention, and where certain people had what seemed a black art in compelling others to satisfy them. Here was a fellow human being asking me to take care of him.

Leo came back with a package of paintings under his arm. He was in a hurry. We began packing his things. I stood at the foot of the bed and looked down at his bag, trying to remember if I had ever felt the same anxiety when Lizzie and I separated for a few days, a week, or a month. It must have been like that at the beginning. I couldn't remember.

At the bus station we asked a man to take a picture of us, and Leo put his arm around my shoulders. In the middle of the vast lobby, we hugged. He lifted up his floppy camouflage hat, smoothed his hair and replaced it snugly on his head. He turned and walked toward the door to the gates. Without turning he raised his hand and waved back at me before the station agent ushered him through the glass doors papered with a black film. In a flash he was gone, out of sight, swallowed up by the giant mouth of the terminal.

19

June 2002

Five months to the day after I left Havana in January, I was back at the Jose Martí airport, inching along in a line at customs. It was mid-afternoon and there were two agents, both women, doing thorough searches of every bag, box, backpack, and shopping bag. Security was tight because of a string of bombings instigated by right-wing Cuban-Americans to strike fear into the tourist industry. Two weeks before, an Italian tourist had been killed when a bomb went off in the lobby of one of the hotels.

The young woman currently in front of the customs agent had four boxes and three large suitcases. The agent pawed through one of the suitcases while the contents, strewn across the table, spelled out the story of the woman's life. I imagined a story about her. She was moving to Cuba, fed up with life in the United States. There was a Cuban boyfriend in the tale, a musician, and she originally thought of bringing him to the States. But when things started going bad back home, she decided a better option would be to pack up and move in with him in Cuba.

How bad would things have to get at home before I considered flight? My secret was out. I had come clean to my family about Cuba, and though I had not completely been absolved, there had come about, after many gut-wrenching conversations, an uncertain truce. Lizzie was first. Her reaction, at least outwardly, was to center attention on my health, the danger of these trips to Cuba, the probable insincerity of Leo. It was easier than focusing on the notion that our life together as man and wife had in many ways been a failure.

On a chilly gray winter's day, Lizzie and I had sat in the living room watching the patio plants getting beat up by the rain and water rolling in sheets down the glass doors. "Are you going to tell me now, or are we going to torture ourselves a few more months?" she said.

"Is it that obvious?" I stared into the green tea that I was holding, the bitter aroma climbing up into my nostrils and the heat warming my hands. But inside I felt a chill I would never be rid of.

"I think the twenty-two years we have lived together does give me some insight. We've never exactly had a conventional marriage, but we've always been able to talk, to share what is going on. This sneaking around and guarding secrets is what I can't stand."

"I didn't want to hurt you. I wanted so much to talk to you, but I've been confused. I couldn't grasp what was happening. It's hard to talk about since it concerns emotions, sexuality." Lizzie's eyes jumped at the word "sexuality," not in surprise, but in recognition, and though expected, still painful. She nodded her head slightly.

"How long has this been going on? Were there others, before Cuba?"

"No, I swear."

"You had to go all the way to Cuba to come out?"

"It wasn't my intention."

"Nothing just happens. You have to put yourself in the place. But I am not going to argue with how you choose to see it. So you met someone. Who is he?"

"He is the one who did those paintings I showed. I'm not going to recount the whole adventure as if you were my college roommate. It is enough to say that he is a young guy, a struggling artist. Lost, I guess, like me."

"You're not lost, at least not in the same way. You're just distracted and foolish. What do you know about him? What does he get out of this?"

"I hardly understand the relationship." Again she shuddered at the word "relationship." "But I know that he is a good person. I have met his mother who was very kind to me after the accident, and his family. As to what he wants, of course, having a foreign friend has its advantages."

"Are you giving him money?"

"It's not what you think. I help him and his family. Why shouldn't I? That's why I brought back those paintings to sell, so he can have his own money from his own efforts. It's difficult for people there."

"Why like this? Why did you have to get involved in *that* kind of situation?"

"You make it sound dirty. We don't always have the luxury to choose how things happen. You start down a road not knowing where it is going to take you. You meet someone and it works. God knows why. Then you realize you have gone too far and there is no way to go back."

"Because you don't want to."

"I did at first. I was crazy to have my life back. But it kept picking up speed. I couldn't stop it."

"God save us from men in their mid-life crises. I'm so sick of hearing all my friends' stories, and now I've got mine. It's disgusting. Did you think at all how this was going to affect your family?"

"Of course I did. You have no idea how I've agonized over this."

"You have a hell of a way of showing agony. You act like this is a fucking tea party." She stood up and threw the *National Geographic* she had been reading at me, hitting me square in the nose. I felt sorry for her. She couldn't fault me for what I was, so she had to attack me as a man trying to find himself in his forties. Later she apologized, tried to discourage me from going back to Cuba, and advised me to get some counseling. I knew she and Tomás were going to gang up on me on that point. I gave in and started seeing a therapist.

Jenny was a different story. I insisted that Lizzie not say anything to her, that I would talk to her when I was ready. Over dinner at one of her favorite Hollywood dives, Jenny detected my nervousness and said, "You're not going to tell me that you and Mom are breaking up, are you? 'Cause I can't handle that right now."

"It's not exactly that, a bit more complicated."

"Something *is* going on with you and Mom, isn't it?"

"Something is going on with me. I guess I'm gay." I shocked myself at how easily it came out.

"Jesus, Dad. You guess? What does that mean? Doesn't someone know?" She groaned and stared at the label on her beer, then at my hands across the table. "Stop fiddling with your damn fork." In her eyes was surprise at her own voice. "I'm sorry. I know this is not the way I'm supposed to act." She stopped and looked straight at me, as if realizing how hard this was for me. "I'm sorry, Daddy, it's so sudden...and...weird. If it were someone else's Dad, I'd say 'Yeah, cool.' But we've been so close all these years and I never knew you had this secret life."

"I didn't, until recently."

"Cuba," she sighed. "Why there?"

"That's what your mother said. You know, the country is screwed up in some ways, but the people, at least with their bodies, are very liberated. Sex is such a big deal there that it's not a big deal. I know that doesn't make sense."

"Oh, Dad," she said, shaking her head. "How is Mom doing with it?"

"It's hard to tell. Sometimes she's more like a man the way she holds things in. It's killing her not being able to talk to you about it. I made her promise not to until I had my chance. Now you two can drag your ol' Dad over the coals."

Her face made a transition from shock to anger, as though what I told her just registered. "How could you do this to Mom?"

"Jen, you know it's not something you do to another person. It's about being who you are."

"Sounds like some crap you got from your therapist."

"That doesn't mean it's not true. You can be mad at me for a while if you want, but I can't live without you in my life. I need your support."

She looked down for a long time at the remains of her veggie burger. "Do you have any idea what this feels like?"

"This is not about you, Jen. I've spent the last twenty-two years trying to be the person you and Mom wanted me to be. Now I have to be who I am."

After a long pause she pushed her plate aside and took a drink of her beer. "You're right. I'm being selfish. I guess I'm not the cool daughter you thought I was."

"Yes, you are and always will be. And I'm still the same father, just a little...different."

She rolled her eyes. "Please, spare me the details. I suppose I'll hear about this person some day. It is one, right? Or a bunch of them? Oh, God. I don't want to know."

Back at the airport the line inched forward, and my thoughts turned toward Leo waiting beyond the double doors. Every time they opened to let someone out, I tried to spot him, but they kept the greeters far back from the threshold. I began to worry he would think I missed the plane and go on home.

Things between us had developed over the last five months, as much as a relationship can develop through phone calls, letters, and emails. The three days we had spent together in January showed us that it was something more than a summer fling, but the true test was yet to come. Could our tenuous bond survive the domesticity of a whole month living together? And if it did, what then?

By phone I was able to give him good news about his artwork. I had brought back ten of his paintings, all about the same size as the one he'd given me. I was convinced he had talent, and my friends in L.A. thought so, too. The paintings were all in the same somber colors, a lot of dark narrow streets, with streetlights, a popular theme, penetrating the gloominess and casting down a yellow cone of light, sometimes on a skeletal figure. But in one the shaft of light fell on a voluptuous woman, her face turned away and her ample naked buttocks appeared like two luminescent globes. There were a couple of female nudes, always with the face turned away, and one of a couple kissing, the man standing over the kneeling woman. The unclothed brown body of the man faded into the brown of the background with just a hint of slack genitals between his legs. But his head floated in the light and his hair shone thick and brown. His wide nostrils were slightly flared, a sharp contrast to her more delicate features.

I had organized an informal showing at my house for a group of friends, only telling them the paintings were by a Cuban artist I had met. They reacted the way I had, unable to ignore them, like eyes on a freeway drawn to a wreck. I put on no pressure to buy, but almost everyone wanted one. I had picked out a couple for myself, but the rest I was able to sell for fifty to a hundred dollars each. Later I regretted letting them go so cheaply. Then before my friends took them away, I showed them around at a couple of galleries. There was some interest, and at the shop where I had them framed, the employees praised them, said they had never seen anything like them.

One of the works I kept, my favorite, showed a stick-figure crowd with circles as heads and lots of movement, perhaps a market day. It was done in grays and dark greens with a church tower in the background and streetlights vaguely sketched in on one side over an empty sidewalk; all the action was in the street. Leo was like his paintings, sinister and full of life at the same time.

I told him that if he would put together a collection, I might be able to get a show in a gallery. But his life was going through the usual emotional upheaval. One day in late February I came home to find an email saying to call him at a Havana number. When I got him on the phone, I found out that he had quit school and moved back in with Yudith though he insisted it was as a companion rather than a husband. She was getting married to a Spaniard in the summer and would leave the country. I talked to him a couple of times over the next few weeks, and then one day Yudith answered and said in an icy voice that I should call him in Holguín.

Before I had a chance to talk to him, a letter arrived explaining that Yudith's apartment was very comfortable—thanks to the remittances from her Spanish lover—but he felt out of place and wasn't free to be his own person. He had returned to his mother's house. Curiously, he never mentioned anything about Sulyn. Leaving the country was more on his mind than ever, he told me, and we would discuss his plan when I came in the summer.

A week before my arrival he was back at Yudith's sending me teasing emails from her computer. He had gone to Havana a week early to arrange an apartment for us to stay in. "I'm crazy for you to arrive," he said in one email. "It has been so long since we were together and each day that I wait seems to be eternal." In another one he said, "I'm desperate for you to come, to have you in my arms." It was saucy, the flavor of pulp romance, and I ate it up even knowing it was typical fare for Cubans.

I had miraculously arrived at the front of the line at customs, but it was a dubious victory because I knew they were going to be in a state of shock when they opened my bag and found a couple hundred bottles of medicine. A lot of them were anti-retrovirals for people with HIV, but there were also antibiotics, painkillers, and an assortment of over-the-counter remedies. It was my third trip bringing meds to Cuba, and I had been able to supply Luka and a number of other people with the "cocktail" of medications they needed. Of course, the customs agents would see me as just another suspicious tourist with a bag full of drugs.

When I took my place in front of the agent and hoisted my bags up on the table, it was obvious that neither of us were very happy people. She may have been dissatisfied with her job, but I had a better excuse. I had just spent nearly an hour in line while someone I was anxious to see was standing just a hundred yards away. She stared at me with her expressionless eyes from a puffy face. She wore a green military uniform, and her mousy brown hair was swept to the back of her head and held with a clip.

"Open your bags," she said firmly.

I didn't get the bag with the meds half unzipped before I started a nervous chatter. "I bring donations of medicine to Cuba. I have never had a problem before. I work with a doctor at the Institute of Tropical medicine. His name is Pedro Sanz."

"Hmm," was all she said as she began to take out the bottles of medicine one by one, looking at each label and putting it on the table.

"What's this for?"

"It's an antibiotic."

"And this one?"

"It's for HIV." We went through several bottles like that, and then she fell silent as she dug into the bag, pulled out something new, scrutinized the label as if she had some notion of what it was, and then casually put it on the table. By the time she got to the thirtieth bottle, my patience was completely stretched thin. But I used all my power to act nonchalant. Then she stopped, let out a sigh, and stared at me again. She had no idea what to do, and she was petrified of making the wrong decision.

"Wait," she said. She walked over to a supervisor, talked to her a moment, and they both looked over at me. My agent came back and again said, "Wait a minute."

"Look, if you want to call Dr. Sanz, I'm sure he will vouch for me. I have his number right here." I held out a business card. She didn't reach for it, only looked at it as if it were a dead mouse, and then stared at something on the other side of the room.

"My supervisor is coming."

I turned around and looked at the people still in line, who gave me the impression of refugees, with all their bags and boxes and their drawn faces. I smiled as if to say I was sorry for the delay, but they only responded with vacant stares.

The pert, younger supervisor with black curly hair arrived, and I started my story again, offering her the card. She didn't look at it, but lifted up the glasses that hung from a chain around her neck and went straight to the medicine, picking up each bottle, staring at the label and putting it down. She sent her hand deep into the bag, rustled around and then came up with a plastic vial that she pondered as if it were going to tell the whole story. One after another after another. She had no more idea what to do than the other woman. After a prolonged silence, she said to her coworker, "Okay, you can let him go."

It took me several minutes to repack everything, while my lovely official stood idle in front of me, my case already forgotten. I grabbed all my things and raced toward the door.

There was a sea of expectant faces looking past me as I rolled my bags out. Then a handsome young man with a goatee came in my direction, and it took me a minute to realize it was Leo. He didn't have a heavy beard, but because his facial hair was so dark, the goatee made him look older and even more handsome than I remembered. He also looked meatier, as if he had gained weight. He hugged me, and I felt my negative experience at customs melt away.

We took a taxi to the place in Vedado where a woman, a contact through Yudith, had an apartment to rent on Calle 17 right across from the giant three-winged Focsa building. The owner, Nancy, was an attractive, dark-haired woman in her twenties who had the air of a savvy businesswoman, though she was casually dressed. Some workmen were putting down a new tile floor in the second bedroom, so she wasn't quite ready to hand over the keys. She suggested we walk around for a bit.

Across the street we had a beer at the outdoor café with its plastic seats—faded from red to rosy pink by the relentless sun—attached to yellow tabletops sticky with spilled ice cream and soda. Leo was all smiles and relaxed, though there always seemed to be secrets lurking behind his soulful eyes. "How's everything in Holguín? How's your mother?" I asked.

"I'm going to be a father," he blurted out, and then laughed nervously.

"You what?"

"Sulyn is pregnant."

I couldn't think of a single thing to say. My eyes grew cold.

"It has nothing to do with us. I just wanted you to know."

"But—"

"But what? Nothing's changed."

"No, nothing," I said. "And everything."

"Forget about it. We can talk about it later." We fell silent and sipped our beers.

Nancy turned over the keys and I paid her for the whole month as we sat in the sparsely decorated living room. There was a giant framed picture of Jesus showing the sacred heart above the sofa, and a three-part lithograph by a very unreligious modern Cuban symbolist artist on the opposite wall. It was the face-off of Cuba's struggle with religion: traditional Catholicism versus a revolutionary secularism.

Leo went straight out on the bedroom balcony that looked down on the busy street life. Nancy's final instructions were, "Don't spend too much time out on the balcony during the day and don't open the door to anyone you don't know. If anyone asks, just say that you're my boyfriend. If I come by, I will knock like this." She demonstrated her two-quick-two-slow knock pattern on the door. She gave me no receipt and didn't write down any of my personal information. That meant she was renting illegally, and if she got caught, would suffer huge fines. I didn't like the restrictions or the feeling of being involved in something that could bring the police asking questions. Aside from the illegal rental, I was a foreign man living with a young Cuban. I didn't know how many rules were being broken. But I also knew that the outlaw culture was so vast in Havana, with a large percentage of the population doing something that was against the law in order to survive, that what we were doing was nothing exceptional, and as long as we were discreet, people would turn the other way.

Leo and I went into the air-conditioned bedroom and fell on the bed. He was affectionate and any tension from our brief talk in the café melted away. I buried my nose in his neck and took in his smell that I had missed the previous few months. His kisses, always full of tenderness and promise, reminded me why I had come all this way to be with him again.

Gerard and his entourage of visiting Americans and Cuban friends arrived twenty minutes late for our rendezvous at the Karachi Club for the afternoon tea dance with seventies and eighties music. There were ten of us at the table, and our group was the only curiously different table in the small club. Most of the other patrons were straight couples. When we danced it was in a big group, so it was hard to tell who was dancing with whom; that way the managers didn't have to panic that we were trying to turn the place gay again. Gerard told me that a few years back it had been a mostly gay club before they closed it down.

One of the Cuban guys at the table had attached himself to the group to sell bottles of rum from under the table, which he pulled out from a tattered flight bag that said Taino Tours on the outside. It was street rum he put in used Havana Club bottles and sold for an inflated price. As the evening went on, he became more and more aggressive about selling his product, and some of the Cubans were also pushy with the foreigners to buy more drinks

Throughout all the negotiations for drinks, Leo was calmly at my side, sitting close so that our legs were touching and at one point he absent-mindedly rubbed my elbow. He didn't talk much and I wondered what was going through his head. Did he see that his countrymen were being obnoxious? Did it trouble him?

No one bothered Louise, an American woman across the table. She was pale and blonde and looked very East Coast top drawer, but Gerard had told me she was more revolutionary than most Cubans in both her social and political life. She asked Leo to dance and later they disappeared. After a respectful amount of time so as not to look as though I was hounding him, I found them out on the front patio sitting at a table, having a beer.

"Martin, sit down. I was just asking Louise if she would go to the wedding as my date."

"Wedding?"

"You remember, Yudith is getting married to the Spanish guy and the wedding is next week. She wants me to bring a date."

"You could take me."

"Would you like to see the fireworks if I showed up with you? Remember what she did with my backpack. That would just be a warm-up."

"Of course I would go with you," said Louise, "but I don't think I'll be here. I'm supposed to go back to the States next week."

"See, you'll just have to take me, and we'll have an early Fourth of July."

"*No jodas, niño*. Don't fuck around, baby. She means business."

"She hates me that much?"

"Let's just say, around her I don't talk about you."

From Karachi, Leo and I went to eat at La Casona de 17 on the same street as the apartment. Prices were reasonable, but it was still the very beginning of a month-long stay, and I suggested we get the chicken plate on special. Leo gave me a wearisome look and cavalierly told me, "Don't worry about it."

"Easy for you to say. I'm going to be here a month, and if I don't budget from the beginning, I'll run out of money in a week." Budgeting was a concept Cubans had no use for.

"Order what you want."

"Are you going to buy me dinner?"

He took out his wallet, dug into one of the pockets and pulled out a folded bill. He opened it up with precise motions, laid it on the table, and proudly pointed to the picture of Ben Franklin. "Yudith gave it to me to buy things for the baby."

"No, we're not using that money!"

"Look, it's my money and I'll use it however I want. Anyway, we're just going to use a little of it, and with the rest I'll buy some baby things."

I still ordered the chicken plate and he got a shrimp cocktail and grilled lobster. Seafood was his favorite food, he announced. He probably liked it so much because it was one of the things that ordinary Cubans couldn't afford.

"I thought you were going to wait to become a father," I said.

"My mom is crazy to have a grandchild. I thought it would make it easier on her if she has someone to take care of when I leave. What do you think?"

"Strange reason to have a kid, to fill a gap. When is it due?"

"November. That guy said that he might be able to arrange my visa by the first of the year."

"You are going to become a father, and then a month later leave the country?"

"How am I going to support my family here? I need to leave so I can give my child a decent life."

"It seems to me that you are doing things backwards. Wouldn't it be more logical to get settled first with an income before deciding to have a child?"

He gave me the vacant look as if he had been transported momentarily to a planet where people say strange things.

And then he was back. "Did you tell your wife and daughter about us?" he asked.

I nodded.

"How did it go?"

"It was hell, but once they sort of accepted it, they didn't understand why I had to go all the way to Cuba to, you know, to be with a man."

"I guess you just wanted the best."

At Miguel and Ricardo's the furniture had all been moved out of the living room and the kitchen was set up like a bar. They were having a 10-peso party. I was a way they could make extra money, charging an entrance fee and selling drinks. Leo swore to me that we would just go for a short time because he had promised he would help them set up.

The beer was already on ice in a large rusty barrel, and Miguel filled bottles with rotgut rum from a plastic jug. The stereo had been moved to a makeshift dance room just beyond the kitchen. Ricardo prepared his DJ station and Leo offered to help him arrange the CDs. There wasn't anything for me to do, so I grabbed a beer and went out on the front porch to watch people arrive.

At midnight guests showed up by the carload—a mix of gays, lesbians, straights and the ambiguous—and the house filled up quickly. It was a young crowd, some of whom I recognized from the Malecón, but I couldn't imagine having a conversation with any of them, certainly not one that would last more than a couple of lines. I felt old, out of place, intolerant, and I hadn't had enough to drink to make me forget I was there for one reason only. And he was so involved playing assistant DJ that he seemed to have forgotten I existed. From my corner of the porch I listened to conversations about the latest conquests, like a pair of jeans at a good price or a boy someone had taken home—both told with the same emotion.

Leo and I ran into each other over the beer barrel. "Buy me a beer, mister?" he said.

"I will if you go home with me. And soon."

"We'll go in a little bit." He looked over his shoulder toward the music.

I followed him back into the suffocating dance room and carved out a space in the corner where I could watch him. Several of the boys had taken off their shirts and their taut bodies were glistening with sweat. I decided to make my way toward Leo. As I brushed up against the wiggling bodies my arms were coated with a sticky dampness and I was reminded why summer parties were so much better outdoors. Thanks to Leo's spinning, the throng was pumping up and down, and my progress was slowed by the press of flesh; but taller and bigger than most everyone in my path, I pushed my way to within a few feet of the DJ station. I waved my hands and Leo looked up. "I need to go home," I shouted. It was already an hour after he promised we would leave.

"We'll go in a half hour." I weaved back through the crowd and returned to the front porch. The place was packed now and I had lost my seat on the ledge that caught a slight breeze. With the thumping music, the high sharp laughter and the shrill staccato of the voices around me, I wondered that the neighbors didn't complain. I supposed that a number of people were paid off so that the party could go on and it irritated me, though it was really none of my business.

Bolstered by a couple more beers I approached Leo again. I had given up the nice-guy approach. "I'm leaving. Are you going with me?"

"Come on. I'm having such a good time. I love seeing everybody happy and enjoying themselves." Ricardo had let him take over as the main DJ.

"I need to go home. Call me when you are on your way so I can come down and open the gate."

"I won't drink too much because we're going to do something when I get there."

"We'll see about that," I said under my breath. I went out and jumped in one of the cabs that were lined up outside.

20

It was two in the afternoon and still no Leo. I needed to get out of the house. Just a few blocks away on Calle 15, Luka was housebound due to a flare-up of the same bacteria in his legs that kept him from going to Spain a couple years earlier. He was staying in a friend's apartment, and since Monica and Cesar had broken up, she moved in with Luka to take care of him. He looked healthy, as handsome as when I met him, but when he got up to change the music, he was in pain. The doctor told him he needed complete rest for three to four weeks.

"How are things going with Leo?" he asked.

"Just great. We went to a party at Miguel's last night and he still hasn't come back."

"Don't worry too much about it. He's young and wants to have a good time."

"Precisely. So what the fuck is he doing having a kid?"

"Having a kid?"

"He went and got Sulyn pregnant. He's going to be a daddy."

Monica overheard and came in from the kitchen where she was fixing lunch. A strand of thick black hair was plastered to her sweaty forehead as she tumbled into one of the easy chairs opposite the couch, and lit up a cigarette.

"Who's having a kid?" she said.

"Leo."

"He's hardly more than a kid himself."

"That's what we were just discussing," I said.

"I'm not going to advise you one way or the other about Leo. I haven't even met him. But I can say that getting involved with a bisexual is very hard. Believe me, I know." She took a big drag on her cigarette and shook her head as she exhaled a cloud of smoke that temporarily obscured her face. "No, I can't do it anymore. I'm so glad that Luka wanted help. I mean I'm not glad that he is suffering, but we support each other. I don't know what I would have done without him. With Luka is where I need to be right now."

"Look at me," said Luka. "I can't do anything. She has to cook, do the dishes, wash the clothes, clean the house. She's a lot more help to me than I am to her."

"At least you appreciate what I do for you. I'm finished with being somebody's slave." At that she got up and went back to the dark and sweltering kitchen.

We sat down to lunch, but she hardly ate, complaining of an upset stomach that had been going on for weeks. I told her that I had some medicine that might help her in my bag of donations. After we had coffee, I returned to the apartment and started digging through the bag.

I had just come up with some physician's samples of Prevacid when there was a knock on the door. I opened it to find Leo leaning on the doorjamb with a disgusted look on his face, but he stepped in and kissed me.

"Where were you?" he asked calmly. "I was here at around nine this morning. I knocked and knocked."

I wasn't sure I believed him, but it was possible that the air conditioning had blocked out the knocking. "I didn't hear you. I was here all morning, and then I went over to Luka's."

In a few minutes we were naked on the bed, listening to Luis Miguel singing "*Cuando Vuelva Tu Lado.*" Leo sang along in his horrible voice. "You are such a jerk," I said, putting a hand over his mouth. There was a long session of play before sex. It had been five months, but unlike the first time in January, he wasn't reticent. "I've been waiting a long time for this," he whispered.

"And me," I said.

For an hour we lay in each other's arms in post-sex oblivion, listening to Luis coo his love songs. Then we got dressed and went over to Luka's to give Monica the medicine. Luka gave me a knowing look, and Monica laughed when she saw us together. The laugh caused her to double over in pain. "*Coño!*" she said. "Shit. This hurts like hell."

"I don't know if the medicine will help," I said. "Maybe you should see a doctor."

"I'll give it a try. You're going to stay for dinner, right?"

"No, no. You don't have to cook for us."

"I have to cook anyway."

Luka brought out a bottle of rum. "I think this calls for a celebration. I can't drink, but you guys can."

We drank our rum and I stared at Leo across the room. He wore a navy blue tank top and his arms looked bigger than I remembered. His skin had taken on a deep cinnamon color from the summer sun. Monica caught me looking at him and twisted her lips, but she knew exactly how I felt. She must have been thinking about Cesar; her eyes went cold and her face turned hard, her chin jutting out in bitterness.

We settled into a casual domesticity, spending a lot of time in the apartment. Every night we slept embraced, or with an arm loosely draped over the other's chest or in some way touching. Mornings were mine. While Leo slept, I set up all my papers and notes on the dining room table. I had waded through *Versos Sencillos* time and again, seeing it as the autobiography of his soul in poetry. I wrote, "For Martí, love of country was love of his fellow man was fighting against racism was history was literature was poetry was political action was life. And yet he was just a man, a man who renounced his one true love, who became estranged from his wife and only son, who was lover to a widow and surrogate father to her four children. He was a man with faults and foibles, but unshakable in his principles and willing to make the ultimate sacrifice for the cause of Cuban independence." Though all my attempts to describe him seem insufficient, I plodded on, trying to capture what Lizzie inspired me to do—find what made him human "like you and me."

Leo spent a lot of time out on the balcony, leaning on the rail, smoking cigarettes. He liked to look at the cars parked just under the balcony where two wiry men with leathery skin lugged big plastic buckets of brackish water out to the street and hand-washed a constant stream of relatively new Russian compacts and classic American cars.

One day he told me, "When I get over there, I want to buy a Mustang." I wondered where he had seen one since all the American cars on the streets were from before the revolution. In movies, he told me, and I had to smile. It fit his image so perfectly—a muscle car for the country boy with the tattoos and a sleeveless T-shirt, a cigarette dangling from his pouty lips.

Into this blissful albeit boring life entered the tricky discussion of a cell phone. For months Leo had been badgering me about getting a cell phone and was disappointed when I didn't bring one from the States though I explained that the system was different in Cuba and U.S. phones didn't work. Yudith knew someone who was selling a phone for fifty dollars—mostly likely stolen from an unfortunate European tourist—and Leo wanted to buy it. I would have to put the line in my name because Cubans weren't allowed to initiate cell phone service.

"How much is all this going to cost?" I said wearily.

"Forget it."

"No, you brought it up. Tell me how much it costs and why you think you need it."

He snorted and got up to leave the room. "I'm doing it for you," he said, going down the hall toward the bedroom. "It would be easier for us to keep in touch. But forget it."

In the bedroom he lay sulking, with the earphones on and his arms crossed on his chest. I let him stew and went back to my writing. Later I heard him rustling in the kitchen. With a sandwich in one hand and a glass of pineapple juice in the other, he came in wearing his silent hurt and sat down on the sofa to eat.

"I refuse to do this," I said from across the room.

"Do what?"

"Let money destroy what we have. It's stupid. I know you think I'm being cheap, but having a cell phone is a luxury, especially here where a lot of people barely have enough to eat. I'm just not sure that's a good way to spend money."

"Do you have a cell phone?"

"Yes, but that's not the point. In the short time we have been together, I've seen you change. You start living in the dollar economy, and it's like an addiction. You want more and more, things that aren't necessary. I give you money and it disappears. I have to constantly worry about my cash flow."

"If you don't want to help me…"

I stood up and walked over to where he was sitting. "Wait a minute. We're not talking about help. We're talking about wasting money. There's no control. It's like play money to you, maybe because you didn't earn it."

"Ouch, that hurt."

"I'm just trying to make you think. And I have this fear that you are only interested in me for what I can give you."

"You know that isn't true."

"I'm not saying what is true or not. I'm talking about gut feeling, a lurking doubt that raises its head every time there is tension between us."

"I've always been honest with you. I told you about the women in my life and they know about you. Of course, I need help. Things are very difficult in Cuba. I haven't hidden anything from you." And then he added, "Unlike you."

"What do you mean?"

"You know. Last summer in the hospital?" He raised his thick eyebrows.

His remark stung me. I *had* kept that crucial information from him, and I didn't know how much longer I would have kept it if he hadn't discovered my pills. But bringing it up in the cell phone conversation was a manipulation, and in that game I was going to lose. Leo was much better at getting his way than I was.

"It wasn't right. I admitted that from the beginning. Do you…do you worry about it? I mean the HIV."

"No, I worry more about something else."

"What?"

"Why are *you* with *me*?"

"Let me guess. You think that I just want you for sex and I'm not interested in helping you."

"I wonder."

"How can you think that?"

"I keep dropping hints about going to the States, but you never say anything except that it is *so* difficult. Maybe you don't want me with you. Maybe you just want to come here and play, and then leave me in this shit."

"You have to be patient. It has only been a couple months since I told my wife. She and I have lived together for over twenty years. What do you expect me to do? And then there is the issue of finding a way, which is far from easy. We need more time. Anyway, you know most Cubans don't stay with the person that helps them leave the country."

"I always imagined that I would stay with the person who—"

"What person? How many offers have you had?"

"You are the only one that I would consider. We're good together."

"I feel the same, but we have to be careful. We have to recognize our gut fears. That's why I'm not pushing you to have sex all the time."

"You're not?" he teased.

"No, I'm not. That's not the reason I'm with you. The sleeping together and cooking together and laughing together are just as important to me as the sex. Maybe more important. I mean, definitely more important. It's the whole thing, the way you make me feel. Sex is a natural part of it."

I sat down by him on the sofa as he gulped the last of the juice. "Do you really love me?" he said.

"You need to ask?"

"Don't answer a question with a question. You're the one that taught me that." He put his lips to mine, and they tasted of cool pineapple. Neither of us was the kind of person that could stay mad at the other for very long. Later that evening I stuck some money in his hand and told him he should buy the phone. He smiled as if he had expected it.

Leo came back from Yudith's house, not with the cell phone that he supposedly went to get, but a shopping bag full of baby things. He proudly pulled the clothes, blanket, pacifiers, and bibs out of the bag and displayed them on the bed. I didn't ask, but I was sure he had used the money I gave him for the phone; the rest of Yudith's hundred dollars had long been spent.

"And the cell phone?"

"We tried to call the guy that has it, but he wasn't there. She'll get it later and I'll pick it up the day of the wedding."

"Do you have money left for it?"

I could see his mind working quickly. He knew that I knew he had used the phone money for the baby things. "She's going to give it to me, a going-away present," he admitted sheepishly.

"But she's the one going away."

He shrugged as if to say that he didn't make the rules.

"Hey, you didn't say anything about my ring." He held up his hand and I saw a garish ring with a large red stone in a square setting of gold metal. I knew nothing about jewelry. Was it real gold? Was the stone real?

"Do you like it?"

"Sure. It's nice."

"It's for you." He took it off and put it on my finger.

I didn't know how to react. It was not my taste at all. "Does this mean we're married?"

"Sure. I feel like I'm *doble casado,* double-married." He was excited. "*Doble casado.* I like the way that sounds."

I didn't particularly like the way it sounded, but he was putting me, at least in a fanciful way, on the same footing as the woman who was going to have his baby.

"Seriously, who am I in your life?"

He didn't take a second to answer. "You're the person I don't hide." Like so many of the phrases that came out of his mouth, it was simple, possibly profound. But what did it truly mean?

Leo and I picked up four cardboard box lunches of meat, rice, and salad that they sold for workers, and went over to Monica and Luka's. In the kitchen Monica whispered, "I'm worried about Luka. He doesn't seem to be getting any better. At first the doctor said four weeks of complete rest, but now they are saying much longer. Yesterday he didn't get up all day."

"But he's not getting worse, is he?" I asked.

"He has his good days and bad days. I'm not going to put the food on the plates yet. He'll probably want to take a shower."

It was almost an hour before Luka emerged in his shorts and tank top, looking clean and fresh, his black curls still glistening. Except for his slow shuffle, there was no sign that he had been suffering. "Sorry to keep you waiting."

At the heavy antique formal dining table, Monica said cheerily, "I have some news. I've been offered a job cooking in a restaurant in Peru."

"Peru?" said Leo as if it was bad word.

"Anyplace to get out of here. I need to leave, especially now after what happened with Cesar. I just want to be where I can work and get paid. I'm not afraid to work. I'll cook and clean all day if they pay me a decent wage."

"It wouldn't be right away, would it?" I said, looking at Luka.

"You know nothing happens fast around here. Luka is going to be fine by the time I'm ready to go."

"I wouldn't go to Peru," said Luka. "Anywhere in Europe or the States, but not Peru. I was in Colombia for a few months. It was hard to find work and you didn't feel safe."

"I am sticking with the USA, Los Angeles," said Leo. Monica and Luka looked up from their food at me.

"Are you a good swimmer?" I joked. I didn't want Luka and Monica to know about our plan.

"People go all the time. Where there's a will, there's a way. Some day I might surprise you and knock on your door."

"What makes you all so sure that you would be happy in another country?" I said to the group.

"It's not about being happy," said Monica. "It's about doing a day's work and getting decent pay. It's about having the opportunity to better yourself without being a member of the party or having a friend who works in tourism."

"Yeah, what kind of system is it when a doctor quits his job to work carrying bags in a hotel so he can support his family," said Luka.

"I'm tired of doing things that are illegal to survive," Leo added. "Just to do a simple business like I was doing these last few months, selling soap, is illegal. I had to get up at 4 a.m., go all the way to Santiago and carry heavy loads in a backpack like a fucking mule around to different towns. And for what? A few dollars, and all the time worrying about being picked by the cops. No, man, what kind of job is that?"

Back at the apartment, we were stretched out on the bed and just beginning to enjoy the air conditioning when a blackout hit. The coolness began to seep out of the room, and there was little left of the day's light. It seemed that the atmosphere might lead to sex, but Leo had other things on his mind.

"I was talking to Ricardo and Miguel the other day," he began tentatively. "They asked if you can get HIV from kissing."

"And what did you tell them?"

"I said I didn't think so."

"You mean you're not sure? Are you thinking about stopping kissing me?"

"No."

"They know about me then?"

"I didn't tell them. I think they found out from Sulyn."

"She's a friend of theirs?"

"She knows Ricardo from Holguín."

"If she told them, she probably told others. Oh, God. Probably everybody in Holguín knows. Your mother?"

"I don't think so. She never said anything."

In the last light we dressed and went outside as most people in Havana do during a blackout, to escape the stagnant air inside. The stores across the street had closed except for the bar on the corner, which had an emergency power generator. We bought a couple of beers and headed for the Malecón where we sat on the wall, caught a slight breeze and drank our beers. From the seawall you could observe that it was a general blackout with only the hotels like the Nacionál in the distance having lights. Headlights from cars passing on the seaside drive pierced the darkness and spotlighted shadowy figures running across the street to the Malecón. It was a moonless night and the salty smell of the sea hung in the air.

It was wedding day for Yudith, and Leo was dressed all in white. He had bought a crepe cotton peasant outfit with drawstring pants and a V-neck top that laced up. The almost see-through fabric clung to his slender frame and accentuated his brown skin. His goatee had filled in and he had gelled his hair into his usual spiky do.

"Yudith is going to be angry with you."

"Why?'

"Because it is supposed to be her day, and you're going to be the most beautiful one at the wedding."

"You're saying that because you want something when I get home."

"No, you're wrong. I want it now." I pushed him up against the wall.

"No, no, no, no," he uttered. "I have to go. She'll kill me if I'm late."

"You're no fun."

"I will be later."

"When do you think you'll be back?"

"In a couple of hours. It starts at five. I should be back at seven or a little after."

Two hours seemed unlikely, an obvious example of what he thought I wanted to hear. By the time he called at midnight, I was unable to control my anger. "Where the hell have you been?" I yelled into the phone.

"Don't be angry. I'll be home soon."

"When?"

"We're leaving now, but we have to take some people home." The playful lilt in his voice told me he was drunk. "I love you a lot. Send me a kiss."

I responded with silence.

"Oh well, see you soon." He hung up.

I went out for a walk to clear my head, and when I came back there was a dark figure dressed in white sitting in front of the gate. I started up the steps. We didn't speak. I couldn't look at him, though I felt the silent barbs passing through the night air. I opened the gate and he followed me in. He took the offensive as if he was the injured party.

"What were you doing out in the street at this hour?"

"You try sitting in the apartment hour after hour. If I didn't go out for a walk, I was going to explode."

"It's not my fault. They wouldn't let me leave. Every time I said I was leaving, Yudith had a fit."

"I can imagine."

"Then I had to drive everybody home."

"You drove everybody home in your condition?"

That got a smile out of him. "Everyone else was worse."

"Why did you have to say two hours in the first place? I don't care if you go out by yourself, just give me a reasonable amount of time you'll be gone, and I can make other plans. That's all I ask."

"Look, it is like I always say to my women. The important thing is who I lay my head down next to at the end of the day, who I caress."

Things were starting to get better, but his unintelligible logic threw me back into fight mode. "Don't ever put me in the same category as your women. Don't you see how ridiculous that sounds?"

"You don't understand anything," he said. He stood up as if he were mortally wounded, went into the bedroom, took off his clothes, and got into bed. It was the first night that we slept on opposite sides of the bed, a whole night of not touching.

21

We flew along in our tiny Daihatsu, and halfway to Pinar del Rio, the wheels began to wobble. I slowed down to a more comfortable speed. Viñales, our goal, was another twenty miles beyond that. The sky was angry and a black pall hung over the west. A hurricane was making its trajectory for the southern coast. Just as we got to the border of Pinar del Rio province, it began to rain and the water beat down until the wipers working at full speed couldn't clear the windshield fast enough. The worst of the storm passed in a few minutes, and through it all I kept driving with Leo wiping off the inside glass that kept fogging up.

After our night on opposite sides of the bed, I was surprised we were making the trip at all.

"I don't know what to do," I had said when he opened his eyes that morning.

"About what?"

"Should I go get the rental car?"

"Why not?"

"I thought maybe you didn't want to go."

He took hold of my hand. "I want to go," he growled. "Go get the car and hurry back."

"You just want to get rid of me so you can sleep."

"*Sí*. You know me too well. Go."

When I returned, he was sitting on the bed with his back to the wall, watching the door. He narrowed his eyes and I braced myself for bad news.

"What?" I said.

"You started something yesterday before I went to the wedding," he said gruffly.

"Me?"

"And now you're going to finish it." Then he broke into laughter and grabbed my arm, pulled me toward him. I landed on top of him with his hard-on in my face. I stared at it, and he looked down. Taking it in his hand, he started waving it about, saying, "El toro. El toro."

"Would that be *el toro feroz, Ferdinando?*"

He laughed. "Except this one likes to fight."

As we came into the Viñales Valley, the lush greenery was shimmering under the sun that had poked its head out again. On either side of the car was an endless expanse of tobacco fields only broken by large tent-shaped thatched shelters used for curing. And rising up from the valley floor were oddly shaped humped limestone formations called *mogotes*, capped with greenery. The soil was a deep rust color and contrasted with the leafy green of the tobacco plants. We opened the windows and took in the damp earthy smell, which inspired Leo to light up a cigarette as if in homage to the acres of tobacco.

On the main street of Viñales there was a large old house with a Room-to-Let sign, and a man sat in a rocking chair on a wide porch. It was painted a rosy color and looked in good shape. I parked the car in front and approached the nice-looking man in the rocker. His eyes followed me up to the porch, but when I started to speak he threw back his head in surprise. I asked about the room and his mouth curled up in a shy smile. Without answering, he got up and went into the house. I heard low voices and then a wiry old man came out, shook my hand, and indicated I should follow him to a stairway around on the side that went up to the second floor.

The room was fine and only fifteen a night, but I knew I had to mention that I was with a Cuban. When I told him, I wasn't sure if he had heard me. Without a word he led me back down the steps and around to the front porch before disappearing inside. I waited for the answer and stared at Leo sitting in the car under the stifling mid-afternoon sun with the door swung open.

A stout woman in a food-stained housedress came out and set to moving her mouth rapidly as though she was talking to no one in particular, complaining mostly, about the inspectors who controlled rentals. She felt she had every right to have whoever she wanted stay at her house, but she just couldn't have another run-in with the authorities or she would lose her license. She launched into a convoluted explanation with appropriate anecdotes and criticism of the local inspectors, but the final answer was no. Then she said she had taken the liberty to call her daughter-in-law who knew better how to deal with these situations. She would be coming by shortly.

The man in the rocker perked up and leaned forward. "Here she comes."

A small woman walked toward the house at a good speed. She was skinny, in faded shorts and a sleeveless powdery blue T-shirt. Her hair was cropped. She bounced up the steps with a cigarette dangling from her lips and offered her hand. Up close I could see she was not young; her pinched face was heavily lined.

"My name's Daisy. How can I help you?" she bellowed in a strong, raspy voice.

"I need to find a place for my Cuban friend and me to spend the night. It looks like that's not an easy thing around here."

"You can't do that anywhere." She sounded definite though sympathetic.

"I've never had a problem in Havana or Holguín."

"No, the laws don't permit it. There could be some big fines and people just don't want to risk it. But I know somebody who might do it."

We drove about a quarter mile outside town and Daisy told us to stop in front of a boxy yellow house. There wasn't a tree anywhere on this stretch of the road, and we began to sweat thirty seconds after the

car stopped in full sun. Daisy got out, and a few minutes after entering the house, appeared at the open door with another woman who
examined us from a distance. Then the two women came out with a
determined gait and climbed in the back seat. There was a tension in
the atmosphere like a drug deal, and Leo had fallen into a brooding
quiet.

The women directed us to turn onto a dirt road and then again
onto an even smaller road that was full of ruts and puddles from the
rain. We drove half a block and pulled into a driveway. Across the
road was a tobacco field. There were old car parts around the yard and
faded laundry hanging on the line. The house, it seemed, was away
from the prying eyes of the inspectors.

A crowd, mostly kids, gathered around the car. We all got out and
Daisy's friend went up on the porch to talk to a large woman with
orange hair sitting in a rusty metal lawn chair. I couldn't hear what
they are saying, but the large woman wasn't smiling. With a grunt and
a pained expression tweaking her face, she struggled out of her chair
and came over to the edge of the porch. "Let me show you the room,"
she said. "Come on."

It was dreadfully cheery with floor-to-ceiling lace curtains and a
bedspread stamped with giant red roses. "How much is it?" I said. My
voice had a resigned quality and her eyes lit up.

"Only fifteen dollars," she said sweetly, then added in a more serious tone, "but your friend has to stay at a neighbor's."

She called her pretty teenage daughter and told her to take Leo
down the street to another house where they rented to Cubans. Leo
meekly followed the rolling hips of the country girl, his head down
as they walked away from the house.

I ran after them. "Wait," I said. The girl turned around and looked
at me as if I were deranged. "I don't like this."

"What?" Leo said.

"This is not right."

"Let's go back to Havana then."

I hated the thought of driving all the way back, but I was anxious
to get away from a place where everybody was staring at us as though

we were an alien species. I turned to Daisy and the woman. "We're going back to Havana."

"Suit yourself," said the woman. Daisy let out a moan.

We got back in the car and I waited for it to be pelted with rocks, but instead we just got the blunt daggers of their vacant stares. The whole neighborhood had come out to see the show.

On the way back we drove up to Hotel Los Jazmines to take advantage of what the guidebook said was one of the most photographed views in Cuba. Set high on a hill, the hotel overlooked the valley with its patchwork of fields and the *mogotes* rising up among them. We walked into the bar and ordered beers. The television was on and Leo started to get pulled into a soccer game, but I grabbed his arm and dragged him outside. It was the perfect time of day—just before sunset.

The terrace overlooked the misty green hills and the red soil below, bathed in the golden light of late afternoon. The rain clouds had gone away, leaving behind large white billowy ones. Right below us was a small *mogote* surrounded by a guard of palm trees and to one side was a peak-roofed tobacco shed. An ageless calm settled over the valley, broken only by the occasional shout from the swimming pool filled with families playing and splashing. I tried not to think about driving the two and a half hours back to Havana.

I awoke to the voice, amplified and angry in the regular pounding cadence of Spanish, knocking out its fury. It rose and fell with the shifting sea breeze, fanning out over Vedado, filling each corner, street, road, dead-end alley, patio. Life was at a standstill. Buses and cars were stopped. Banks, stores and offices were closed. The voice bounced off the nearby walls and into our bedroom. I knew that voice, had heard it on TV. It crackled with age, but still full of fight. It climbed, climbed up to lofty peaks, and at each one was *revolución* or *socialismo.* The crowd responded with a roar. Lots of little people with a big voice. They were two blocks away, but I trembled. And then I heard the rallying cry of "Elian Gonzalez."

I pictured the scene on the Malecón, the throng occupying the Tribuna Anti-imperialista, a large square where they held almost daily demonstrations demanding that Elian be returned home. The square was opposite the large building housing the United States Interests Section. They stood in a face-off, the open-air plaza and the steel and concrete monolith, the tropical island David against the sea–to-shining-sea Goliath.

I untangled myself from Leo's embrace, legs crossed here, arms there, and all the sweaty places where our skin touched. I got up and looked out the slats of the balcony doors. The street was full with over-flow from the demonstration, hundreds of red T-shirts and miniature flags, a red sea with splashes of the red, white, and blue of the Cuban flag. Brown hands held soft drinks or ice cream cones from the corner bar. They worked hard on their cones against the heat of mid-morning, and their faces were further contorted by lines of guilt. A day off for the rally, but they had strayed, like bad puppies, not hanging on the word, the voice.

Leo woke up with a snort of disgust. "They don't even let me sleep." His face was puffy and his thick black hair looked like a battle helmet. One hairy leg stuck out from under the sheet. A dark hand against the whiteness, caressed a bulge between his legs. He stared at me, scanning my nakedness through the slits of his barely open eyes. From deep in his throat came a gravelly "Come here. Tell me what you see." He nodded his head toward the street.

"A bunch of people in the street."

He patted the bed next to him, and I kneeled on the spot looking down, down, down into the dark depths of him. He reached up and pinched my nipples, and then using them as handles, he pulled me on top of him, taking a bite of my neck. "Go on. Tell me what's out there. I wanna know. Tell me."

"People in red shirts and lots of little flags…" He squished my face between his hands and kissed me hard. He probed. A surprising ur-gency. With our lips still locked he rolled over on top of me and began grinding his hips into mine. Sunlight streamed in where I had left the slats open and it landed on the foot of the bed, warming my toes.

"What do you hear? Tell me what you hear." His voice was rough, scratchy, riding on hot breath. "Tell me. Tell me. Tell me."

"I hear Fidel and people shouting and…ah, ah…" Now he was tonguing and chewing on my chest, taking away my voice.

He stopped, looked into my eyes, and said, "Tell me what you hear, *coño.*" He sounded angry. I laughed. "Come on. You're making me crazy. Stand up by the window. Look out. Look at the people. Look at the funny people on the street."

I was at the doors again, peering through the slats. He came up behind me and started biting the back of my neck. His tongue plunged into my ear. My knees were weak until he wrapped me in his arms, pulled me close.

"Look at the people. Look at my country," he whispered, his mouth on my ear, the hot wisps of air tickling deep nerves. "All right," he said. "Now. Do you feel it? Do you feel it? Look at the people. Can you see them? Come on. Look. Look. Look."

A pair of eyes down in the street seemed to be watching us. Leo pushed harder. "*Todo para tí, amor.* It's all for you, love. And they can see us. Yes. Yes. Everybody. Look at them. Look at them. They see us. This is the revolution. The revolution. Here. You and me. You and me. We are it, baby."

I reached up and grabbed the top slats of the door with my hands curling around the thin old wood. The door rattled. Puzzled people looked up. In the distance the voice said *libertad* and something about the *imperialistas.* Big applause and all the lost people on the street turned their heads away from the rattling door and toward the roar of the crowd.

The voice went on and on, building, building. It was feeling its power. Leo was in sync, rising, rising, rising, then slowing down and rising again.

"*Socialismo o muerte,*" shouted the voice. "*Viva la revolución. Viva la revolución.*"

"*Coñooooo…*" screamed Leo. Explosion. I answered on the flowery Spanish tiles of the floor. We collapsed on the bed, twin towers falling down. He was still holding me tight. His body twitched and jerked, twitched, jerked, twitched. Then ripples in a pond fading into eternity.

"Oh, God. Oh, shit," he said. "Shit. Oh fuck." He started to laugh. I laughed, too, and both our bodies shook to the beat of the cheering and clapping of the crowd, the cheering and clapping, the clapping and cheering. Then the noise died down. Silence. No voice. No crowd. And we went still, too.

The steamy air from his lips moved closer, found my ear. He whispered, "We are the revolution, baby."

Playing tennis before it got too hot sounded like a good idea, but I failed in getting Leo up at a decent hour. We didn't get to the Hotel Nacional until noon, but the one well-maintained court, set off by towering trees, was free. Leo started off hitting poorly and complained of being sore from the paddleball we had played at the beach the day before. But then he began controlling the ball and hitting forehands that I had a hard time getting to. A smile soon brightened his cranky features and his confidence soared. I was amazed at his rapid improvement since the first time we played in January.

At one side of the court was a hole in the fence and a group of four young boys—seven or eight years old—appeared at the opening and stuck their heads in. Gradually they worked their whole bodies through and were on the court. If a ball came near them, they picked it up and threw it back to us. Little by little they became bolder and started chasing balls. Though they weren't quite up with ball-boy etiquette, it was a relief not to have to chase down the balls in the hot sun. Our bodies were soon covered with sweat and our shorts soaked through, but we forged on with the tennis game as Leo was determined to improve.

We stayed the full hour we had paid for, but were exhausted. Our ball boys followed us down the hill from the hotel, and we gave them a couple of the balls that were going dead. They joked with us and kept asking how much the rackets cost. One boy continually bounced a ball, seeing how high he could make it go. Another boy took hold of my arm as we walked along, and kept calling me *Señor*. His hands were rough, but his touch was gentle. He had several scars on his brown scrawny arms.

"*Señor*, where are you from? *Señor*, do you throw away your clothes when you take them off at night? *Señor. Señor.*"

The question perplexed me. I understood the words, but not what he was asking. Leo explained that they thought foreigners were so rich that they never wore the same clothes twice. At night you threw your clothes away and in the morning put on new ones.

"See these shorts," I said to the boy. "I've worn them for ten years."

"No, you're joking with me," he said in disbelief, still holding on to my arm. His shorts were dirty and too big. He used a piece of rope for a belt and his dusty tennis shoes were without laces. Then as suddenly as they appeared, they were gone, running up one of the side streets. My new friend stopped in the middle of the street, turned around, and waved. Then he ran and caught up with his friends.

"Do you like kids?" asked Leo.

"If you remember I have one, though she's not a kid anymore. She's the light of my life. I'm sure I'll like your child. Don't worry."

"I just wondered." That he was going to be a father was still a vague concept. I imagined it would be my job as *Tío* Martin to spoil the child rotten.

Back at the apartment I got a phone call from Julie's friend, Madelin. Julie was a colleague who had been in Cuba the summer I met Leo. She invited me over one afternoon for lunch and I met Madelin. Every time someone was going to Cuba Julie made up little packages to send to her friend. She wanted to come over and pick up the package that I had brought for her.

During my conversation Leo was out on the balcony, smoking a cigarette. When I got off the phone, he came in and said with a half-suppressed grin, "I'm going out for a minute. They called me from down on the street."

"What?"

"Don't worry. You know I don't like black girls."

"I don't know what you're talking about." He was half out the door and didn't explain. I thought he was kidding and just going across the street to buy cigarettes. I stepped out on the balcony, and with a knot in my gut, stared at him sitting on the corner talking to two young black girls. They looked up, and I quickly turned to go back inside.

I had often pondered the fact that since we had been together, he had displayed little interest in women. He never gawked at women or made comments as many Cuban men do when an attractive girl passes by on the street. In my memory he had never made a single remark about the attractiveness of a female on TV, on the street, or anywhere we had been. I had never seen him flirt, and only with Sulyn the summer before in Holguín had I seen him be physical with a girl. So it was a mystery why he would go out and talk to two strangers who called him down from the street.

He came back in a short time with his nonchalant stride, approached me like a hesitant puppy, and kissed me quickly.

"What was that all about?"

"Nothing. Those girls motioned for me to come down and talk to them."

"You're that easy, huh?"

"No harm in talking to them. I told you I don't like girls like that. They said they were looking for this handsome guy with spiky hair and a goatee they had seen on the balcony a few times." His hair was natural today, and he had just shaved off his goatee. "I told them it was me and they acted surprised. Then you came out and looked at us."

"I wasn't spying."

"They asked me if you were my boyfriend."

"And what did you said?"

"Of course. I told you that I don't hide you from anybody."

"And what if they had been pretty white girls?"

"Same answer," he said without hesitation. "You should trust me more. By the way, where's your ring?"

"It's safe in the drawer."

"I didn't give it to you so that it could sit in a drawer."

"I took it off when we went to the beach the other day. It's loose and I didn't want it to fall off."

"I want to see you wear it."

22

Ricardo and Miguel showed up for dinner in matching outfits—faded jeans and red shirts, Miguel's a T-shirt that had Levi's across the front and Ricardo's a buttoned-down shirt of a clingy fabric. They wore pointy cowboy boots that were all the rage.

We were lucky to finish dinner before the power went off for the third time in a week. Leo grabbed a bottle of Havana Club and we took some chairs out on the balcony. He poured the first few drops onto the tile floor for the *orishas*.

Gerard arrived for an after-dinner drink and announced that his friend who made the documentary *Gay Cuba* was in town. We were invited to a screening in his apartment on the weekend. From there he steered the conversation to gay life in Cuba. His eyes swung out over the room in an exaggerated arc. "I guess I should say, men who have sex with men." He never tired of the subject.

Miguel was surprisingly open about his relationship with Ricardo. He had been married, and his wife and two kids lived just a few doors down from him. Several times I had seen a boy and a girl playing at his house. They often crawled into his lap. I thought they were neighborhood kids, and just hung around his house because he had video games and a nice TV. I now realized they were his children. He said that he and his wife were still close, the kids saw Ricardo as a third parent, and everybody in his family knew about his relationship with Ricardo. Ricardo, too, said that his family back in Holguín knew he was living with Miguel.

Leo, who had been very quiet, piped up. "Martin has only just told his family about me. They think I am a hustler or something." He threw the words in my direction and caught me off-guard. "See, he doesn't even deny it. He doesn't want them to know anything about me."

"I don't want to upset them any more than I already have."

"Does your mom know about Martin?" Gerard asked Leo.

"Of course. She met him."

"But I mean does she *know* about Martin?"

"She knows that he is my friend and that I love him. That's all she needs to know."

"That's the problem," Gerard said. "People here know, but they don't want to talk about it." There was a creaking sound from the balcony next door, someone shifting in a chair. We turned to look as the middle-aged neighbor in the shadows inched toward her door. Just on the other side of the balcony wall, she had been listening to our conversation, probably heard every scandalous word. We looked at each other with twisted smiles.

"Gerard," Leo said in a lowered voice, "think about where my mom lives, what kind of education she's had. She doesn't interfere. The one thing I can't stand is people trying to tell me what to do."

"That's right," said Ricardo. "People are always butting in. They look at the way I dress and think they know me."

Leo sat up in his chair and said with a sense of pride, "I've always tried to dress cool, look good, you know, and for that people ask me if I'm a *pinguero*."

"And what do you say?" Gerard said menacingly.

"Fuck you, Gerard," said Leo.

"Take it easy. I'm just kidding."

"Hey, *callado*," Leo said to me. "You're so quiet. Say something. Defend me in front of your friend."

"I always defend you. Ask Gerard if I don't."

"Martin would do anything for you," Gerard said. "Don't doubt it. And I suppose if you hadn't met him you would probably be sitting around the TV with your wife and mother back in Holguín, thinking about having kids."

"You said more than you know," I pointed out. "Leo wants to have it all, apparently. His wife is pregnant."

"Oh," Gerard said and held up his glass. "I guess I should have said congratulations."

"Save it. It's not until November." Leo let me know with a hard stare that I shouldn't have brought it up.

Leo offered to go get another bottle of rum.

"Count me out," said Gerard. "I want to be able to ride my bike home without falling off."

Miguel and Ricardo prepared to leave, too.

Everybody stood up, and then, in a block-by-block chain of emerging lights, the whole neighborhood became illuminated. A rumble in the bedroom brought the air conditioner to life, and Leo and I breathed a sigh of relief knowing that we would be able to sleep.

The air at the farmer's market at Calle 19 and B was heavy with the smell of coffee, black beans, and pork from the prepared food vendors. Along the main aisle the produce sellers were sluggish behind piles of plump mangoes, muddy bunches of carrots, and long stringy beans, and would only get up off their crates if it looked like you were going to buy.

The only sellers that seemed to have energy were the butchers, who sent out hawkers to reel in customers. "How much meat do you want? We have a good selection. You want lamb? Here, leg of lamb." A young man pulled us over to his partner's stall, grabbed the leg, and stuck it in our faces.

"I don't know," I said.

"What do you mean, you don't know?" Leo said. "How much do you want to buy?" He'd woken up with a scowl and had been in a foul mood all day.

"You decide." I wasn't used to buying meat in open-air markets with flies swarming all over bloody carcasses.

He rolled his eyes. "Do you want some meat or not?"

"Relax. What's the big deal?"

The seller had been hovering, but stepped back as if witnessing a domestic quarrel.

"The big deal is that he's waiting and that's the last leg of lamb." Cubans hated looking silly and indecisive in front of other Cubans.

"Get it if you think it's a good buy." The guy weighed the leg and the price sounded like a lot of money, probably a lot more than a Cuban would pay. I peeled off the worn peso bills and paid the butcher with a smile.

Buying the fruit and vegetables was easier. It's likely I got overcharged there, too, but it was a matter of a few cents. We loaded everything into my pack and he slung it on his back. He was sullen on the walk home, and when I asked him if he wanted me to carry it a while, he shook his head and said it wasn't too heavy.

He started cooking as soon as we got home. He was a fan of using the pressure cooker for everything, so he cut some of the lamb meat off the bone, and threw it into the pot with some onions. I went to work on my notes, and he sat on the sofa, staring at the wall.

"What's wrong?" I asked.

He got up and left the room.

I lost track of time, and then raised my head to the smell of burning meat. "The lamb is burning!" I shouted.

We both ran into the kitchen from opposite ends of the house, and he dragged the scalding pot off the burner and into the sink. It was too hot to open up, so we left it and went into living room to be away from the acrid smoke.

"Were you upset by the conversation with Gerard, Ricardo, and Miguel last night? I mean the gay stuff?"

"I'm always interested in hearing other people's opinions."

"You didn't have a lot to say."

"I'm comfortable with who I am, and all I ask is that other people respect that. I thought what Ricardo and Miguel said was cool. They never talk about those things around me alone. I think in a few years, I'll be like Miguel."

His words hung in the air between us. So many times he seemed on the brink of acknowledging being bisexual.

"You mean living with a man and having your family close by?"

He shrugged. "Why not?"

He went back into the kitchen.

"Shit," I heard from the other room. The lamb was burnt beyond recognition. I suggested we get some of the box lunches from the place across from Luka's.

Luka was upstairs on the enclosed rooftop terrace, propped up on the rattan sofa watching a rented video, *The Green Mile*. It was well into the film, and Leo and I got hooked right away. By the end, Leo and I were sniffling.

Monica came up the stairs with a tray of coffee. " Oo-ee. What's going on here, my teary-eyed babies?"

"A sad movie," I said.

"That's just like guys to cry over a movie, but not real life."

"Who's crying?" said Leo.

"Forget it. I've got an idea. I'm crazy to go out tonight," she said. "There's a place right on the corner called La Red that gets very good on Friday nights. Do you guys want to go? I hate to leave Luka alone, but I'm sure he'll be all right."

"Don't worry about me," said Luka.

"I'd like to go," said Leo. He turned to me with the first hint of brightness I had seen in his face all day.

"I have to get up early tomorrow. They're picking me up at eight to go on a tour of the sanatorium in Santiago de Las Vegas. But you two should go."

"Sure you don't mind?" said Leo.

"I know you're bored staying home every night."

He reached over and touched my forehead. "Are you feeling all right?"

"Very funny. Just go."

I woke up early in the morning to find that Leo had not returned. I lay in bed and thought about the mercurial nature of Cuba, how life on the island is a reflection of the Caribbean climate. A blue sky can quickly go black and dump buckets of rain on your head. The sea, so azure and inviting one minute, can suddenly churn and toss boats over on their sides. A wind can appear from nowhere and take the roof off your house. I knew it and yet wasn't prepared for it. Leo was the Caribbean, erratic and unfettered. And I was a product of my culture that simply saw him as irresponsible. It didn't seem that either of us was going to change.

Dr. Sanz, whom I had met on the last trip, invited me to bring my medical donations, meet with the staff, and then have lunch in Santiago de Las Vegas. It was a chance to visit the best-known of the HIV sanatoriums, the rapid response system set up in Cuba when the first soldiers returned from Africa with the disease. Luka had told me about living in a sanatorium, and then Tomás explained to me in more detail about Cuba's controversial reaction to HIV, at first a mandatory quarantine. Not surprisingly there was an outcry in Miami, calling it a human rights abuse.

"Like the Miami Cubans actually care," Tomás said bitterly, "about a few soldiers fighting in Africa and queers fucking around with tourists. But along with the fanatical voices of Miami, there were also more rational voices from within and outside Cuba that questioned such a strict policy. Going to a sanatorium isn't obligatory anymore, and I think it was wise to change the policy."

Upon entering the sanatorium grounds, I was immediately struck by the tranquil beauty of the place. There was a long palm-lined driveway up to the main building with tropical plants and flowering bushes on both sides. In front of the administration center a white statue of a naked wood nymph stood on a marble pedestal. The front of the whitewashed building was a series of wide, red-trimmed arches and the roof was of sun-faded Mediterranean tile. Two young men leisurely walked by. One had his hand on the other's shoulder, and they stopped their conversation and smiled at the passing car. A pair of nurses in starched white uniforms, one male and one female, hurried across the spongy green lawn from one building to another.

With my large duffle bag full of medicine in hand, the driver escorted me quickly out of the hot sun and into the shade of the arches. We passed through an inner courtyard into a bare outer office where they had cranked up the air conditioning to Siberian temperatures. I was asked to wait outside Dr. Sanz's office while he made his rounds. After a few minutes, a tall young woman with a head of cascading brown hair came in and introduced herself as Elizabeth Paniagua, Chief Psychologist of the center. "I'll be meeting with you later, but I just wanted to say hello and thank you for all the aid you have brought us."

"It is really Tomás. I'm just the donkey," I said, and she laughed.

Dr. Sanz burst into the office a short time later. About my age, he was short, stocky and full of nervous energy. He greeted me, talked about his rounds, asked an assistant to bring us coffee, and led me into his office all at the same time.

"There are some soft gel tabs in there," I said, pointing to the bag. "I'm concerned because they were out in the sun while I was waiting to be picked up."

"Oh, sorry you had to wait. I'll have somebody come and take out the things that need to be refrigerated."

We had coffee and he asked about Tomás and some of the other people he had met in Los Angeles when he had been there on a speaking tour several years before. After a few words, he stood up. "I've asked my assistant to take you on a tour, and then we will get together for lunch with Elizabeth and some of the other staff."

In the private dining room for the higher-level staff, we had beans, rice and salad like the patients, but with the addition of grilled fish filets and ice cream for dessert. Elizabeth wanted to know about my research on Martí, but I told her that it seemed far less important than the work she was doing. "I'm curious," I said, "how effective you think your education programs are here. I mean, how do you know people are actually practicing safe sex?"

"The numbers prove it. Let me speak frankly with you. Cubans are very sexual people. Some of our residents report having large numbers of sexual partners. Divorce rates and incidences of extramarital sex are high among the heterosexual population. Yet Cuba has one of the lowest HIV-transmission rates in the world. People are educated and they use protection. Have you seen the publicity for condoms?"

"It's great, but I've heard people say condoms aren't always available, and some of the Chinese ones are bad."

"What you say was unfortunately true for brief periods in the past, but we are working hard to correct this situation. Only last week a huge shipment of good quality condoms arrived."

Cubans who are part of the system always balk when you bring up something that isn't working, especially in the areas of health and education, the two pillars of socialist progress in Cuba. They will admit when something is obviously wrong, but are quick to point out the positive, even at the risk of sounding as if they are just spouting the official line.

When the car pulled up in front of the building, Leo was leaning over the balcony, smoking a cigarette. He was shirtless and his hair glistened in the sun. I gave him a small wave and trudged up the stairs weighing my options. Tamping down the anger was the best I could come up with.

He opened the door and kissed me. "How did it go?"

"It was great. I met some nice people and ran into a friend of Luka's I met only last year, but he has gotten bigger and quite muscular. I hardly recognized him."

Leo looked at me strangely and we retreated into the bedroom, closed the windows and turned on the air conditioning. The circles under his eyes were more pronounced than usual.

"Did you get any sleep?" I asked.

"A few hours. I fell asleep on the sofa at Luka's. We had a good time in La Red and then when it closed, we went over to La Rampa. I ran into that guy, Diego, from Holguín, remember the one we went to the party with in January? He just arrived in town yesterday."

We lay down on the bed in a loose embrace, and Leo quickly dozed off. I got up and worked on my notes, but when I went in later, Leo was sitting up in bed, staring at the wall. There was a chill in the air.

"I'm going to Holguín." He spoke as if it was the final solution to a horrible dilemma.

"What? When?"

"Today. I have to deal with some construction issues on the house. You know my mother is there alone and they could try to cheat her. There needs to be a man around to make sure everything is okay."

I sat down on the bed with my back to him. It felt like the end. I got an eerie, imploding feeling. I could hear myself breathing.

"I promise I'll be back in a few days. Maybe a break will be good for us. Help me pack some things. I'll leave most of my stuff here. Don't be sad." He moved close to hug me.

I shook off his embrace and stood up. "Take all your stuff if you want. You don't have to pretend that you're coming back."

He grabbed my arm and pulled me down. He put his mouth close to my ear and whispered. "I'm coming back. I promise. And you better wait for me."

I let out a groan as if the possibility of not waiting for him were remote.

We put a couple pairs of underwear, some T-shirts, a pair of jeans, and his toiletries in a bag. I reeled in my emotions, and at the door gave him a hug. But I fantasized packing up the rest of his things and asking Ricardo to come and get them the following day. I, too, had the urge to escape. I marched over to Luka's house, beating up the sidewalk with my feet, and punched the doorbell.

Monica let me in and I kissed her on the cheek. "*Como estàs?*" she said.

"*Más o menos*," I said. It took her about two seconds to change the expression on her face.

"What's wrong?"

"I need to talk to Luka." She pointed toward his bedroom.

"What happened?" Luka asked. "Did Leo do something?"

"He went back to Holguín."

"What?"

"He just left. Said he needed to deal with the construction, that he couldn't trust the workers."

"Do you believe that's the reason?"

"I think he just wants to get away."

Monica came and stood in the doorway.

"Did he said anything to you last night about going to Holguín?" I asked her.

"Not a word. Did you guys fight?"

"Well, I wasn't happy that he never came home last night."

"He never came home?"

"He told me he fell asleep on the sofa here." Monica looked at Luka and scrunched up her face as if she had stuck her foot in her mouth. "Did he sleep on the sofa or not?"

They were both silent. I had put them in the impossible position of ratting on a fellow Cuban. "Look," Monica said, "after we left La Red, we went to La Rampa and he ran into a friend from Holguín."

"He told me that much."

"Then I was tired and I came home. I left him sitting there talking to his friend. Now if he came back here later and somehow got in and slept on the sofa, I don't know."

"I can't say," said Luka. "I was asleep with the doors closed."

"So he didn't sleep on the sofa." I got up to go.

"Why don't you stay for dinner?"

"Thanks, but I need to go home. Maybe we can do something later."

Shortly after I got back to the apartment, the phone rang. It was Leo, saying he couldn't get a ticket to Holguín and was coming back. He would try again the next day. When he arrived, the first thing he did was drop his bag and kiss me. I took him by the hand into the bedroom and we sat down on the bed.

"You didn't sleep on the sofa at Luka's. Why did you tell me that?"

My directness surprised him and he hesitated. "I didn't want you to think I was out with someone else."

"Were you?"

"No, of course not. I'm not looking for anybody else. I told you I was with my friend from Holguín, and you know, sometimes you just need to have some space and go a little crazy. We were drinking and sitting on the wall like the night I met you."

"But lying doesn't accomplish anything, especially a lie that is so easy for me to discover. Why can't you just tell the truth?"

"I'm afraid every time you go back to the States that I'm never going to see you again and that you aren't going to help me. It has happened to plenty of people I know. I have to protect myself."

"And I have to protect myself. I've tried to explain what I've gone through in the last year, the problems with my wife and daughter. Sometimes I wonder what it's all for. It's so hard for me to know if you—"

"If I what? Love you? You still have doubts? You'll never trust me. Maybe it's better that we just end it. You need to find someone who is not such a burden on you, someone who doesn't need help."

His conclusion shook me. There was a minute of silence. He was giving me a way out. Wasn't that what I wanted, never having to deal with this uncertainty again, the long separations, the financial drain, the fears of traveling illegally? I could be free. He was presenting it as a logical conclusion, not in a fit of anger. I imagined myself saying yes, that he was right. His bag was already packed. It would save us both a lot of pain and suffering. I opened my mouth several times to agree to his suggestion, but the words wouldn't come out. The thought of never seeing him again seemed stupid.

I turned to him with a funny grin on my face. "Now explain to me again why we are breaking up. I'm not sure I get it."

"You don't get it because you don't want to."

"Do *you* want to break up?"

"I thought I should make the offer."

"You're a pain in the ass."

"Oh, yeah. I'll show you what a pain in the ass is." He pushed me back on the bed and jumped on top of me, holding my hands with one arm and with the other hand tickling me. I screamed and squirmed, which only made him go at it harder. In a short time we moved through a field of emotions, from the fear of breaking up to the joy of laughing to the peace of holding each other for a long time. We slept stuck together all night.

Madelin called to ask if we were still interested in playing tennis. She was having a lesson at five o'clock, so we could play at her club, and then have dinner at her house. Leo was still asleep and I didn't know what his plans were. I said I'd call her back. When he got up, I told him about Madelin's invitation and he liked the idea. There was no mention of going to Holguín.

Madelin arrived at the Pan-American tennis complex, looking like a star in her short white skirt and Adidas top. She had the kind of attractiveness that my younger brother would fall for. Her curly hair looked naturally blond, though I knew it wasn't. Like most Cuban women, she dressed to accentuate her sexuality rather than hide it. She was tall, long-legged, had large round breasts, and carried herself as if she had been trained as a model. Yet she was one of the sweetest and most natural Cubans I had met.

We played on the court beside her and after the lesson walked over to her house a few blocks away where she lived with her mother. The block-long apartment building smacked of socialist architecture with its concrete walls and lack of adornment. The treeless grounds were littered with garbage and tattered plastic bags fluttered in the breeze. Children played stickball in the trampled dusty grass, and on the sidewalk rolled about on homemade skateboards. It was hard to imagine that this was where the stylish Madelin lived. Once inside the apartment, the depressing exterior was forgotten. The walls were lined with framed art prints and photographs of Madelin and her brother, who lived in Spain. The modern furniture had the sleek and functional flair of the 50's, and a new TV and stereo system were visible.

Madelin's mother, Elena, greeted us warmly and asked about Julie. I could tell right away that she was not from Havana. She had the down-home demeanor of Eastern Cuba and took to Leo right away when she found out that he was from her hometown of Holguín. As we sat down to a dinner of lobster in a tomato sauce, corn fritters, fried bananas, rice, and a salad of avocado and tomatoes, I was amazed at how normal it felt. Elena doted on Leo like her long-lost son and listened with glowing smiles as he told about the upcoming birth of his child. For an outsider looking in on the table scene, one might think that Elena and I were a couple, Madelin our daughter, who had invited her boyfriend, Leo, over for dinner. At the same time, I couldn't imagine too many Cubans being shocked when they found out a quite different reality. Like Madelin and Elena—listening to Leo talking one minute about becoming a father and the next how I snored too loud—everybody we encountered seemed unfazed by our friendship. In Cuba, relationships with foreigners have a particular set of standards.

I came to dread the phone ringing. It always seemed to bring problems. Leo got an early morning call to go have lunch with his ex-wife, which he accepted without consulting me.

"Is there any coffee?" he asked.

"As soon as you make it, there will be."

"Come on. You know how hard this is for me."

"What? Leaving me behind to go have lunch with your ex?"

"No, that's torture. I mean getting up." Even in his morning stupor he could come up with something clever. "If it were my choice, I'd just stay in bed all day with you."

"What a bullshitter!"

Later, after he showered and put on a navy blue shirt with white dragons and Chinese characters on it, a pair of tight jeans, and a dab of cologne, I said "You don't need to look that good."

He kissed me and headed out the door. "I'll be back in a few hours."

The terrace-louvered doors were closed, and I looked out through the slats. He was sitting at an outside table at the place across the street, a beer in one hand and a cigarette in the other. I was a harem girl looking out from the latticework vents, the only view to the outside world from my sheltered life. I could see the people on the street ambling by, but they couldn't see me. I watched Leo and watched what he watched. I tried to catch him following girls with his eyes as they passed by, though all he did was look toward each car that pulled up to the curb to let people out. Two young, scantily dressed girls walked by and gave him the eye. He glanced at them, and then back to watching the passing cars.

The phone rang and I went to answer it. It was for the neighbor on the shared line, so I told them to call back and I let it ring. When I went back to the balcony door, he was gone. I felt cheated. I missed seeing him get in the car, maybe hug and kiss her, missed my chance to feel like an utter jerk in a hot flash of jealousy.

I went out for a walk, but people looked at me like I was a freak, a foreigner alone in the city where no one was alone. The pavement radiated the stored-up heat from the day, and there was no hint of a cooling rain in the air, but looking down La Rampa, I made out a mirage of puddles in the street near the end of the gentle downward slope. From one of the cafes, dance music was blaring—Los Van Van grinding out the song, "Quién no ha dicho una mentira?" I thought about the lyrics—"Who has not told a lie?"—and wondered why people told so many. Five hours had passed since Leo left. Why would he go off with his ex-wife, who supposedly meant little to him, and leave me wondering and waiting? Maybe our whole relationship was a lie.

From the cafeteria, a pungent mélange of fried chicken and coffee wafted out and hung in the air. I walked, eyeing the pavement until the keen sense of eyes boring into me made me lift my head. An athletic young man in a baseball cap, shorts, and a tank top passed by, and when I looked back, he had stopped. If it was all lies, what did it matter if I had a little fun? He waited, brown muscular arms crossed in front of him, an aloof expression on his face now that the bait had been taken. He reached down, touched his crotch, focused in on me and raised one eyebrow. I froze in his icy stare.

He motioned with the slightest tilt of his head for me to join him, and I floated toward him with a churning in my gut. The bright lights of the cafeteria were at his back as he faced the much softer light of the street, and I couldn't see his face well, couldn't guess his age. Did it matter? I got close and took notice of his long sideburns pointing down like arrows, and his teenage attempt at a goatee. He was handsome despite his pockmarked skin.

He addressed me, "Hi, how are ya doing?" in authentic street English.

"Okay," I croaked.

"You from Italy?"

"No, from the U.S."

"Good, because my Italian not so good. I like USA."

"Probably more than I do," I mumbled.

"I have an uncle in New Jersey." He took out his wallet and went through a stack of little pieces of paper with names and addresses scribbled on them until he found the one from Union City, New Jersey and showed it to me. I marveled at this practice, which I had witnessed several times. Were a few scraps of paper supposed to convince me that he was a reliable person?

"I also have a friend in Kentucky." He showed me another address.

"I bet you have friends all over," I said.

He gave me a suspicious glance. "Not so many. No one special."

"Are you looking for someone special?"

"I just like to meet new people. You never know what is going to happen. What about you?"

"I have someone special." There I killed it. The spark of interest for a man other than Leo always died quickly. Was it possible to be gay for just one person?

"Does he know you are out wandering the streets?"

"No. He's probably on his way home, so I need to get back."

The boy let out a small snort of disgust as if I was wasting his time. "You'd better go then."

I pushed my glasses up on my nose. "I hope you find what you're looking for."

"I'm not looking for nothing."

When I got back to our street, there was a light on in the apartment, and I bounded up the stairs, put the key in the lock, and pushed the door open with, "I'm home." And then I remembered I had left the light on. The silence was oppressive, and I raced into the bedroom to put on some music.

23

With a sour taste in my mouth I opened a suspicious eye on the morning and confirmed that there was an empty space next to me in the bed. In a few minutes I had a plan. He had offered me my freedom and I had failed to take it. But after his latest disappearing act, I felt I had no choice. I dragged myself out of bed and began to move in a flurry, packing up all his things. I carefully included everything that I brought him as gifts, but excluded any of my belongings he showed an interest in and probably would have ended up with at the end of the trip had things gone better. I carried the bag to the living room and set it on the sofa by the front door. When he arrived, I would hand him the bag.

I sat down with his things next to me, under the giant Sacred Heart of Jesus picture, and draped my arm over the bag, giving it one last hug. Though I was convinced my action was right, my heart had an irregular gait. Then the phone rang and I jumped. It was Gerard.

"How is everything, dearie?" he said in a chipper voice that made me want to strangle him.

"Oh, just great!"

"Uh-oh. Tell me what's going on."

I told him the latest episode of my sad-ass saga, including the part about packing up Leo's bag and putting it by the door.

"You sure you want to do that?"

"I can't let him treat me like this. He hasn't even called."

"How much longer do you have in your trip?"

"A week."

"How were things going before he left on his adventure?"

The question brought to mind the several times we had had sex in the last few days. "All right, I guess."

"My advice is to unpack that bag as quickly as you can. The kind of confrontation you're headed for rarely has a good result. You're forcing him to react, and it could be very unpleasant. You risk embittering your last week, and if you regret it later, you might have gone too far to resolve things between you. He may be immature, but he's only done what almost every Cuban man does on a regular basis. Not an excuse, just a fact. What I would do is the opposite. When he comes back, and he will, just act as casual as you can. Act like you had a wonderful time without him, but now that he is back you can pick up where you left off."

I let out an extended breath, fingering the zipper on the bag, and thought about what he said. "It just drives me crazy when he disappears like that."

"You have to be the mature one. You don't have it in you to play the jealous Cuban wife role, so if you want to enjoy the rest of your vacation, just let go of the anger. Believe me, I know."

I knew as soon as I got off the phone that he was right. It was my wounded ego that wanted to make a scene, not me. I hated scenes and I wasn't much good at them. They always brought out a side of me that I disliked. In record time I had everything back in its place. When it was all done, I felt better and called Luka to make lunch plans. Monica answered.

"Luka is still sleeping. Do you guys want to come over for lunch?"

"It will probably be just me. Leo has disappeared again." I told her about packing and unpacking the bag, forcing myself to laugh about it.

"You did the right thing," she said. "Just act like nothing is unusual at all. And don't expect an apology. He knows he has done something wrong, but he doesn't know how to deal with it. I've seen it a thousand times. It's his ex-wife. Give him a break. Show him why you are much better for him than she is. I think he has already made his choice, but he is probably having a hard time completely separating himself from her."

"Thanks, Monica. I appreciate your advice. Tell Luka to call me when he gets up."

I had a very short time to ponder my new plan. There was a knock at the door, and he was all smiles and kisses, as if he had just been gone a couple of hours. I held my tongue.

"She wouldn't let me leave. Every time I tried, she got upset. She insisted I go with her to the immigration office this morning."

The conversation moved to the island of our bed. I sat, leaning against the wall with a pillow at my back and he put his head in my lap. "I wanted to be with you, you know. But sometimes you just get caught. She's been very good to me over the years, and I feel I owe her something."

"Is she still in love with you?"

"Do you think so?"

"Don't tell me you don't know."

"But I'm not in love with her."

"I know. It all ended when you met me."

He laughed, but didn't answer. I absent-mindedly ran my fingers through his thick slightly damp black hair. He closed his eyes and I knew he could be asleep in two minutes. "Don't go to sleep," I said.

"Why not?"

"Just don't go to sleep."

"Mmmm," he said as he pulled me down into a lying position. He got on top of me and put his mouth on mine. His tongue slipped past my teeth and probed deep inside. He pulled it out and started chewing on my lips. "So you missed me, huh?"

"Did I say that? If I did, it was just to seduce you."

"You're a bad boy. Were you a bad boy last night?"

"How could I be? You weren't here. I only want to do bad things with you."

The streets were noisy with late-afternoon traffic, and the sidewalks bustled with a post-siesta exodus from shaded parlors. Leo kept his eyes on the distant objective: the Cubacel office on La Rampa. We had gotten his phone charged and were going to activate service. I took in everything: the people walking by, the number of easily identifiable foreigners, how people were dressed and if they looked poor, the ratio of new cars to old ones, if people looked as if they were getting enough to eat, and in general, sizing up the country. At times I tried to justify the difficulty of life on the island by looking at the big picture, the successes, the tiny steps toward progress. At other times I saw a society of absurd contradictions, a people with boundless energy going nowhere at a dreamlike pace. Was it really much different than where I was from? People in Los Angeles certainly looked as though they knew where they were going and were much better decked-out for the journey, but where were they headed? And then for a moment I imagined I was back home as a car pulled up alongside with Latin hip-hop music booming so loud I could feel the bass in my chest. I turned to see if Leo felt it, too, and realized we had gotten separated.

Near the corner of Calle 23 and L, he had stopped and was talking to someone whom I immediately knew to be a foreigner. My shoulders locked up as he motioned for me to come back.

Leo mumbled a quick introduction, and though I missed the name, I guessed that he was Italian. He had a hooked nose, curly dark hair going to gray, and sad droopy eyes. A significant paunch was visible under his Lacoste shirt and skinny white legs stuck out from his khaki Bermuda shorts. He looked stunned and about to buckle under the weight of Leo's hand resting lightly on his shoulder. With his other hand, Leo patted the man's stomach and smiled broadly as if to say, "Isn't this great fun?" I put my hand on my stomach, thinking that it wasn't the flat board of few years back, but it wasn't nearly so prominent as this fellow's. I quickly felt superior and confused at the same time. Why was Leo touching this person?

I backed away from something I didn't understand, and bumped into a passer-by, who gave me an annoyed look. Leo slid his hand off the man's shoulder and reached out to catch me as I stumbled.

Leo said to the Italian, "We should have a beer some time, next time I run into you." He grabbed the man's hand and shook it while the Italian stood like a zombie. Leo touched my arm and steered me toward the green light for crossing the street.

"Who was *that*?" I asked, as if we had just encountered a beggar with viscous liquids oozing from multiple lesions.

"That is the Italian guy that I told you about. I'm surprised he recognized me after so long. I look different now."

"Oh, the one you…oh…." The tip of my sandal caught the edge of the curb as we stepped up on the other side of the street, and I faltered a second time.

He took my arm. "What's the matter with you?"

"It must be the heat." He looked at me suspiciously, and I forced a smile.

I had just looked in a mirror and seen a ghost, a ghost of the future, some years hence, when I might run into Leo on the street with his new lover. My belly was in a knot and the air was too dense to breathe.

"Snap out of it. You can't be jealous. I haven't even seen him in a couple of years. That's all in the past."

"Of course. It's the past." I again scrunched up my mouth in a weird imitation of a smile.

When I had observed Leo next to the Italian, it looked like the clichéd mature foreigner with his local boy, pure sexonomics, as Tomás called it. I had always believed that Leo and I fit together in a different way, that we were as innocent as two boys lost in the woods, helping each other find the way out, that we were two guys bound together by love. I couldn't bear that others saw us in the way I had seen Leo standing next to the Italian.

"I wish I had my cap," I said. "My scalp is getting burned."

He took off his and put it on my head. I immediately felt protected from the sun and less vulnerable to the quizzical eyes of the people around us, who might not share my vision of Leo and me. After another couple of silent blocks, we ducked into the Cubacel office, escaping the crowd, letting the soothing air conditioning settle around us.

We had the rental car another day and I had promised Gerard a trip to the beach with what I called his orphan boys, a few teenagers from poor families he liked to help out and take on excursions when he could. Two of them were younger brothers of an ex-boyfriend and another was a neighbor who often came by his house to play video games. The six of us piled in the Hyundai—the three boys were so small and thin they took up little room—and soon we were on the crowded highway toward Santa Maria del Mar.

It was the hottest part of the day when we got to the stretch of sand between Mi Cayito and Guanabo, and Gerard set about first thing to build a shelter to protect his white skin. He sent the boys out to scrounge for the longest branches they could find, and then he knotted the four corners of a large beach towel to the stakes, though the branches the boys dragged back were short, making for a squat tent.

The two older boys ran to the water's edge, but then stopped with a sense of trepidation, as though it had been a long time since they had experienced the sea and weren't quite sure they could trust it. Ojelis, a couple years younger than the others, settled down next to Leo, who sat on our towel outside the tent. Ojelis kept looking at Leo adoringly, while Leo pretended not to notice. He lit a cigarette and stared at the waves. Gerard feigned sleep from under his canopy, but kept a wary eye on the developing scene. He enjoyed his role as Pied Piper and was reluctant to give up one of his devotees to another idol.

"Do you know how to swim?" Leo asked the boy.

"Not very well," he answered in almost a whisper.

"Come on. I'll go in the water with you."

Ojelis rose hesitantly, unable to control the beaming smile on his face. Leo ran ahead and beckoned him on. The other boys had made their entrance and splashed in the frothy waves churned up by the breeze.

I followed after them and when Ojelis was almost to the edge of the water, a wave pounded the sand and moved in rapidly, forcing him to run backwards to avoid the water touching his little brown feet. He looked so tiny and vulnerable next to the great roaring sea, his body a rich chocolate color and all his ribs showing. With his shoulders bent forward, he looked as if he was trying to fold up into a cocoon, his head hanging limp.

"Don't be a baby," Leo chided. And then on a softer note, "I'll protect you."

Leo coaxed him into the water and helped him swim by putting one hand under his stomach to support him. In a spastic dog paddle, he kicked and slapped the water with his hands, holding his head above the waterline. Leo turned his head to avoid getting the sea splashed in his face, his expression a combination of resignation and accomplishment. I detected the emerging instincts of a father in him, and at the same moment felt him drifting away.

From under the covering Gerard called us to lunch, but most of us were only able to have our heads and upper bodies under the towel with our legs sticking out all around like spokes of a wheel. The red-and-yellow towel cast a warm and alien light on the faces of the group while Gerard cut up pieces of drippy mango and squirting oranges. The sandwiches were warm and we worried about the mayonnaise, but ate them anyway. Then the light under our shelter turned gray as the sun passed behind a cloud and stayed there.

Leo stuck his head out to give us a report. "There's a big black cloud coming our way."

"It's not supposed to rain today," Gerard protested.

I put my head out, too, feeling a couple of drops. "Tell that to the sky. We could wait it out. Maybe it will be a light shower."

Leo stared at me as though I was from another planet. "Hello? A summer afternoon in Cuba. Light shower? I don't think so." His words heralded a round of bigger, fatter drops.

"We'd better go to the car," said Gerard.

By the time we had gathered up all our things and were halfway to the car, the real downpour began, and we started running. We threw our wet things in the trunk, piled in the car, and slammed the doors. The windows fogged up immediately and we listened to the rat-a-tat-tat on the roof.

"If we're going to sit here, I'm going to run and get some beers," announced Leo.

"You'll get all wet," I said.

"I'm already soaked."

"Right. Go then."

Fresh from the beach we approached the massive fort, La Fortaleza de San Carlos de la Cabaña in the fading light of dusk. Two red-coated guards with tricorner hats and crisscross canary yellow sashes stood at each stone pillar of the entrance to the bridge which led to the arched double doorway. They held nineteenth-century rifles with bayonets, wore shiny knee-high black boots, and looked very solemn. It was the nightly *Ceremonia del Cañonazo* where they fired a cannon to commemorate the blasts that used to signal the closing of the city gates. With everybody standing at the entrance to the fort, I snapped a photograph. Leo stood in the back, a head taller than the boys, but at a distance from Gerard as if he didn't belong in the group. But as soon as we turned to go through the gates, Ojelis was at his side, reaching up to put one hand on his shoulder, smiling contentedly.

It was still early, but a crowd of both tourists and Cubans had begun to form around the rampart area where the ceremony took place. We sat on the wall and looked across the bay to the old part of Havana. The hues of evening light softened the harshness of the decaying buildings, and with the stillness of the air there was a dreamlike romantic feel to the view. Then the sky started to perform its show of color with just enough clouds on the horizon to add spice. The constantly changing pinks and purples and golds hung over the entrance to the bay and the round lighthouse tower of El Morro—the fort at the mouth of the bay—penetrated the ruddy flesh of the sky.

The boys scampered on the ramparts in the receding light, and as soon as darkness fell, a drum roll rose above the chatter of the large crowd jostling for position. A hush came over the assembly and men bearing torches appeared from one of the doorways in the courtyard below us, and with dramatic fanfare accompanied by the drummers, lit a series of kerosene lamps along the path. Soon the harsh smoke reached our nostrils and the beating got louder as the uniformed soldiers approached the cannon, calling out a warning that the gates of the city were closing. The small group of brightly attired soldiers lined up near the canon, and orders were shouted, all in military fashion. Then a couple of the soldiers broke off from the group and began to pack the old canon on its wooden cart.

The packing turned comical as they thrust the plunger into the long barrel, and with an alternating hollow thump and sucking withdrawal, they pounded the plug—not a real cannon ball—into the cannon. Yet it seemed that they couldn't get it beyond a certain point and they jumped high in the air before the thrust to increase their power, but to no avail. It was difficult to say if they were really having trouble or working the crowd. They repeated the scene several times, and each time the spectators tittered and looked around to see if everybody was thinking the same thing. I leaned over to Gerard and said, "Only in Cuba could they turn a military ceremony in period costume into a titillating pseudo-sexual event."

"Honey, any chance they get." It sounded at the same time like a condemnation and the explanation for why he was living here.

At long last one of the packers leaped into the air and with a mighty thrust, we felt the lodged plug give way and descend into the depths of the canon. The crowd let out a communal sigh, and then cheered. With another drum roll, the fuse was lit, and even though I was prepared for it, the boom came as a shock. I felt the momentary pressure on my chest and the resonation in my ears. A small smoke cloud and the smell of gunpowder lingered around the canon.

We left the area in something like a post-climax haze and went into one of the fort museums that had an abundant display of torture devices and crude weaponry. Leo was fascinated by the swords and knifes, and I winced as he held his head against the glass cabinets and studied them. I wondered if he looked at knives differently than the average person, if he thought about the night that disfigured him. But I saw none of it in his face.

From the weapons we went to the small baroque chapel, which by contrast was serene. I lit a candle for my grandmother. The flame flickered and then grew strong, adding to the brightness dancing on the wall. Leo had disappeared, but I located him outside, smoking a cigarette in a dimly lit alley. He smiled when I approached him. Then he lifted the glasses off my face and started cleaning them.

"Who's going to take care of you when you go back to Los Angeles?"

I let out a gigantic sigh.

"Don't be sad." He put the glasses back on my face and turned me around. "Let's go. We'll lose the others." He patted my butt and chuckled.

24

I was jerked awake by a shout followed by low guttural sounds that were neither Spanish nor English, no earthly language, but rather a primitive mumbling that might announce the arrival of the devil. I was petrified, and the very real rumble of the air conditioner told me it was not a dream.

I could barely make out the form lying beside me in the dark, but I knew the sounds were escaping from what *had been* Leo, now a possessed creature of unknown origin. I was about to reach for the bedside lamp when there was a shift from grumbling to whimpering, a mournful, wounded animal noise more disturbing than the other. There were a few rapid sniffs and gurgles, and then the whimpering again. The terror I had felt before became a need to console. If I could wrap my arms around him and hold him close, I could make the pain go away. But when I touched him, he shouted more unintelligible syllables, and began to flail and kick. He landed a good one on the side of my head and kicked me to the other side of the bed.

"Leo," I shouted and fumbled for the lamp switch. With the blast of light, he sprung into a sitting position like a cadaver being brought to life with a bolt of electricity.

"Hey," he yelled. It echoed around the room. His eyes were frantic with confusion and he stared at me without recognition as I hovered on my side of the bed out of reach. He tumbled back on the pillow and let out a knowing sigh.

"Are you all right?" I said.

"What happened?"

"You knocked the shit out of my head for one thing."

"Sorry. Come here. Hold me."

I hesitated.

"Come on. I won't hurt you. It's me, baby."

I moved over and embraced him.

"Does your head hurt?"

"A little."

"Show me where." He rubbed the spot lightly.

"What were you dreaming about? It must have been awful."

"The same."

"Same?"

"Same as always."

"Tell me."

"I can't."

"Is it like in your paintings?"

"A dark street…it's hard to talk about."

"Does it have anything to do with this?" I gently ran my fingers over the long scar on his neck.

He didn't answer. I pulled him closer still, and he settled. I stroked his head as he buried his face in my neck like a piece of a puzzle that had found its match. I reached for the sheet to cover us against the cool air.

When I awoke later, the room was chilly, and we were on opposite sides of the bed again. It was as if the long separation had already started. I moved over and wrapped myself around him. He grunted, but didn't wake up. At least we had one more day…and one more night. We would have lunch with Luka and Monica, play tennis in the late afternoon, and then have a going-away dinner at Luka's that evening. I had invited Madelin to join us.

I returned from the market with lunch and Leo was on the phone. "No, I told you tomorrow." And then. "Why do *I* have to go?"

He kept insisting that he would leave the next day, but the conversation ended with an abrupt, "Okay." He hung up the phone precisely before turning to me. "I have to go today." He got up to turn on the air conditioning, but nothing happened. "Shit, the power's off."

"They always win, don't they?"

"What do you mean?"

"The women in your life."

"If that were true, I wouldn't be here with you."

"But in the end."

"Don't talk like that. It is just one less day. She has to go to the doctor tomorrow and I need to go with her."

"Sure, that's fine." I tried not to look at him, but he came around and squatted in front of me. I sat on the edge of the bed with my hands between my legs. He rested his arms on my knees and wrapped my hands in his.

"Look at me. I love you, love you, love you. Nothing is going to come between us." He was so good at it. He could rip my heart out and I gladly let him. "Let's not make this any worse than it is. Help me get my things together. Will you go to the bus station with me?"

"You're going to pack up and go right now? Just like that?"

"If I go now, I should be able to get there by tomorrow morning."

The lights were still off when we got to the station and in the vast interior the people moved about like phantoms. I had so much I wanted to say, but nothing came out, nothing about the future that we needed to get settled. He joked that the next time I came at the end of the year, we would be able to leave together. The person who was fixing the visa said it would take about four months.

Questions filled my brain. How would it work in Los Angeles? How would I break the news to Lizzie and Jenny? Would Leo and I live together? It was bizarre that I was even thinking about something that clearly wasn't going to happen, or was it?

Near the outside doors where there was more light, Leo plunked his bags down. He had an hour wait for his bus. We sat with our backs against the wall, not talking, but sitting close, his hand discreetly rubbing my leg.

"I should go," I said. He looked at me painfully. "Madelin is coming at five."

I stood up and he held on to my hand and wouldn't let it go. Then he pulled himself up and hugged me tight, again unmindful of what people around us might think. "Call me on the cell phone tomorrow. Tell everybody I'm sorry about the dinner tonight."

"Sure. I'll call you."

"Now go. I hate this."

As the taxi pulled away, he stared out with his head against the glass door. His gaze was haunting as the glass magnified the sad circles under his eyes. I wanted him to wave, to raise his hand, but he stood stiff, far away.

Madelin showed up an hour late in an aqua tight-fitting sleeveless top and body-hugging white jeans with white high-heeled sandals. Her thick blonde curly hair looked both wild and perfectly coiffed, while subtle make-up brought out her full lips and soulful eyes. We walked along quiet streets still darkened by the blackout, and talked of love and relationships.

Luka's living room looked like a chapel, a host of votive candles haphazardly placed around the room. Monica came out of the kitchen where she had been cooking by candlelight and I introduced Madelin. Monica looked her up and down and I wondered if she was even going to kiss her; to not do so would have been an incredible snub in Cuba. In the end Monica allowed a light air kiss and returned to the kitchen, calling out, "Kiko, get some glasses. Time for some rum." To round out the party was Monica's 16-year-old nephew, Kiko, who frequently spent time at the apartment to get away from his parents.

By the time we sat down to dinner, we were all feeling good from the rum, and though Luka only drank a little, he was more animated than I had seen him in a while.

"I'm afraid the fish is overcooked," said Monica as she brought it out on a big silver platter. She looked at Madelin as if daring her to say something.

"Looks fine to me," said the younger woman.

Monica seemed unsatisfied with her sweet answer. "How can you tell in this light?"

"Don't worry about it," said Luka. "Nobody is expecting a gourmet meal under the circumstances."

She let the platter drop in the center of the table with a loud clang. "It's not my fault. I couldn't see."

"Forget about it," Luka said, reaching up and hugging her around the waist.

"You see why I can't leave this guy? He's worth all my ex-lovers and husbands put together."

"Just one problem, *Tía*," Kiko said to his aunt. "He's not into women."

"I'll give up sex," Monica offered.

"Yeah, right, *Tía*. I would, too, if I had to do it with that thing you brought home the other night." Kiko was testing his bravado brought out by the rum.

"*Oye, chico*. You'd better shut your mouth or I'm going to send you home." She sounded mad, but she wasn't. "He *was* pretty bad, but he was sweet. A German guy. You wouldn't understand, Kiko, but you get to a certain age and other things are important."

"You were singing a different tune a few months ago when you were with Cesar," Luka reminded her.

"I don't want to hear another word about César," and then she added. "Shit, he was hot."

"He still is," I threw in, and everybody turned to look at me since I had been so quiet.

"Not you, too. Every gay man falls for him," said Monica.

Her referring to me as a gay man was like a kick in the stomach; it was the first time I had heard anyone say it. "I didn't say that I fell for him. Can't I just recognize that he's good-looking?"

"Humph," she said. "And what about your cutie? Is being with someone that hot worth all he puts you through? Did you meet Leo, Madelin?"

"Martin brought him over for dinner. My mom loved him. He's a sweetheart."

"But even the sweetest Cuban men pull the same shit and if they're bi, it's worse. I'm sick of it."

"Give Martin a break. It's not what he needs to be hearing right now," said Luka.

"She's got a point," I said. "This is a perfect example. Why isn't he here? Because his wife called and he went running."

"He has a wife?" Kiko said in disbelief. He had seen us a number of times affectionately curled up on the sofa.

"Come on, Kiko. He's hardly the first Cuban guy that plays on both sides of the fence," said Monica.

"You guys looked like a solid couple," Kiko said to me.

"He's good at loving the one he's with," I said, even though I appreciated the comment immensely.

"My mom thought you guys were cute together, but she also said she understood his desire to have a child."

"A lot of people want to have kids, but I'm not sure it is always the right thing to do," said Luka. "You should be in the right circumstances."

"God, thanks for saying that!" I said. "Everybody acts like it's fabulous that he's having a kid. Nothing pulls the heartstrings like a little bundle of joy. Of course he's put no mind to the practicality of it. Like who's going to support the child?"

"*Tío* Martin," said Luka and got a laugh out of everybody except me.

"We'll see about that," I croaked.

"You have to realize, Martin, that people here don't think the way they do in the States, especially not people from the country," said Madelin. "Couples just have kids because they think it is the natural thing to do. They figure out how to take care of them later. Anyway, it's not as if they worry about kids interfering with a career."

"What's next for you two?" Luka asked me.

"I'll be back for New Year's. By then he'll be a daddy, and we'll see if anything changes."

Being midweek and early morning, the Havana airport was quiet and most of the waiting-area seats were empty. Even the colorful snappy architecture and pleasantly cool climate control didn't improve the gloominess I felt. There hadn't been time to eat breakfast before I left the apartment, and I was further disheartened by the dismal offerings at the snack bar—dried-out sandwiches or packaged cookies. With a watery cappuccino and some chocolate cream-filled cookies, I found a solitary corner.

I took stock of the past month with Leo, remembering the good things and trying to forget the bad. There was his affectionate companionship; the long soapy massage showers; the tennis games where I watched him improve day by day; the afternoons at the beach under the golden sun; and the many meals we prepared and ate together. I even had time to get a lot done on my book. It reminded me that relationships are made up of simple things shared rather than great events, and I was already missing those simple things.

Should I, against the judgment of almost everyone I knew, try to help him leave the country and come live in Los Angeles? I had to make a decision. He wasn't begging me to help him leave and in fact mentioned it less and less. Sitting there on the uncomfortable plastic seats under the blaring airport light with the faintness of early morning outside the windows, I made a decision to help him. The next time I talked to him I would tell him to contact the person who could make the visa arrangements and find out how much it was going to cost.

25

December 2002

Back home in Los Angeles, my crisis of what to do about Leo took second billing to the continuing decline in Lizzie's parents' health. Her father was in the hospital with a blood clot in his brain and Lizzie was in Santa Barbara almost full-time, shuttling back and forth between the hospital and taking care of her mother at home.

I roamed around our empty house wondering what it would be like not to live there anymore. Jenny called to welcome me home and tell me that she had decided to move in with Jack, the tattooed boyfriend. We both had tattooed boyfriends now, I reminded myself.

"Aren't you going to yell and scream and tell me it is a stupid thing to do?" she said.

"When have I ever yelled and screamed at you?"

"Right. I guess I have you confused with a father that isn't so caught up in his own issues that he can worry about his daughter."

"Are you still mad at me?"

"No," she said with a big sigh. "I was never mad at *you*, just life."

"Let's forget about my situation right now and talk about what is going on with you."

"With everything that is happening with the Grans, and you and Mom, I need the stability of living with someone."

"Do you think living with Jack is going to provide that stability?"

"Jack is not what you think."

"I'm not saying anything against Jack. I like him."

A month later in the midst of my furious editing to finish the book before school started, Lizzie's father died. After the funeral, family and friends came back to the house to eat and drink tequila, the drink Jenny had decided was what we all needed to drown our sorrows.

Jack was out on the patio smoking, and I was having one of my every-six-months urges for a cigarette.

"Marty, have a seat." He knew I didn't like that name, but persisted in using it. His first attempt at bringing the lighter to my cigarette missed by a couple of inches until I held his hands and we got the thing lit. He took off his jacket and I stared at the tiger tattooed on his right forearm.

"I spose you're worried 'bout me an' Jen movin' in together."

"She knows what she wants. Didn't get that from me."

"Marty…sorry, Martin. You're all right. You're cool."

"I hope Jen doesn't hate me for what I'm doing."

"No way, man. She thinks you're the coolest dad on earth. It's just that she feels bad for her mom."

"I do, too. Change is hard."

Jen stuck her head out the door and said, "Would you guys put out those cancer sticks and come in here. People are beginning to leave."

"Yeah, baby. Right away," Jack said, winking at me.

"Now," she reiterated and closed the door. Jack jumped up and offered me a hand.

"Come on, ol' man."

"Ol' man yourself, " I said, grabbing onto his arm. I got halfway up and we both lost our balance. Next thing I knew he was hugging me, squeezing me hard. We had never done more than shake hands before, and it felt strange to have a big muscular guy holding me, my daughter's boyfriend.

"You're all right by me, Martin. If anybody tries ta tell you difernt, just send 'em ta me."

"Thanks, Jack," I said with a flushed face, separating myself from his bear embrace. Then he kissed me on the lips, even lingered a moment, pressing his lips to mine. It was one of those moments in life that you later wonder if really happened. It was so sudden and strange and forbidden. Then just as quickly it was gone. He put his arm around my shoulders, and we walked into the house.

I never told Lizzie about the possibility of bringing Leo to the States and I was glad since it fell through. We avoided the topic of Cuba as her life was more than full—moving her mother into a managed-care facility and dealing with her father's business affairs. When I said I was going to Cuba for New Year's, she looked at me blankly as though it hadn't even occurred to her that the holidays were only a couple of weeks away.

"I'll be here for Christmas," I added.

"Oh," she said.

One of my bags was full of baby clothes that my sister had given me. Some of them looked as if they had never been worn, and Leo's daughter was going to be the best-dressed baby in Holguín. Optimism was in the air as Leo came toward me at the airport, eyes smiling and a buzz cut making him look younger than ever. He seemed to have an inexplicable compulsion to change his look every few weeks.

In the apartment he grabbed me and moved me slowly toward the bedroom. Almost to the door he pushed me up against the wall and leaned into me with all his weight. I slipped my hands under his shirt and felt his smooth warm skin, and then brushed over his nipples, which were like pebbles of excitement. Bending his knees slightly, he wrapped his arms around my waist, lifted me off the ground, and carried me through the door as the top of my head grazed the doorjamb. A few steps into the room we started falling and landed on the bed with a crash. The bed scooted against the side table and toppled a lamp.

He was the playful lion that had trapped its prey, but was not quite ready to devour it. I rolled up his T-shirt so that I could pull it over his head, and he turned passive like a little boy.

"You look so young with your hair cut short."

"You don't like it," he said with a pout.

"I like it. It just makes you look boyish, like one of my students at school."

"Is this how you treat your students?"

"Only the bad ones."

"*Descarado,* you are shameless."

Sex had none of the hesitancy of the first nights of my other trips. His repeated expressions of affection for me now had a life of its own, a history. I was determined to avoid the problems we had the summer before, and I made it clear that he was not a prisoner in the apartment. But I had never been very successful at establishing ground rules. Even as I heard myself outlining what we needed to do to keep things sane and happy, I sensed I was going against the impulsive nature of Cuban men. He agreed to my rules, but there was a lack of conviction. At the same time it appeared that Leo wanted things to be good between us, was ready to make some sacrifices. That was the duality of Leo.

We walked down Paseo toward the Malecón, and the sun shined brightly. Only in the shade could you tell it was winter, feel the coolness of the breeze. The sea churned and the wind whipped up great walls of white water that pounded against the seawall with an audible boom, sending up spouts that rained down on the sidewalk, and then spread out on the street, forming a lake. A crowd had gathered in front of the Galerías Paseo shopping center. Mouths gaped and wide eyes stared at the power of the sea just a hundred yards in front of them.

"A cold front is coming in," said one man and several others nodded their heads. It sounded funny since everyone was decked out in tank tops and shorts.

Inside the supermarket I fell into a quicksand of complaining, starting with the poor quality of the rattling shopping cart, the surliness of the clerks, and ending with the paltry supplies. "Look, they only have one brand of flimsy toilet paper, and it's pink!" Leo stared at me and shook his head. He was about to say something, but then turned and walked out of the store. I stared after him a moment before leaving the empty cart in the aisle.

"Wait, Leo. I'm sorry."

"You're beginning to sound like Gerard, always complaining about Cubans. Why do you come here then?"

"I come here for you."

"You always say you come here because of the book."

"You *and* the book. I could probably finish the book back home."

He blew out some of the angry air inside him and looked down. When he raised his head, his eyes had softened a bit.

"What are we doing? Do you even want to be with me?" I said.

We were in the middle of the Galerías' spiral ramp with shoppers swirling all around us. It was not the place to have this discussion, and I could tell that Leo was painfully ill at ease. "I do want to be with you," he began slowly and in a low voice, "here or there or anywhere. But I can't spend all my time thinking it's going to happen. When you grow up here, you learn to just deal with what's in front of you, what you can see. Everything beyond that isn't real. My whole life I've heard how things are going to get better in this country from…" he made the sign for beard, which was a common way to refer to Fidel without saying his name, "but nothing ever changes. There's no future."

"I want to give you a future."

"I know," he said. His voice faded to a whisper.

"Anyway, you've got your whole life ahead of you. You shouldn't be talking so hopelessly at your age."

"I don't feel so young anymore."

I laughed. "Believe me. You're young."

In the walk back to the apartment we fell into silence as we often did, each into his thoughts. But after a time I had to say what was on my mind.

"Remember the night we met?" A spark of a smile crossed his face. "I think about it often."

"Why is that?"

"It was totally unexpected. I wasn't looking for anything. I didn't even want to be there." I was sure he didn't fully appreciate how that night changed my life.

"Uh-huh," he said. He wasn't ready to jump into the conversation, but by the glint in his eye I knew he wasn't bored by it, either.

"You worked your charm on me."

"I didn't do anything." His smile was growing.

"You're partly right about that. It did happen naturally. I felt a connection when you first put your hand on mine."

"You did?"

"Didn't you? Feel anything?"

"I thought you might give me forty bucks to go to Holguín."

My feet came to an automatic stop, and my back tensed. I felt as if I had been punched in the belly. Never again could I pretend that our meeting was some serendipitous cosmic bonding. Yet the way that he said it was so nonchalant, so cool and honest. He might have been pointing out that the street was wet after a rain—the obvious that I had failed to notice.

"What?" He searched my eyes that lingered on an oleander bush just beyond his left shoulder.

"I guess you got what you wanted."

"And you, too." he laughed.

"When *did* you start to feel a connection? I'm assuming that you do."

He gave me the look of exasperation. "In the hospital. I began to feel affection for you. I began to care about you, and I knew you needed me."

As much as the previous revelation stunned me, this one touched me. They were both said with the same matter-of-factness.

None of the rental agencies had any cars to get us to Holguín. We were told over and over, "*No hay nada en toda Habana.*" There was no room on buses either. Leo went out with Ricardo to look for a private car to rent. He had it in his head that we were going to his mom's house for New Year's. Nothing could shake him.

In the afternoon there was a knock on the door and I opened it to find Leo leaning with his arm up on the frame, looking both seductive and sheepish. I stared right into his dark hairy armpit.

He dropped his pose and slid into the room. "I got a great deal on a car. Only twenty-five a day. Had to take it for a week, though."

"What's it like?" I said.

"It's okay. Not a BMW, but it'll get us there."

"Are you sure?"

He didn't answer, but went past me with a big smile and started to pack in the bedroom. "I thought you were going to pack my clothes for me," he said in a whine.

"Didn't know what you wanted to take."

A light rain was falling when we got down to the street. At first sight of the car, my bag went kaplunk on the ground, and my mood sank with it. Leo quickly picked up the bag and hauled it over to the trunk. The car—a badly abused Moskvitch built in the '70s—was worse than anything I had imagined. It had been painted a slimy yellow—they probably used house paint—that even under the low streetlight looked hideous. Parts of the body were rusted out and the back fender was off. The tires were bald and the wheels probably hadn't seen hubcaps in a decade. One taillight was cracked and the other was plastered over with red tape. The lid of the trunk looked as if someone had taken a hammer to it in a fit of anger. Leo lifted it with a jarring creak and stuffed our bags in. I got in the back and observed that the inside of the door was down to the metal and missing the handle for the window. The interior reeked of oil and gasoline, and parts of the torn ceiling fabric hung down with a haunted-house effect.

Ricardo was in the driver's seat—not a comforting thought—and Miguel was in the back with Fernando. Fernando was a rake-thin beady-eyed guy in his late thirties who was hanging around Miguel's house trying to put the moves on Leo before I came into town, and then had had the audacity to continue his pursuit, though more subtly, after I arrived. Leo thought it was amusing.

I imagined breathing exhaust fumes for the ten-hour-plus drive, trying to make conversation with this creep who was trying to steal Leo away, keeping one eye on Ricardo's driving, and sitting on a seat whose upholstery sunk to the hard metal frame. I was gripped by an eerie panic that I might not survive the trip.

Ricardo turned the key and there was a sickly grind until the engine chugged to life. We pulled out into the empty street with the shush of the tires on the wet pavement, and at the corner we turned left and started up a small incline. Ricardo downshifted, but the motor struggled, coughed, and then came to a halt. My first reaction was guilt as if I had willed it to happen.

"*Coño!*" said Leo.

Ricardo turned the key and got a high-pitched whine. "Pump the gas," shouted Leo. He stomped on the pedal a couple of times and tried again without result. I took a deep breath. I was not one to believe in preternatural signs, but if there was a time to believe, it had come.

Leo jumped out of the car and opened up the hood. "I need some light." He came around my side of the car for the trunk. I got out, too, while Miguel and Fernando huddled on their half of the back seat. Leo popped the trunk and rummaged around to get the flashlight out of his bag. My bag was on top, so he lifted it out, but hesitated to put it on the wet ground. I grabbed it and threw it over my shoulder. Something scampered over one of the bags. "The car has rats, too?" I cried.

Leo picked up the little animal and cupped it in his hand. "It's not a rat. It's Benny."

He shouted to Ricardo, "Benny's out of the box." The creature stuck its head out of Leo's hand and looked around. Ricardo got out of the car to take charge of the hamster while Leo dug for the flashlight. I stood in the middle of the street in a catatonic state with the weighty bag on my shoulder. A voice told me to walk away. Leo went back under the hood and fiddled with valves and levers. Ricardo, back in the driver's seat with Benny on his lap, tried again, but it wouldn't start. Leo closed the hood and said, "I'll push and you pop the clutch."

I stood off to the side and watched the car roll back down the hill. It picked up speed and Leo said, "Now." Ricardo let out the clutch and the car lurched, but didn't start. I walked down where Leo was standing with his hands on his hips and a frown on his face.

"I'm not going," I said quietly.

"What?"

"I'm not going in that car," I said more forcefully.

"That's the only car we've got." Rage was just under his tongue.

"I'm not going." I had the feeling that the glass tower of our relationship was crashing down around us, and I was surprised how little I cared.

He walked around to the back of the car and opened the trunk again. "Come on, put your bag in."

"No. I don't feel good about this trip."

"Now it's the trip. I thought it was the car."

"It's mostly the car."

"Mostly the car," he repeated. He closed the trunk with a bang that made everyone inside pop his head around. "I'll see you next week, or month, or maybe never. You'd better go." It started to rain again. He came over, hugged me loosely and kissed me on the cheek. The lackluster kiss stung like acid.

"Will you call me?" I asked.

"I don't know." He walked to the front of the car.

"Don't call me," I yelled. "I don't want you to call. All you care about is yourself and this fucking trip. You're the most selfish person I've ever met."

He walked back toward me with a beast taking over his face, making me unsure if he was going to hit me or have a seizure. His shoulders arched and his fists folded into hard little balls.

"You're the one that's fucking up our plans, not me. In this car everybody's going to suffer equally, but we are going to be together. But no, it's not good enough for you. You're the selfish one. You make promises, but don't keep them. Probably the same will happen with me coming to live with you. You'll decide at the last minute I'm not good enough for you. You're like all the rest. You come here and take, satisfy yourself and then go back to your life, leave us here in our shit." His face was close to mine and I could feel the spray of his anger, or was it the rain sputtering down from the sky?

"It is all about you and what you want. All your relationships have failed because you can't give yourself to anyone. You talk about love all the time, but you don't even know what it is."

"If you loved *me*, you would get in that car. How can you say you love me when you won't accept certain things about me, the whole me? And you never will, so what's the point? Go have your life and forget about me, because I'm tired of this."

"I'm tired, too. I won't be here when you get back."

His eyes burned into me, then he turned and jumped into the car. I hadn't walked ten yards before I heard the engine turn over, but it was too late to do anything. The car started up the hill and the gears strained and grated into second. I turned around and as my eyes followed the car I had the same sickening abandonment that I had felt at the age of seven when I came out of the gas station bathroom in a town far from home and watched in horror as my parents and brothers and sisters, my whole life, pulled away and drove up the street. I was utterly alone. My small skinny legs kicked into gear and I took off after the family station wagon. It was like running in a dream as I made no headway while the car streamed out of sight. I must have been a heartbreaking sight because when my family came back for me—my brother had finally let out the secret that I wasn't in the car—my mother was more hysterical than I had ever seen her. She was laughing and sobbing and screaming all at the same time.

I didn't run after Leo's car though a part of me wanted to. And I couldn't claim abandonment since I was the one who had decided not to go. He wasn't exactly family either, but he was the reason for being in this place so far from home. I stood in the rain staring after the car now gone from sight, wondering how I could be missing him already when a few minutes before we had been screaming at each other. It was all broken, and I didn't see any way to repair it.

The street was dark and very quiet. I had no place to go since I had given up the apartment. I stood under the rain dripping off the leaves of the laurel trees and with the damp darkness wrapped around me. I felt old, the greater part of my life having passed even if I stayed lucky with my compromised immune system. And the way I had chosen to live was likely to bring me pain as bad or worse than what I was suffering. Still there was no choice but to go on. I hoisted my bag higher up on my shoulder and walked toward Gerard's house. A crescent moon emerged from behind rapidly moving clouds, and hung just above the treetops, reminding me that on this path there was also the possibility of great joy.

Several people were standing around the bed, ghosts in the eerie blue glow coming from the computer screen. I recognized Luka and Gerard, but the other three were unknown to me. Pale and decidedly glum, Gerard opened his mouth to speak, and though I couldn't actually hear what he said, I felt it, a heavy wet blanket on top of me. Something was wrong. My vision turned blurry and my body was under a tremendous weight, making it impossible for me to lift my head.

"I need to sleep," I said. I heard the wind rattle the window. "Can you turn off the computer?" I pulled the sheet over my head, but I could still see the blue light, stronger than ever.

"Martin, we have to tell you something," Luka said in a voice full of gloom.

"Can't it wait until morning?" I lowered the sheet just enough so that I could peek out.

"No," said Gerard, "we want you to know."

"Know what for Christ's sake? You are being very *pesados*."

"Something…has…happened…to…Leo." Each word came out like the beat of a slow drum, as if he thought I didn't understand English.

"What?" I said.

"There was an accident near Santa Clara. The road was slick from the rain. The car went off the road. It turned over a couple of times. Leo was thrown. He wasn't wearing his seat belt. They rushed him to the hospital, but he didn't make it. I'm sorry."

"This is not funny," I yelled. "Not funny at all. Leave me alone."

"*Es la verdad*," said Luka.

I went back under the sheet and thought that maybe if I was very quiet, they would all go away.

The mattress sunk down as someone sat on the bed and started stroking my head. I knocked the hand away, then there were others touching me. I started hitting and kicking through the sheet. My shouts sounded like the faint squealing of an infirm mouse. The terrifying sound of my own voice made me want to see, to remove the sheet, which now seemed made of a dense material. Somehow I was able to break my hand free and make contact with the hard bone of someone's jaw.

With a flash of light I opened my eyes to Gerard standing over me. "What's going on?" he asked. I was twisted up in the sheet.

"Did I hurt you?" I asked guiltily.

He looked confused. "I heard you shouting and came in to see if everything was all right. You were having a bad dream."

I felt a terrible dread, an unbearable weight on my heart. "And Leo, is he…?"

"What are you talking about? Leo's on his way to Holguín."

I became aware of where I was, in the back bedroom, the former maid's quarters and now the computer room, in a single bed in which I couldn't even stretch my legs out. "I'm sorry. Was I making a lot of noise?"

"Not that much. I probably wouldn't have heard you except that I was in the kitchen getting a glass of water. Did something happen to Leo in your dream?"

"No, we were fighting or something."

"Are you all right now? Do you need anything?"

"Do you have any rum?"

"The perfect Cuban remedy. I'll be right back."

He came back with two small glasses, shots of the good stuff. I noted the rich amber color and the way it clung to the sides of the glass. Then the smell, like burnt honey tickled the inside of my nose. We touched glasses and I let the smooth liquid slide over my tongue. It coated my throat while its fumes rose calmly upward to my brain. "Havana Club?" I asked.

"*Añejo. Siete años.* Just what the doctor ordered to make you sleep like a baby."

"From what Leo's been telling me, I don't think I want to sleep like a baby. Little Anabela wakes up all the time. She cries and cries until Leo gets up and gives her a bottle."

"Is he cool with being a daddy?"

"Hard to tell. Sometimes he sounds genuinely pleased when he talks about her and at other times it sounds as if he's talking about a video game, describing her as entertaining or comical. He doesn't seem to take the whole father thing too seriously. It's like everything in his life. He accepts it, coddles it, looks at it from different angles, makes it part of him, yet remains in his own world. He is so totally giving or absorbed in what is around him at the moment, but when it or the person is gone, he detaches himself and moves to the next thing without a backward glance."

"You make it sound like his feelings don't go very deep."

"I don't mean to say he is superficial. Or even that he is acting. Believe me, I've spent a lot of time trying to figure out if it *could* all be an act. But no, I don't think so. He feels deeply, and at the same time, has a detachment mechanism. He never asks me about my life back home. Still he will tell me that he is crazy to see me, that I am his partner, that he wants to live with me no matter where."

"I hope you're not thinking about spoiling whatever you have by trying to take him to Los Angeles."

I stared at him for a minute. What he thought on the matter was obvious and he was backed up by the dismal track record of relationships between foreigners and Cubans outside of the country.

"How could I not think about it? Coming here every few months is a nice getaway for me, but it's hardly a relationship."

"Why does it have to be a relationship?"

"Because you get to a certain level of feeling with someone and you have to either take the high road or you drop it. All the reasons I think of for dropping it come from society, not from inside me. If I thought there wasn't love between us, or that I couldn't trust him, or that he was using me—"

"You don't think he's using you?"

"No more than I'm using him. I could never have a friend like him back home."

"Never say never. You are a perfectly lovable and attractive person. There are cute guys in the States who dig older men."

"I don't know how to go out and meet guys there, and I'm not sure I want to learn. You know, his bad-boy good looks and sexiness are just the packaging. What keeps me coming back is the hum in the air when we are together. It's not just sex. It's the caring, the playfulness, the affection. Anyway, it's done. We broke up."

"Are you sure it's over?"

"It certainly felt like it when we argued out in the street. Maybe I should count my blessings, but it makes me unbearably sad to think of not seeing him again."

Gerard looked at me with a pitying smile. Into the silence a rooster crowed and I glanced at my watch. I thought of Leo out on the road. If all was going well, they were somewhere near Sancti Spiritus.

"I need to get some sleep. Can you believe tomorrow is New Year's Eve?" Gerard said.

"You mean today," I pointed out. "It's already today."

"I'm not ready for today. And we're having a big party tonight. Got a lot to do."

As Gerard went off to bed I heard the cock crow again, and I mused how unexcited I was about New Year's. It was the second year in a row I had tried to spend it with Leo and failed. Yet deep in the darkness of my uncertainty, there was a glimmer of hope. Leo and I had a good history of getting through crises. I imagined him showing up at my door in a few days with his enigmatic smile and a kiss. With only a few hours sleep, I went back to the apartment and told Victor I needed it again. He happily unlocked the door for me.

26

They were already out playing in the street, probably the same kids as the New Year's before, but a year deeper into the alliances, desires, and rules of engagement that would carry them into adulthood. I wondered what I had learned in the past twelve months, a year deeper in with Leo and nothing to show for it. I stared at the black velvet painting on the wall, an antelope galloping through a lush forest, the bright colors against the black background creating a sense of foreboding that a predator was about to pounce. Just below the painting sat the telephone. It beckoned me with the number of Leo's neighbor in Holguín beginning its loop through my brain, telling me that the freedom I had been anticipating was lost.

When I kept getting a message that the lines were busy due to holiday telephone traffic, I called Miguel's house in hopes that friends staying there might have news of Holguín. Miguel answered in his telltale, bored monotone.

"What are you doing in Havana?" I said in shock.

"Martin, uh, how are you?" He was surprised, too, and something else. "I just flew back. Ricardo and I weren't getting along."

"You mean Ricardo and Leo are still there?"

"Well, yeah."

He was holding back. I thought of my dream. "What's going on? Is Leo okay?"

"I shouldn't be the one to tell you this, but—"

"Miguel," I shouted, "tell me."

"There was a problem with the car. An accident. I…"

"What?" I shrieked. "Shit, don't tell me. Leo?"

"He's all right. I mean, he's bruised and scratched, but it's not too bad."

"What do you mean 'not too bad'?"

"It's nothing. They took him to the hospital, but they didn't even keep him."

"Swear to me he's all right!" I said.

"I swear."

"And the car?"

"You'd better talk to him about that."

As soon as I got off the phone, I ran to the rental agency on Paseo to see if any cars had come back.

The Ocho Vías highway stretched out in front of me like a giant landing strip—flat, wide, and almost empty. At various points there were hints of lane markings, so that you could actually count the eight lanes, but most of the line paint had faded in Special Period neglect, and you had to guess where to drive. There was so little traffic it hardly mattered. It had turned a balmy winter warm, and the sun, already high, beat down on the lonely pavement in front of my Toyota Yaris, a small 4-door coupe I had rented just an hour before.

I popped in one of the cassettes I had borrowed from Luka, the Trio Los Panchos harmonizing their way through heartbreak after heartbreak. They had a way of glorifying the tragedy of love that made me feel my journey was both inevitable and futile. And outside the car was a melody of a different kind, countryside vibrating with an assortment of greens, fenced by tall, skinny palms that rattled their fronds at the sky, angry with the God that had abandoned the island.

In the nothingness of blank road, cruising at eighty miles an hour along the magnificent stripe down the backbone of Cuba, the first few hours flew by like a meditation—my eyes fixed on the gray pavement plowing the green, my position frozen with a singleness of purpose. But the road petered out a little past Sancti Spiritus. Once you pass the Holy Ghost, you're on your own, let down from eight lanes to two on the Carretera Central that drops you off in the middle of towns and forces you to pick your way to the other side; signage was poor or nonexistent.

Constant attention was needed when I reached the outskirts of a town and fought for road space with trucks, cars, horse-drawn carriages, tractors, bicycles, motorcycles, motorcycles with sidecars, and pedestrians. To further distract me were people at every intersection flagging down rides, many of them waving peso bills to show they were willing to pay.

The first time I stopped to pick up riders was in Ciego de Ávila. I was lost. I had followed the first two signs, but had driven through a good part of the town without seeing another one. A young couple with a baby stared longingly into my car when I was stopped at a light, and I waved for them to get in. The young man put himself in the front and his petite wife and tiny baby in the back. They mumbled, "*Gracias*," but said no more. The dad was as slender as the newly planted saplings on the side of the road, about twenty-five, wearing faded jeans and worn-out sneakers. It was all I could do to stop myself from laying my hand on his bony knee to reassure him he would get home all right. He stared so straight ahead that his gaze seemed to arrow into a distant future, so I smiled instead at the mother in the back through the rearview mirror. I figured it would break no conventions since I appeared to be smiling at the baby. She held my gaze a second before looking down at the bundle in her arms. I imagined that they could be Leo and his little family.

"I'm lost," I announced. "Can you direct me back onto the highway to Camaguey? I hope it's the way you're going."

The young man spoke in the clipped, scratchy Spanish that told me we were getting into Eastern Cuba. "No problem. I can tell you. We are going to Florida."

"Oh, really? Miami?" I joked.

The man pursed his lips and continued to ponder the road ahead. "Our city is Florida, here in Cuba."

The woman repeated with equal sincerity, "Florida, Cuba."

The conversation didn't pick up much from there. I asked about the baby. She was three months old and her name was Mayalín. They had been to visit the woman's father in Ciego de Ávila, who had seen the baby for the first time. They showed a peculiar lack of interest in me, as if being picked up by a foreigner in an off-the-grid town was an everyday occurrence. I told them my name anyway, and that I was from Los Angeles. California. USA. Their faces appeared incapable of showing life and we fell silent.

Soon we escaped the jam and jumble of the city, and though we were on the open road, it didn't mean we were moving very fast. There were still the horse-drawn taxis and tractors that slowed traffic down, making it hard to pass. When we got to Florida, I pulled over and the family slipped out of the car like phantoms. Their parting words were "Go straight." I stayed the course through the town, miraculously finding myself on the road out in the direction of Camaguey. A few minutes later I wondered if I had imagined the whole incident.

An hour outside of Holguín, I got Leo on the phone, and we exchanged tentative hellos. Then I revealed that I was a short distance away.

"Martin, you're crazy," he said roughly with just a sprinkle of being pleased. "When you get into town, ask how to get to the Carretera de Gibara. Everybody knows where it is. Look for me on the side of the road near the clinic."

The usual mishmash of vehicles and pedestrians kept the traffic moving slowly, and I had no trouble spotting Leo walking in my direction with a slight limp like a cowboy who had fallen off a horse. I pulled over, and he got in with his freshly showered scent and shiny damp hair. We did one of those always unsatisfying driver-to-passenger hugs. I slipped back into the snaking traffic, keeping one eye on the road and the other on the beguiling smile taking over his beautiful face, no longer holding back being pleased with himself. He knew that he had me again, and he knew that I knew that he knew. Just being in the same car with him made me feel I had a purpose in life. I put my hand on his leg, and he slid his fingers in between mine. It was like the first night we met, and I felt the same crackling sensation.

"You look fine to me," I said. "You didn't make all this up just so I would come and get you, did you?"

He turned his face and pointed to a bruise just under his eye on the right side and a cut on his forehead. "Most of what hurts is what you can't see."

"Your aching heart from missing me so bad? Or do you mean down here?" I said, slipping my hand onto his crotch.

He squirmed, removed my hand, and looked out the window. "I'm sore all over. Anyway, I didn't ask you to come."

"I know."

We turned into his gravelly, potholed street and he said, "Wait, let me drive." I stopped the car and we changed places. It was a big deal for him to be seen driving a new car down his street. We proceeded at a snail's pace past the crude unfinished dwellings. To several people trudging along the dusty road, he waved almost imperceptibly, and they ducked down to peer into the car.

He stopped in front of a house with a corrugated plastic roof and a couple of scrawny bushes out front. He turned the car off and got out. "Come on," he muttered.

We climbed the bare steps, and Leo pushed aside a dingy curtain. Inside were several women sitting wide-eyed on a few mismatched rusty chairs under a bare bulb that hung precariously on unraveling cords from the ceiling. The brick walls were exposed and not for a trendy effect. I recognized Sulyn, holding a tiny thing wrapped in a blanket.

I had barely gotten into town and I was slapped in the face with the 3-D, living-color reality of his life. I tried not to act shocked. I kissed Sulyn on the cheek and cooed at the baby whose eyes were pressed shut in a grimace. There was a smell of fried onions hanging in the air and a faint whiff of urine from the open bathroom door. He introduced me to Sulyn's sister, whom I kissed dutifully, and then her mother, who gave me a hard, cold stare and stuck out a rough hand.

"Let's go," Leo said to Sulyn. She followed his lead without asking where or why.

I offered Sulyn and the baby the front seat, but she waved me off and meekly crawled in the back. It seemed that becoming a mother had tempered the fiery eyes I remembered from my last visit a year and a half before.

We drove the two blocks to Leo's house and his mom rushed out when she heard the car. She hugged and kissed me, but called me "*Sin Vergüenza*. Shameless."

"I'm still mad at you," she said, wagging a plump finger at me. "You should have been here for New Year's. All the family was here except you."

I didn't know how to respond to her calling me part of the family and chastising me at the same time.

Inside the house Sulyn unwrapped the baby from her thin blanket, and Leo held her up for me to see. I noted that she was *not* wearing one of the outfits I had sent with Leo. She was awake and looked around with a distinctly curious expression.

"Do you want to hold her?" said Leo. He put her in my arms. She weighed almost nothing, but her face seemed ancient and wise. She had her father's deep brown eyes and full-lipped mouth, and a wisp of dark hair that stood straight up. I made silly faces at her, and after a look of consternation, she began to react.

"Look," said Lisbeth. "She smiled at her, uh, *Tío*." Everybody laughed. I was an honorary uncle. But what did it really mean?

Leo and I sat down to dinner. He invited Sulyn to join us, but she sat instead in the corner of the living room and rocked the baby. Lisbeth loaded food on our plates and pressed me to eat. Leo beamed like the king of the mountain surrounded by his loyal subjects.

When we finished, I carried plates into the kitchen and Lisbeth corralled me between the sink and the refrigerator. "I'm worried about that car," she told me in a low voice. "You've got to help him. If the owners don't think he can pay for the damage, they might come after him. None of this would have happened if you had come with him."

She had left me speechless twice in less than an hour. So it was my fault.

Leo came in the kitchen and gave us a suspicious look. "What are you two talking about?"

"I have some things I need to discuss with Martin. Nothing for you to worry about."

Leo frowned. "I should take Martin to the room I rented for him. I'm sure he's tired. You can talk tomorrow."

"I thought we were going to the beach tomorrow," said Lisbeth.

"You can talk at the beach then," he said with his jaw falling open in exasperation.

On the way to the rental place, he explained what had happened. The day after they arrived from Havana, he took the car over to show Pedro, a mechanic friend of his. The man fiddled with the carburetor, changed the oil, and put air in the tires. He said he wouldn't charge anything except for the oil, but that he needed a big favor. His father was dying and lived in the small town of Banes about forty-five minutes from Holguín. He asked Leo to take him. They had some rum, and then got in the car. Pedro insisted on driving, but after a few minutes Leo told him to pull over, that he was too drunk. They got in a fight, and Pedro called him a *maricón*. Leo tried to grab the wheel.

"One second I was looking at his ugly mug, and the next I was upside down. It was like the movies. We went off the road, a steep embankment. The car turned over two times and landed on the roof. The windows were all smashed, so it was easy to crawl out. I was bleeding from a cut on my head, but we were all right for the most part."

"God protects drunks and babies. I'm not even going to mention how stupid that was."

"Don't rub it in. But you should have seen that asshole. He had his fat self there on the ground sitting like a Buddha. He was blubbering and carrying on, saying he was sorry and all that shit."

"Is he going to pay for it?"

"With what? Chicken feed?"

"Jesus, Leo!"

"Don't be mad at me, baby. I'm sorry." He reached over and stroked my leg.

We got to the address, a fifties-era bungalow on the corner in one of Holguín's nicer neighborhoods. The owner, Roberto, was a short, skinny, likeable guy about my age. He lived in the house with his plump wife, his aging mother, and a teenage son. He was educated and had a good command of English.

The room was clean, simply decorated, had its own entrance and private bathroom. Comfortable. We filled in the paperwork, and Leo said that he wanted to be registered as the companion. Roberto gave him a doubtful look. "Are you planning on spending the night?"

"Not tonight. Tomorrow."

"And you don't mind being on record?"

Leo scoffed as if he didn't care what the government or anybody thought. "I have nothing to hide."

"No problem. It's your call," said Roberto.

As soon as we were alone, he grabbed me and planted his mouth on mine. I squeezed him and he winced. "Whoa, boy. Remember the accident."

We undressed and he showed me his bruises, which I kissed one by one. He was beautiful, all of him, his scars, bruises, and tattoos. I wanted to protect him, save him. We lay down on the bed, and continued kissing, touching in a fiesta of skin on skin. I was losing my head again, off in some fantasy land, drunk on his breath. It seemed so right, so perfect. Yet another voice inside me told me to get every last drop of the moment. Relish it. Wallow in it. Because tomorrow we could be on opposite sides of the country, the continent, the world.

We lay in the post-sex stupor, neither one saying anything. My head was on his chest, listening to his heart slowing down as he ran his fingers through my hair. I opened my eyes and the room had gone dark in another blackout. A motorcycle roared down the street as if opening a wound, and then the darkness returned to silence, covering it up. Leo's hand stopped and went lax. After a few minutes, his body jerked, catching itself from falling. It was so dark I couldn't see his face, but I felt his smile.

"I'm falling asleep," he said like a little kid. "I have to go."

"No you don't."

"Yes, I do."

"No you don't, damn it."

"Yes, I do, damn it."

It was useless to argue. I knew I wasn't going to win. He raised himself up and started to dress.

Unlike the road to Gibara, the highway to the beach town of Guardalavaca was wide and well maintained. The Toyota flew along despite the heavy load—Leo at the helm, me as the co-pilot, Lisbeth and her boyfriend, Sulyn and the baby, and Leo's cousin, Adita. It was a perfect sunny day and warm for January. It was a day to feel optimistic and part of something.

We passed through the hilly countryside, the road lined with sugar cane fields like rows of Tropicana showgirls in green plumed headdress. From the crest of one hill the blue sea was poured out along the horizon, and we dropped into the town where groups of blonde, pasty Canadians wrapped in colorful attire made their way to the beach. They flew in by the planeload and took over the resorts of Guardalavaca.

Our modern extended family descended the steps to the beach of fine, sugary sand with stands of palm and sea grape trees offering shade. The water was aquamarine, broken only by rolling white lines of gentle surf. We spread our towels under the shiny leaves of a sea grape tree, and Leo set up his family closer to the trunk in full shade. The ring I had given him hung on a gold chain and bounced on his chest as he collected rocks to secure the towels. Sulyn stared at the bouncing ring with a scowl, while Leo remained oblivious, concentrating only on the comfort of his daughter. He sat down and cuddled little Anabela in his arms, spoke to her in soft baby talk.

Lisbeth leaned toward me and suggested that we take a private walk. Leo looked up and squinted in our direction, but quickly returned to cooing at the baby.

To keep pace with her I slowed my steps, her Rubenesque body filling out the red one-piece bathing suit—she had asked me several times to bring her diet pills from the States. Her bundle of dark hair was tucked under a red USMC baseball cap. She turned to me with beads of sweat on her forehead and said, "He's all I've got. He's my whole life." She spoke in a breathy, desperate voice, and I was afraid I was going to get the stay-away-from-my-son speech.

"I know," I said softly.

"There is no life for him here. He seems lost. One day he is selling soap on the black market, and the next he is raising roosters for cockfights. I am constantly worried he is going to get into trouble."

"I wish he would focus more on his painting."

"They are so dark. I wish he would paint happier things."

"That's why they're good. He is reaching down into his soul, not just painting what people want to see. That's what art is all about."

"You know about such things, and I appreciate you trying to encourage him. I know he thinks a lot of you. If he comes to live with you, all I ask is that you take care of him. It would break my heart to see him go, but I know he needs to develop as a person. He has a lot of his father in him and if he stays here, he will end up like him."

"I'm surprised. I never thought you would want him to be with me, especially after having a daughter."

"I want him to be happy. I know he's not happy with Sulyn. She doesn't give him the support he needs. He's not always an easy person to be with, but he has a good heart."

"Lately he's been kind of quiet about the leaving plan. I thought it was because of you. Now I see that the struggle is mostly with himself."

"I guess I've spoiled him. Always tried to give him everything I could, which wasn't much. But when he has to, he'll work, and work hard. You're right, though. He struggles a lot with decisions and sometimes makes the wrong ones."

I wanted to point out that having a kid at this stage of his life wasn't one of his brighter decisions, but as she was one of the main instigators of him becoming a father, it was better not to bring it up. "We all make some bad ones."

"I think being a father has changed him. It has forced him to grow up."

To be honest, I didn't see it. He was loving and responsible in taking care of the baby, but it still seemed a way to postpone what he needed to do in his life. And I wasn't helping much, supporting him, allowing him to not face the financial reality of being a new father. I couldn't tell her everything I was thinking, but I *was* content with the fact that she was in a sense giving her blessing to our friendship.

When Leo came to pick me up, I hadn't showered yet. The sun had sapped my strength, and I had crashed on the bed with the sand still in my trunks and between my toes.

"Come on. They are waiting for us for dinner."

"Who? What?"

He rolled his eyes. "Wake up, sleepyhead. My mom fixed dinner for us. Then we're going out with my cousin and some friends. And guess what?"

"What?" Question words were all I could manage in my grogginess.

"We'll go out, and then I'll come back and sleep here. I'll say I was too drunk to get home." He hugged me, thrilled with his plan.

"And Sulyn?"

"No way. She's not going. She doesn't even like to go out."

On the way to his house we stopped to pick up Sulyn and the baby. I stayed in the car, and when they came out, the tension stripped their every step of its weight. Leo grimaced as he started the car, and Sulyn looked rather dressed-up for a simple night at home.

As soon as we got in the house, Leo and Sulyn took the baby into Lisbeth's room, and everybody pretended that we couldn't hear them arguing. The atmosphere worsened around the dinner table. Lisbeth sighed and looked nervously at Leo as she served our plates. Sulyn was perched on a corner stool with the baby on her lap and a half-smile on her lips.

In the Pico Cristal discothèque we got a bottle of rum and some Coke to mix Cuba Libres. The DJ put on the ubiquitous Reggaton, the music of choice wherever young people congregated, and it fit well with the bump-and-grind sexuality of Cubans. Leo danced with a group while Sulyn sat at the table with her head slightly bowed, not talking to anyone, her back to the dance floor. He motioned for me to join them, and I gave her a little smile as I shuffled past.

Leo moved close to me. "How's it going?"

I shrugged, but didn't answer.

He tilted his head and gave me his sweet-as-pie look. "Come on. There's nothing I can do about it." We bobbed up and down, leaned close together as we talked. The rest of the group drifted away exposing us as the only male-male couple on the dance floor. Though it didn't seem that anybody minded, I felt uneasy while Leo appeared not to notice. He put his hands on my shoulders. "She insisted on coming. I tried to talk her out of it. In a few days we'll be in Havana, and everything will be back to normal."

I nodded my head, amused that "normal" meant us being alone together. I felt a smile invading my uptight face as the music pumped "*La batidora, la batidora…*" And the rum relaxed me enough to enjoy the absurdity of life, the uncommon destinations when taking the road less-traveled.

The few days we spent in Havana passed much too quickly, and before I had a chance to prepare myself for the separation, I was crawling into a taxi at dawn to catch my flight. Leo was with me, but said he didn't want to go to the airport, that he couldn't stand the sadness of goodbyes. We stopped at Miguel's, and when I got out of the taxi, he motioned for me to carry one of his bags up to the porch. The early morning chill of tropical winter was in the air. On the porch, surrounded by plants and semi-darkness, we dropped the bags and held each other tightly. Birds timidly greeted the new day with melancholy songs as I tore myself away, carefully descending the broken steps in the shadow of my already emerging loneliness. I didn't look back as I got in the taxi and slumped into the silence of the back seat.

27

June 2006

A rapping on the door stirred me, subtle enough that if I had wanted to sleep through it I could have, and yet firm enough to be the hand of a man. It had the mark of Leo, who I assumed had gotten Anabela to sleep and found his way to my door. Was it three years too late? I didn't let myself dwell on whether it was the right thing or not. It was the right thing for the moment. The love we felt had never died. With the anticipation of being alone with Leo, my doubts blew over like a warm and mildly disturbing tropical breeze. The clock showed just past midnight, earlier than I thought.

With a big smile on my face, I opened the door, ready to grab him and pull him in. From the shadows, two figures came at me, forcing me back into the room. One got behind me and locked my arms, while the other put a hand over my mouth. I could smell the acrid tobacco on his fingers as he stared hard into my eyes, telling me not to make a sound. A pale light from the street allowed me to see the silver in the stubble of his heavy beard and the glint of the knife he held near my face.

I nodded that I understood as he reached around with his knife hand and gently closed the door. Fear incited my heart to gallop, but the stronger emotion of anger took hold, making me furious that they weren't Leo, that Leo wasn't there to save me, that their breath stank of alcohol, that they were probably going to fuck me up for the measly forty dollars in cash that I had on me.

"*Dónde está el dinero*?" he hissed.

I motioned with my head to the bedside table. The one holding me from behind released my arms and moved toward the table, but the one with the knife, still with his hand over my mouth, clutched the blade where I could see it and backed me up against the wall. Hate rose up in me, all the hate I had ever felt for being bullied, hate for all the pain I had suffered, the dreams unrealized, the disease I carried. Hate became my weapon, and I raised my knee up as hard as I could into his groin.

"*Pinga*!" he shouted and doubled over, the knife clanging on the tiles.

"Help! Roberto, help!" I screamed and I kept screaming until a blow landed on the side of my head. I had the sensation of falling, but not the actual fall before I blacked out.

When I came to, I was in the back seat of a car with my head in Leo's lap. He pressed a towel to my head and it felt wet. There were red stains on his shirt, a white shirt that I had given him years before.

"Talk to me, baby. Say something." He ran his hand softly over my cheek. The look in his eyes scared me. My head was pounding, but I didn't feel that I was going to die.

Roberto turned around from the front seat, his face lined in worry. "Hold on, Martin. We're almost there." His words came from the end of a long tunnel, stretched and hollow. I went out again.

I next opened my eyes and saw a name tag on a white lab coat that said Jonni Martinez. His face was grotesquely broad and blurry, and vaguely familiar in an unsettling way. "Oh, no," I said, thinking I was in hell. But someone held my hand. Did devils hold your hand? I turned my head, despite the pain it caused, my eyes falling on a face I loved. He was anxious, but tried to smile.

Jonni put a hand on my shoulder. "Hello, my friend. You're back again. Don't worry. I'm not going to take your passport and you won't be charged for anything." He laughed.

I didn't understand what he meant, but I was able to focus my eyes enough to realize that I was in the emergency room of a hospital. I had a fuzzy remembrance from the past. I lay on a gurney and squeezed the hand, unsure of who he was, but I could tell by the way it felt that I didn't want to let go.

"They caught them," said Jonni.

"Who?"

Jonni gave Leo a funny look as they hovered over me.

A doctor approached and took Jonni's place in the aura of light. "Can you tell me your name?"

"It's…it's…Martin." They smiled, so I must have gotten it right. I had more trouble with my age, and I failed with the date.

"It looks like you have a concussion," said the young businesslike doctor. "I want you to stay in the hospital for 24 hours for observation."

"I'll get your room ready," said Jonni.

"My room?"

"It's just as you left it. It will feel like home."

When I next gained consciousness, the TV was on, but the volume was so low that I could barely hear it. I watched in amusement as the characters gesticulated wildly and distorted their faces, accompanied by tiny voices. Leo was in the chair next to the bed with the remote in one hand, tucked up under his chin; his other hand was on top of mine. I twitched my fingers to get his attention. I was now fully aware of who he was. Leo was my caretaker once more, but so much had changed since the last time.

"Hey, sleepyhead," he said with a broad smile, the worry fading from his face. "You've been out for a long time. Let me call the doctor."

"No, wait. Not just yet." I squeezed his hand.

"Do you remember things?"

"I remember you."

"That's good because I wasn't sure there for a while."

"Unfortunately, I remember the bad, too—the attack, those men.

Who were they?"

"The police got them. They think they followed you home. I'm sorry. I should have been there. I arrived a few minutes later."

"Is Anabela all right?"

"She's fine. She was here this afternoon. She kept staring at you and asking when you were going to wake up."

"God, how long have I been out?"

"About fifteen hours."

"Thanks for sticking by me…again." I reached up and touched the stiff tape of the bandage on my head. "Can we turn off the TV? The picture is making me dizzy." He banged the power button against his chin and the picture was gone.

"*Que mala suerte tienes aquí en Holguín.* What bad luck you have here in Holguín."

"The universe is trying to tell me something."

"What's that supposed to mean?"

"I shouldn't be here."

"Don't say that." The worried look had come back, and he withdrew his hand from mine.

"I shouldn't be in a place where I can't control my feelings…with you. I have someone. Back there."

He squinted his eyes and spoke through clenched teeth. "You found your perfect boyfriend?"

"There's no such thing."

"You always hide things from me."

"We haven't exactly had time to talk. I wasn't going to call you. That's true. I thought it better that we just live our lives. But when I ran into you by chance, it seemed like a sign."

"The universe trying to tell you something?"

"I had wanted to see you since the moment I stepped off the plane, but I was determined to be strong."

He backed away from me, and his face went through a brief distortion, and then his forehead smoothed out, his jaw settled. I even thought I could see his teeth relax as he began to speak. "It wasn't an accident, you know, that day."

"What are you talking about?"

"It wasn't like I planned to hurt you. Something took hold of me, a crazy idea. It wasn't meant to be anything serious. When you started into that curve and I felt your panic, I did something. If I had leaned the right way, we could have made it around the curve. But I didn't. I threw you off. I wanted to."

"It was an accident. Why are you doing this?" I shouted.

"It's true. I did it. I made us crash. You were going away the next week, going back to your country, leaving me in the mess of my life with no way out."

"You were trying to kill me?"

He let out a pathetic laugh. "No, just something, you know, to make you stay around a little longer. I could take care of you. I didn't think it through. It just seemed like an opportunity to change my life."

"You are completely out of your fucking mind!" I screamed, sending what felt like splinters of shattered bone through my head. "You could have killed us! Neither of us was wearing a helmet. Did you think about that?"

"It's not like I made a plan. It was just…"

"And the rest of it—the letters, the emails, the calls to get me to come back after that first trip? Was that all part of a plan, too, a deception, a manipulation? You had a foreigner in your hands, and it was all about how best to make use of me. You sensed that I was weak and you knew exactly what to do to have me."

"You knew what I was when you met me."

"No, I didn't. And I don't know what you are trying to be now. What you did was stupid and wrong, but you can't rewrite the history we shared. I have to believe there were real moments. Maybe that's just the way I am, the way I have to look at life."

I was already at the point of forgiving him, but the romanticizing had come to a halt, the desperate fear of losing him waning. He was only a mortal now. I could walk away and not look back.

"Don't hate me." His voice was deadpan.

"You'd better go."

He nodded. Even now, he couldn't walk out the door without

giving me a peck on the cheek. In the doorway, he flipped a cigarette from the pack to his lips, and I heard the click of his lighter as he moved out of sight.

28

July 2003

The rain thumped against the wood planks nailed to the outside of the balcony doors. The brunt of the hurricane had passed, leaving us with a lake in the middle of the living room and without gas or electricity. All night the wind had whipped the rain against the shutters, rattled the glass and howled through the cracks. It was mid-July and hurricanes were rare this early in the season. But this one hit just two days after I arrived in the country.

Leo and I were in a new seventh-floor apartment overlooking the Malecón. He was still sleeping after he had spent most of the night peering out through the louvers to watch over the lone palm tree down on the corner, its narrow trunk bent over and its fronds thrust outward by the fierce wind. I fell asleep before I knew if it survived. Now it was a somber mid-morning, and I stared at the water on the floor. With the plywood blocking out the light, and the half-inch-deep puddle covering most of the floor, the living room was a damp, stuffy cave. And the dank air I breathed convinced me that something was wrong, that the storm had imposed its disturbed atmosphere on Leo and me. Leo had been restless since the first moment of my arrival, a short temper here, a lukewarm kiss there, the hint of doubt on his face. It was the pressure beginning to spiral inward toward the center of the low.

I went across the hall to the apartment where the owner, Berta, was staying, and knocked on the door. "There's a lake in the living room," I told her.

"Oh, dear," she said. "I'll get a mop and bucket. At least it's only water. I guess I'm lucky. The balcony of one of the apartments in the neighboring building fell and landed on the roof of the little market. Nearly made a pancake out of Benito."

While she cleaned up the puddle and Leo slept, I went down to the street. The rain was now a drizzle, but the storm's residual waves crashed over the seawall and flooded the drive along the Malecón. People were out dragging fallen branches into piles next to the street. Down by the hotels on Primera and Paseo, uniformed workers swept up glass from blown-out windows.

I had hoped to find something open, but the shopping center, gas station, corner bar, and cafes were all closed, gated, boarded-up. I drifted along with the dazed sense of a post-catastrophe survivor, imagining that I was alone in the world, until a patrol car pulled up beside me. They asked me where I was staying and told me to get off the streets.

When I got back to the apartment, Leo was up. We slapped canned sardines marinated in tomato sauce on bread and washed it down with lukewarm cola. Everything in the refrigerator was only slightly cooler than the air temperature, and strange odors that the cold normally kept at bay wafted out every time we opened the fridge door. I tried to get Leo to laugh at our predicament, but his lips coiled up into a nasty frown. "If this is all we have to eat for the next few days, I'm going to die." Again he was in a foul mood, acting as if I were responsible for the angry air.

We ate sandwiches for a couple of days until the gas came back on, and then we heated up canned meatballs to pour over spaghetti. Every time we sat down to a meal, Leo looked skeptically at the food and ate it begrudgingly. We played a lot of cards and he usually won, bringing a rare smile to his face. Three days after the hurricane, it was still raining and we were lying, hot and sticky, in bed. Neither of us felt like getting up to face another day of no electricity, which meant no air conditioning, no elevator, no TV, and no music. The phone rang. I heard him agree to meet someone.

His father, a truck driver, had just arrived in town from Holguín. Leo and his father were friendly, though not close. They didn't see each other often in Holguín, so I didn't understand the pressing need to get together in Havana. I knew they would get drunk, and he would most likely disappear, but if I said anything I would look like a jerk. So I bit my tongue and shoved the breakfast eggs around in the pan, while he got ready to go.

He took a few bites of the beat-up eggs and then stood up with a look that he was dying to make his escape. I gave him the all-too-familiar exasperated look, and he forced a half-smile.

He leaned into the apartment with half his body through the door. It was seven in the morning. We both waited to see how the other was going to react.

"I couldn't call you," he said. "My battery was dead."

I stepped aside. He entered, took out a cigarette, lit it, and walked out onto the balcony. I went back to bed. He came in later, took off his clothes, and got under the sheet. I was on my side, turned away from him, and he didn't move to hug me. Soon he was snoring, and I chewed my lower lip without a chance of going back to sleep.

In the day we tried to talk it out as we had always done before. He was defensive and gave nothing. I was incapable of making him see that if we ever found a way to get him to the U.S., he would need to modify his behavior. He protested that I wanted to keep him a prisoner, and we were back to square one, back to the same discussion we had had a year ago and a number of times since. After an ugly silence he stood up and went in the bedroom.

One minute we were talking about living together in Los Angeles, and the next he was packing his bags for Holguín. I made no attempt to talk him out of it this time and was surprisingly calm. He walked out of the bedroom with his bag slung on his shoulder saying, "I hope you find your perfect boyfriend."

"If I were looking for the perfect boyfriend, I certainly wouldn't be here with you," I called after him. The apartment door slammed.

I wanted it to be over. For two years he had been in my thoughts and dreams, no matter how hard I tried to shut him out. I had rearranged my life so that I could be near him, if only every few months. In the time between the January and July trips, I had convinced Lizzie it would be best if I took a small apartment. She didn't want to be alone in the house and made the point that not much had changed, that we already had our separate rooms and to a certain extent our separate lives. She wanted to keep on living together, but I couldn't.

"Lizzie, you've got your life back now." Her mother had died within three months of her father. "You should go out, start seeing people."

"Date?" She hurled it at me as if I had suggested a satanic ritual.

"Why not?"

"Don't patronize me. You want to alleviate your guilt. I'd rather take up knitting."

I found a small, furnished, one-bedroom in Hollywood. I took my clothes, the Volvo, and my dog, Yuni, a few remnants of my past life, as I embarked on a new one. Even when I fought with Leo and thought things were finished, I knew that I couldn't go back to my old life.

After Leo left, the large seventh-floor apartment seemed an extravagance and I had the idea to dump the whole trip and go home. What was the point of paying rent for the privilege of climbing up and down seven flights of stairs, suffering through nights of no air conditioning, and wondering if the food I bought was going to go bad in the refrigerator? I told this to Luka, and he said that the mother of a friend of his had a room that she might rent out. It would be cheaper, was nearby, and on the ground floor.

"We hardly ever have blackouts, and there is an air conditioner in Dany's old bedroom," said Liliana. "I'll only charge you twenty-five a night, and I'll cook if you buy the food."

I hadn't mentioned anything about Leo, and I wondered how much she knew. What if we did work things out and he came back to stay with me? "You know I'm living with a friend here," I said hesitantly.

"I know. Luka told me. Your friend is welcome, too. No problem."

"He's gone to visit his mother for a few days, but he'll be back." Here I was opening the door when I should have been closing it.

I moved into Dany's old room with a lumpy mattress, a laminated cabinet unit behind the bed, and a double-window with diamonds of stained yellow and white wavy glass. Liliana said that since her son had left for Spain, a niece and a nephew had occupied the room at different times. The décor was a bizarre collection of Shakira posters, a coatrack painted with balloons and rainbows, and plastic stars and moons stuck on the wall and ceiling that glowed when the lights were off. There was a pink princess phone and a small boom box. What else did I need?

"I put those sheets on the bed that a friend gave Dany a few years ago," she said. They were in a rainbow print and looked almost new, as if she were preserving them for when he came back.

"That's very nice of you." I stared at the bed and immediately had an image of Leo and me having wild sex in the midst of the paraphernalia of childish dreams with Liliana in the next room.

"Turn on the air conditioner if you want. Cool things down."

I smiled.

I had hardly gotten my clothes unpacked when the doorbell rang. Then I heard Liliana say, "Martin, please come to the door."

Standing outside in the patio was Leo, smoking a cigarette in short anxious puffs.

"I thought you were in Holguín."

"I didn't go." He looked at me with sad, droopy eyes and a hang-down lower lip. "Why didn't you call me? It has been two days."

"I don't know. Thought I'd give you time to cool down."

"Are you going to make me stand out here all day?"

"When you left, you sounded so final."

"You know me better than that."

"I don't know what to expect anymore."

He stepped heavily into the kitchen, and I closed the door behind him. There was little light and I couldn't read the expression on his face. I led him into the living room, and then into the bedroom. We stood at the foot of the bed, and he looked at everything in the room but me.

He took a step toward me, his eyes still fixed on the Spanish-tiled floor.

"Wait. You can't just run off every time things are not going well."

"I didn't go very far."

"Over there, there's no Holguín to run to."

"You still want me to come and live with you?"

"You have to want the same thing, or else it's no good."

"I do. I want to be with you."

I listened to his words. They sounded sincere. I looked into his eyes. They were true. But why didn't I believe him? He had two months before I arrived to get his passport and papers in order for the visa. He didn't do it. He studied English for a couple of weeks, but dropped it. I wrapped him in my arms. We lay down and held each other without saying anything. The fit of our bodies together was like a cool salve on a burning wound.

It was the eve of my birthday. We had spent a lot of time around the house because Leo had a cold and didn't feel like going out. We'd eaten well and Liliana was motherly though she still looked at him apprehensively and made comments about him when he wasn't in the room. "Why does he have all those tattoos? He sure likes his rum. You mean he doesn't work at all?" I refrained from pointing out that she could have been talking about her own son when he lived in Cuba. Luka had told me that Dany had tattoos, didn't work, and drank a lot.

Leo's cell phone had been ringing all afternoon. He let it ring the first couple of times, but they continued calling until he gave in and answered. He never told me who it was and I didn't ask. After dinner he took a shower and got dressed. "You don't mind if I go out for a bit, do you?"

"You're sick." He was still sniffling, coughing, and feverish.

"Don't worry. I'll be back before midnight so I can be with you when your birthday begins. 10:30 or so."

"Who are you going out with?"

"You don't know them. Friends from Holguín. They keep insisting. I promise I'll be back." He flashed his most winning smile under a reddened nose. "Just a couple of hours."

I walked him to the door and when I came back to the living room, Liliana was sitting in front of the TV, watching the news. It was the biggest holiday of the year, and she was dressed in a long embroidered Arabic dress to go to a neighborhood party. I almost got by her before she said, "He's going out?"

"Just for a while."

"He'll back for your birthday, I hope."

"He should be back before midnight."

"We have a lot of work tomorrow to get ready for your party."

"I know." I escaped into the bedroom.

About a half hour later I heard her go out and breathed a sigh of relief. It was much more difficult to excuse Leo's behavior when she was looking over my shoulder. A couple of nights before, he had cleared the table and washed the dishes. I waited for her to praise him or at least mention it, but she didn't. I wanted her to like him. Most people fell under his spell easily. Liliana resisted.

I was in the cool air of the bedroom trying to read, thinking maybe it was a good thing that Leo went out. Maybe he would expel what was troubling him. There had been times recently when the old Leo shined through, but most of the time I was dealing with a new and angry version of the carefree boy I had met.

I dozed off with the book resting on my chest, but was awakened by the doorbell. It was still before midnight. I opened the door, and he gripped a bauble in his outstretched hand. It was two small purple fake roses trapped inside a sphere of glass. There was a piece of white ribbon tied around the plastic stems of the flowers and a message attached. I stared at it in disbelief. In a flash he was kissing me full on the mouth and wrapping his arms around me. "Happy Birthday, baby. I told you I'd be back before midnight." His beer breath was all over my face. Then he stepped back and put the bubble corsage in my hand.

"Thanks. That's sweet."

He ran to the bathroom and peed. When he came out, he started kissing and hugging me again. "I love you so much," he said.

"Come on in the bedroom where it's cooler."

"I can't stay," he said in a quick shift of mood, taking an awkward step back.

"What?" I thought he was joking.

"My friends are waiting outside. We're going to a free concert on the Malecón."

"But—"

He put his hand lightly on my mouth. "Ta..ta..ta. Wait. I'll be back in a couple of hours. Go to bed. I'll crawl in with you and give you the birthday present of your life. You're gonna love it."

"You're drunk."

"Now, be nice. I promise. As soon as the concert is over, I'll come home." He went out the door before I could protest. I stared after him dumbfounded. In a normal universe he would at least have asked me to go with him.

I went in the bedroom and set the glass-enclosed roses down on the dresser with the attached message staring up at me. It read, "Love does not end with a simple failure nor begin with a single caress." I plopped down on the bed and turned off the lamp, which brought to life the iridescent stars on the walls. Above me was the Big Dipper.

At midnight the phone rang. Leo sang Happy Birthday in his off-key, scratchy voice. "Love you, baby. Gotta go. See you soon."

If someone else was going through our bumbling attempt at creating a relationship, it might seem funny. He appeared convinced that his behavior was normal, that cute gestures and promises of sex wiped out any bad behavior, that you didn't actually have to be with your loved one for his birthday, just acknowledge the day. It was to be the year we were going to spend my day together, maybe play tennis, have a nice lunch somewhere. We had a party planned with all my Cuban friends. Things were going to fall into place on this trip. Yet I saw it all fading away.

Liliana and I were making miniature ham-and-cheese sandwiches for the party when Leo popped his head of disarrayed hair out of the bedroom. He had come home at nine in the morning. It was now late afternoon, and he scratched his scalp as if trying to think of what to say. I kept working without looking at him, even though I knew that he was impervious to my cold shoulder.

"*Oye, niño,*" said Liliana. "You certainly know how to sleep. There's some chicken and rice on the stove if you're hungry."

"Is there any coffee?"

"I can make some." It was an unwritten law in Cuba that no matter what trouble might taint the air, coffee could not be denied a guest. With great effort and a grimace of pain, she rose to her feet. "These damn knees," she groaned. Then she shuffled into the kitchen. I glanced up and he was at the double door, holding on to the still-closed portion. I could feel the chilly air escaping from the bedroom as he stared at me with a mixture of cool tenderness and confusion.

"Do you want to help?" I said.

"Let me wake up first. What time is the party?"

"I told people to come around eight o'clock."

He stepped out of the doorway and flip-flopped to the bathroom.

Liliana returned to the dining room with a tray of demitasses. We all took one and downed them quickly. "I'm heating up the rice," said Liliana. She took a faded plastic placemat and set it in a space that she had cleared, pushing aside the piles of bread and plates of cut-up ham and cheese. Then she went to the kitchen and brought out a plate piled high with steaming rice and chunks of chicken. We went back to our work while Leo shoveled in the food. The silence was too much for him, so he asked if he could turn on the TV.

At 8:00 no one had arrived. I was showered and dressed, and anxious for the festivities to begin. I cracked open a bottle of Havana Club and poured out an offering on the floor. I served Liliana a shot and then took a glass as a peace offering into Leo, who was still dressing in the bedroom. I sat down on the bed, and he took a couple of sips, then smiled at me as he handed me the glass. I overlapped my fingers on his for a moment. He leaned down and kissed me on the forehead. A few minutes later, the rum began to work its magic; it stopped the loop in my head that was whining about the future and let me just deal with the present.

All the guests showed up late. Gerard arrived with Louise, who was back in town, and a couple of other friends. He didn't bring Giovani and I didn't ask. Then Madelin arrived with her boyfriend, Luka with Monica and three other friends. Ricardo, Miguel, and another group showed up even later, so by 10:30 there were about twenty people. We only had the small boom box from the bedroom and Leo put on a new Mariah Carey CD, which got everybody moving. The house was filled with noise and smoke, and Liliana looked overwhelmed. I poured her another shot and made the rounds. Leo was talking to Louise, and I came up beside him. He put his arm around me, and in a second he was my lover again, squeezing me and pulling me back when I tried to move on to the next group.

At one in the morning, there were only a few guys and Monica left dancing around the box. Liliana had gone to bed, and I convinced everybody that it was time to wrap it up out of respect for her. I thought I was going to have to fight to keep Leo at home, but he was as complacent as a lamb. The next morning I awoke after a night of sweet cuddling, feeling that we had turned a corner.

29

June 2006

"Ham and cheese again?" I said to Jonni as he dropped the sand-wiches on the bedside table, the bread highlighted a plastic shininess by the shrinkwrap over a milky cloud of Styrofoam.

"You said you didn't want fried chicken," he shrugged, halfway out the door.

"I think I would be better off eating what the Cuban patients eat."

"Most of them get their food brought from home. I don't think you'd want the hospital food." He looked down the hallway and said, "*Hola, Reina.*" He winked over his shoulder to me. "Guess you won't have to eat those sandwiches."

Anabela peeked around the doorframe, ignoring Jonni, who had crouched down and was trying to embrace her. She hugged the frame instead, her tongue out and twisted to the side.

"*Hola, Tío* Martin." Her innocent voice churned the sea of emo-tions that had just begun to calm, and welling up inside me was an automatic anticipation that Leo would follow her through the door. At the same time I knew his impromptu revelation about the accident and subsequent departure just a couple of hours before had a finality to it.

"*Hola, mi vida.* Come here and give me a kiss.

"Go on," Lisbeth prodded from just behind her, still in the shadows of the hall.

Her sneakers sent off little beams of light as she ran over to the bed, and I leaned to gather her up in my arms.

"Oh, Martin, you shouldn't." Lisbeth rushed over and nearly let the plate with its savory smells of garlic and black beans slip to the floor.

"She doesn't weigh much." She crawled into my arms and hugged me tightly, and then sat on the edge of the bed, looking with adult concern at my bandaged head. Lisbeth leaned over to kiss me.

"I brought you some chicken, rice, and beans."

"You're an angel."

"*Abuela* isn't an angel," said Ana.

"Who's the angel? You? Are you your daddy's angel?" I asked.

She nodded her head.

"You weren't an angel the other night," I laughed.

"I cried. *Papi* never cries." I looked at Lisbeth with an apprehensive grin, and she shook her head. Anabela rested her little hand on mine. "*Te quiero mucho, Tío.*"

Her tiny voice was a hook that went inside me and yanked out five years of pent-up emotion. My shoulders began to heave, and I put a hand over my face. Lisbeth grabbed my watch off the bedside table and lifted Ana to the floor. "Ana, take *Tío's* watch over and show Jonni."

Jonni stood in the doorway. "Show me the watch, *mi reina.*"

Lisbeth took my hand. "He's not a bad boy. He's confused."

I took a few deep breaths and was able to refrain from completely embarrassing myself. I wiped my nose on the corner of the sheet.

"How could I feel so close to him one minute, and the next not have the faintest idea who he is? It's always been that way with him."

"Sometimes I don't know him myself." She thought a minute. "He loves you very much."

To hear her say it was a bittersweet victory, too late to change anything. "It's over, Lisbeth. I didn't come here to start with him again. I probably shouldn't have come to Holguin."

"Now you listen to me." Her voice was stern and motherly. "We all love you. You are part of this family no matter what happens with Leo. You are always welcome here."

I nodded my head, touched by what she said, yet my tears were already dry. More than anything right now I wanted to be home with David. I pictured the dark-haired little daughter we would adopt. I would love her like I had wanted to love Anabela.

"I won't disappear. I have to follow Ana's growing up. She will always have her *Tío* Martin."

She stared at me a moment as if she was trying to gauge the possibility of a future visit. Her eyes went blank. "Ana, come over here and give Martin a hug. We have to go fix your *Papi's* dinner. Take care of yourself, *mijo*." I squeezed the hand of this woman several years younger than me, who had just called me her son.

30

July 2003

The heat was a prison wall keeping us in the cool cell of the bed-room. We lounged on the bed and listened to music, cranked-up to drown out the groan of the air conditioner. Darkness had fallen, and it was almost bearable enough to go out. "Let's take that bottle of tequila over to Miguel and Ricardo's," said Leo. I had bought a bottle of Cuervo Gold in Mexico to drink for my birthday, but then had forgotten to bring it out at the party.

"I don't want it to turn into an all-night drunkfest."

"We'll just go over and drink the tequila. That's it. One bottle and we'll come home." I put out my hand, and we shook on it.

At Miguel's, Leo's cousin Yordani and his girlfriend, Daniela, and several others were already at the house. I glanced at the group and then the bottle. If Leo was good to his word, we would be out of there in about a half hour. I showed them how to do shots with lime and salt, and the bottle was gone in ten minutes less than my prediction. I looked at Leo. "We can still catch the movie on TV." He was not amused. Ricardo got on his bike and took off to get a bottle of rum.

During the tequila chugging, I had managed to get in a couple of shots, so I was feeling relaxed and the company became more tolerable. We went out on the front porch to escape the heat of the house. Leo was antsy. He sat with me a few minutes, and then was up running around. He and Daniela went in the house to talk, and Yordani kept peering through the open door from time to time.

We broke open the bottle of rum and everybody talked at once, shouting over each other to get in a word. Yordani got the floor and started telling about his experience with his boyfriend. Did he say boyfriend? His revelation was something like a lion announcing that he was going vegetarian. There seemed to be absolutely nothing gay about him and it underscored how youth in times of need were somehow given license to push boundaries. He had spent a great couple of weeks with a guy from Italy, he explained, who sent him clothes, money, and a cell phone so they could speak frequently. Mr. Italy hinted that he might invite him to Milan. Everything was going great.

"Then," Yordani continued, "he comes to Cuba again. He calls me up, and I rush over to see him. He acts like a stranger. Can you believe it? He gives me an envelope with two hundred dollars in it and tells me to get lost. We didn't even do anything. I'm like, what the hell is going on? He just tells me to go, so I go. I'll never figure these guys out."

"I guess he was just bored with your dick, honey," said Miguelito. Everybody laughed, including Daniela who had rejoined the group. Leo was still inside the house.

Miguel continued, "You know, it's like this. Two gays get together. They love each other. Like I love my friend, Beto. We have a lot in common, share a lot of the same tastes. So two gays get together and decide they are going to make a go of it. They cook dinner together every night, and they start fixing up the house, everything very tasteful of course because we have that talent. So after six months the house is looking great. They've run out of ideas for improvements, and the TV shows are getting boring. One night they sit and look at each other and wonder what the hell they are doing. The next night they are both out looking for *pinga*. I tell you, relationships between two gays just don't last. I'll be the first to admit that Ricardo and I have a pretty fucked-up relationship. But here we are two years later, and I'm as hot for him as ever."

His speech felt like spiders crawling up my back, but the others smiled and nodded their heads. Leo came out and Daniela gave up her seat so he could sit beside me. I felt dirty, like I was just one more sordid player in Miguel's tragicomedy. Leo put his arm around my shoulders.

"Are you okay, baby? We can go if you want 'cause I promised you." He said it with the tinge of hope I would say no.

"Yeah, let's go." He frowned, but honored my wish

When we stood up, Miguel said, "What's the matter? Was it something I said? Don't pay any attention to me. I was just babbling. You don't have to agree."

"Don't worry about it. I'm just tired."

"Do you want to play tennis later?" I said

"Sure. When it cools down."

"But not too late. You know we're invited to Luka's for dinner."

"I remember."

We were in the living room. His eyes scanned the entertainment center and lit on an almost full bottle of rum on the bottom shelf. His face shined as if he had stumbled on a pot of gold. "Have you been hiding that from me?"

"Hiding? It's been right there since the party."

He went straight to the kitchen and got a glass. I had a few sips, but in the next couple of hours he finished off the bottle, sitting in front of the TV. It was late afternoon, and he got up to go out and get another one.

"What about tennis?"

"Tomorrow."

After a long time he came back with the bottle in one hand and his cell phone in the other, staring at the screen like a zombie. He took off his shirt, sat down, and tapped out a message. Liliana and I were playing cards, and she raised her neatly plucked eyebrows. In a few minutes he got an answer and then he sent another one back. When he felt our stares, he got up, took the bottle and sat in the open doorway that led to the alley off the kitchen.

"I wish he wouldn't do that. That looks terrible. His tattoos, those scars, and with a bottle of rum in his hand. What will people think? Was he in prison?"

"Why?"

"The scars, and those tattoos."

I told her a brief version of the story of the scars and tried to make him sound as innocent as possible. "And the tattoos? Everybody has tattoos these days."

After we finished our game, I went out to the kitchen and stood behind Leo. He quickly erased what was on his phone screen and gazed up at me innocently. His difficulty in focusing told me how high he was.

"Don't you want to rest a little bit before we go to Luka's?"

"Rest?" he said, as if it was an absurd idea. "No."

Liliana entered the kitchen and began to prepare herself something to eat. Leo stood up and started into the alley.

"Where are you going, young man?" asked Liliana.

"Sit out near the street."

"Not with that bottle you're not." He came back, filled his glass, handed me the bottle, and went off with the full glass.

"I'm going to lie down," I said to Liliana.

I dozed off, but was awakened by a knock on the door. Liliana stuck her head in. "Aren't you going to dinner at Luka's?"

I looked at my watch. It was 7:30 and we were supposed to be there at 8 o'clock. "I'm getting up. Where's Leo?"

"He's still out there by the street, playing with that phone. I don't know what's going on. He came back to fill his glass and I said, 'You being very inconsiderate to your friend, drinking so much like that.' And he said, 'I was like this when he met me. He knows me like this.' You need to go out and get him. I don't like him wandering around the neighborhood in that condition."

He was sitting on a low wall near the street at the entrance to the alley. He still had the phone in hand and the glass of rum at his side.

"Come on," I said. "We have to get ready to go."

He scowled as though he was about to tell me to fuck off, that he wasn't going. Then he focused his eyes on me, as if suddenly remembering who I was. "Okay, let's go. I need to take a shower."

I stared at him a minute. He was hardly there. He still said the endearing phrases, still touched me in the same playful way. But in his eyes I saw that he had gone to some other place and the realization hadn't hit him yet.

Since it was late we showered together, though we barely touched. When we were drying off, he leaned over, nearly losing his balance, kissed me, and tweaked my nipples.

"No time for that," I said.

"Later. We do something later." He spoke English. He never spoke English.

As we dressed in the bedroom, he continued. "I want be wit' you tonight. You like to me. You be mine... *como es?...* forever."

"That's more English than I've heard from you in two years."

"I need speak in Los Angeles, no?"

"It'll be easier when you have to use it every day."

The only taxis in front of the nearby hotels were open-air taxis built to look like classic old cars and priced for tourists. I tried to steer Leo away from them. I hated looking like a typical tourist.

In a playful mood, Leo approached one of the cars. "We take one car this. Very romantic." He picked one with a young woman driver and bargained for a three-dollar fare. Almost immediately after getting in the back, he started chatting with the driver. He had one arm draped over my leg and complained to her that his partner didn't like him to go out and have fun, that he had to stay in the house all the time.

"That's not true," I said, and she laughed.

"No, I am like a prisoner." His speech was slurred, and it all appeared to be a big joke, but I still wondered why he was sharing this information with a stranger. Then he asked her for her cell phone number so she could pick us up when we were ready to go home. She said that her boyfriend lived near the address and she might wait at his house until we wanted to be picked up.

We pulled up in front of Luka and his sister's new apartment. They had traded the one in the huge apartment block for a smaller one in a much better neighborhood. Trading homes was allowed by the government, but outright selling was not.

Inside Leo threw himself down on the gaudy print couch next to Luka and flirted with me from across the room. The rum had made him animated and funny. He started teasing Luka about a guy he saw him with one night on the Malecón.

We sat down to dinner and Olga brought out the food. When we invited her to sit with us, she declined, saying she has already eaten. Leo jumped up and insisted she sit down, and when she still didn't, he embraced her and started dancing her around the room. Luka narrowed his eyes in disapproval. She escaped from his grasp looking flushed, though amused.

With Leo's inebriated state, the dinner conversation didn't go beyond sexual banter, music, and tattoos. Luka prodded Leo to show his body art, and he clumsily unbuttoned his shirt, and stripped to the waist. Olga hurried in from the kitchen to catch the show, but she stared at his scars more than the tattoos.

"Leo, put your shirt back on."

"See, just like I was telling the taxi girl. You don't want me to go out and have fun."

"We're eating dinner."

He stood up and put his shirt back on, but instead of sitting down, went out the open door to the balcony, which ran the length of the building. He lit up a cigarette and then walked down the balcony, out of our view, cigarette in one hand and his cell phone in the other. We finished dinner and Luka brought out a flan that Olga had made, showing it to us like a game show hostess. I called Leo to come in for dessert, but he didn't answer.

"Let's go ahead," I said, "if he is going to be so rude." Since we had all had a couple of beers, I could ignore Leo's bad behavior and hoped the others could, too.

With our dessert nearly finished, Leo walked by the door in the other direction and I called to him again, but he kept walking. Coffee followed, and Leo's sat going cold on the table next to his flan. The balcony was now quiet, no pacing or cell phone jabbering, so I went out to find out what was going on. He was nowhere along the balcony. I went downstairs and out the front door. I didn't see him and guessed that he had gone to get a pack of cigarettes. I reported back to the others, and we shrugged off his strange behavior.

After another fifteen minutes, Olga went down to the street and talked to the neighbors who had been sitting on their porch the whole evening. She came back with the news that the neighbors saw a young man leave in the same strange taxi we had arrived in.

"He's been acting weird all day," I offered as an explanation, but inside I was seething.

"Why don't you call him?" said Luka.

In the other room I dialed his number and got a message that his phone was turned off. Returning to the living room I said, "Turned off. That's one button he is going to wish he never pushed. I apologize for his rudeness."

"Don't worry about it," said Luka.

And his sister chimed in with a smile, "He's young."

Luka's answer to the evening's events was to go to the Malecón, and I agreed to tag along in hopes of distracting myself from Leo's latest disappearance. I should have been used to them, but I knew it was something I would never accept.

In our initial stroll the length of the crowd, I spotted Monica, hard to miss in her white jeans and frilly yellow top. I sat down next to her. I had avoided talking to her at my party, not comfortable with the slanted eye she always put on my relationship with Leo. Now I spewed my wrath and she heard me out, nodding her understanding. She responded with a lot of wise things for a woman who spent so much of her time hanging out in the shady underbelly of the Malecón. A lot of what she said made sense, but mostly she tried to make me see it wasn't my fault. While listening, I cranked my head around every few minutes to see if Leo had turned up, and Luka kept passing me a cup of rum and soda from which I took unusually large gulps. It burned down my throat, an antiseptic to the despair coursing through my body.

With the alcohol, the sharp images of the last few hours began to dull, and I forgot about rushing back to the apartment with the hope that he was there waiting for me. A hawker came by with a tattered travel bag—I recognized him from that afternoon at the Karachi Club—containing bottles of rum, the cheap stuff he had poured into discarded Havana Club bottles. I gave him three bucks. He wanted five, but I stuck the bills in his hand and grabbed a bottle, waving off his protests.

"You'd better slow down," said Luka. He had never seen me set out so deliberately to get drunk. Usually I was the one holding back, pacing myself, ready to be at least half-sober if someone needed to take charge or drive a car.

"I'm in Cuba," I heard myself say in a loud voice that didn't appear to be my own. "You don't slow down in Cuba, unless of course you're working." Luka chuckled with me, while Monica gave me a look of admonition. A foreigner wasn't allowed to say that? For a moment I was cowed by her stare, but I turned away, and with the unscrewing of the cap I regained my courage.

Glasses were thrust in my direction and I filled them, and then took a swig straight from the bottle. Along the length of the bottle I caught the stare of a short hairy man sitting on the wall a few feet away. I had seen him several times over the previous couple of years, noticed his hyper-masculine face with a heavy beard and square jaw that people liked to call rugged. His jet-black wavy hair was combed back, exposing a squashed forehead—his only obvious flaw. I heard my grandmother telling me to stay away from people who had a short distance between their eyebrows and their hairline. I could have been looking at a cretin, but at that moment his intelligence was of little concern to me. Then his hard look turned to a smile, and he sweetened it with dancing espresso eyes. I walked over to him.

"Do you want a drink?" I offered him the bottle.

"You don't have a cup for me?"

"No, sorry." But I wasn't sorry. If he was so damn masculine, why was he being prissy, not wanting to drink out of my bottle? Then the person next to him produced a white plastic cup.

"Anybody got soda?" he said.

My attention waffled, drawn to a guy coming my way who looked like Leo. I tightened up before realizing it wasn't him.

"Are you going to pour me some or not?"

"Yeah, sure." I was back with him, and it took some effort to steady my arm. "Don't look at me," I said with a screwed-up smile. "You make me nervous and I might spill it all over you."

"I make you nervous?" He took a sip from the nearly full glass.

"A little. I've seen you before."

"I know, but you never talked to me."

"So les talk. Ya wanna walk with me." God, I couldn't get my tongue around my words. I was running solely on hard liquor and the fumes of impulse.

We started down the Malecón in the direction of the apartment, though I knew I couldn't take him there. As we got farther away from my friends I felt the veil of darkness and the dumb bumper of drunkenness closing me off from them. I was cast out in a boat with no line, on my own with this neo-Cro-Magnon man. I glanced at his solid torso, noting how it stayed in place while his short legs moved it along as if it were a tank.

With my eyes on him I didn't notice a big chunk of cement that had tumbled from the seawall onto the sidewalk, and he grabbed my arm just in time to lead me around it. His hands were rough, a workman's hands.

"Thanks. I'm Martin, by the way." I shifted the rum to my left hand and extended my right.

"Eliades." He buried his hand in mine and I felt the calluses again.

"What?"

"El-i-a-des. That's my name."

"You're from the *Oriente*, right?"

"Yeah. I know, the accent. I'm from Moa."

We were far from the crowd and only a few couples were perched on the wall, wrapped in conversation or an embrace. Cars passed on the drive and lit us up from behind, throwing our giant shadows momentarily on the pavement in front of us, mine an elongated head taller than his. We got to a part of the Malecón that was deserted. Eliades led me over to the wall and we sat.

Facing the sea we looked out onto the black water dotted with the lanterns of fishing boats bobbing several hundred yards offshore. Small whitecaps rolled toward us and slid over the rocks below our dangling feet. We sat so close our thighs were touching. I filled the cup and we drank, without soda, just the rum.

"Let's go down there," he said. There was about a seven-foot drop down to the rocks, some of them relatively flat, a place where people swam. One day I had stood, watching in near horror as young boys dove from the rocks into the murky polluted water, and somehow managed to avoid smashing their heads and scraping their thin bodies against the craggy surfaces.

He jumped down and beckoned me. I half-jumped, half-fell, lost my footing on the rocks slippery with oil from passing boats, and he caught me. I was pressed up against him and smelled his cologne— Armani. That was Cuba: studly boys bathed in European fragrance. We held each other a minute, then separated. We were in a new world, cut off from the city and invisible from the other side of the wall. It smelled of salt, dead fish, and urine. The crevices of the rocks were littered with plastic bottles, beer cans, and shopping bags, twisted and torn, their supermarket logos faded.

I looked down at his blue-and-white jersey with yellow lettering, the word Sweden emblazoned across his chest and the number 10 underneath. In a flash he pulled it over his head and stuck it in his belt loop. I wished he hadn't done that. In front of me I had a perfect torso and arms. He grabbed my hand and put it on his chest. It was firm, unyielding, perfectly sculpted like a Greek statue, but warm with life and covered with black fur. His nipples peeked out from the mountains of his pectorals, and I ran my fingers over them like reading Braille. Maybe a message where I should go next. He pulled me closer, and I hid my face in his thick neck, listened to the water lap at the rocks just a few feet from us. At his neck the Armani was strong, but it mingled with an earthy spice that was uniquely the creation of his own body. I felt dizzy with his scent, the alcohol, the unsure footing, the adrenaline of danger and the heat from his body. He embraced me; I knew he wouldn't let me fall. I wanted to stay like that forever, holding him, burrowing deeper into the essence of his neck. So odd, a stranger, supporting me, giving me strength and making me weak at the same time.

"*Estás bien*?" He twisted his head and tried to look in my face. I lifted mine and our lips were a few inches apart. I didn't imagine him to be a kisser, but his thick lips were on mine in a second. It was more than a kiss, a desperation trying to escape from deep inside him. Then he undid his belt buckle and slid down his tight jeans to the point where they caught on the muscular ridges of his thighs. I was moved to reach into his bikini underwear, and silently rolled my eyes. Wasn't it enough that he had a perfect body and a classic Mediterranean face? Did the gods have to make him the rival of Priapus, too? I crouched down in front of him, easing him into my mouth, inhaling his musty odor.

The air was completely still, and I heard the struggling engines of broken-down cars approach, pass, and fade away. I heard voices, too, a group walking by, just a few feet away beyond the wall. I stopped, and he pulled me up. We were stuck in a few tense seconds. They went on. I glanced down and spied a condom splayed out on the rock like a beached jellyfish, pearly white in the pale light of the moon. He stared at it, too, with his hands on my belt. "Do you have one of those?"

I shook my head. "Not here."

He nodded, but continued to undo my belt and pull my jeans down. We kissed again. He put his hands on my ass and pushed our crotches together. With one hand he reached around and started jacking off, while he kept my backside cupped in the other, pressing us close together. I started pulling on mine, too, all the time our lips locked, as we breathed short gasps into each other's mouths. It didn't take long, and we turned slightly toward the sea. We broke our kiss. He went first, growled and jerked, and I soon after with a moan and a shot.

A moment of nothingness followed, and then we were strangers once again. What lust had given us, it quickly took away. I reached down and picked up the bottle that I had left on a flat part of the rocks next to the slime-covered lower part of the wall. I took a drink and passed it to him. He put it to his lips and looked out to sea.

We hoisted ourselves back over the wall and into the fuzzy light, the blurry apartment blocks staring down at us. They seemed unreal, a Hollywood set that I viewed from underwater. Back on level ground, I felt shakier than ever.

"I should get back. My friends are waiting," he said.

We stared at each other. He was out of focus. Was that a smirk or a smile? I reached for my wallet.

"*Ni pensar.* I don't want your money."

"I didn't mean…"

"Don't worry about it." We stood about five feet apart, and he continued to stare, his mouth gaping a bit. My eyes fell to the ground. In a low voice he said, "You could see me tomorrow."

"It is tomorrow." I tapped my watch or somewhere in the vicinity. "Where should we meet?"

"Cine Yara at 9 p.m."

"Does it have to be there?" The hub of gay Havana, I thought.

"It's central."

"Right. Sure. Why not?" I stuck my hand out. He took it, did a quick survey of the surroundings, and brought his lips to my mouth. Then he walked away, and I didn't know what to do. Goddamn fucking Leo. Why?

Eliades was swallowed up by the shadows, and I turned to walk the other way toward Liliana's house. I finished off the last few swigs of the bottle and tossed it over the wall. It hit the rocks with an explosion that startled me and seemed to reverberate all along the Malecón.

I passed the street to turn for Liliana's house and instead headed for the taxi stand, the place where just a few hours before Leo had ushered me with his hand on the small of my back into that woman's funky old car, the one that later took him away.

There were few taxis at that hour and only one from the same classic car company. I got close enough to see it wasn't her, but rather a young man sprawled across the front seat asleep with his shaved head uncomfortably propped up against the door.

"Hey." It came out much louder than I intended and it made him bolt upright. I put my hand on the door to steady myself.

"What?"

"Where's that girl? The one with the taxi like this. I need to talk to her." I was surprised how rough I sounded, how ridiculous.

"She went home, man."

"I gotta find her. I lost something. Yeah, my passport. I think it fell out in the cab. A passport from the U.S. of A. Do you know what that means? If I don't get it back, I'm fucked. You understand me?"

"You're drunk."

"No, I'm serious. You gotta help me. Like tell me where she lives. Please, man. This is life or death." I fished for my wallet and held up a twenty. He stared at it with his head cocked to one side, and then stuck out his hand.

"You gonna take me there or not?" I said, pulling it back.

"I don't know. She's at her boyfriend's house." I started to back away, but he looked around and motioned me back.

"Come on. Get in. Just don't tell her I brought you. I'll let you out at the corner. You'll see the car parked in the driveway.

"What's her name?"

"Juliet."

At first the air rushing into my face in the open car felt good, though soon I was ready to barf with the bouncy motion of the suspension. I managed to hold it back until he let me out, but then puked all over the curb before he was a block away.

The house was dark and I imagined that they were going at it like dogs. Maybe Leo was having a nice little three-way. Or maybe she made him do it to her in the car before she kicked him out and told him to get lost. Crazy notions skewered my brain so that by the time I got to the door, I was ready to kill somebody. I pounded on the door. "Juliet." I pounded some more.

I kept pounding until a light went on, and she opened the door a crack, saying, "Who is it?" over the chain lock.

"Where's Leo?" I said, reducing everything to a simple question.

"You are mistaken. You've got the wrong house."

"No, I've got the *right* house. You took us in your taxi to a place not far from here. Then you came back and picked him up. Is he here? Leo?" I shouted.

"Quiet down. You're crazy. Of course he's not here." A shadow came up behind her.

"Leo?" I shouted again. The door closed enough so that she could release the chain, which clanged to the side. When it reopened, a beefy guy filled the doorframe.

"Shut the fuck up. Who the hell are you?" the man said.

I stepped back, but I wasn't giving up. "Who are *you?*"

Juliet looked petite beside him. She had on a long T-shirt that said "Daddy's Girl" across the front. He wore baggy gym shorts. His belly hung over the waistband and he had gray in his chest hair. Nothing like Leo. He stepped toward me.

"You'd better leave *now.*"

"Wait. Wait. Wait. I'm sorry. I just want Juliet to tell me where she took my friend."

"Get the fuck out of here. She's not going to tell you anything."

In an insane gesture I moved toward him, and he reacted by shoving me so hard I fell back on my ass on a little patch of bare dirt and gravel. He slammed the door.

I hugged my knees and took in big gasps of air to get my breath back. Picking up a handful of gravel, I threw it at the door. Maybe he would come out and beat me up. I didn't care. Goddamn you, Leo. I started blubbering as if I was the most-wronged person on earth. I reverted to my five-year-old self, sitting in the dirt with a sore butt, crying and wanting to puke after losing a fight. Then I heard steps coming toward me, and I raised my eyes into the beam of a flashlight.

"*Levántase,*" said a harsh voice. I put my hand over my eyes and stayed on the ground. With a swift motion they jerked me up, one on either side. They were in uniform.

"Wait. I'm sorry. I'm sorry." I sobered up quickly, but my voice was still mucousy.

"You a foreigner?"

"Yes. I'm sorry. It's just a misunderstanding."

"Show us your passport."

"That's the problem, see. Uh, excuse me. Could you not grip me so hard? It hurts." They loosened their grasp a tiny bit. "I don't actually have my passport here. I thought I lost it, maybe in that taxi over there. Maybe at home. I'm not sure."

"Is it lost or not?"

"It might be lost."

"Come with us." I almost laughed. Where else was I going to go? They had a vise-grip on me as they led me to the patrol car.

"Get in the car."

"Wait. Where are we going?" I had enough wits about me to start feeling scared, and my stomach was in a knot. I leaned over and barfed again, some particles of Olga's dinner speckling the shoes of one of the officers.

"*Coño,*" said the cop.

We had to stop one more time before we got to the police station on Zapata, but it was mostly dry heaves. I was an empty shell with a sour taste in my mouth.

At the station I sat doubled-over on a gray metal chair and waited with three young men from Guantánamo who were suspected of the heinous crime of being in Havana without good cause. Our conversation didn't go beyond the basics of where from and what happened. One of the guys had a cell phone, and I gave him a dollar so I could call Gerard. I dreaded waking him up, but even more what he was going to say. He didn't chastise me over the phone, though I was sure it would come later.

In a half hour he arrived in a taxi. The police hadn't talked to me since I had gotten there. All they had done was relieve me of the photocopy of my passport I kept in my wallet and my tourist card. Gerard started yelling at them. Go Gerard.

By the time we were in a taxi sailing along Havana's empty early morning streets, Gerard had calmed down and wasn't too hard on me. "It is not the first time I've had to go collect someone at the police station, but I never imagined I would be going there to get you." I felt like the wayward adolescent, and my dad, Gerard, was going to ground me.

"Don't give me a hard time. I'm pretty low the way it is."

"We'll talk tomorrow. I want to know everything that little bugger did to get you to this state because I know it had to be something bad."

"I suppose it's just an accumulation of things and not all his." I left it at that, letting my head roll against the door. Sleep, just give me sleep.

I entered the house as quietly as possible and went into the room, which was stifling and heavy with the evidence of Leo—his clothes, his shoes, but not the body. I looked down at the several changes of clothes on the bed he had decided against as we got ready to go out the night before. I picked them up in a big heap and tossed them on a chair. I made my way to the bathroom and as soon as I opened the door, I heard, "Is that you, Martin?" coming from the darkness behind the half-open door to her room.

"Yes."

"And *el niño?* Is he with you?"

"No. I haven't seen him since about ten o'clock."

"*No me diga.* What happened?"

"We'll talk in the morning. Don't let me sleep too late."

The first thing I did in the morning was call the airline to see if I could change my flight for that afternoon instead of my scheduled departure in five days. They couldn't confirm space on the flight, but there was the possibility of standby. Over café con leche I gave Liliana an unemotional account of what happened, leaving out the part of my encounter with Eliades and glossing over some of the details of what led to me getting picked up by the police. She became frantic when I mentioned the police. "You didn't tell them you were staying here, did you?"

"I gave them Gerard's address."

"They could fine me. They could take my house, the place I've lived my whole life." The high whine in her voice sent the nerves in my brain into vibrato. If my brain went, my queasy stomach was sure to follow.

"They're not going to take your house," I said in almost a whisper. "There is no connection with this address. Anyway, I'm leaving."

"Where are you going?"

"Home."

"Are you sure that's what you want to do?"

"I have to do something."

I had stuck it out the summer before when we went through the rough patches, and I was glad I did. This time was different. Things were out of control, and I didn't know how to reel them in. The trip had been rocky since the beginning, and I couldn't expect it to improve over the next few days. I did what I had threatened to do several times before. I packed up all his things and told Liliana that I was leaving his bag with her until he came to get it. My flight was not until the late afternoon, so I had a couple of hours before I had to leave for the airport. I paced, wondering what I would do if he showed up and gave me the look with his head slightly tilted, smiled his devilish smile, and then touched me.

At the airport while waiting to get on my flight, I thought about Gerard and the speech he probably had planned for me, and Eliades standing in front of the Yara convinced I was another lying foreigner, but mostly I thought of Leo standing in the doorway of the empty room. What would he see first? His large bag huddled in a corner or the bauble of fake roses he gave me for my birthday abandoned on the desk? Would he feel something? How would his face look? I called his phone and got the message that the party couldn't be located. Insufficient funds. Such a cold, cold message when you were reaching out one last time. I headed toward the desk to check on my standby status and got the last seat on the flight. They held the plane for me until I got through immigration and ran to the gate.

I looked down from the plane and saw the great green ship of hope, sailing away into the big blue sea. My recollection of my brief voyage on its decks was already losing its sharpness, its vibrant color, and by the time I reached Cancún it would be as if awaking from a dream. I wouldn't recall the name of that street in Havana Vieja where he tenderly reached over and brushed a crumb of ice cream cone from the corner of my mouth, or the precise breadth of his smile afterward. I wouldn't quite remember if that little speck of gold was in his left or right eye, if he had two or three small birthmarks on his neck, or if that childhood scar when a friend shot him with a homemade arrow was just above or just below his kneecap. By the time I reached Los Angeles, I wouldn't be able to conjure up an exact replica of him in my mind without looking at a photograph. I would forget exactly how his eyes rolled back and his jaw dropped when he was on the verge of an orgasm. Fading away would be the image of that morning after his nightmare when I walked into the empty second bedroom and saw him sitting in the corner on the cool tile floor with a sketchpad on his knees. I would fight to remember precisely how the shaft of sunlight stabbed through the solemnity and fell on his face lost somewhere between agony and ecstasy.

But memories I would have, as imperfect as they were. Oh, and the paintings, which were part of him and not part of him. Still they would bring me no consolation because paintings had a life of their own, had been pushed from his nest, fledglings that had to make it alone. For me the experience of Leo was his touch, the magic of it. And despite my dread of the coming loneliness, the invisible mark of his hands would be on me when all else had dissipated. They had awakened what I could not feel before. To know the joy, I also had to know the pain. And even for the latter I had no regret.

Then I walked down the dimly lit, endless hallway of my apartment building in West Hollywood. It was like the narrow street of the first painting, but there was no person waiting for me in the shadows. This was not right. But it was too late. Nothing could be done. I walked on and a commanding ache hit me, like a big gaping hole in my heart and I marveled that I could keep walking, walking into a future that appeared to get narrower with each step as the walls closed in around me. I put my key into the lock and remembered the night we first met, when he opened a door completely new to him with such ease. I opened my door, and Yuni scampered down the hallway and looked at me guardedly for about two seconds before he ran and jumped in my arms. He got his licks in.

Vincent Meis lives in San Francisco where he is a teacher, editor, and writer. And when he gets the chance, he is a traveler looking for the setting of his next story. He has published two previous novels, *Eddie's Desert Rose* and *Tio Jorge*. His website is: www.vincentmeis.com.